The Fallen Race

by Kal Spriggs

Published by Sutek Press

The Fallen Race Copyright 2013 Sutek Press
Cover Image Copyright 2013 Sutek Press

Books by Kal Spriggs

The Shadow Space Chronicles

The Renegades

Renegades: Origins
Renegades: Out of the Cold
Renegades: Out of Time
Renegades: Royal Pains*

The Lightbringer Trilogy
The Fallen Race
The Shattered Empire
The Prodigal Emperor

The Lightbringer's Sister
The Sacred Stars
The Temple of Light
Ghost Star
The Star Engine*

The Eoriel Saga

Echo of the High Kings
Wrath of the Usurper
Fate of the Tyrant
Heir of the Fallen Duchy*

The Star Portal Universe

Children of Valor

Valor's Child
Valor's Calling
Valor's Duty*

CHAPTER I

June 1, 2402 Earth Standard Time
Venture System
Nova Roma Empire

The seven remaining ships of Convoy 142 writhed at the heart of a maelstrom.

Baron Lucius Giovanni clutched at the arms of his command chair as the enemy fire battered the *War Shrike* yet again. The short, dark haired man peered at his displays with dark, almost black, eyes. His black and silver vac suit bore the eagle symbol of Captain's rank on the collar, and his shoulder bore a patch with the snarling wolf's head of Nova Roma. He acknowledged the fresh round of damage reports. His eyes went to his Executive Officer, "Tony, can you get anything past their cruiser screen?"

Commander Doko shook his head. The confines of the battleship's bridge seemed even tighter with the acrid stench of ozone and shorted electronics. "No, sir. Their cruiser's firefly systems are too strong."

Lucius rolled his tongue around a mouth that felt dusty and tasted like ash. His eyes went to the sensor plot that showed what remained of the ships of the convoy. As he watched, the destroyer *Sicarius* dropped out of the formation in a broad cloud of debris and far too few escape pods. "Very well, keep hammering their cruisers."

Lucius looked over at his brother in law, "Any new orders from Commodore Torrelli?"

"No, sir," Commander Reese Giovanni-Leone said from the communications section. Everyone on the bridge had expected one command from Torrelli ever since the initial ambush. One battleship couldn't take on six dreadnoughts, not with any chance of survival. But if they charged into the enemy formation they would disrupt it. That might save the convoy.

The hell of it was, Lucius would rather take that chance than watch the convoy slowly vanish under the enemy guns. Soon enough they'd lose enough sensors or weapons and the enemy missiles would get through. They'd already had the bad luck to jump in on the Chxor force in close vicinity to Venture's refueling station. The escorts couldn't survive that firepower much longer and the merchant ships would not survive after that.

"Don't know why he's waiting," Lucius muttered. His ship rocked again under multiple impacts. "Not like the bastard can't be happy at the chance to give *that* order."

***

Commodore Vito Torrelli grimaced as the *Augustus* shuddered. The elderly dreadnought had held up far better than the convoy's other escorts. The forty year old dreadnought had far more resilience and armor than any other ship in the convoy. Even so, an early hit had opened the bridge to vacuum and slaughtered most of his navigation section. Other hits had wrought serious damage on the old ship. Commodore Torrelli was well aware that his ship was bound to Nova Roma for extensive refits even *before* all of that damage. "Order the *War Shrike* to close in on *Regal*'s aft quarter." He grimaced as he saw Lucius Giovanni's ship swing into position immediately.

He could almost see the aloof expression of the other ship's commander. *He wants me to send his ship into the throat of the guns, wants to die a hero's death*, Torrelli thought... *as if that could ever make up for what his father did.* "I won't give him that honor," Torrelli muttered. He noticed a flicker on one of the enemy cruiser's firefly systems. "Guns, focus on cruiser three, hammer me a gap so we can hit these bastards!"

The enemy dreadnoughts hid behind the massive, pancake-shaped defense screens of the cruisers. Those overlapped screens and the massive jamming of the cruiser's firefly systems counteracted the better targeting systems of the Nova Roma warships.

As Vito Torrelli watched the displays, he could hear the unvoiced criticisms from his rival. It felt like he could feel Lucius's breath on the back of his neck. "Dammit, get me a shot!"

***

"That bastard can fight," Lucius said. The *Augustus* had received the brunt of the enemy's fire. A comet's trail of debris, air, and water vapor trailed behind the battered dreadnought, but Commodore Torrelli continued to fight.

"Cruiser three just went down, sir, I've got a shot!" Commander Doko shouted. A moment later both warships poured their fire through the suddenly opened gap and into the dreadnought left exposed. Every remaining gun and missile tube aboard the *War Shrike* fired into the gap.

Lucius snarled as explosions rocked the enemy vessel. A massive cloud of debris enveloped the lead Chxor dreadnought. "Looks like we gave them something to remember us by!" The Chxor formation adjusted though, and a moment later the damaged dreadnought disappeared again behind the defense screen of another cruiser.

"Sir! *Augustus* just sent Code Black!" Reese said.

Lucius felt his stomach drop. The other warship lay only a hundred kilometers distant, close enough for visual. He looked at his sensor repeater just in time to see the dreadnought's port side engines erupt in a chain of explosions. The massive ship began to rotate as its starboard engines threw it into a spin. The stresses over-taxed the ship's frame and the midships section ripped apart in a slow-motion avalanche of sheering steel.

Lucius watched as four thousand crew died... and he could do nothing.

Lucius let out a tight breath. Only five ships left remained and Convoy 142 had a new commander. His eyes raked across his navigation display. The civilian ships didn't have the acceleration to escape the Chxor. They didn't have the time to calculate a jump through shadow space to take them elsewhere. Even if he threw his ship at the Chxor, the remaining transports couldn't elude the enemy, not without someone to screen them.

"Message to all ships," Lucius said, his voice suddenly hoarse. "Prepare and execute blind jump immediately."

There was a sudden silence on the bridge.

"*Solarius Endeavor, Unicorn,* and *Trade Enterprise* acknowledge," Lucius's brother in law said. "*Regal* reports damage to their jump drive and that they'll have it up as soon as they can."

Lucius felt a cold mask settle over his face. The *War Shrike* couldn't take the full firepower of the Chxor, not for long. "Tell them to expedite and that we'll cover them until they jump." He watched as the other three civilian ships jumped away into shadow. He wondered if any of them would emerge again.

As if on cue, a fresh barrage swept in from the Chxor ships. Alarms wailed and Lucius felt the deck heave as multiple beams tore into his ship. His eyes focused on the inbound missile tracks. Without the *Augustus,* they'd lost most of their interceptor fire.

Lieutenant Livianus's hands flew across his station. He took the sensor data and picked off the missiles one after the other. His precise shots almost stopped them all.

Two missiles slipped past his fire. One swept past as the helmsman continued his evasive maneuvers. The proximity fuse detonated only five kilometers in front of the *War Shrike*. The Chxor used missiles based off of captured human munitions. Fundamentally identical to the pilum ship-killer missiles, they packed a sixty megaton fusion warhead.

The sudden burst of radiation hammered into the *War Shrike's* magnetic fields that held the plasma defense screen in place. The massive induction coils exploded like bombs at the massive surge of power.

One exploded out into Engine Room Three and killed fifty-eight crew. The other detonated only fifty meters away from the bridge. The four armored bulkheads between there and the bridge absorbed some of the effect. The aft bulkhead of the bridge shattered.

Shards of steel whipped through crew members and equipment alike. Half the weapons techs died before they knew what hit them. The concussion ripped Lieutenant Livianus out of his shock chair and smashed him against the forward bulkhead hard enough to leave a red smear.

One shard flew like a spear and slammed into the back of the communications officer's chair. Lucius's brother-in-law let out a scream of agony as it bit through his left shoulder.

Lucius's gaze locked on the shard of metal that pinned Reese to his seat. He felt something twist in his own guts as he heard Reese's scream.

The explosion itself vaporized fifty meters of armored hull and opened the ship's entire forward section to vacuum. The hard radiation and the wave superheated plasma took the lives of two hundred more of Lucius's crew in an instant.

The first missile's simple tracking system lost the *War Shrike* and continued past.

The *Regal* had no countermeasure systems to prevent that missile from acquisition. The missile detonated on top of the unarmored transport. It vaporized the aft end of the vessel and sent the ship's fusion plant into overload. Lucius grunted in anguish as the seventy five civilians aboard died almost instantly.

Lucius shook his head. His sensors told him that only his ship remained. He cut his seat restraints and staggered through the smoke and noise of the bridge. He shoved a corpse off the top of the navigation station. Lucius flipped up the clear plastic cover, the surface slick with blood.

His fist hammered down on the jump initiation.

***

June 1, 2402 Earth Standard Time
Deep Space

When a ship plotted a jump through shadow space, it took hours for a navigation computer to run the calculations. The complex nature of shadow made up most of this time. Other factors of that time, however, lay in the gravity-induced shear forces and changes in relativistic frame involved in transitioning from one part of the universe to another without passage through the space between.

On a blind jump, a navigation computer input a null code for the destination. The ship could emerge a thousand kilometers or a hundred light years away, if it emerged at all. And a blind jump didn't take those other factors into effect. A ship might emerge only to be ripped in half by tidal forces. Or it might hurl into some bit of space detritus at a huge difference in relative velocities.

Fortunately, the *War Shrike* emerged in empty space. Unfortunately, the tidal forces sent the ship into a sharp axial spin. The ship's inertial compensator adjusted, but for a moment the crew experienced fifteen gravities of acceleration.

The harsh tang of ozone and the arrhythmic staccato of arcing electricity brought Baron Lucius Giovanni out of a delusional nightmare and into a nightmare of reality.

Consciousness brought with it a spitting headache and nausea. Lucius retched all over the deck and his vac suit. The shriek of damage alerts and the cries of the wounded began anew. He lost only seconds to his brief lapse of consciousness due to the unguided transition from real space to Shadow and back to the real universe.

His sister's husband hadn't yet bled out from the shard of steel that pinned him into his chair. "Medical team to the bridge," Lucius croaked into the intercom.

Injured and dead men lay scattered across the bridge deck. One or two others stumbled to aid the worst wounded. Lucius moved forward to help Reese, but at that moment the bridge medic team moved in and one of them shook his head at him, "We'll handle this, sir."

Lucius nodded and retreated to his command chair. He swept a hand across the front of his vac suit. That only smeared the filth that caked him. He took a few breaths to calm himself and forced himself to focus. First thing to do, he knew, was to run a diagnostic of his ship.

From his chair he activated his command displays. The three dimensional projections were visible to him, but would appear as only blurs of light to someone else. Life-support, engineering, defense systems and weapons; all the absolutely necessary systems retained most of their functions or would, at least, for the next six hours. He hadn't known the extent of damage to the ship before he made the jump.

His lips drew up into a predatory snarl. The *War Shrike* remained intact; the ambushers hadn't smashed the his ship entirely. And with time, he would return to gift the Chxor with *that* knowledge.

Reports came in from the damage control teams as they tried to get systems up. Petty officers directed repair crews and medical support to where they were needed most. Someone, Lucius thought he heard his XO's voice, dispatched repair teams to the essential areas of the vessel. With the certainty that his ship would not explode or dissolve beneath him, Lucius had a moment to study the space that in all probability would be his final resting place.

"Navigation, what do we have?" He asked, his throat feeling raw. He looked over at the man at the navigation console. He felt a shock to see a tech at the main console. *Ensign Camila and Lieutenant Divore and their petty officers are* all *down?*

"Not much, Captain." The navigation tech's hoarse voice answered. "I'm confirming our location now, but the initial run shows us only five light years away from Venture. The nearest inhabited system is Fey Darran."

Lucius grimaced at the short distance they had gained. A blind jump could have taken them a thousand light years as easily as five, but the tiny distance covered made it more likely that any Chxor forces that searched would discover them soon enough. "Fey Darran?" Lucius asked and his eyes narrowed. "That's a quarantined world, correct?" He forced his gaze away from where the medical team worked frantically. Commander Reese Giovanni-Leone would live or die; Lucius had to save his ship. Alanis would understand. *I have to stay focused...* he thought. Fey Darran lay out on the very edge of human space, and the world had gone into quarantine before Lucius's birth, if he remembered right. *Some kind of plague, one dangerous enough that the survivors maintained quarantine.*

"Yes. It's only a few hours away in Shadow. The next nearest world belongs to the Republic, Anvil, and that's five days away in Shadow."

Lucius shook his head. He forced his eyes to focus on the symbols. There wasn't a good choice between the two. Fey Darran would prove no refuge with a plague. At the Anvil system, the Colonial Republic would be as likely to open fire on sight of the *War Shrike* as welcome them. For that matter, half of Anvil's security forces were little better than pirates. "Anything else that's closer?"

"No, sir. I'm reading only a handful of systems nearby, but our logs for this area are old. Mostly uncharted systems. The Imperial Fleet hasn't had much interest in this region."

That was something of an understatement, Lucius knew. Nova Roma's Imperial Fleet had ignored this section of space as a backwater for decades. Lucius sighed, pinched the bridge of his nose and tried to think. They needed time and that was something they just didn't have. He looked at the list of systems, almost all of them listed only an alphanumeric rather than a name. All but one. That caught his eye: Faraday. "Nothing else on this system?" he asked as he highlighted that one.

"Negative sir. No worlds or stations listed, just a name, and the type of star, G-class."

"How far?" Lucius asked. If the star had a name, perhaps he'd find something there worth naming.

The navigation tech remained silent for a long moment, "Seven hours."

Lucius looked at his control screen. He opened a channel to the engine room. A haggard old man met his eyes. "James, how long do we have?"

Commander James Harbach had been a professor at the Academe of Science on Nova Roma, before being drafted to the Fleet. His lank white hair, well out of regulation cut, hung down in his eyes. Soot and stains covered his engineering vac suit. Deep lines cut his face and made him look even older than his already considerable age. "Well, I might keep the reactors up, for ten more hours or so. After that… I just don't know. We can make shadow space, for now. But once the containment coils go, and I'm not sure how they're holding, we won't go anywhere." As always there was a whine to his tone that set Lucius's teeth on edge.

"Ten hours? Make your men ready for shadow space." Lucius closed off the channel.

***

June 2, 2406
Faraday System
Unclaimed Space

Alarms wailed as the ship exited shadow space. More alarmingly, the floor heaved, and the ship itself groaned. Lucius had not moved from the bridge, "What was that?"

"Gravitational anomaly, sir, it pulled us off course. It looks like the system is a lot more active than we thought."

"How much more active?" Lucius asked as he took his seat.

The navigation technician shook his head, "I'm not sure, sir.

I'll have to complete my scans. We based our jump to shadow off of a standard G-class system. Eight worlds, three or four of them gas giants."

"There's a lot of margin for error programmed into that estimate," Lucius said, "Mass estimates would have to be off by—"

"Two hundred percent at least, sir. I'm getting the astronomical scan in now. I've—I've never seen so much in a star system." The navigation tech shook his head, "Lieutenant Divore would have been better at this, but there's at least a dozen gas giants."

"A dozen?" Lucius asked. Lucius took a breath of stale air that felt thin and couldn't help but glance at his helmet. "Sensors get me a scan of the system, priority is spectral scans, you know what we're looking for." *It's just my mind playing tricks on me,* he thought, *the War Shrike couldn't bleed air out fast enough for me to notice it yet.*

"Engineering, how much time have we got?"

Commander Harbach came on screen, "I need to shut the reactor down as soon as possible." He gave a look over his shoulder at a hiss of steam, "We lost a lot of primary coolant earlier. That means we're cycling the same coolant through more rapidly, and it's retaining a lot more heat than I like. The secondary coolant system isn't taking it well." He shook his head, "I need to shut it down before we lose secondary coolant systems."

Lucius nodded, checking the incoming scans. They held little promise. "How much time?"

Harbach grimaced and Lucius could tell the old man wanted to get back to his work, "Two, maybe three hours."

"What about environmental?"

"Back-ups will be online, but we've vented a lot of atmosphere as well. Our reserves will take us four or five hours." Harbach jumped slightly at a loud pop behind him.

"Thanks for your time, Lieutenant Commander. I won't take any more of it. Let me know if—"

"Yes, yes, I will." Harbach turned away from the screen.

Lucius sighed, "Damage Control?"

Commander Doko's voice came in, "We'll have the rest of the leaks sealed up in the next twelve hours. I'd better get back to work, sir."

"Thank you, Tony. Out, here."

"Flight Operations, what's your status?"

"Uh, Lieutenant Naevius here, sir." The Lieutenant answered. "Both port shuttles, airlocks, and the docking clamps are gone. One of the starboard shuttles is damaged, but we might get it back up in a day or so. The other one is fully operational. The refueler took a couple of light hits, but we've patched it up. It's fully functional otherwise. The launch tubes for the fighters took hits. The fore tube is totally destroyed, and the rear launch tube is damaged."

"Have the refueler crew on standby, if we find someplace, they're going to be getting us air." Lucius felt another surge of relief that they hadn't lost the refueler. The light craft could skim a planet's atmosphere and draw in hydrogen for their fusion reactors. Both the refueler and the shuttles docked to the external clamps, which made them more vulnerable in combat.

"Yes, sir. They'll be standing by and ready to launch at your go." The Lieutenant sounded more confident already. Perhaps all he'd needed was direction, Lucius thought.

"Roger, Lieutenant, continue the good work, Bridge out." Lucius took a deep breath and ran one hand through his short, curly black hair. It felt sweaty and oily, and Lucius tried not to think about how he must smell. He had forced himself to leave the bridge long enough to rinse down his suit and eat some ration bars. He had already rotated crew through twice for rest and food. "What's the status on the scan?" Lucius asked

"Sir, most of our sensors are gone. We've got thirty percent effective scan, and we're spinning the ship to get that." His sole remaining sensor tech's voice snapped, "I'm doing what I can, sir, you should be getting a list... now."

Lucius unclenched fists he didn't remember making. He forced himself to take a breath. "I've got it, thank you, Tech Brunetti." Tearing the head off his remaining sensor tech wouldn't get him anywhere, even if it would ease some of his own tension. Lucius had never appreciated superiors who took out their frustration upon their subordinates, now was not the time to emulate them.

"Astro?"

The navigation tech looked up, "It's not looking— wait sir, I've got something that might be within range." He brought a diagram on the main display, "A moon of the nearest gas giant. Spectroanalyzer scans show significant amounts of oxygen in the atmosphere. Best possible time is a hundred and forty minutes out."

"Helm, engines to full and adjust course."

"Adjusting course, Captain."

***

"Atmospheric pressure is close to standard. Temperature is low, ten degrees Celsius at the equator on this side. It looks to be tidal locked with the gas giant. There's a significant temperature differential, causing some rather odd weather patterns." They had just taken up a stable high orbit around the large moon. The braking Maneuver had seemed to take forever, but it had given the sensor techs time to work, at least.

"But it's inhabitable?" Lucius asked, just as the hum of the engines died. As did half the control panels on the bridge.

Thankfully, sensors didn't and Tech Brunetti spoke in his staccato voice, "It's something, sir. There's air, looks to be plant life of some kind, animal life as well. Visual scans are recognizing a little bit of Terran-origin life. Looks like it was seeded a long while back."

"Excellent," Lucius nodded. He opened a link to Lieutenant Naevius, "Flight Ops, launch the refueler."

"Roger, sir, refueler is launching." Lieutenant Naevius's hoarse voice answered.

Lucius opened a ship-wide channel. "All hands, we've reached an inhabitable world. With the shuttle and the refueler, we can begin restocking our supplies of air. The crisis is past. Department heads, put your personnel on quarter watch. Mess, I want a good meal for our people and then all non-essential personnel should get eight hours of down-time." He smiled, "Department Heads to the conference room in one hour." *No rest for the wicked*, he thought.

He stood from the command chair. His stiff muscles complained. Lucius nodded to the only other officer on the bridge, his brother in law's assistant. "Ensign Tascon, you have the Conn, I'll be in my quarters." The ensign was a new arrival, transferred over by Commodore Torrelli. A brief stint in charge would give the ensign a chance to prove himself, both to Lucius and to the rest of the crew.

Lucius stepped from the bridge. He manually levered open the hatch to the hallway beyond. He nodded to the two Marines on guard outside and continued down the corridor to his quarters. The Marine sentries outside came to attention as he moved past and Lucius gave them a nod, "Carry on."

He stepped into his quarters and levered the hatch closed. Alone at last, he sagged against the bulkhead. "Oh, thank God." His breathing dissolved into a ragged pant and he stumbled over and toppled into a chair.

Seven years, he thought, *seven years since we haven't been fighting non-stop.* There had been short leaves during that time on conquered planets or ones they defended, always far from home, far from the Nova Roman Empire's core worlds. Those brief respites had been short, tension-filled, clouded over by the threat of uprising or invasion, and all too often, cut too short by the same.

For a moment, he saw the ranks of his dead as they paraded past in his mind. He wondered if any of the other ships in the convoy had survived.

***

There were times when Lucius praised the ability to instantly contact fleet headquarters or another ship using the ship's ansible. It provided amazing abilities at vessel coordination on both the tactical and strategic control.

Most times Lucius cursed the damned thing. It allowed senior officers, many of whom had not seen combat in over thirty years, to micromanage ship deployments and movements. Furthermore, it took away the initiative of ship's captains and chained them to the whims and fantasies of senior flag officers. *Or in this case,* Lucius amended, *to their political masters' delusions.*

Lord Admiral Duke Stravatti's words were flat as he addressed Lucius and the remainder of the *War Shrike's* officers. "I understand your vessel has taken heavy damage, and that you are currently cut off from our forces. That doesn't change your orders. The Emperor and Senate have spoken, we are to take the offensive against the Chxor, to push them back once and for all." The holographic image had enough detail for Lucius to watch a bead of sweat curl down the Admiral's forehead.

"Sir, as it is, we can't even make shadow intact. There's no way we can fight the dreadnought squadron they have on our trail." Commander Anthony Doko responded. "And we certainly cannot get through that much hostile space to support your forces."

Stravatti's gaze flicked to the side. His eyes focused on something or someone off screen. "You have received your orders. Lucius Giovanni is to be arrested and brought in for his negligence and cowardice in the face of the enemy. He's the son of a traitor and from his current actions is obviously a traitor himself."

Lucius closed his eyes, *why did it always come back to this?* "Admiral, as soon as we make our repairs we will rejoin-"

Stravatti's face paled and he shook his head,"Your ship is to rejoin the Fleet at once! If you are not in formation with the rest of our forces when the time comes to launch our counteroffensive, you will be listed as renegade and declared pirate." The admiral nodded to someone off-screen and the transmission ended.

Lucius sighed. "That's that." He rotated his chair to face down the table at his assembled officers. He met the eyes of each of them in turn. To his right sat Commander Anthony Doko, who'd been with him since Lucius had first come aboard the *War Shrike* as the Executive Officer. The short, raven-haired officer met his gaze with a an unusually somber expression. His captain, at the time, had told him that they could have passed for brothers. Lucius's hair tended to curl if he let it grow out and his XO had straight hair that tended to grow out. They'd worked together for fifteen years and Lucius trusted the man like family. *Tony will back me no matter what,* Lucius thought.

Lieutenant Cato Naevius had come aboard only three months earlier, a replacement from after the battle of New Berlin. As the senior remaining flight officer, he commanded the ship's fighters and light craft. Tall for a Nova Roman, the Lieutenant had dark brown hair and an olive complexion. The Lieutenant looked ill at ease, but his brown eyes met Lucius's gaze without even a flinch. He understood that the Admiral's orders were suicidal at best.

Commander James Harbach had his normal pinched expression. He could be angry over Lucius's decision or just annoyed that he had to leave his engine room for the meeting. Either way, the man would be a pain in the ass and Lucius doubted anything could make him more of a problem than he already was.

Major William Proscia commanded the ship's Marine complement. Of all his crew, they'd suffered the least attrition, and Lucius knew that Major Proscia retained the loyalty of all the Marines. What that man decided, the remaining two platoons would follow, and they possessed the training to take the ship if it came to it. The Major's weathered face showed his normal calm mask. Lucius wondered what glittered behind the Major's dangerous blue eyes. His close-cropped white hair, bushy white eyebrows, and weathered face showed his wealth of experience in the Imperial Marines, and the toll that years of war had taken.

The other department heads were either dead or seriously injured, as in the case of Lucius's brother-in-law. For that matter, they had run well short of a full crew for the past six months.

Lucius sighed, he returned his gaze to his engineer, "We can't even get moving unless we have defense screens. You are absolutely certain that we can replace the coils?"

Commander Harbach nodded. "Well, it's going to take a lot of work. I can start on a replacement within a week, if we stay here. I could be finished with another five weeks on top of that."

Lucius nodded. "If we have that much time, we may as well get our other repairs underway. Cato, how long until you clear the fighter launches?"

Lieutenant Cato Naevius didn't need to look down at his notepad. "The technicians give it at least a week on the aft launch. The fore launch will have to be torn out and the rails recast. There's no chance of getting a fighter out of there."

Lucius winced. "A week is a long time without shields or defenses."

Lieutenant Naevius nodded slowly. It looked like a huge effort for him to lift his head back up, "I would suggest towing the fighters out of the ship, except we'd have to cut away several bulkheads. I think though that it would be faster just to clean out the aft track."

The fighter crews took the worst losses in many battles. Of the two squadrons--twelve fighters total--only three craft had returned to the *War Shrike* before the hit that smashed the launch tubes. The others, to include both squadron commanders, had boarded the

Augustus.

Lucius swept his eyes across the department heads, "We've been through a good deal. I won't lie and say we're safe. By disregarding the Admiral's orders, we're doing the unthinkable." He felt the ghost of his father's treason as he said that. He knew, without question, that many of his fellow officers had expected such action of him long before. "We've been through hell together. And whatever anyone might say about the decision to disregard those orders, it is my decision and it will be me who will accept the consequences."

He stood, "Gentlemen, you are dismissed. Major Proscia, please stay after."

Lucius watched them depart; they looked like the walking dead, with hollow eyes and exhausted expressions, but they moved with purpose. He turned his gaze on the Marine commander. The silence drew out as they studied each other.

Proscia was short and broad of shoulders. Bushy white eyebrows overhung icy blue eyes. He kept his white hair cropped close. He wore the perfectly starched uniform of the Imperial Marines. At full strength, he'd commanded sixty-four Marines aboard the ship. After this last battle and the previous engagements, his two platoons were down to fifteen men each.

"You were quiet during the meeting, Major."

"Not much reason to speak, sir." His calm voice could have come from a recording. Not for the first time, Lucius wished he were a psychic and could read the Marine's mind.

"I need to know how you feel about—"

"If you're worried about some kind of mutiny by my boys, you need not, Baron." The Major said. "Our loyalty is to the ship and you. It has been since you pulled us out of Danar." The Major rapped his knuckles on the table. "It was a bastard like Stravatti that ordered a ground assault there, and it was you and your crew who sent shuttles down for the survivors, against orders."

The Major smiled coldly, "As to what I feel about leaving Nova Roma? I can't do anything about it, sir. I've been with you long enough to know you don't plan to let the Chxor do as they want, but..." The Major's smile died, "It's been seven years of fighting. We had two years of peace before the Chxor invaded. Four years of war and expansion before that. On and off, I think I've fought for thirty of my forty years in the service."

Lucius opened his mouth, but the Major raised a hand, "Let me finish, sir. I was in on the invasion of Ghornath Prime, where we sacked an allied planet and left it defenseless. I was part of the infiltration teams we sent against the Saragossa to draw the Chxor away from our borders. I've done some pretty terrible things in the name of the Empire." He closed his eyes, "Frankly, sir, I'm tired. More than that, I'm ashamed of some of the things I've done in the service. There's a big part of me that doesn't trust *any* senior officers right now... but I trust you, sir."

The Baron stood, "Thank you, Major." He cleared his throat, "Now that we've made orbit, we'll begin operations on the moon. I'll want some of your men to set up a base camp."

The Marine nodded. "It would do the men good to get down on a planet. I can get the men ready and we'll do our best, sir."

"Excellent." Lucius smiled, "Major—"

Alarms began to wail.

Lucius bit back a curse. He and Proscia hurried to their battle stations.

***

Lucius stepped onto the bridge. He moved to the command chair and brought up his display. The *War Shrike* was in orbit above the nameless planet. "What's our status?"

"Primary power systems are down, engines are down, shields are down, weapons are down," Ensign Tascon spoke with a sneer.

Lucius turned cold eyes on the Ensign. Tascon had transferred aboard the *War Shrike* from the *Augustus*, and it seemed some of Commodore Torrelli's views on Lucius had come with him. Either that, or he severely overestimated his own position.

Lucius held the Ensign's gaze until the younger man looked away. The medics had told him just before the meeting that Reese still lived. Hopefully he'd be back in his normal place soon. Until then, the Ensign would have to do.

He shook off those thoughts and looked at the sensor display. He checked it twice before he pressed a stud. "Naevius, are you near Flight Operations?"

"Yes sir, I'm looking at it on screen. How'd we miss this?"

Lucius raised an eyebrow and gazed at Tech Brunetti.

"Sir, it was on the far side of the moon. It appears to be in low orbit, which just now brought it around to our side. We couldn't see it, even if we had all our sensors up." The technician shook his head, "I should have asked for an approach that let us get a look."

Lucius shook his head, "Not your fault." He stared at his screen for a long minute. The damaged sensors gave little data. "What can you get from the computers?"

"Looks like a battleship, sir. Maybe a battlecruiser. Computers are having difficulty identifying the origin, it's been damaged and I'm not getting a lot to work with," Tech Brunetti said.

"Captain, we can launch the shuttle to check it out," Lieutenant Naevius said.

"No, Lieutenant. Just because it doesn't show power signatures, it doesn't mean it isn't armed." Lucius brought up the sensor data on his own console. "Launch one of our recon drones."

Tech Brunetti winced, "It's our last one, sir—"

"And if we're not destroyed by that ship, we can recover it."

There was a few seconds wait. A few minutes after launch the probe flooded the bridge with information.

The Ghornath battlecruiser lay at rest, on a lower orbit than the *War Shrike.* It seemed to all intents and purposes abandoned and lifeless. "Lieutenant Naevius, I'll have the recon drone turned over to your control. Try to get me as much information on that ship as possible."

Ensign Tascon spoke up, his voice tight with nervousness, "Sir, what should we do?"

Lucius looked up at the communications officer, "Ensign Tascon, there's not much we can do. If their ship's in any better shape than ours I can't tell." If they weren't… well, a Desperado-class battleship was only slightly more powerful than a Ghornath battlecruiser. The *War Shrike* could take higher accelerations and was bolstered by more powerful weapons, although they were considerably fewer than what the Ghornath battlecruiser would mount.

Of course, intact did not really describe the *War Shrike*. With no shields and the weapons systems doubtful at best, Lucius figured he'd do as much good out on the hull and throwing rocks as going to battlestations. "Commander Harbach, I need you to look at your repeater—"

Harbach interrupted him in a nasal whine, "I'm busy down here! These idiots nearly lost containment on the reactor just a few minutes ago. I may have to shut everything down. You would be advised to conserve power and air—"

"Commander Harbach!" Lucius barked, jamming his finger on the override switch. He waited for a moment in silence. "Air will not be an issue, but we have a vessel and I need your opinion of it. I need an estimate of its status. Turn your attention to the repeater." He removed his finger from the switch and took controlled breaths.

A few seconds later, Naevius's recon drone circled the battlecruiser. It beamed sensor data to the *War Shrike*. He reported in audibly as well. "Some life signs, port engine core destroyed, weapons systems inoperative, communication's nodule appears to be completely destroyed. The shield coils look to be intact, but they've no power to use them, both reactors are gone, completely destroyed." There was a long pause, "You know, some of the damage looks to have originated from the inside."

"Secondary explosions?" Lucius asked.

"No, no, the damage is all wrong for that!" Harbach interjected. "The engineering sections are nowhere near the external hits they've taken. Far more likely to be an attempt to scuttle, you know, or maybe sabotage the vessel."

Lucius nodded. He opened another channel, "Major Proscia, I need you to prep a boarding party, it looks like you'll be going to the surface some other time." He thought for a moment. "Initial entry team as a scouting operation only. I need to be kept informed, try to use non-lethal force when possible."

"Captain, you remember what we did at Ghornath Prime, correct?" Ensign Tascon said. Tascon's Adams-apple bobbed nervously. "We didn't exactly make any friends after our victory there."

Lucius felt his lip curl up in disgust. "Might as well call it what it was. The fight's sole purpose was to loot the Ghornath technology base. We betrayed our allies to buy ourselves some more time against our enemies." The *War Shrike* herself had engines, weapons, and power plants built off technology stolen from the Ghornath. "We owe them for that. Perhaps we can make some of that right."

***

Lucius stood over the massive, bullet riddled corpses of the Ghornath, and wondered how things had gone so horribly wrong.

Of course, he didn't really stand there on the alien ship. He sat on the edge of his command seat, and stared at the projected holograms from the Marine boarding team. He watched and let Major Proscia do his job. Lucius knew his own skills; commanding a boarding operation was a task he knew Major Proscia would handle far more effectively.

The camera feed from the Marines' helmets shunted into the ships computer. That feed combined with shipboard sensors developed a three-dimensional overlay of the vessel.

As a courtesy, Major Proscia relayed that to Lucius, keeping him informed of the operation. "Looks like Ghornath weapons," the NCO in charge of the team spoke, his voice seemed close. "From the way they lay... they killed each other."

Lucius nodded, it looked more and more like sabotage--or perhaps--a mutiny.

"Proceeding deeper into the ship, heading towards the bridge." The view expanded as the team of Marines proceeded deeper into the ship, the sensors on their suits gathering information on the environment around them. "There's a group of heat signatures ahead."

A harsh, guttural bark issued from the corridor ahead. The computer translated it, even as the NCO responded to the challenge, "My name is Sergeant Govi, I'm—"

A rattle of weapons fire and a hail of bullets ended the brief confrontation. "Returning fire!" The repeater view altered, quickly forming a close overlay of the area. Enemy heat signatures appeared and faded as the Marines returned fire. A cluster of them on the bridge surged forward. They charged into the weapons fire of the boarding team. Lucius shook his head at the waste. They weren't here to fight, these Ghornath had thrown their lives away for nothing.

"We've secured the bridge, multiple enemy casualties, most of them are dead. One Marine wounded, we've performed first line aid. We need a medic ASAP."

Lucius spoke, "Major Proscia, we'll send the shuttle back

immediately."

"Thank you, sir. The medic team is a priority, but I'd like to get more personnel in there to secure the area. We still don't know what's going on, and the situation is likely to get more confused rather than less." Major Proscia's voice was steady, but a rough edge of excitement lurked just under his words.

Lucius got a jolt as he realized that this was what the Major lived for. For him, the prospect of a dangerous boarding operation must be what commanding a ship in battle was to Lucius.

"Very well, Major. Have any of your personnel you're sending assemble at the shuttle airlock. Lieutenant Naevius is standing by."

"Yes, Captain. I'll be going over myself to maintain better control. We're boarding the shuttle now."

Lucius realized the other Marines must have been waiting. "Lieutenant Naevius here, sir. They've been standing in their gear waiting outside the airlock." There was a pause, and Lieutenant Naevius's voice was slightly more restrained, "Uh, Major Proscia informs me he's ready to go."

"Very well, Lieutenant, take them over."

***

"Well, Captain, I've got some organization here, finally." Major Proscia said, a couple hours later.

"Do you know what happened yet?" Lucius asked. He felt a little light-headed and he fought to keep his eyes open. He couldn't afford to sleep now, too many lives hung on his decisions. Lucius had already taken stimulants twice now, he didn't want to have to take them again. He hated the jittery, disjointed feeling the drugs gave him.

"Yes, sir, it looks like some kind of mutiny, though I've never heard of the like among the Ghornath."

"It has happened before, but rarely," Lucius said. He felt saddened to hear it. "Most of the time it occurs over incidents of honor."

"Well, Captain, that's actually understandable." Major Proscia said. His voice suddenly sounded more confident.

Lucius restrained a sigh, "Any details?"

"Negative, sir. We have three of the individuals from the

bridge, all of them are badly injured. We've also found six others, all of them restrained and confined to a storage room just off the bridge. Two of them have senior officer rank. I'd like to transfer them over to the *War Shrike*, if possible." Major Proscia paused for a second, "Prisoner manifest reads Fleet Consul Feydeb and Strike Leader Maygar. There is also—"

"Major did you say Strike Leader Maygar?" Lucius asked, his voice tight.

"Uh, yes, sir. I don't read Ghornath well, but that's his name and rank."

"I'd like him brought to the conference room immediately, if possible." Lucius said. He felt suddenly much more alert and awake.

"Perhaps the interrogation room—"

"No, Major, have him brought to the conference room as soon as your Marines get him aboard." Lucius said. "My apologies, Major. I know that particular Ghornath. I… I owe him better than to meet him in an interrogation room."

The Major cocked his head, "Understood, Captain. I'll have my men notify you when they've got him secured there."

"Thank you, Major. Please continue to keep me informed." Lucius cut the circuit and stared down at his hands for a long moment. After a moment's reflection, he turned to the sensors tech, "Brunetti, that ship, its registry is the *Gebneyr*, correct?"

"Uh, yes sir." Brunetti's startled voice came a moment before he looked up from his console, "How'd you know?"

"I've seen her before, a long time ago."

Lucius stared at the battle-scarred hulk. Craters and gouges pitted its armor and, here and there, the inner structure of the ship lay open to the cold void of space. Something in Lucius wanted to weep when he remembered the sleek, predatory vessel he'd encountered twenty years ago. "I wanted to destroy that ship the first time I saw her."

Time wrought its changes on everything.

Lucius wasn't aware he'd spoken until Ensign Tascon answered him with a leer, "Shouldn't be too hard, now, eh?" Lucius turned an unblinking gaze on the olive-skinned officer. Tascon flushed and looked away.

"Captain, Sergeant Alsan here. We have the prisoner in the

conference room as you requested."

"Very well, I'm on my way." Lucius stood, "Tascon, let me know of any developments." He stepped off the bridge and closed the heavy hatch behind him. He didn't see the two Marines snap to attention as he passed. He walked in a haze to the door of the conference room. One Marine stood outside and the sergeant himself stood inside.

The heavy alien sat, his hairless skin rough. He looked like an aged stone statue. Two silver eyes peered from under a heavy brow. A heavy muzzle filled with dull, triangular teeth, and absurd, almost comically pointed ears finished the ensemble. Most Ghornath looked the same to humans, and vice-versa. Even so, Lucius felt a start of recognition as he stared on the face of this once-enemy. "Hello Strike Leader Maygar."

"You have the advantage of me," the Ghornath's flawless Terran might have surprised the Marine guards. It did not surprise Lucius. "Who are you?" The alien squatted at the end of the table. His cuffed hands rested on the table surface. If he were to stand, he would have to hunch over in the room. Few human ships were designed for three meter tall aliens.

Lucius narrowed his eyes when he noticed the bandages swathing the alien's left shoulder, "Did my men wound you?"

Strike Leader Maygar shook his head. "I repeat my question, who are you?"

"Twenty years ago, hours after the fall of Ghornath Prime, a dozen Ghornath ships made a break for the edge of the system. They could have escaped undetected, save they stumbled across a damaged Imperial corvette." Lucius seated himself at the near end of the table. He stared down its length into those mirror-like eyes. "It was drifting without power, with no communications and little air. They could have taken revenge on their enemy. No one--on either side--would have thought anything of it. Instead, the Strike Leader ordered the ship boarded and its crew was taken prisoner and then dropped off on a neutral world."

The heavy alien head hung low. "You recount the past, well, human. Is there anything else?"

"You spoke to the human commander. You learned that his ship was in the initial attack on Ghornath Prime. You learned that his ship helped to destroy the defenses that opened your world to attack. Even then you didn't jettison him or his crew into space. You treated honorably a foe who deserved none." Lucius said the last with sadness at the man he had been. It had taken him years to erase the anger and bitterness about his past and how the Fleet had treated him. *Even now,* Lucius thought, *there's a part of me that is grateful that I have an opportunity to prove my worth.*

"And the wheel has turned, I see." The alien stared at him for a long time. "You are Lucius Giovanni, then? Has the wheel turned so far that you are now the fleeing refugee?"

Lucius started, jerked out of the past. "I am Baron Lucius Giovanni, Captain of the Nova Roma Imperial Warship *War Shrike*." His response came automatically, an echo of the past. "I was once your prisoner, and now, you are mine. I hope you will be a better prisoner than I was."

"But a prisoner, nonetheless, correct?" The alien showed no expression.

"For now. My men are trying to find out what happened. Some of your people on the bridge opened fire on them when they boarded. They returned fire and they found you confined near the bridge—"

"Those weren't my crew... not anymore." Strike Leader Maygar growled, anger flushed his face with color. His skin color fluoresced red as rage flooded him. "They mutinied, out of false declarations of honor. They abandoned hope, and they betrayed me and their people."

"So it is a mutiny." Lucius murmured, shaking his head. "What happened?"

The Ghornath regained control immediately. "I must know, are we enemies?"

The question had deeper meaning than the immediate situation. The war with the Ghornath had not ended. The Imperial Fleet still had shoot-on-sight orders for a number of Ghornath 'terrorists.' Lucius knew for a fact that Strike Leader Maygar lay near the top of that list. To disregard that order meant a far more direct mode of treason than his earlier actions. "The *Gebneyr* acted as a raider for the past twenty years. You are confirmed in the destruction of over fifty ships of the Empire."

"The number lies closer to a hundred." There was no denying the pride in Magyar's voice. As well he should, without a base of operations, with no resupply besides what he took off of Roma Nova merchant ships or military vessels, he had continued to fight a war that others had already written off as lost.

"Yet... the Nova Roma Empire has... fallen." Lucius found the words bitter in his mouth. "A true warrior once taught me that when all else is lost, a warrior has only his honor."

"A bit naïve, but true."

Lucius smiled a bit, "I am not your enemy, Strike Leader. Not now and hopefully never again." He sighed, "I think we are in similar circumstances. Right now, however, I have the ability to help you. I have a company of Marines, and the facilities to help repair your ship."

The silver eyes stared at him for a long moment, and then the Ghornath spoke. His voice was emotionless, but a blue-tinge of sorrow came to his brown hide, "My ship came to this system seeking a rumor of a refugee ship that had come to this area. We found this moon, and then an inhabited world. The humans there call it Faraday."

Lucius had to interrupt, "There's an inhabited world here?"

"Yes... unfortunately." The Ghornath's coloring switched to a brilliant crimson, "They told us the ship was damaged, but that they'd sent it away anyway, after allowing them to make some repairs." His skin practically glowed with anger, "They fired on us when we insisted they give us more information."

Lucius waited, watching the Ghornath's skin darken back to a neutral brown.

"It was... unexpected. They didn't have much of a defense force. They claimed to be an Imperial world, but they did not show any of the known ship classes, just older warships, crudely made and armed. Even so, they caused much damage to my ship. We did not have weapons armed or defense screens raised. My crew was not even in suits." The Ghornath's skin turned a deep blue of sorrow. "It was an act of treachery. One that many of my crew believed deserved retribution. I believed differently, I thought it was more important we discovered the refugee ship before its systems succumbed and more of our people were lost."

"So they mutinied?" Lucius asked, shock in his voice.

"It was merely an excuse for some." The dark blue skin lingered, as the alien remembered the past. "We have done some damage to our enemies. We have even had our victories," the Ghornath mirrored a human smile, his shark-like triangular teeth glinting in the light, "But for some, the loss of our world struck too deep a blow. There are a handful of refugee colonies, but their defenses lay in their own pitiful squalor. They are not worth eradication. Even the Chxor often ignore our enclaves in their expansion. We pick at the scraps of other races and we barely survive."

"They wanted to return and destroy the cities from orbit. Nearly a quarter of the ship mutinied. They seized the armory and the bridge before I knew what was happening. I had only seconds, so I ordered our engineers to destroy the reactors."

Lucius winced, "You had to know that was a death sentence for all on-board."

The alien nodded, "We had already taken orbit over this moon. I had hoped that many would abandon the ship, and survive below. The loyal crew did descend. Some stayed to fight the mutineers."

"And the two groups have turned the *Gebneyr* into a charnel house." Lucius shook his head, "I hope many took refuge on the planet below. We're finding less than thirty life signs remaining on the ship."

The alien hung his head again, "Then my crew are dead and I have failed them."

"You have not failed them, Maygar." Lucius said, his voice firm. "You helped me once. I will help you now. I need your help now," Lucius stood, hands clasped behind him, "Tell my men how to identify your loyal crew, so we don't shoot them. Tell your people not to fight mine."

"And then what?" Maygar stared at Lucius for a moment in silence, his stiff face and brown skin showing no sign of emotion, "Then we will be allies?"

"Maybe. Maybe we'll fix these two ships and fight out a last battle, finally finish our empires' collapse." Lucius sighed, "I hope that we could be friends."

Lucius held out his hand.

"What do you say?"

***

Lucius and Maygar rode the lone operational shuttle to the

Gebneyr several hours later. Lucius finally took the time to catch some sleep, though his mind had buzzed with partially formed ideas.

The hatch cycled open, with a hiss of escaping air. The rank fumes of stagnant air and the heavy metallic odor of the Ghornath filled the shuttle.

There were several Ghornath on the far side, not quite armed to the teeth, but close enough to make no difference. Lucius stepped forward, arms raised in the nearly universal sign of peace. "I am Baron Lucius Giovanni, Captain of the *War Shrike*—"

"Strike Leader!" The leader of the group barked, "You've been injured!" A number of the holstered weapons suddenly became aimed weapons.

"Not by the humans, Burbeg," The Ghornath Strike Leader answered. His calm voice cut through the sudden tension as much as the words he used. "I was, indeed saved by them."

"Oh." There was the slightest disappointment in the Ghornath's coloring. "In that case, welcome! As you can see, we have triumphed against the mutiny. The few remaining mutineers are prisoners. We have also contacted the loyalists who abandoned ship and we can recover them soon!" Burbeg's rough voice shouted. Lucius had the sinking feeling that Burbeg shouted everything.

"Yes, so I understand, the humans have been most helpful." Maygar's hide might have shown the slightest green tint of humor. "Are you ready to hear my orders?"

"Yes, Strike Leader!" Burbeg braced to attention, still holding a pistol clenched in each massive hand.

"The humans will send repair teams aboard, assist them, and show them what areas need the most attention. Their resources are limited and their own ship has received damage, consider that when judging what needs immediate attention."

"Yes, Strike Leader!"

"Good. Captain Giovanni and I will go to the bridge. Has Fleet Consul Feydeb returned aboard?" Maygar's skin tone was neutral brown and Lucius reminded himself to ask about the senior officer's purpose aboard the ship.

"Yes, Strike Leader! He has returned to his quarters!" Burbeg paused for breath, "Strike Leader, do you wish an escort?!"

Maygar shook his head, "No, Burbeg, I will be fine."
***

The Marines and the remaining crew had cleaned the worst of the gore out of the bridge. Even so, red stains remained spattered across consoles and control panels. The Strike Leader stomped around his bridge. He set one massive paw on the control couch. "I had not thought I'd return to command her."

"It is a pleasure to be able to return your favor." Lucius said. He rubbed his jaw. "Perhaps you could tell me about the ship, and your crew."

Maygar shrugged, "Weapons Commander Burbeg is the remaining officer behind me." A series of colors rippled across his skin, too quick to catch. "He was born after... He was born on one of the refugee worlds. He can be a bit impetuous."

"As in?" Lucius raised an eyebrow.

"In truth, my orders to him were 'disable the ship's reactors, so the traitors cannot use the ship.' He directed the crew to destroy both reactors to accomplish this task."

"Ah..." Lucius' eyes widened, "Perhaps a bit eager?"

Green amusement suffused the old Ghornoth's skin. "Yes, a bit. Very talented, though. Extremely ingenious. If circumstances were different, he would be a Strike Leader himself... probably."

"Not many ships to command, I take it?" Lucius asked. "Perhaps Fleet Consul Feydeb might know something about that?"

Maygar's mirror eyes gave away less than his emotionless face as he answered, "He might."
***

"You know, I'd have to say that whatever they ran into, I'm amazed that they got out of it." Commander James Harbach stated. The chief engineer's whining voice grated on Lucius' ears. His nasal pronouncement of 'well' in particular set Lucius's teeth on edge. "*Well*, there appears to be two separate incidents of damage. The first was what knocked out the port engine, damaged the port broadside, and hit the communications nodule. The second was the internal damage. The sabotage destroyed the primary and secondary reactors and the communications nodule. Most of the other damage is dated before those two incidents."

Harbach sighed. "Frankly sir, I don't see how they survived so long without power. Their air systems are in terrible shape. The temporary fix we put in place has kept the atmosphere from getting worse, but it still has a dangerous level of toxins."

"Perhaps it is, but that isn't a question right now. The Ghornath have respirators and your repair teams are all suited up, anyway." Lucius rubbed his jaw for a second in thought, "I'm not liking your best estimate on repair times." Lucius had met both Commander Harbach and his assistant, Lieutenant Meridan, in his cabin. Lucius was very familiar with the chief engineer's experience and eccentricities. The Lieutenant had worked under Harbach for the past year. That was longer than any other engineering officer had managed, which said a good deal for his knowledge *and* his patience.

"Captain, that ship is nearly fifty years old. It hasn't seen a shipyard in at least five years..."

"Five years?" Lucius demanded, "The Ghornath haven't had any shipyards for twenty years, where did they find one to take the *Gebneyr*?"

Commander James Harbach shrugged, "How should I know? *Well...* it might be more than five years. It might be as many as ten, but not any more than that." He pointed at his data-tablet. "You know, it has seen a lot of damage in the time since. Some of that damage has been there for years. Some of the primary systems have run continuously for years, the secondary systems scavenged for parts for the primaries!" The engineer threw up his hands and his nasal voice climbed an octave, "It's a mess, all of it!"

Lucius rose from his chair, "You can fix it, correct?"

"Well... yes, of course *I* can." Harbach held a hand out to either side and jiggled back and forth. That annoying habit and his pot-belly had earned him the nickname 'Jimmy Wiggles.' "But I *also* need to work on the *War Shrike*. You know, I can't do both at once. Frankly, I don't trust anyone to do most of these repairs without constant supervision—"

"Commander, need I remind you that time is not on our side. Sooner or later someone is going to wonder what two large vessels are doing in orbit over this moon." Lucius' voice was stern.

"*Captain*, need I remind you that I can only do so much—"

"Uh, Captain?" The assistant engineer interrupted, "I think the time estimate is a little long. I could—"

"Don't interrupt me, Meridan, or—"

"Harbach, shut up." Lucius snapped, "Lieutenant Meridan, what is your suggestion?"

The Lieutenant gave a nervous look over at his superior, but spoke up, "Captain, I think we could cut down on the work time if we split the work crews. Lieutenant Commander Harbach wants to directly oversee several projects that don't require as precise a tolerance as he says."

Lucius raise and eyebrow, "Such as?"

"Well, sir, like the fuel regulator for the fusion reactors we're mounting in the *Gebneyr* . Tolerances within the milliliter of hydrogen input will be sufficient for a substantial amount of time—"

"That's absurd!" Harbach's voice was shrill He threw up his hands, "You might as well say that the fuel consumption doesn't matter! The fuel inefficiency will be catastrophic!"

Lieutenant Meridan continued on, "Captain, at worst, the reactors will consume fuel at twice the rate they should. I majored in engineering, but you don't need a degree to do the calculations, even at that kind of fuel consumption, the *Gebneyr* will have eleven days of fuel on her tanks."

That was one of the weaknesses of many warships, they rarely carried fuel for longer trips, not without external fuel pods or refueling auxiliaries. Ghornath warships, due to their single system nation, typically had smaller fuel reserves than most. Lucius nodded, "How much time will that cut from the refit schedule?"

"Each of those regulators is scheduled in at four hours a piece, with Chief Engineer Harbach overseeing production to his exact tolerances, and we'd need eight of them." Lieutenant Meridan didn't dare to look over at his boss any more. "I've got a dozen other fixes that will save us time, short term, and get these ships up and running." His voice dropped back to not much more than a murmur, "That's not including the break time he's scheduled in for himself."

"I see." Lucius turned his eyes to the former professor's puce-colored face. "What do you think of this?"

The Commander sputtered, "*Well...* This is ridiculous. This... this *idiot* doesn't know what he's talking about. He hasn't spent nearly enough time considering the cumulative failures he will build into the engineering systems by cutting corners like this!"

"We don't have to leave the systems like that. We can do repairs of the systems over time." The Lieutenant sighed, "It just doesn't make sense to spend four months doing *everything* perfect when we can get it good enough in a lot less time."

"I see." Lucius stroked his jaw, staring at Harbach for a long moment. A fix that would let them get operational in a short time would be better than one that took months. Given time to do full repairs, they could bring those systems up to full efficiency. "We'll implement your plan, Lieutenant. Get to work on it." Both Engineering officers rose, but Lucius raised a hand. "James, stay here a moment." Lucius waited for the Lieutenant to close the hatch behind him before he spoke. He looked up at the taller engineer, "I've cut you a great deal of slack, in the years you've been here."

The engineer interrupted with a shrill protest, "I get things done! This fool will leave you—"

Lucius slammed a hand on the desktop. The crack startled Harbach into silence. "*Enough!* You get things done, but you try to make things damned perfect! That may work for an engineering professor, it does not work for an engineering officer. Sometimes 'good enough' is all I ask."

Lucius sighed, "I need you, James. I really do. I need you at one hundred percent. The margins of survival are... they're not good."

"I'm doing my–"

"No, you are not doing your best. You're afraid, and you're not thinking straight, so you're going back to how you did things as a professor." Lucius shook his head. "Frankly, James, you're a teacher, you're not meant for this kind of life. But that's what you have, and that's where we are. As soon as we find a safe haven, I can put you off, I'm sure with your skills-"

"I'd like to stay, please." Harbach's said.

Lucius paused, "Why? You've never shown anything but disgust with the military."

Harbach slumped a bit. "I—I just don't have anything else. I hated teaching. I hated my students. They didn't care, they had no *passion*, they had no drive!" The engineer's face twisted in bitterness. "They wanted me to pour information into them like they were plants, receiving rain. They didn't want to work for it. It was hell." He shook his head, "They didn't know what it was to learn, and they hated me for making them work." His face took on a look of smugness, "I had a thirty percent pass rate in my classes."

Lucius stared at him, and spoke slowly, as if to a child, "To me, that means *you* failed seventy percent of the time." He shook his head. "I see, among other things, we disagree on teaching too." He looked at the bitter man in silence for a while, "What do I do with you? You're terrible as a department head, you know?"

The Chief Engineer waved a hand, "I've kept this ship flying, and you know it! My knowledge and expertise—"

"Has persistently been a pain in the ass." Lucius responded. "In any case, for the time being, I'm assigning you to oversight of the areas that specifically require your expertise. Lieutenant Meridan will take over in Engineering."

"I won't work under—"

"You won't be working under anyone but me." Lucius said. "But you will do as I say, James Harbach, or I will vent you out the nearest airlock, is that clear?"

Lucius watched Harbach's face go from bright red to pasty white. The other man nodded, finally.

"Very well, you're dismissed," Lucius watched him leave and wondered how long until the engineer's next problem. Unfortunately, personnel issues lay with many other areas besides his engineering department.

The *War Shrike*'s full crew was just over a thousand; the *Gebneyr* 's was six hundred and forty. His present crew, split between the two ships, was four hundred and fifty. Seventy of those were Ghornath, the rest humans from his own ship.

Those depressingly low figures meant twelve to eighteen hour shifts for his recently promoted officers, huge gaps in some vital places and a low number of people to make the repairs he needed.

He sighed again as he picked up the next report.

***

July 31, 2402 Earth Standard Time
Faraday System
Unclaimed Space

Lucius stepped into the crowded sickbay and moved down the rows. He paused now and then to give a word to the wounded as he passed. He felt like a man twice his age, though he kept cheer and warmth in his voice. He congratulated some on their recovery, told others they'd be cared for, and made promises that he hoped he could keep regarding their futures.

His destination was the fair-haired commander at the end. Lucius could no more have not spoken to each of his men as he passed than he could have cut off his own hand, so it took him some time to reach him. He knew that some part of him welcomed the opportunity to delay the conversation he expected.

"Hello, Reese. I hear you've made a rapid recovery." Lucius's voice was slightly hesitant. He saw that Reese picked up on it and the other man's face clouded over.

"What's this rumor about us not going back to Nova Roma!" Reese snapped. "You have to quash these things! Tell me, when do we return?!"

Lucius shook his head, "Reese, the *War Shrike*'s been hammered, we've barely held on, we're in no shape to go anywhere yet." He couldn't meet the younger man's eyes.

"Look, Lucius, I can't stand the thought of... well you know how bad it will be if the Chxor break through. You know what will happen to Alanis if they take Nova Roma. The way people have spoken, they think it's foregone. I know you, I know you can stop it. I know you can make a difference. We have to go back!" Reese burst into a coughing fit, his blue eyes clenched in pain.

"Reese..." Lucius began.

"Look, I know I'm no damned good right now. But we need go back. I know you took me on because Alanis wanted me safe. She wanted me on the best ship and we're it! We-"

"Reese, there's nothing to go back to." Lucius interrupted. "I haven't told anyone yet, I had to tell you first." His voice was low. "The Chxor broke through Nova Roma's defenses yesterday morning. The Senate surrendered just before noon. The Chxor executed the Imperial family in a live broadcast. They've claimed to have arrested and executed ninety percent of the nobility and all of the senior houses."

"Alanis is dead, Reese. I wish it weren't so. I wish there was something I could do. If I could push this ship there to stop it, I would," Lucius said.

"No." Reese shook his head. "No, we still need to go back! You don't know she's dead!"

"Reese, I hope she's alive, but you know what life will be like under them. Give it five years and she'll wish she was dead. Give it ten as a slave—"

"The only way we can be sure..."

"I won't kill the rest of the men for a forlorn hope!" Lucius snapped. "We'll have enough problems surviving on our own. I won't throw their lives away for nothing. You aren't the only man who has lost someone they loved. Half the crew has family and friends on Nova Roma. Do you think they feel any better?"

"Get out." Reese turned his head away. "Just get out."

"Reese..." Lucius sighed. "Look, if you want to talk..."

"You abandoned your sister and my wife because you're a coward, and I never want to see you again. Your father was a traitor, I see you inherited that." Reese's voice was hollow. "Get out or I'll kill you."

Lucius stared down at the other man. He felt an ache in his chest. The weight of command seemed to increase a bit. The uniform seemed to constrict a little tighter around his throat.

Lucius shook his head and turned away.

***

CHAPTER II

August 3, 2406
Faraday System
Unclaimed Space

"Attention inbound craft," the patrol ship announced, "this system is the property of the Colonial Republic, if you do not turn aside you will be intercepted and destroyed by CRA Fleet assets."

Lucius smiled a part of him wondered if anyone in the Colonial Republic could ever be so courteous. It didn't matter. The Colonial Republic had *not* claimed the system. He switched his communications to tight band and made a circuit of communications between himself, the patrol craft and the jury-rigged contraption on the *Gebneyr*. He also activated a second line. This broadcast everything from the first to the planet. "Very interesting, tell me, I assume you have a task force within easy hailing distance, at least a couple dreadnoughts, correct?"

The speaker showed no sign of hesitation, "Four dreadnoughts as a matter of fact, escorted by a number of destroyers and light cruisers."

"Ah, now, please explain to me why the Colonial Republic Liberation Forces would be using dreadnoughts." Lucius said with a smile. "As they have never used them in combat before, and they don't have the shipyards to build any?"

The speaker on the patrol craft didn't answer for a moment. "Attention inbound craft, turn aside from your course immediately or you will be attacked by all craft in-system."

"That's what?" Lucius asked matter-of-factly, "Two destroyers, a patrol cutter, maybe a squadron of fighters or so, and a couple of corvettes? If that force couldn't destroy a crippled battlecruiser, what exactly do you think it will do to two fully armed and operational capital ships?"

There was a longer pause on behalf of the patrol craft. "I repeat, turn aside from your course or you will be fired upon."

Lucius smiled even more, "Patrol cutter, you seem to be losing forces as we speak." One of the destroyers and both corvettes began to break orbit, not in the direction of Lucius, but in the opposite direction.

"No doubt they are going for reinforcements?" Lucius asked. "You just cannot trust mercenaries anymore, can you?" He let that bit of information sink in, and then he turned up the heat. "Our ships will move into a high altitude orbit of your planet in a little less than an hour. We will not initiate any hostile moves and we hope that you will not. Any use of force against us will bring instant retaliation."

Lucius waited.

"What do you want?" the voice was subdued now.

"I want to talk to whoever is in charge down there." Lucius replied. He kept his voice level. He did not want to sound hostile, merely strong.

"The Contractor is a busy person–"

"Whom, without a doubt, will want to meet with the commander of the two ships that can turn your colony to cinders," Lucius answered. He didn't like making threats, but he had to make it clear who held the better hand up front.

"I'll see what I can do."

***

The planet was quite beautiful, Lucius decided upon arrival. No pleasure world, to be sure, no West Eden or Hannishland, but beautiful all the same. Just beyond the spaceport he saw a dense forest, with hills and mountains rising beyond. The spaceport could adequately be described as 'quaint,' from the simple concrete pads and metal-roofed sheds to the small brick customs station squatting next to the gate.

In the distance, however, he noticed what looked like a scrapyard, dozens of ships, mostly tramp freighters, squatted in a large field near some large structures. He wondered at that, particularly since he saw a great deal of activity in the area. *Almost looks like a refugee fleet,* he realized.

He stepped off the shuttle, followed by two Marines in full battle armor. He didn't expect anything as… foolish as an assassination attempt, but Major Proscia had insisted. Lucius hadn't wanted to argue and a part of him had agreed.

The group of well-armed men who awaited him suggested the wisdom of that decision. They wore dark green uniforms and several wore body armor. "I am Captain Giovanni, I've come in good faith."

The group that faced him stood still, obviously hesitant to start a fight with Marines in power armor. A couple of them looked back, as if they weren't sure what to do.

In his ear bud, he heard Major William's voice, "Baron, my men have the second shuttle ready to launch with the rest of my Marines. I spoke with your escort. You will now have a full squad accompany you while on planet."

"Who is in charge?" Lucius snapped at the waiting men.

Finally a uniformed officer stepped around the armed men gathered at the ramp, "I'm Captain Beeson of the Faraday Defense Forces." He was a tall, beefy man, with dark brown hair and a ruddy complexion.

"Captain Beeson, I am Captain Giovanni. I was assured I would be granted access to your Contractor and would not be harmed along the way," Lucius said.

The other man flushed, "We do not negotiate with pirates."

Lucius walked down the ramp and extended his hand. The other man towered over him, and not for the first time, Lucius wished he stood at least a little taller, "Good. I'm not a pirate. I'm a military officer. As a military officer, I know that the military is bound by a code of honor. Will you honor our agreement?"

The other man spat at Lucius's feet, "We'll honor our end, leave your men here."

Lucius ignored the insult, though he mentally made note of the man's behavior. Either he was some kind of hothead or he was willing to deliberately provoke Lucius and his men into a firefight, possibly because he had additional forces ready to commit. The first spoke poorly of his temper, the latter suggested that he was brave and dangerous. Lucius shook his head, "They accompany me."

"Or else?" Captain Beeson's eyes narrowed.

Lucius sighed, "Captain, I have no intentions of harming your world. I want to make an offer to your Contractor, one that I believe, will make your world safer."

"*Oh...* you're a merc." Captain Beeson sneered and he looked as if he'd stepped in something foul. "Well... follow me."

***

The Office of the Contractor lay at the top of a high-rise.

The relative lack of ostentation surprised Lucius. Most fringe worlds had peacock-like dictators or corrupt oligarchies that luxuriated in wealth. The offices did display wealth and power, but nothing more than a powerful corporation's offices.

He stumbled a bit, on entering the Contractor's presence. He had not expected anything so progressive as a female leader, not on a backwater colony off the books. The Contractor was a woman of medium height with closely cut blonde hair and blue eyes. She was not classically attractive, Lucius decided. Her nose was too long and her jaw too strong, though there was a strength about her that he found attractive. She did not rise from her desk to greet him or offer him a seat in one of the chairs. She remained behind her desk, her blue eyes evaluated him. She absently brushed a lock of her blonde hair out of her eyes, "I am the Contractor."

He nodded politely, "I am Baron Lucius Giovanni, until lately of the Nova Roma Empire, and I've come to you with a business proposition."

She looked him up and down. He could see her eyes dissect him from his perfectly polished dress boots to his impeccable black dress uniform. Her eyes ranged over his service ribbons, though he doubted she recognized any of them. "You're a little short to be a warlord. You're a mercenary?"

He felt a bit of tension relax in the muscles between his shoulder-blades. He realized that she didn't care about who his father was, or what he'd done. "I was once of the Imperial Fleet."

"So you're a deserter then, and probably a pirate."

Lucius's polite smile went away. "I did not desert. Nova Roma fell to the Chxor four days ago. We took too much damage in a recent battle to make it back in time."

She paled, "Nova Roma fell?" He could see her drawing the implications to her own world's security. They weren't good, Lucius knew, not with an entire sector of space now under the control of an expansionist alien power. "Four days ago, you said?"

Lucius nodded, "There will probably be a number of ships fleeing the fall. It's probable many pirates will take advantage of the chaos."

She grimaced, "You Nova Romans aren't much better. We've a number of Saragossa refugees here. I've heard what you did there."

Lucius shrugged, "I didn't make the foreign policy of my world. Every nation has done what it must to survive, since the fall of Amalgamated Worlds. At the time, we hoped turning Saragossa into a target would buy us a decade before the Chxor turned their attention to us."

"Well, we see how that little debacle turned out, don't we?" the Contractor replied dryly.

Lucius gritted his teeth, "Look, we can snipe at each other all day, or you can listen to my offer, and then go back to whatever business you do on this backwater colony."

She smiled icily, "Well, then, state your business."

"Thank you," Lucius nodded, "Simply put, I've two warships. You could spend hundreds of millions of whatever currency you use building a shipyard large enough and then hundreds of millions more building the ships. You can outfit those ships for millions more, and then spend millions paying upkeep." Lucius smiled, "Or you could pay me a few million to stick around and defend your system."

The Contractor's eyes narrowed ,"Captain Beeson said one of those ships fired on us not too long ago."

"The Ghornath aboard said your people fired without warning when they questioned your people about a Ghornath refugee ship," Lucius held her gaze until she looked away.

"The last mercenaries we hired, the ones who fled your arrival, did the firing. Their captain assured us the Ghornath could not be trusted," she cocked her head at him. "It is hard to get hired guns that aren't either bullies, opportunistic pirates, or cowards."

Lucius held out one hand, palm upwards, "Then you see the importance of having someone trustworthy around."

"Can you be trusted?" The Contractor arched an eyebrow.

Lucius sighed, "Madame Contractor, if we work out a deal, I will honor it, I swear."

They locked gazes for a long moment. Lucius could see determination and strength in her blue eyes, but he wondered what she saw in his own dark eyes. "Very well," she sighed, "What are your terms?"

"Money is the first issue. We will, of course, accept the local currency, so long as we can use it to buy supplies and some items we can't build aboard ship," Lucius said. "I'm unsure of the value of your currency, so, for the first payment, I'll accept what you paid those fellows who just ran off."

"Their rates were extortionate."

Lucius shrugged, "You will recieve more for your money."

"We already paid them this month."

"Well, you can ask them for a refund," Lucius said with a slight smile.

She sighed, "What do you know about the politics of Faraday?"

Lucius smiled slightly, "Until we got to this system, I didn't know Faraday *existed*."

"We have a three party parliamentary system here, Captain. The Liberals, the Moderates, and the Conservatives. I'm a Liberal." She shrugged, "The Liberals want change here on Faraday."

"Change can be bad or good," Lucius said, uncertain where this conversation led.

The Contractor snorted at his neutral answer, "Right now, you might consider yourself an immigrant. Do you think you might want to become a citizen?"

Lucius shrugged, "It's not inconceivable."

"Under the Contract, under the law, it is," the Contractor's voice was flat. "Immigrants are not citizens. Citizenship on Faraday requires being born on world, to at least one Faraday citizen." She shook her head, "On top of that, if you don't have citizenship, you have no legal rights. You can't be represented in court, you can't press charges for a crime, you have no rights. We have tens of thousands of refugees here, you may have seen the boneyard near the spaceport. They've no rights to speak of and Faraday's wealthy extort them for labor."

Lucius raised his eyebrows, "That's... interesting."

"It's barbaric," the Contractor snapped. "It's unacceptable. Right now, my party is trying to change that, and we've got a number of Moderates on our governing council, the Shareholders, leaning our way. We've had power for only five years, and the Conservatives have fought ever move we've made tooth and nail. They'd still have power if not for an incident we had here five years ago that exposed some of their more severe corruption. That's how I came to be the Contractor."

"I'm seeing implications with this I'm not liking," Lucius admitted.

"You should. The Liberals also believe in a stronger military and increased foreign policy. In short, we believe that Faraday cannot stay on the fringe, alone and without allies for long."

"And the Conservatives?"

"They like the status quo," the Contractor grimaced, "I would call some of their factories slavery, but at least a master cares for his slaves somewhat. The Conservatives control much of the industry, and they view the refugee populace as a resource to be used."

"I see." Lucius frowned, "So not only will I be representing something they won't like, that being a strong foreigner, but I'll also have to purchase things from them?"

"Yes."

"Well, thank you for the warning."

"You still wish to tie your future to Faraday?" The Contractor looked surprised.

"Madam, I've seen worse systems. Frankly, some of Nova Roma's frontier worlds were… worse in a way. And if my presence causes the corrupt here discomfort, maybe even a loss of political power…" Lucius grinned, "So much the better."

"Well…" She cocked her head in surprise, "In that case," She rose offering her hand, "I'm Kate Bueller, and I have to ask… are you *that* Lucius Giovanni?"

***

"So, Captain, is this payment satisfactory?"

Lucius looked up from the paper at the monitor, "Most satisfactory. There remains only one other thing I'd like to ask. As you have no doubt read, both my ships are low on crew. I wonder if you would allow me to send out recruiters."

The Contractor's face grew cold. "There will be no drafting of our populace."

Lucius shook his head. "We'd like to sign up some of your people voluntarily. We will sign them up only for the length of the contract and any who stay aboard longer than that will be purely voluntary as well."

The Contractor nodded. "Faraday was founded as an

isolationist colony, you understand, so if I took any direct action in assisting young people to foreign ideas, it could mean my job." She frowned, "However, you would do good to buy some airtime on the radio, or on holovideo, and you can probably get a number of recruits." Lucius nodded. "And Captain, do you think that different sexes as well as races would be a good idea?"

Lucius thought for a moment. "Yes, that probably would be a good idea." Lucius typed a reminder to himself on his console. The Nova Roma Fleet's rather homogenized enlisted ranks consisted entirely of human men. It did have some, albeit few, female officers. Lucius had served under a female commander aboard the *War Shrike*, before he became Captain.

"There is one other thing…" Lucius said, somewhat hesitantly.

"Yes?" Kate Bueller said.

"I wonder, madam Contractor, if your world has… currency speculators."

She frowned, "Unfortunately so. They're a persistent pest and they've caused devaluation of the Faraday dollar several times."

"I wonder if you've let the knowledge of the fall of Nova Roma out yet?" Lucius asked.

"I've kept that pretty close, for now. That kind of knowledge can have—oh." She narrowed her eyes, "You want me to point you to some currency speculators to get rid of some Drachma?"

Lucius shrugged, "I'd assume, seeing as the Conservatives are very strong in the economics of your world, they would logically have their hand in currency speculation."

"A safe assumption," She growled.

"What hurts them economically…"

"You're talking about what's essentially a confidence scam, you know?"

"I prefer to think of it as turn-about. I have just under fifty thousand Drachma of ships funds in hard currency, and my crew has around the same in personal funds."

"You'll be lucky to get sixty percent of its worth," she cautioned

"It's worth nothing now. I might as well vent it out the airlock. But if I sell it to the currency speculators, who don't know of the fall of Nova Roma yet…"

"What you're proposing is illegal and immoral." She said, her voice stern. The edges of her mouth however, curled upwards slightly, "I'll see what I can do to help."

"Thank you Contractor, *War Shrike* out."

***

"Strike Leader Maygar," Lucius bowed slightly. "I hear you wanted to see me."

The Ghornath nodded, slightly, "I must yield command of the *Gebneyr* to Burbeg."

"I see." Lucius frowned, "Have I caused you some insult?"

"No." The old alien's hide rapidly shifted through colors, returning to a neutral brown. "I cannot say why I must leave, only that it comes at the urgings of Fleet Consul Faydeb." The Ghornath paused, "He has allowed you the loan of the *Gebneyr* for now, pending its return and a suitable payment at a later date."

"Ah." Lucius said. "That payment would be what?"

"It remains to be determined." Maygar said. "He has, provisionally, promoted Burbeg to Leader rank, your equivalent to Commander, I believe."

"Yes, close enough." Lucius said, frowning. "I must ask, do the Ghornath possess shipyards?"

"I think, Baron, we should not discuss this, right now," Strike Leader Maygar said.

"Ah." Lucius frowned. "Will you need money for passage?"

"An… agent has arranged for our passage off-world. There is a merchant vessel headed towards Anvil. We will not need currency." The alien turned to depart. He stopped. "Thank you, Lucius, for repaying my actions with honor. I hope, one day soon, we can work together."

"But first you need to get Fleet Consul Faydeb back to Ghornath high command?"

The alien's hide briefly turned a pale tan shade that Lucius guessed meant surprise, "As humans say: no comment."

"Thank you for your help, Strike Leader. Best of luck with your journey." Lucius said.

"And yours. I think yours will be the more difficult."

***

August 17, 2406
Faraday System
Unclaimed Space

Lucius had several plans for the refit and repairs aboard his two vessels. The cost for both was a minor problem, at least, until the next month's payments arrived from the planet. Currency differed from planet to planet, which meant that the pay Lucius's ships received wasn't worth the plastic it was on, unless he spent it on Faraday or converted it to Republic Denari.

The first payment and the currency exchange had given him some money to work with, which allowed him to pay his men and he had to initiate the sign-up bonus for the new recruits and fund the new training program. After that, there remained a tidy sum left over that he could address to his own plans and to initiate repairs of his ships.

Despite the hard work of his crew, both human and Ghornath, he had been unable to repair some very sensitive and extremely necessary machinery. The Ghornath communications nodule was now structurally sound, but many of the communications systems required a large industrial base to even contemplate production. The *War Shrike* desperately needed a new sensor computer, equipment for his port sensor tower, and machinery in the refueling gantry. He also needed fighters. The machine shops and fabrication units aboard the ship could produce those. He would rather give his personnel shore leave and, far more importantly, training. He thought it would be easier and cheaper to hire out the contract. Lucius found a contracting firm that he thought wouldn't screw him too badly on price, and moved on.

And, after all those costs, Lucius could look at the remaining money, and seriously hope that banks lent credit to foreigners.

Of course they didn't.

So Lucius had to turn to other means. He couldn't afford to buy a respectable, or even a semi-respectable business firm, so he looked for a firm on the verge of bankruptcy. He found a number of those, some owned by embezzling cretins and others by the bigger corporations who used them as tax write-offs. Then Lucius found the perfect one.

Matthew Nogita's father was a trained engineer from Tau Ceti.

His father had immigrated to Faraday and taken a job at one of the larger companies. He'd been skilled enough at his job and apparently impressive enough a human being that he married into the family, which made his son a citizen, although something of a societal outcast. Young Matthew Nogita had taken some of his father's ideas and started up a firm of his own. The competition had disliked both his entrepreneurial enterprise and his pedigree and had done everything they could to destroy him... but he had still managed to scrape by, working niche jobs that the bigger companies couldn't compete with.

It took Lucius a few days to arrange a meeting, but they finally had begun to discuss the contract... and what Lucius wanted to do.

"It's very simple, I supply some cash, some machinery, and some designs, and you run the business and build the craft." Lucius explained to him. "I won't own the business, but I will be an investor. You can buy me out when you get the funds."

Nogita looked down at the documents before him. "I don't mind taking the money you offer to buy the business, but, well, I don't see how you'll make any money building ships and selling them to yourself."

Lucius sighed. "Look, here, at this engine," he pulled up the schematics on the display. The secret stamps all across it would have made showing it to a foreign civilian treason, if the Nova Roma Empire had still existed. "This engine can attain accelerations twice that in your military craft, right?" Nogita nodded dubiously. "Well look at it this way, here on Faraday there is a very large market for race craft, right?" Again the nod, "Now what if we started putting these engines or worked down versions of these engines into some racing hulls?"

Nogita's eyes widened, "Racers would pay anything for those engines, they can afford to anyway. Why, we would be able to charge whatever we wanted!"

Lucius nodded. "As long as you register these patents, the engine–and the profits—are yours… and mine. The money we earn on the racers will easily cover the cost of the fighters. So, do we have an agreement?"

Nogita frowned, "You know, here on Faraday, I could take your money, sign that paper, and if I blew you off, you wouldn't be able to do anything legally, right?"

"True. If a man dishonest enough to do that did so, it might be wise to remember who has a bunch of Marines willing to break things," Lucius said.

Nogita smiled, "Just warning you. I've seen too many people taken advantage of."

"You're my insurance against that."

The man nodded. "Yeah, boss, we have a deal."

***

August 30, 2406
Faraday System
Unclaimed Space

Lucius shook hands with Matthew Nogita and nodded acknowledgement to James Harbach. The older engineer hadn't even bothered to hide his bitterness with Lucius. Even so, Harbach knew he had it about as good as he could expect, given the circumstances.

The office held a startling quantity of print-outs, hand drawn sketches, and scribbled columns of figures scrawled on scraps of paper.

Lucius looked in vain for an empty chair to sit in, then gave it up as futile, "So what's today's crisis?" The workshop and trial runs had gone successfully, but he'd received numerous calls from both engineers about a number of matters.

"We're screwed," Mathew Nogita said.

"There's no way we can finish the ships under construction, much less all the orders we've received," James said. He seemed almost jovial in that news. He wiggled his hands back and forth.

Lucius looked between the two. "Explain."

Nogita spoke, "Someone bought up all the palladium, boss. We need the paladium for the drives."

"Palladium?" Lucius asked.

"Palladium," Jimmy Wiggles said, and his voice dropped into his toneless lecture mode, "It is a metal of the platinum group, used most commonly in industrial applications for its properties to absorb and hold hydrogen--"

Lucius scowled, "I know what palladium is. Why can't we buy more?"

"That's just it, boss." Matthew Nogita shrugged, "Someone bought it all. Every ounce of it available in the star system."

"Every ounce?" Lucius shook his head, "There are mines, right? I know for certain the planet has some merchant traffic and a little bit of orbital mining going on too, what about that?"

"There's not a huge trade in it," Nogita shrugged, "The little bit of mining taking place was enough for the small amount of new construction. And most of those constructions don't need nearly as much palladium as your drive does."

"Can we substitute something else for it?" Lucius asked.

"It's theoretically possible," Harbach said. "We're not using it for its unique properties, but we'd probably have to use platinum." He turned to a dusty chalk board and began scribbling as he muttered to himself. "No, no... hmmm."

He turned around, "Well, you know, this is actually very interesting. We'd have to use about three times as much platinium as palladium, but it might actually increase efficency of the drive by three tenths of a percent!"

Lucius frowned, "That sounds expensive."

"Boss, we're talking metric tons of platinum, that's not expensive; it's financial suicide!"

Jimmy Wiggles hummed to himself and did a little dance as his chalk flashed across a board. Lucius shook his head, he gestured at Matthew and they stepped out into the hallway, and left the other engineer to scribble and mutter behind. "Do we have an alternative?" Lucius asked.

Mathew Nogita hung his head, "I don't know, boss. It's bad, either way. We just picked up six more contracts yesterday. When I went to place the intial orders, that's when I found out."

"So, what are the odds this is random?" Lucius asked.

"I wouldn't put any money on it," Nogita said. "There just isn't any project going on that would require that much, not unless you were the one doing it."

"So it's sabotage," Lucius felt something dark stir in his gut.

Matthew couldn't meet his eyes, "I'm sure whoever's doing it thinks they're just making a bit of money--"

Lucius felt a jolt pass down his spine. "They're directly jeopardizing the same business that produces fighters to defend their planet. I don't care who they are, they deserve a quick trial and a quicker execution," Lucius said. He let out a calming breath, "Very well, so give me an overview of how bad this will be."

"Very bad, boss." Nogita shook his head. "It couldn't have come at a worse time. I *just* signed a contract for six ships with Schultz Enterprises. All six are large freighters, with fifty percent higher a profit margin than our other contracts and a huge bonus for early delivery."

"And a huge penalty for late or non-delivery?" Lucius asked.

"Well, yes, but we haven't had any problems before--"

"Which is why they knew you wouldn't choke on it, especially with the bait of the early delivery bonus." Lucius grunted, "We've been set up."

Nogita didn't take more than a second to catch on, "Oh, crap. They bought up all the palladium. We default on the contract, they bring the whole thing into court."

"How would the courts react?" Lucius asked.

Nogita scowled, "If we got lucky, we'd keep a partial stock in the company and Schultz would 'oversee' our operations, after we built the ships at cost, of course." He shook his head, "If it goes to a judge Schultz bought, then I'd end up in jail, Schultz would receive the whole company and all our assets."

Lucius nodded, "So... what can we get done with the palladium on hand?"

"That's the problem, the little bit I've got on hand is enough for one engine, we've got five other contracts, twelve ships total, all coming due in the next two months. That's the early delivery date to Schultz, as well."

Lucius stopped. He stared out a window, not really seeing the factories or the river or even the shanty town that squatted in the boneyard. "So we need palladium, and fast. How about us doing the mining?"

Nogita shook his head, "There's strict import laws. Add in the time in getting that kind of thing set up, mining the right asteroid and accumulating more than trace elements of it... we just don't have *time*, boss."

Lucius stood silent for a moment. His eyes followed the course of a laundry line from the shanty town that extended to one of the hulked refugee ships. Every time he tried to get anything working it seemed more and more like the human race seemed destined for the scrap yard, just like one of those ships. In a few decades, the handful of survivors would be picking across the skeleton, looking for spare parts...

Lucius' eyes widened, "Parts..."

"Boss?"

"Palladium is used on older ships too?"

"Yeah boss. Not as much as we need on one of these new ones, but some."

"Go get Harbach, tell the professor we're going on a field trip."

***

The trip took a bit more preparation than Lucius had hoped. Even so, the next day, he arrived with a small Marine escort at one of the larger refugee ships.

A scrawny boy escorted them into the dimly lit bowels of the old ship. In a room that had once served as a ship's lounge, Lucius met with two dozen men and women.

They were a mixed lot. Lucius recognized the scraps of uniform that some of them wore as old merchant uniforms. Others wore whatever civilian garb they could afford. A couple looked decently fed. None of them looked remotely prosperous.

"Good morning," Lucius said, his gaze swept across them all. "I'm Lucius Giovanni and I have a business deal for you."

"That like the rent we're paying for our landing facilities?" one of the men grumbled.

"Rent?" Lucius asked. His gaze went to the shanty town beyond the port hole.

"We pay rent for the land we occupy on a per-meter rate." A grey-haired woman said. Her lined face and hard eyes bored into Lucius. "Utilities too, if we draw water and power, or a 'safety' fee if we run our reactors and power our recycler systems."

"How can you afford that?" Lucius said. He couldn't keep the surprise off his face.

"Most of our... benefactors accept manual labor as payment," one of the younger men growled. He had black hair with a gaunt, pinched face, deeply seamed with lines. "Of course, they pay us in food for any excess man hours we contribute."

"That's abominable," Lucius said. He had heard that Faraday's elite used the refugees for labor... but he hadn't expected they paid them in just food. That was almost as bad as some of the worlds with slavery.

"It's that or starve or try to find refuge somewhere else," An older man said. He looked like one of the few that ate often enough. His civilian suit looked to be well-cared for, if old. "Others have left. Some have returned with tales of piracy and war."

"Just because some people have sold their fellows into slavery doesn't mean the rest of us need to be grateful, Alec!" The younger man said. "They may cottle you as their lapdog now, but-_"

"You would have done the same had you arrived here generations ago instead of in the last decade, Nyguyen." Alec responded. His response started a shouting match between several of the groups. The babble of different dialects and voices made it almost unintelligible.

"Enough!" Lucius's voice cut through the compartment. "It's obvious there's bad blood between you and the factory owners... and more between some of you." He cleared his throat, "I'm in a situation not unlike yours." He held up a hand before anyone could object. "I have more resources at my disposal, to be certain. But I am an outsider, I've come with only my men and my ship and I am without a home to call my own."

Lucius looked around at the faces. He saw suspicion, cynicism and doubt. He discarded his original plan to bargain. While it would probably be cheapest, he would gain no allies and most likely alienate the only faction with which he felt any similarity. *Besides, these people have been treated like trash, some of them for generations,* Lucius thought darkly. They deserved better than for him to treat them the same.

"The truth of the matter, is that like you, I came here looking for a new life. As you might know, I put some money into a factory, one whose owner I trust, Mr. Nogita, here." There were some grunts of acknowledgement. "When we began to find success, someone set us up. They've bought up all of the resources we need to finish our contracts. If we default, then they'll take over the factory."

Lucius saw no softening of any of the audience. He hadn't expected it. "So here's my offer. We need four metric tons of palladium. We can't mine it, we can't buy it off the market, and we can't import any. Palladium is found in your ships in the power systems and engines of your ships. In exchange--"

"You want to gut our ships?!" A big man from the back interrupted. He barged forwards, "That's all we've got left. We've sold ourselves and our children into slavery for food, but we will not give up our ships, not for--"

"In exchange, we will refit all of your ships with our new engine systems," Lucius talked over the interruption, his voice level and calm. "As soon as our current contracts are cleared."

They stared at him in silence.

"Your new drives, they're military grade, aren't they?" Nyguyen asked.

"They are." Lucius said. "To be clear, I'm not offering to do a one-for-one size swap on your ships drives. The drives we'll build you may be significantly smaller. But you'll have at least the same acceleration. We're not custom-building each one, just building a number of identical drive systems, which we'll install for you."

"What if we don't want them installed?" Alec asked. The expression on his face suggested that the drives would be sold... and the money would go towards himself, rather than any refugees that he managed.

Lucius grimaced, "If you want to sell the drive rather than install it, that's up to you. The installation is a one time deal, though."

The big man who'd interrupted snorted, "His ship's in such bad shape at this point it won't hold air, much less lift off the ground."

The old man looked around at the others, "As long as we can get some kind of assurances as to the validity of the agreement, then I will go along with this." He smiled nervously, "Now if you'll excuse me, I'll speak with my engineer to make preparations."

Lucius watched Alec step out with narrow eyes. A man who'd sold out his own people would have no hesitation about selling out someone else. He made a mental note to have someone keep an eye on him.

"I'm certain each of you will have to speak with your crews and your passengers about this decision. It will be at least two months before I'll be able to make good on the offer," Lucius said. "As a proof of my intentions, you may select two of your number to monitor our construction. Additionally, we'll probably be hiring, and paying cash, for anyone willing to work hard and help to get our current construction completed."

The group still looked distrustful, if not as hostile as before.

Lucius nodded at them, "Contact me with your decisions by tomorrow morning."

On his way out, he noticed the decay of the ship even more. The tired, miserable faces that peered at him from the corridor seemed even more downcast and afraid.

"Hey!"

Lucius turned. The big man and Nyguyen both approached wearily, their eyes on the pair of Marines flanking Lucius. "Yes?"

"I was wondering," the big man said. "Those enlistment advertisements you've been running, are they open to us too?"

"What?" Lucius asked.

"What my friend Aaron Dallas means," Nyguyen offered, "is that the Faraday Defense Force doesn't allow non-citizens to join their ranks... not even to enlist."

"Bastards don't even let us own weapons," Dallas said. "That was one of the terms for our entry. They also disarmed any defense systems aboard ship."

Lucius shook his head, "That's ridiculous." Even after the Imperial Security Act, Nova Romans retained the right to bear personal weapons. To disarm whatever pitiful weapons a freighter might carry was not just ridiculus, it was insulting.

"The recruitment is open to all who apply. I'll take anyone willing to serve, you can tell your people that." Lucius shook his head, "And I'll treat every recruit the same. They'll receive the same pay, same food, and same quarters as any other recruit."

***

September 27, 2406
Faraday System
Unclaimed Space

"So, Matthew, what's the news?" Lucius asked. After almost a month of work, and what had looked like tens of thousands of man-hours of labor, his business partner looked exhausted. Lucius had been more deeply involved in the training of the new recruits than he had expected. Fortunately, Major Proscia's Marines and a select group of ship's crew had served admirably in the basic training.

Where Lucius had worked hardest was with his remaining officers in the selection of recruits for officer training. They'd studied the recruits and looked for that spark of initiative and the ability to think outside the box. They didn't have time to put them through months or years of additional training, they needed the best and most capable to fill the roles right away. Those recruits received additional training, and Lucius had been personally involved in many of the classes and exercises.

His experience at the Nova Roma Military Academy had proven an excellent resource to draw on. Lucius had discovered that some part of him actually *liked* teaching, especially to enthusiastic students. He had a training exercise to attend later in the day and Lucius actually looked forward to it... and to the nasty surprises he and Anthony Doko had worked up.

Even so, between the training and the continued repairs aboard the *War Shrike*, he hadn't had time to follow up with Nogita. One thing he had come to value about the man, once he got a tune for Lucius's hands-off approach, he simply got to work. Lucius had felt certain the other man would warn him if anything serious needed his attention. For now, it appeared that he'd been correct.

"Well, boss, we got it all done," Nogita shrugged, "It's been a month that if I ever repeated, my wife would kill me." The engineer settled slowly onto the edge of his desk. "As soon as it became clear that we found a source of palladium and that we'd be producing the ships not only on time, but early, Schultz Enterprises flooded the market with palladium."

Lucius gave a snort, "I hope that didn't help them."

"It didn't," Matthew Nogita smiled. "As a matter of fact, between the loss they took between the buy price they paid and the sell price we got, they lost somewhere upwards of a hundred million. Combined with the twenty million dollar bonus for early completion, and the hundred million dollar price tag, I think they're having a bad year."

Lucius smiled in return, "Good. *Very* good. I suppose it would be too much to hope it ruined them?"

Nogita shook his head, "No, Baron, unfortunately not. They're one of Faraday's largest corporations. That chickenshit Schultz owns controlling interests on half the space industry. It hurt him, it might make it so he can't do anything to us any time soon, but he'll recover."

Lucius shrugged, "Then we keep an eye out for him. I think the loyalty base we've developed with the factory workers will work in our favor in that regard." He nodded out at the busy factory floor.

Matthew nodded, "Agreed. I never held with the standard practices around here. But I've never seen these people so motivated. I wouldn't have bet even money that we could finish those ships, but when you let on how much it would hurt bastards like Schultz..."

Lucius nodded. "They've suffered through a lot, Matthew." After his talk with the ship's captains, he found more than enough recruits and the factory floor had flooded with workers. He didn't fool himself to think their hard work came from anything besides a hatred for the rich who'd mortgaged them to wage-slave status, but he hoped they had at least gained a working relationship now.

"Good job, Matt, and be sure we give those people out there a decent bonus, I can't think of a better use for the profit we've made on Schultz's behalf."

***

"Captain, the first shipment of fighters is here." Chief Petty Officer Winslow reported.

Lucius nodded, "Excellent! Alice send someone forward to open the hatch and tow them in."

It was with no little awe that he watched his new fighter squadron XO go into motion. Just two weeks ago she, and half her squadron had been the female racing gang known as the Raging Lionesses. They had signed up, in masse, after the first day of his advertisements. Their presence was at once both startling, amusing, and, to some of his crew, contemptible.

Faraday considered itself an enlightened culture, above such things as gender or racial discrimination. This of course, flew in the face of their xenophobia of those born off world.

The culture of the Nova Roma sector, on the other hand was fairly primitive. Even the most Egalitarian oriented of Nova Roma never considered co-sex dining halls, sleeping quarters, and even bathrooms. In this respect, a number of his crew experienced embarrassing and even harassing incidents. Lucius had found the need to hammer more than one individual for behavior that was unacceptable. He had hoped that such behavior would be isolated to a few of the lower enlisted, but Ensign Tascon had proved him wrong. Lucius had felt more than a little satisfaction to slam the Ensign, especially after the initial counseling had failed to yield the desired results.

The Faraday recruits had issues of their own. Right off he had to release seven well-trained but inadequate officers. The three men and four women had shown potential, but they treated the Ghornath with disgust, and handled the other non-human recruits with contempt. They all had prior service with other militaries, five from the Colonial Republic and two from the Centauri Confederation. Two non-human Wrethe received discharges as well, because of their inability to follow orders from their officers.

Then again, perhaps trying to integrate Wrethe went a little too far, Lucius acknowledged. The two meter tall, bipedal aliens were known to be both territorial and violently individualistic. Still, from what he had heard, they functioned well in hand-to-hand combat and Major Proscia had been optimistic about their use in boarding operations.

Faraday had a large refugee population, which hadn't found it easy to integrate into their new home. With Faraday's unfair policies towards immigrants, Lucius's recruiting went well. Many recruits signed on for several years, and some signed on 'for the duration.'

Lucius looked over at his new Chief Petty Officer. Chief Winslow's colorful military background in the Nova Roma Imperial Fleet lasted thirty years, right up to the day he shot and killed his last Captain on his homeworld of Gio Toro. A wanted file remained on the ship's computer for his capture and return to face a court martial.

The *War Shrike* hadn't had a real Chief Petty Officer since the death of Chief Lagrano. Lucius, reading Chief Winslow's records, had had initial doubts. On meeting the proper, polished, and professional Chief, he no longer had any.

Whatever pushed the man to murder his Captain, three decades ago, lay in the past.

Other military refugees, some of them deserters, others less so, also bolstered his new recruits. Major, now Colonel, Proscia, had even ventured to smile when a platoon of Centauri Marines showed up, en masse, to volunteer. Lucius didn't doubt they'd done mercenary work to keep themselves fed since the dissolution of the Centauri Confederation. They had a hungry look about them, however, that suggested they'd refused more than one unfair or illegal offer... and suffered for it.

Lucius shook off his thoughts, and turned back to the simulation monitor. The recruits had finished their basic training and they'd begun their training at their ratings. The newly commissioned officers had also received enough training that they notionally knew their duties. Lucius had felt it time for an evaluation of their progress. Throughout the ship, he'd integrated the trainees with his more experienced crew.

He'd split them into several smaller crews, in the simulator, though, so that the inexperienced officers would have less to manage and so that the crews would have more individual responsibility.

He winced internally at the statistics. The gunnery stations had taken severe losses in the the *War Shrike's* previous engagements and that was where he had the least amount of experienced personnel to train the recruits. Lucius plugged into the communications of both crews, watching the simulated battle on his console's holovisual unit.

"Port broadside on third quadrant target A. Lock…. Fire!" the acting Commanding Officer shouted. A third of the shots actually struck the computer-generated target. One well-aimed shot actually slipped through the defense screens. "She's altering course, maintain gun lock, we'll match. Prepare to roll ship, rolling." The barrel roll that the acting CO threw the destroyer into kept the enemy ship in effective firing range, but it also left his rear harder to defend from small craft, such as fighters.

The computer saw that, analyzed the situation, and the fighters swept in.

"Fighters inbound in second and third quadrants, port side guns pick your targets and fire at will. Starboard, fire on target A, fire." This second broadside was dealt from closer range, and just under the equatorial plane of the enemy corvette. A near perfect shot, at five thousand kilometers, less than knife range. This broadside tore the lighter ship in half. But the fighters had the same shot, an entire squadron that faced weak defensive fire, with an under-equator shot, and a full payload of missiles.

The destroyer vanished in a ball of fire less than two minutes after its prey.

***

"Can you tell me what you did wrong?" Lucius asked.

Lieutenant Daniel Beeson sighed, "I didn't cover myself from the fighters, I never thought the computer would sacrifice a ship to take out mine."

Lucius nodded, "Don't forget that. Anyone can spot a feint or a trick, but an experienced commander will notice when a bad situation can be turned to the better. The computer did that; the corvette was doomed from the moment it altered course. However, the computer realized that, and adjusted so that its loss would bring victory." The simulation had gone very much like a skirmish Lucius commanded at the attack on Ghornath Prime. He'd never have thought anyone would sacrifice one ship for another. That decision nearly cost him his life.

"Isn't that sort of, well, disgusting… sir? That war is just two people sacrificing lives?"

Lucius nodded. "Yes, it is vulgar, but so is war. It is impossible to keep all of your people alive, but your efforts should make sure they don't die in vain. There will be days when you can live with yourself only because you took out the enemy, no matter the cost. It never, ever, gets easy, but then, nothing ever is easy, is it?" Lucius shook his dark humor off. "You did much better than last time though. Your port side batteries are still rough. Another thing, you always have to keep an eye on all of your enemy's units, no matter where they are. You chased off the fighters early on, and you expected them to keep running instead of coming back in on your tail. Don't count an enemy out until you have a kill, and even then be cautious."

His new Assistant Tactical Officer nodded. "Yes, sir." He'd been the weapons officer aboard Faraday's patrol ship, which made him experienced, but marginal on Lucius' list of officer recruits. Lucius had put more of the experienced crew aboard the *Gebneyr*. Lucius trusted himself bring the less experienced recruits up to speed quicker.

"Overall, however, you did very well. Most of those we will be facing out here won't be the dedicated and selfless warriors of the real fleets. Pirates, mostly. Congratulations on passing this exam and I look forward to seeing you on the bridge, right beside Commander Doko... once you complete your training. You're dismissed, Lieutenant Beeson."

The Lieutenant stood and snapped off a sharp salute before he turned and left. Lucius knew that the younger Daniel Beeson's decision to sign on with him had caused an estrangement with his father. The tall, ruddy faced young man had a sharp mind and seemed to have something to prove, either to himself or to his father, though Lucius wasn't sure that the boy knew which. *Captain* Beeson commanded the the Faraday Defense Force's elderly destroyer, though from what Lucius had heard, he apparently served as a military adviser to several members of Faraday's Moderate Party.

Lieutenant Beeson filled out his officer complement. His enlisted crew was still learning their duties, as evidenced by their efforts in the simulation. Lucius figured another month would be just long enough to bring them up to his minimum training standards. Endless drilling and practice would, hopefully, tighten them down and make them as good a crew as any who had served aboard the *War Shrike* before.

Morale had started to climb again, a combination of the new and energetic recruits and the effort that Lucius had dedicated to rebuild the ship's morale. Most of the original crew had come from Nova Roma or one of her daughter colonies. The blow over their homeworld's loss had hit hard. Families, friends, everything and everyone they had known off of the ship were gone, lost to the Chxor. Hardest hit was his brother-in-law, Lucius knew. His former friend went about his tasks, but the normally cheerful man had become bitter and angry.

His XO, Commander Doko was also hit hard, but Lucius knew that was as much about something that never could have happened as actual loss. The lowly-born officer knew he never would have stood a chance, especially not as close as he was to Lucius.

Politically, his affections were absurd. *Still, he loved the girl and she him... and now they'll never get a chance to get over one another,* Lucius thought. He wished, not for the first time, that the convoluted politics of Nova Roma and their noble houses had never come to be.

Might as well wish that my father never betrayed the Empire, Lucius knew, *or that my grandmother fell in love with Emperor Romulus I.*

Lucius shook of that thought and forced his mind back to the task at hand. In addition to training the new crew members, Lucius had to design battle plans for eventualities. He had to allocate his resources to make certain that any attack could be dealt with. With the *Gebneyr* repaired and an aged freighter purchased to act as an improvised fighter carrier, the force would be something to reckon with, should anyone attack. Lucius hoped for quiet times as long as possible, however.

He feared things wouldn't stay quiet for long. Lucius had finally gained access to some Faraday Defense Force records. Two previous Colonial Republic forces steered clear after bluffs and threats over retaliation. The previous mercenaries had run off a disorganized pirate raid. Those occurrences suggested that even someplace as remote as Faraday wouldn't stay lost for long.

The Chxor Empire continued to expand.

The threats made Lucius anxious. Faraday had the potential to work out very well, or to go very badly indeed.

***

CHAPTER III

November 5, 2402 Earth Standard Time
Faraday System
Unclaimed Space

The ships of Nova Roma and the other stellar nations didn't match the power of the fallen Amalgamated Worlds Fleet. They had built ships of scale and power, with overlapping defense screens, antimatter reactors, and advanced weapons.

Nevertheless, the designers of the Nova Roma ships of the line had done their best. They managed to create defense screens that protected, if not all of the ship, three quarters of the hull, leaving only the full aft hemisphere, and the 'khon' sections open. The khon sections being four eddies in the forward area of the screens, caused from the tension of stretching the energy as far as was needed.

The *War Shrike* was a Desperado-class battleship, designed for the quick, fast, and furious clashes of skirmish lines, convoy raiding, and recon in force. She had two sets of turret-mounted dual exotic particle cannons, an over-powerful armament for her size, and her intended duties. The later decision to put the Desperadoes to work in the wall of battle against larger ships proved a fiasco. They inflicted heavy damage on their opponents but – invariably -- lost. The most notable example was the Battle of Khon, where the lighter but more numerous guns of the enemy found the forward shielding of the Desperadoes to be inadequate in four specific locations. Those four sections bore their namesake from that battle.

The reasons for the horrendous losses, both in that battle and others, was that the Desperado-class lent most of its energy in offense. When it came down to taking damage itself, the lighter battleships lost against more massive dreadnoughts. Desperadoes such as the *War Shrike* carried only two squadrons of fighters, mounted only a small amount of electronic countermeasures, and in the end, simply didn't have large enough power plants to produce the strong defensive screens of larger ships.

They proved extremely effective in defending convoys, both singly and in groups, from raiders. It was when Nova Roma Fleet

Command ordered the remaining Desperado-class battleships to begin raids at the will of the captain and whatever opportunities arose, that the true glory of the battleships arose. The *War Shrike* had killed over forty-three convoy escorts, and at least three times that number of convoy vessels. In fact, the *War Shrike* had one of the most-feared reputations to the enemies of Nova Roma.

Perhaps that was why Task Force Seven of the Chxor fleet made the *War Shrike* its primary target.

Perhaps... then again, perhaps not.

Squadron Commander Kleigh drove Task Force Seven after the *War Shrike*. Kleigh, being a typical Chxor, was very logical minded, structure oriented, and ultimately, a perfectionist. He had faced the *War Shrike* in no less than three occasions. On all three, despite overwhelming numbers, distinct firepower advantage, and in the end, even complete surprise, the *War Shrike* had escaped him.

It made no sense, it followed no pattern; the *War Shrike* was an anomaly, completely atypical of the logic and order of the universe. The Chxor were superior. The Chxor destroyed all who opposed their inevitable expansion, the Chxor created order out of disorder. Nothing, *nothing*, could long oppose the Chxor Empire, Squadron Commander Kleigh knew.

Therefore, Kleigh decided that the *War Shrike* must be eliminated.

Kleigh felt no personal loathing towards his prey; nor respect either. The Chxor had long previously abandoned emotion as inferior to the necessary structure and order of a modern society. However, an objective observer may have noted that Kleigh held a perverse fixation on the destruction of the *War Shrike*. Many xenothropologists considered this blind dedication to a goal that the Chxor often underwent a natural outlet for the suppression of their emotions. Most other people without the benefits of such a brilliant education simply understood the Chxor sometimes went insane.

Regardless, Kleigh performed with maximum efficiency as he gave his latest command, in an orderly and calm voice. His crusade for order would soon be over. Hours spent in trying to detect the escape course of his prey had finally paid off. There had been interruptions, as the task force dealt with any enemy ships they located in the search of their main target, a good many number in actuality, far too many for the sector to remain unmanaged by the Chxor. Order should be maintained, after all.

The two corvettes and single destroyer that the force encountered had attempted surrender. Squadron Commander Kleigh saw little to gain in the capture of human pirates and mercenaries, and a potential for live gunnery practice in the engagement. Afterward, the escape pods and individual humans in their vacuum suits had proven of further use in as a drill for the missile and fighter interceptor gun crews.

The engagement would provide a marked improvement in discipline amongst the non-Chxor conscripts as well, Squadron Commander Kleigh knew. They obviously saw the fate of those who opposed the Chxor and would not wish to join them.

If Kleigh were so inferior as to feel emotions he would have been pleased at the outcome and efficiency. And, after his crew had searched the enemy ships for intelligence, they had found exactly what they wanted on their sensor computer. The enemy ships had seen his target, and their computers knew what star system. He would backtrack the course of these renegade humans and soon he would find more.

Granted, it was only a scrap of recording. A bit of voice which Kleigh recognized as Captain Lucius Giovanni and sensor readings which matched the *War Shrike*. Still, that was enough to tell Kleigh that his squadron was on the correct track. He had technically exceeded his initial orders to engage Nova Roma forces on the periphery of their Empire. In truth, he knew, he had gone beyond their borders. Still, this latest encounter showed that he had continued a logical progression. His Fleet Commander had yet to order him to return, and he still served the efforts of the Benevolence Council and the Chxor Empire.

The efficiency involved in the service of their interests and to achieve the restoration of good order to the universe in the destruction of Lucius Giovanni and the War Shrike *is most excellent,* Kleigh thought. Best off all, to achieve it soon would be the epitome of efficiency.

***

Lucius wasn't sure what to make of the Contractor's curt request for him to meet with her privately at her office. When he found her red-faced and pacing, he still didn't know.

"Fortress Faraday," the Contractor snarled. "The Conservatives are calling a convention; they want to 'see to the gross violation of the Contract.' They're rallying behind the call of 'Fortress Faraday,' calling for us to sever all ties with the outside. The fools think we can build down our naval presence, and buy off anyone who comes through! They don't understand anything!"

Lucius blinked at the vehemence in the Contractor's voice. "I wondered what you called me down here for. Anything I can do to help?"

The Contractor rolled her eyes in apology. "You can't do a thing, I'm afraid. I wanted to warn you in person. While you have finally gotten things in order upstairs, the shit will be flying down here."

Lucius raised an eyebrow.

The Contractor sighed, "I know a bit about how difficult things must have been for you, and that was with my unofficial help. Right now, the Conservatives will be pulling out all stops to prove that I sympathize with you; I can't afford to help you without losing control down here. I've got to keep control down here or they'll throw away all the progress I've made over the past five years."

"I see," Lucius nodded. "I'll do my best to keep things quiet upstairs."

The Contractor nodded and for once she seemed to relax. "Honestly, it has been good to deal with someone who knows what they're doing." She straightened her spine. "But now to business. Get up there and at all costs avoid anything that could put things in a panic down here."

Lucius's comlink began to ring and a second later the Contractor's did as well. They both went for them. They listened for a moment, Lucius to the bud in his ear, the contractor to her handheld.

They looked at each other for a moment. "Madam, I believe that we have a problem."

The Contractor nodded, her face pale as the person on the other end continued to reel off a list of ships.

Lucius didn't need a categorical listing, he heard enough in the

four words. "Chxor task force inbound."
***

Lucius arrived at the shuttle pad, and stopped in surprise to see his brother in law at the shuttle ramp. "Reese, when did you--"

"I'm leaving."

Lucius noted the two duffel bags at the man's feet, "You can't be serious."

"There's a Chxor fleet coming in, right?"

"Yes..."

"I'm going to stay here and fight." Reese said. "I don't expect an Academy failure and a disgraceful traitor to understand that, but that's what I'm going to do."

Lucius bit back a retort and spoke slowly and levelly, "Reese, we're going to fight them. We're going to do our best to get them to follow us. I need you—"

"And I needed Alanis. You left her to die." Reese's cold voice cut him off. "I'll stay here. Odds are, the Chxor will win, as they've won before. And then they'll come here. This gets me away from you and the opportunity to kill Chxor."

"Dammit, Reese, you should still be in sickbay—"

"I'll manage." Reese looked away. "Anything else?"

Lucius clenched his jaw, and stiffly came to attention, "Commander Giovanni-Leone, you are dismissed."

Reese returned the salute, jaw clenched. "I stand dismissed." He grabbed both duffel bags. Lucius watched him stagger under the weight.

"Good hunting," the bitter man muttered grudgingly as he passed.
***

"Sir, it looks like four Dreadnoughts, and twelve cruisers," Doko informed Lucius as he stepped onto the bridge. "I'd say it's the same group as hit us at Venture, same group that was after the convoy."

Lucius nodded, "I'd hoped that the jump would throw them off." It was impossible to track a jump through shadow space. "They must have searched every system in the sector." He studied the information on his console and then turned to Cato Naevius, "How many fighters do we have available?"

The Nova Roma Harasser fighter-bomber carried the largest missile capacity of any conventional human fighter. One fighter could carry up to twelve conventional Hunter missiles, useful for killing fighters and missiles as well as larger ships when used in large numbers. Alternatively, they could also carry three of the larger Pilum ship-killer missiles. Those missiles carried sixty-megaton fusion warheads. They also mounted pulse lasers for a close engagement against fighters or missiles. A normal squadron of six fighters could unleash hell on any type of enemy.

The Harasser's versatility in combat load-outs had done much for Nova Roma's predominance in human space, until the coming of the Chxor. Which meant Lucius wanted his fighters ready to unleash against the enemy.

Naevius paused in thought. "Second Squadron is off training with the *Gebneyr* , between the fighters down on the surface and the others on patrol…" He sighed, "Well, really all we've got is First squadron on board, Captain."

Lucius winced, and then grinned ruefully. "So much for those plans, I suppose I should have kept at least two squadrons on station here, but…" He shook his head. "Alright, we obviously can't fight these ones head on, and from the course they're laying, they'll easily detect the local communications within a few hours." The Chxor arrival in the outer system meant that the dense magnetic fields of the outer gas giants would at least mask the local radio broadcasts somewhat. Short of a high frequency burst or military grade broadcast, the Chxor would have to clear the nearest gas giant and that would take them some time, he knew. He thought for a moment. "Our best hope is to draw them off in a pursuit, convince them we're still heavily damaged. Have the *Gebneyr* and our fighters head back here to take up a defensive position, take out the picket they leave in-system. They can use the sensor shadow of the gas giants and their moons to mask their movement." He looked over at Anthony Doko, "Plan Gamma Three?"

Doko winced, but gave him a nod.

He looked around the bridge at the new faces that stood at the old stations. He restrained a sigh. This was suicide in all but name, the fly baiting the bull. "Plot your course for Gamma Three on this little joyride."

***

"I understand fully the orders you give me, fellow warrior, and I shall carry them out," Burbeg roared into the comm. As he turned away to begin giving orders, Lucius thumbed off the screen and turned his attention to the oncoming ships.

There were four dreadnoughts. They swept in-system arrogantly, escorted by a dozen light cruisers. The cruisers deployed so as to intercept any fire on the dreadnoughts with their own hulls. Lucius never understood what went through the minds of the Chxor when they decided to make only the two classes of warships. It did make a sort of weird logic that mass-produced defense ships could screen mass produced attack ships. He knew --from experience of tearing apart the unwieldy formation-- that it didn't always work. The Chxor just thought too slowly and reacted too slowly to change. With two wings of fighters and his own ship to lure the enemy around, Lucius could bleed the enemy dry, smash their offensive ships to scrap and then run slashing attacks against the largely unarmed cruisers.

He sighed, though. Lucius possessed only three full squadrons, and didn't have the time. If that task force cleared the gas giants they would pick up the civilian transmissions. Chxor doctrine from that point would take them directly to the planet. The Chxor would assist the populace in seeing things their way. Perhaps they would only use threats, but probably they would utilize nerve gas attacks or tactical nukes and swiftly turn it into a Chxor outpost. From there they would begin to 'process' the populace and import Chxor colonists to replace them.

"Fifteen seconds till full power to engines." That was the calm call from Lt. Meridan, at the engineering station. Commander Harbach was in the engine room.

"Main weapons up in ten seconds." Lieutenant Beeson announced from his station.

"Life Support and Medical systems online and stable," Dr. Varene murmured. She had taken the position as the ship's doctor, a slot which had been empty for over a year. Lucius had been impressed with her background and experience and she'd been of tremendous benefit in treatment of his injured crew thus far.

"Communications and Electromagnetic Countermeasure

systems fully operational." Lieutenant Palmer drawled. He was a very adept user of both systems, but his nasal twang drove Lucius to distraction at odd times, such as when he was worrying about an upcoming engagement. He'd served in the Centauri Confederation fleet, and claimed he came from Earth, though Lucius felt certain that his accent had to be an affectation.

"Astrogation and Helm at standby, damage control teams are ready, and all Battle Support systems are standing by, Captain." Doko said with crisp perfection.

"Alright," Lucius took a deep breath, preparing to "let's be—"

"Sir, intercepting a message to the Chxor!" Lieutenant Palmer snapped. "Originating from Faraday, I'm patching it in, sir."

"...again would like to welcome you to the Faraday System. We understand you are in pursuit of a pirate vessel known as the *War Shrike*. It has looted our world and now lies in orbit at these coordinates-"

Lucius overrode the signal, "Find me the origin of the broadcast. Jam the frequency." He brought up a line to the office of the Contractor. "What are your people doing down there, someone is broadcasting a message to the Chxor, if they've heard—"

The Contractor shook her head in resignation. "The Shareholders met in an emergency meeting. They've deposed me. They have decided to bargain with the Chxor, for Faraday's surrender." Her shoulders slumped in defeat, "The fools think they can bribe them off."

Out of the corner of his eye, he saw that the tactical section had updated the Chxor squadron's course. The icons of the Chxor forces had changed heading to one that would be a least-time run to the planet. Lucius swore savagely, "I'll launch shuttles to the surface, I'll evacuate who I can."

"The Shareholders and the Contractor will prohibit anyone from leaving," she answered tiredly.

"They can't prohibit my Marines, and there will be a team on each shuttle to provide escort. Get your people moving, get landing coordinates to Lieutenant Naevius so he can order the shuttle pilots and escort them down."

She nodded, some light of hope returned to her eyes. "I won't be able to get many, but some people will listen."

Lucius brought up a screen to Cato Naevius, "The Contractor is getting you landing coordinates for your shuttles, launch them as soon as you have them." As he spoke he typed orders to Colonel Proscia for the team's deployments.

He looked at the screen again and then sighed and opened a channel to Burbeg. "There has been a change in plans."

***

Lieutenant Jessi Toria grimaced as the shuttle settled into one of the only clear areas on the spaceport. A sea of people had washed over the normally empty expanse of stained concrete. "Sergeant Ferch, get your team out there and try and put some order into this."

She was a ship's officer, not a Marine, but the Baron had sent her down with the shuttles to take charge of the evacuation. She would rather be aboard the *War Shrike*, doing what she had trained to do... yet at the same time, she felt a surge in pride that the Baron had selected *her* to be in charge of such an important task.

She heard the Marine NCO bark out orders and she turned her gaze to the south, where the expanse of the refugee ships and shanty-town lay.

She could see a hive of activity around several of those ships. The Baron hadn't specifically said to warn them, but she'd messaged them on the way down. Those were *her* people, not the swarm of Faraday citizens that surrounded the shuttle.

But she'd do her duty by them anyway.

***

It didn't take long for the first problem to come up.

"We have to charge them for passage, how are we going to make anything off this otherwise?" The irate freighter captain sputtered.

Jessi recognized the voice of the Contractor, but only from the news, "Mister Ganske, we have a lot of people to load and not much time..."

Jessi stepped forward through the crowd, flanked by Sergeant Ferch and two of his Marines. "What's the problem here?"

"Mister Ganske is refusing to allow anyone to board before receiving payment for passage. He also refuses to lift off without guidance from someone at Schultz Enterprises." Lieutenant Toria felt a sudden spurt of jealousy for how the politician managed to make her voice clearly heard through the crowd.

Jessi looked between the Contractor, surrounded by a half dozen security guards and the ship's captain, who stood with a man whom she assumed was his first officer. The woman she'd seen before on the news, the only politician of which she felt even the slightest respect, stood calm. She met the Lieutenant's brown eyes with a calm gaze of her own.

The ship's captain's florid face was flushed with anger. His mouth hung open in a bovine expression of either stupidity or shock at the very idea not extorting people in need.

Lieutenant Toria felt her own face flush. Her nostrils flared, "Mister Ganske, you will allow these people to board or you will be forcibly removed and you can seek other means off this planet."

"You can't do this, I'm the Captain of this vessel and it is owned by Schultz Enterprises! We have laws here!" The captain's jowls waggled back and forth as he spoke. Lieutenant Toria thought of the captain of the refugee ship she had come to Faraday aboard. Captain Nyguyen had shared his last ration bar with the hungry young girl who had lost her parents.

"Sergeant Ferch, remove Mister Ganske from the spaceport area," Jessi turned to face Ganske's first officer, "Mister Floyd, do you feel you can work with us?"

The other man watched his former captain as a Marine dragged him away, "Yes, Lieutenant, I think I can."

Lieutenant Toria felt a bit of the tension ease in her gut. "Excellent, start loading these people." She nodded at the Contractor, "Ma'am."

"Thank you for your assistance... Lieutenant?"

"Yes, Ma'am. Not a problem, the Baron sent us to help. Excuse me," Lieutenant Toria turned away as her com unit chimed. She felt sudden gratitude for the interruption, "Yes?"

"Ma'am, we just got a message from Ensign Tascon over at the factory. He says that a number of people have shown up and they're requesting passage. He's told them to seek passage on the refugee ships, but they said some of the ships aren't space-worthy."

Jessi swept her eyes across the mass of people gathered at the spaceport. They might, *might,* all fit aboard the ships gathered here now.

She felt an icy hand grip her heart. She fought off the sudden urge to order the Marines to clear out enough room for the people she'd grown up with. She opened up a channel to Tascon, "What's the status of the loading of the machinery?"

"I can't get any more with these damned people here in the way," Tascon said.

Jessi's eyes narrowed, "Ensign, make room for those people."

"What?" Tascon said. She could almost see his olive-toned face with the automatic arrogance she so hated. "The Captain ordered me to load up the machinery from the factory."

Jessi closed her eyes. For a moment, she prayed for the patience to deal with any further situations. She shouldn't have felt surprise at Tascon's... difficulty grasping the situation. She hadn't missed the fact that he was the only of the Baron's officers to *not* receive promotion since their arrival here. In the rapid brief she'd received from the Baron, he'd made it clear that he wanted the Ensign at the factory was to avoid situations where his arrogance might cause an issue.

Machinery, by and large, didn't take offense.

Jessi focused on her commander's calm voice. *How would the Baron handle this?* "Ensign, that machinery is replaceable. Those people are not. Have them unload whatever cargo necessary and board the transports immediately."

"I should ask the Captain--"

"Baron Giovanni is preparing for a battle, Ensign, he doesn't have time to hold your hand. Follow my orders, or I'll have the Marines over there do so." *And then,* she thought, *I'll bring your ass on charges so fast your head will spin.*

"Yes, ma'am," The Ensign's sullen voice answered.

Toria let out a deep breath and turned to face the orderly lines of refugees as they boarded. Her eyes caught on the face of a little girl, who held hands with her mother and father as they moved up the line.

Her own memories flashed back to her childhood. To the mad scramble where her mother had tearfully pushed her into the arms of a stranger just before the doors had closed.

That would not happen today, she thought, *not if I can do anything about it.*

***

The three squadrons of fighters swept in on the flank of the Chxor cruisers.

Since there was no longer the option to lure the Chxor away, Lucius had gone with the decision to bloody their forces enough to, hopefully, stop pursuit. He'd pulled in all of his fighters for this strike, in a hope to crack some of the Chxor defenses. He had staged them and the makeshift carrier in the shadow of one of the small moons of a gas giant, which made it unlikely that the Chxor would track them back to their origin.

The fighters took only sporadic intercepting fire, none of it near the mark. They launched their missiles in one crippling point-blank salvo that lashed through the gaps in the overlapping cruisers' defense screens to slam home on the hulls of the vessels. The three targeted ships took multiple hits from the eighteen fighters.

The two hundred sixteen missiles in the initial burst exploded in one long chain. The cruisers were designed to take and absorb damage. Their massive, flat planar screens were magnetically sealed bands of plasma fifteen milimeters thick. The hulls were heavily armored against missiles, lasers, and even projectile weapons.

If Cato Naevius's squadrons carried the heavier Pilum missiles, any of those hits would have gutted a cruiser. The effect of that many light missiles startled even Lucius.

Lucius heard snarls of satisfaction from the pilots as the warheads detonated in a chain of explosions that rocked those three ships.

One cruiser bucked as three of its ten engine pods ripped apart. Plasma vented and power couplings ruptured and detonated to rip larger holes in the hull. The second vessel rocked with the explosions, the crippled ship staggered through the inferno. Video from the recon probes showed secondary decompression and fires raging on the ship.

The third Chxor cruiser shuddered from several secondary explosions. The ship continued on without any visible sign of further damage for several seconds. Then the defense screens flickered. The engines stuttered. A single bright flare engulfed the entire vessel. Seconds later, only a field of debris remained.

Fusion reactor overload, Lucius thought to himself, *lucky hit on that one.*

The three squadrons wheeled away, their ordinance expended. They could have gone in on strafing runs with their plasma cannons, but Lucius ordered them out, satisfied with the results.

It was more than he had hoped for, without a single casualty, and good combat experience. Although... an attack on the Chxor's cruisers in a fighter was slightly less dangerous than a live fire training run. Training missions became routine over time if officers didn't plan out complex engagements, and that caused pilots to grow bored, which led to accidents.

It was the Chxor dreadnoughts that one had to watch.

With that cue, the Chxor dreadnoughts finally began a belated broadside at the retreating fighters. They did not slow or alter course. That would have no point, they would not catch the fighters. In any case, the Chxor wanted the planet, not the fighters. As the cruiser screen maneuvered to maintain a solid protective layer about the dreadnoughts, the two wounded ships drew to the rear of the formation. The most heavily damaged fell out of formation, its engines unable to maintain the acceleration.

"Time to play matador," he muttered to himself. *Time for one last gambit,* he thought. If this plan worked, then he could save the evacuation fleet and possibly damage the Chxor. If it didn't, then he would lose his ship for certain and the evacuees might not make their escape. "Execute Bravo Bravo Seven," Lucius ordered.

The *War Shrike* gave a slight shudder as her seven gravity matrix impellers engaged. The amount of energy they drank from the vessel's fusion reactors was tremendous. The thrust they produced was highly efficient when compared to a mass-based reaction drive. The size of the *War Shrike* required incredible amounts of power to propel it through space. A certain amount of energy always went to entropy, and when dealing with the power requirements of a warship, a paltry five percent of the power drain dissipated as electromagnetic noise. That five percent was enough to make the *War Shrike* light up like a small star, if someone had the sensors to see.

Evidently, the Chxor did.

The Chxor formation altered again. The new formation put the cruisers into a blocking screen against this new and greater threat.

The dreadnoughts moved to place themselves in better firing positions in the battle line.

Any single one of those massive dreadnoughts out-massed the *War Shrike* three times over. They also packed an insane amount of firepower, which outweighed anything the *War Shrike* could throw back by an order of magnitude.

The *War Shrike* mounted virtually identical missiles, but even there, Lucius was at a disadvantage, for while the *War Shrike* mounted four tubes to the dreadnought's two, there were four dreadnoughts, and the enemy dreadnoughts had three times the missile storage than his own.

In short, a lone battleship had no business whatsoever getting in the way of a Chxor dreadnought, much less four of them.

The Chxor didn't alter course, they didn't have to. Their target was the planet and their other target, the object of their hunt, was located in orbit above the planet. An ideal situation for them.

Lucius could run through the mental calculations the Chxor must be undertaking. First they would calculate the cost of destroying the battleship, find it minor. Then the commander would consider any possible defenses that the planet held, and decide that the casualties involved in neutralizing them to be minor as well. It wasn't logical that an out of the way planet might possess serious defenses.

Those two casualty lists would be added together, and the final cost tallied up. To a Chxor, it was only logical that victory was assured, if not now, then later.

Lucius was of another school of thought, one that used logic as a tool for people, not people as a tool for logic. While to the Chxor it was unthinkable for a ship to continue to fight after defeat was assured, Lucius didn't think much of assured victories. He had cheated death and had victory snatched away too many times from guaranteed battle plans. Lucius didn't know how this day's fight would work out, but he did know that he would hurt the Chxor. The *War Shrike* would move forward to engage the enemy.

Plan Bravo Bravo Seven made almost a head-on course. The enemy task force would pass the *War Shrike* just within twelve thousand kilometers, at the outermost limit of Lucius's secondary battery. His main battery would bear at twenty thousand kilometers, outside the Chxor's own range. He had felt the temptation to use his own speed and maneuverability to stay outside of the Chxor's range.

His course angled to allow the Chxor the option of altering course to lengthen the engagement, which would be brief at the speeds they traveled. If they altered course, it would draw them away from the planet. They couldn't hope to catch Lucius, he had a far higher acceleration than their vessels, almost four times faster. They could, if they altered their direction now, maintain an engagement for several minutes, which would give them a number of shots at the *War Shrike*, perhaps enough to destroy her. Lucius wasn't willing to gamble on their taking that chance. They were too cautious, too drawn to certainties.

But their commander would be tempted, very tempted. He might even think of an alternative…

"Captain," Lieutenant Palmer looked up from his sensor station. "Two of them Dreadnoughts peeled off, along with their escorting cruisers. It looks like they're goin' on course Charlie Delta Seven."

The Chxor were doing exactly what made sense to them. Two Dreadnoughts would be enough to crush the planetary defenses. Two might be sufficient to destroy the *War Shrike* in a passing engagement. Therefore, it logically made sense to divide forces to accomplish both tasks.

And it might yet work, if Lucius got too smart for his own good. The Chxor might have made the right decision. "If not…" Lucius smiled. "Laser com message to the *Gebneyr*, Plan Bravo Bravo Seven is a go."

***

Kleigh watched the screen as the enemy vessel closed. He did not try to think of what was going through his enemy's mind. He saw no reason to make such attempt. The enemy had acted in ways to defy logic time after time in the past, as he seemed to do now. Why a commander would take a ship away from a planet, which presumably held some strategic and tactical bonuses, and lead it against overwhelming odds was beyond Kleigh's mental outlook. There was no logic to his opponent's actions, unless he looked for escape and had panicked. That was a solid assumption, Kleigh decided. Such illogical beings were driven by emotion, too often.

He showed and felt no emotion while he ordered two of his five-class dreadnoughts and their escorts to alter course in order to maintain a longer engagement window with the battleship. If the battleship altered course, it would make little difference. Such a border world would have little in the way of defenses, two dreadnoughts and their escorts would suffice.

The two dreadnoughts on their intercept course began deceleration. They slowed their velocity relative to the closing battleship. They had only four escorting cruisers to absorb the damage that the enemy ship would be dealing out, but, again, that should suffice. The limited time of the engagement at those closing rates would not allow the battleship to do any particular amount of damage.

The fighters from the earlier attack had withdrawn outside of sensor range. Perhaps they planned to reload their missiles. It didn't matter. Eighteen fighters would raise the cost of the engagement, but by only a slight amount. They could not break through the cruiser screen by themselves

Kleigh felt the utter dispassion which, for a Chxor, passed for satisfaction. Another victory for the Chxor, another world conquered, another enemy defeated.

***

Lucius awoke from a short nap and returned to the bridge. He had rotated the crew through, giving them plenty of rest. The level of tension would make sleep difficult, but rest would be needed. Even now the closer group of dreadnoughts, with their six cruisers, was just over an hour outside of missile range. At his current course, he would brush past them, at eleven thousand kilometers for a period of a couple minutes, and then be in missile range for another hour, approximately thirty minutes before the second group reached missile range.

Lucius had one serious advantage in that area. The missiles that the Chxor used were virtually identical to the ones he would be firing at them. However, they limited themselves to their shipboard sensors. Lucius had four probes to track the enemy forces. He had watched them and had firing solutions on the enemy ships since just after he broke the *War Shrike* out of orbit.

His missiles didn't have the power to travel that distance, but he could see everything the enemy did quite clearly. The Chxor never used probes. Their technology base had the capability, but their ships didn't mount the equipment. A simple oversight in the design phase made for a crippling tactical disadvantage. To the Chxor it didn't make sense to redraw the designs for probes, especially since none of their commanders complained of the lack.

To them, he would be a contact, readily identifiable as a battleship, with an electromagnetic profile to match that of the Desperado-class. They could find his course and speed by watching where he went. If he hadn't lit off his engines, they wouldn't have seen him until they reached the outer limit of their shipboard sensors targeting range. Even then they may not have seen him, since he could have kept the ship's emissions to a minimum until they got very close.

The Chxor, all in a group, could squash him at that close of range, though. If his shadow drive went down, it made a viable, go-down-fighting plan.

It wasn't necessary. In fact, the planet he was paid to protect had told him to get lost. Approximately sixteen thousand people had chosen to run. Those twenty-nine ships hid themselves in the sensor shadow of Faraday as they crept out of the system. Even those slow cargo ships would easily outpace the Chxor, given enough time.

Time that Lucius would win them.

The Chxor, with their built-in handicap, wouldn't even know the ships had departed.

Lucius began to smile. He was going to give the Chxor a number of lessons on the importance of long range sensor systems.

***

Kleigh typed in notes to his shipboard log as he waited. Some of the non-Chxor crew had begun to make mistakes and he made another note that aliens, especially Humans, needed more conditioning to remove some of their illogical habits. It made no sense to worry about one's self before or during a battle. This war for Chxor's logical supremacy required no less. The inconsequential individuals must make themselves tools for the greater good. Those that made illogical errors and blamed them on weaknesses of their bodies showed a failure in dedication.

More discipline was in order.

He noted that the fighters had returned and begun harassment of the wounded cruiser, which fell further behind. They must not have missile reloads, he noted, because they engaged the lamed cruiser with their pulse cannon. The ineffective fire accomplished little against the cruiser's armor. The enemy's actions grew more and more irrelevant and illogical.

The enemy battleship grew closer. Squadron Commander Kleigh's sensors didn't yet have enough data to pinpoint a firing solution, but he had the vessel's course plotted accurately. The enemy made no move to alter course or speed. That maintained the brief weapons pass on Kleigh's force as well as the separated dreadnoughts. The path would take it directly into the fire of the other two dreadnoughts. If it didn't change course, it would actually pass between two of the dreadnoughts and their cruiser escorts. Logically, the enemy ship should have altered course to avoid such close and lasting range with the two dreadnoughts. That the ship hadn't suggested panic and illogical emotional responses.

It didn't bring satisfaction to Kleigh. That would have been as illogical as his opponents' panic. He foresaw the most probable outcome of this situation and saw only success and victory for the Chxor. Squadron Commander Kleigh expected significant rewards and his genetic line would receive benefits for its clear and logical thoughts.

Something resembling irritation came to Kleigh then when a series of missile tracks appeared on radar. The human was defeated, why did it continue to fight? The battleship, unlike the Chxor, must rely on remote platforms or drones to pinpoint the location of the task force, to allow it a range advantage.

The Chxor realized after a moment of reflection that he had not considered that possible tactic, something which he should have. If the Human altered course now, he might stay ahead of the task force and avoid any real dangers.

Of course, the Human's actions, while possibly damaging, could not continue for long. The battleship would eventually run out of missiles. At that time, it would have to depart the system or close the range. So, Kleigh decided, his mistake was not so great as to be necessary to go on record. That was good, his reward and genetic descendants would be of great service for the Chxor. And the Human was still doomed.

Kleigh ordered the cruisers to interdict themselves between the missiles and the dreadnoughts. He then ordered the main batteries to hold their fire, but granted the secondary batteries permission to engage any missiles which bypassed the cruiser screen.

Yes, this battle would continue to its logical conclusion and that would be that.

***

Lucius watched the Chxor maneuver. He had used their weaknesses against them before. There were serious gaps in their tactical doctrine. Only a handful of their commanders ever adapted those tactics. "Give me a fleet and I could rip them to pieces."

"Sir, why didn't the Fleet ever do that?" Commander Anthony Doko asked. "I mean, we've done so much with hit and run tactics... why didn't the Admiralty ever change the doctrine?"

Lucius grimaced, "Because the political appointees of the Admiralty like big ships. Until we fought the Chxor, we had the advantage in ship size against the majority of our opponents. Hell, if they had time to get the *Emperor Romulus* and the other ships of her class produced, they might well have turned the war around. Honestly, my tactics pull a lot from the good Colonial Republic Fleet officers... even a bit from the old Provisional Colonial Republic Army, back when they were rebels against Amalgamated Worlds." Lucius shrugged, "And there are some commanders who have pulled off victories against the Chxor without rewriting our doctrine."

Anthony Doko scowled, "If you're talking about Admiral Vibious—"

"Not *him*, necessarily," Lucius shook his head, the late Admiral Vibious had won victories by attrition that favored only the Chxor and cost too many lives, too many ships, and left Lucius with a foul taste in his mouth. "But there were others."

Not many, he privately admitted, but there were some. Lucius saw that the clock had run down. "Prepare to fire missiles," Lucius said.

"Aye, sir," Doko said, dubiously.

Lucius watched the first volley of Pilum missiles go in and sighed. The Chxor cruisers served their purpose. Two of the four exploded against the cruiser's ridiculously oversized defense screens, which flickered but held. A third was picked off short of the ships by a last minute shot from a laser battery.

The fourth made it through the screen, but a dreadnought swatted it out of space without a problem.

As he'd suspected, the enemy defense was too strong for some piecemeal fire. He immediately regretted throwing away the four missiles. He only had twenty-eight left now.

"I know, Doko, it was a waste. It was worth a try though," Lucius said to his frowning XO, who manned the missile station.

"A lucky shot out here would have been nice. Continue to close the range. Hold missile fire until Plan Alpha One is in effect."

The range ticked down. They were inside the Chxor targeting range now. Any moment now...

"Multiple missile launches, Captain!" Lieutenant Palmer somehow managed to drawl even when he was tense. "I count eight launches, sir." The man claimed he hailed from Earth. Lucius suspected the Lieutenant feigned the drawl.

Lucius kept an eye on Lieutenant Beeson, who manned the defensive weapons. Eight missiles was everything the Chxor could launch. Lucius felt confident that the Lieutenant could handle the handful. If even one of them made it through, though, people would die. Beeson had proved himself in a simulator.

Real life was something else altogether.

A few minutes later, he realized he needn't have worried. Lieutenant Beeson shot down all the missiles well clear of the *War Shrike*. The next eight died well clear of the battleship as well.

The Chxor dreadnoughts held much larger magazines, but they didn't use their tubes as if they felt confident of resupply. After Beeson picked off the third flight of missiles, the Chxor ceased fire.

That, at least, made sense. The missiles would be more dangerous to the *War Shrike* from the rear, rather than from head on. From the rear, they wouldn't have to worry about getting missiles to flank the defense screen.

The enemy held their fire. The range ticked down. The Chxor

main battery would have the range on him for a total of just over eighty seconds. His own main battery had greater range, which extended his own engagement time. That would give the *War Shrike* time for two extra shots.

The main battery of a five-class dreadnought was twenty four colossal fusion cannons, on six turrets that rotated to present all in a massive broadside, or twelve shots from the bow or the stern. They'd have range for two shots from each of those massive cannons. Lucius's crew would have time for four shots with their own longer-ranged heavy exotic particle cannons, and only two shots from the light EPCs. Unfortunately, the *War Shrike* only mounted three turrets, each turret containing four of the long range cannons. Also, unfortunately, the EPCs didn't have the all out punch of the enemy weapons.

He looked over at Doko, a slight smile on his face, "Remember the battle at Endway?"

Doko groaned, "When Admiral Gavetti commanded?"

Lucius frowned, "Was that his name?"

"Yeah, he didn't last long, did he?" Doko snorted. "Wasn't it that final hit on his ship that went *through* to hit us?"

Lucius grimaced, "Yes, that would be the one." He stared at the screen, "Last chance to turn aside."

No one on the bridge said anything. The option now to break off and clear weapons range tempted him. But if the Chxor made it to Faraday unharmed, they would have time to build up too strong an infrastructure for any possible counterattack to work.

"Deploy chaff, commence jamming." Lucius commanded.

A moment later, the *War Shrike* disappeared in a ball of static, surrounded by electromagnetic fuzz. The enemy probably would lose tracking, if only for a moment. The enemy's firefly systems aboard the cruisers kicked in a moment later. This time, at least, the enemy jamming did no good. Lieutenant Palmer had managed to not only put recon probes above and below the Chxor formation, but he had one stealthily coasting *inside* it.

"In range, firing now." Doko's voice was calm, precise. It was the voice of a surgeon in surgery. The ship thrummed as the EPCs fired.

Lieutenant Daniel Beeson was somewhat less restrained, "Hit, multiple hits, Captain!"

Lucius watched as debris intermixed with enemy chaff. Doko fired again, followed by Lieutenant Beeson. Again, debris blossomed from multiple hits. The Chxor fired for the first time, the colossal guns and the dreadnought's secondary batteries fired on the *War Shrike*.

Jamming scrambled radar and chaff distorted the battlefield. Doko, at the controls for the main battery, was hunched over his console. Forty-eight colossal fusion cannons fired a second time.

The restraining harness bit into Lucius's shoulders and the universe spun for a horrid instant. A moment later, the distant thud of pressure doors slamming shut gave ominous note of damage taken.

Lieutenant Meridan looked up, "Captain, direct hit on missile tube three, plasma mount six, and life support in section F is gone."

Lucius waited for the list to go on, but that was it.

They were out of range now, and Doko looked up, "She really is one lucky ship, Captain."

Lucius nodded. The loss of a missile tube hurt. Better there than on the missile magazine. A glancing blow, he guessed, partially turned by the defense screen, rather than the huge hole in the side of the ship he'd feared.

Well, not yet anyway.

As he drew away from the first group of dreadnoughts, Lucius gave a mental sigh of relief. He wore his command face. It wouldn't do to let his people think that a mere two dreadnoughts had their Captain nervous.

Damage reports came in. Lucius gave orders for repairs, but half his mind was on the upcoming clash, while some of it evaluated the sensor data that Lieutenant Palmer delivered. Ghastly casualties reported in the sectors hit. That one hit had killed forty people outright, leaving another fifteen wounded in the sick bay. Most of the dead came from the actual impact. They, like the number three missile tube, were gone, vaporized completely. The bunkrooms and fuel tanks had taken the rest of the damage. They didn't take any of Lucius' crew with them.

Of the enemy, Doko did an excellent job. It looked like four good hits on one dreadnought, which leaked a lot of water and oxygen, sure signs that pressurized cabins took serious hits. One of the cruisers also leaked quite a bit and its emissions drop suggested that it lost one of its power plants.

"That'll give them something to think about," Doko said with satisfaction.

The first force of dreadnoughts finally passed out of missile range, even as the final damage reports concluded. The Chxor saved their missiles. Perhaps they worried they might face a missile engagement with planetary defenses. They could realize that the planet would not put up a fight.

Now the range closed with the second group. These came closer at a slower rate, for the Chxor had actually reversed directions and traveled a similar course to his own now, albeit at a slower velocity which allowed him to overtake *them*. The commander of their force would expect him to break away and avoid such a confrontation. The *War Shrike*'s luck in the last engagement could only go so far. Up close, he wouldn't stand a chance against those two dreadnoughts. But he maintained his course.

Unlike the Chxor, he had sensor probes, and he could see what was behind them quite clearly.

***

Kleigh typed in more notes and commands. He took his time and felt secure in the knowledge that victory for the Chxor was at hand once again.

True, the battleship had damaged Kleigh's command ship, as well as Dreadnought 510114. Damage happened in combat, it was illogical to expect some kind of gain without loss. And while it would take time to repair those damaged sections, they would have time.

Also true, the enemy battleship had much better aim, a situation unfortunately familiar to the Chxor. It was faster to produce a number of identical ships, and much easier to produce them with simpler command systems. Fire often enough and the guns would hit.

As the Chxor had hit the enemy this time. Granted, a lower percentage of hits than Chxor gunnery normally had, but at such range, that was acceptable. That was not to say that those gunnery stations that missed wouldn't be punished. In fact, Kleigh made special note to execute one member from each station that hadn't scored a hit. It would incite them to train harder.

The enemy battleship altered course now, but only slightly. Kleigh knew from previous engagements the enemy had the capability of much greater accelerations and maneuvers. That battleship could nearly match the acceleration of the fighters it carried.

Still, there was no reason not to use an opponent's irrational decisions against them. Kleigh ordered the second group of dreadnoughts to match the maneuver. He noted that the new course would take the ships even closer to a small, rocky planet.

Perhaps the enemy ship hoped to retreat behind the cover of the planet when it took excessive damage. A sensor reading also showed that the fighters finally broke off their futile attack on the damaged cruiser. They raced to meet the intercepting dreadnoughts. Had they not expended their ammunition before or had they reloaded instead of their harassment the cruiser with their main guns, Squadron Commander Kleigh might have found them of greater concern. Neither of those were the case, obviously, else they would have used their missiles earlier.

Inevitably, the Human fighter pilots engaged in pointless activities. They allowed their eagerness and aggressive nature to get the better of them. That weakness made them useless in battle. Now at least, he wouldn't have to chase the fighters down over time, but could instead rely on them to die with the battleship.

Victory would come to the Chxor once again and very soon now.

***

As the two dreadnoughts and their cruiser escort drew closer, Lucius breathed a long sigh of relief. He looked over at Doko, "It looks like things might work out." The enemy task group lay in the box now, no matter where they maneuvered, he had the Chxor pinned.

They'd been in missile range for some time, but both sides held their fire. The missiles were much more effective at close range, with less time to react to the launch.

Because he approached head on, the enemy dreadnoughts would have 'only' their forward turrets in position to fire. He had the option now to cut across their bow, and fire both of his heavy turrets, and to a Chxor, that would have made sense, or at least, as much sense as this situation would grant.

Instead, he kept an almost dead on course. Bow to bow, with the escorting cruisers to intercept his fire, he wouldn't be able to do much damage until he passed through the enemy formation. Neither he nor the Chxor imagined that his ship would last under the withering fire that close to those behemoth ships. The ridiculous charge into that formation seemed inevitable,

Lucius waited a few seconds more, and then spoke, "Signal to the *Gebneyr*, execute Plan Alpha."

The Chxor had just passed a small, rocky, unremarkable planet. It had no atmosphere, no moons, and a rocky, cratered surface. The Faraday colony never gave it anything more than a numeric for a name. However, a planet didn't need to be remarkable to cast a significant sensor shadow.

If Lucius possessed a fleet, he couldn't have hidden it in that shadow.

He didn't possess a fleet, he had the *Gebneyr*.

The battlecruiser rounded the planet behind the Chxor formation just as the three squadrons of fighters reached their optimal firing range for missiles.

The *Gebneyr* and the three squadrons had a perfect firing solution. The four cruisers lay in the front of the formation, ahead of the dreadnoughts. They provided no protection to any attack from astern. The Chxor, in maneuvering to intercept the *War Shrike*, had left their clouds of chaff behind. They hadn't yet deployed new chaff because neither side would throw away missiles at this range. The *War Shrike* hadn't drawn close enough for the main weapons batteries yet. Both dreadnoughts' jamming focused forward, towards the apparent enemy's sensors. The fighter squadrons separated from the *War Shrike* and apparently without missiles did not constitute a threat.

The fighters had reloaded their missiles earlier. An older freighter served as their reloading platform. Thirty-six ship killer missiles lanced out from the three squadrons.

The *Gebneyr* was a different story. It lay only five thousand kilometers behind the two dreadnoughts, well within range within its primary and secondary and tertiary weapons batteries.

It also mounted four missile tubes and external missile racks which allowed it to fire twenty four Pilum missiles in one opening salvo.

The six shots from the primary battery and the six from the secondary battery slammed into the rear of the nearer Chxor dreadnought. Twelve more lighter beams from the tertiary battery quickly followed. The beams punched into the rear of the dreadnought, well aimed at such close ranges.

No ship could take such fire at such close range.

Engine pods ripped apart. Power plants detonated as beams ripped through control systems and containment fields. Turrets and gun mounts blew off, twirling off into space.

The aft end of the dreadnought dissolved into nothing more than shredded wreckage.

The other dreadnought still had its rear mounted weapons and sensors, and fought to get a lock on the battlecruiser. The Chxor technicians had just enough warning to see a total of sixty fusion warhead missiles fired from short range at the two dreadnoughts.

The dreadnoughts tertiary battery could engage missiles, fighters, and light vessels. They had no time for the sensors to gain a lock on the inbound missiles. The gun crews of the X-ray lasers fired blindly at the inbound, evasive missiles.

Fifty nine missiles survived to engage the two dreadnoughts.

The chain of explosions enveloped the two ships. The two dreadnoughts disappeared from Lucius' sensors beneath the massive energy release from those missiles.

When the radiation cleared, thirty seconds later, nothing remained where the two dreadnoughts once lay besides rapidly expanding clouds of superheated gas.

The bridge of the *War Shrike* erupted in cheers and Lucius felt a broad smile spread on his own face. "One half of the enemy's firepower destroyed," Lucius said. The remaining cruisers of this force were essentially unarmed. Lucius could alter course and destroy the vessels at his leisure. The ships were slow and, without the guns of the dreadnoughts, were no longer a threat.

Lucius pondered letting the vessels go, but discarded the thought as the ships continued their courses, the Chxor commanders unable to comprehend the destruction of their force.

"Captain, I'm receiving a signal from the damaged Chxor

cruiser." Lieutenant Palmer said, his drawl harsh. "It's a human."

Lucius frowned. How had a human got aboard one of the ships, much less the one which had fallen out of the Chxor formation? He pulled up the signal on one of his screens.

A woman in a battered and bloodied ship suit stared back at him from the screen. She had removed the helmet from the suit, to reveal brown eyes and a shaven scalp. She also carried a heavy rifle, slung across her shoulder. Behind her, he saw two other armed humans drag a Chxor corpse off the bridge. "Captain, we wish to signal our surrender, and ask for asylum with you. We mutinied against the Chxor." She waited, clearly nervous.

Lucius looked at her for a long moment. "I hadn't realized the Chxor used human crews."

She stared at him for a long moment. When she finally spoke he could see the tendons stand out along her jaw, "They draft people from every world they control. With them, it's either learn your assigned duties or be put out the airlock as useless. Most of the cruisers have significant numbers of human crew."

A dozen questions flitted through his mind, but he pushed them back. "Did you take the ship intact, and can you pilot it through shadow space?" That was the most important issue.

"Yes," she answered. "A lot of the other crew went along with us, in the mutiny. Even some of the lower Chxor officers."

"I'm detaching a shuttle to your vessel. I'll have Marines to take charge of any prisoners and some crew to lend assistance."

"There aren't any prisoners." Her answer was coldly satisfied.

Lucius suppressed a shiver at what he saw in her dark eyes. There was anger, and hurt, and a terrible desire for revenge. He wondered what horror it would be to live beneath the Chxor. Never mind that, he had a hard enough time sleeping as it was. He *really* didn't want to know what burned behind those eyes.

"Well, the Marines can help you take charge. Who is the acting Captain?"

She shrugged, wearily. "I don't know."

"Who is in charge?" Lucius demanded.

She looked around, clearly in an attempt to force her brain to work. "Matty was, but he's dead. Alice took over then, but they killed her when we stormed the bridge." She stared off into space for a long moment. "I guess I am."

"And who are you?"

"Computer Technician Seventeen," she answered instantly, then shook her head, "That's what my rank was with the Chxor. I'm Lauren Kelly."

"Well then, Lauren, you keep things together over there, and we'll detach some people to give you a hand." He cut the connection, then spent a moment in thought. He opened another connection. "Major Proscia."

"Yes, sir?" The connection had no visual, which suggested the Marine was on the move.

"I've a mission for you and a question."

"Go ahead sir. My men are helping out with damage control, but they've got everything under hand at the moment."

"One of the Chxor crews mutinied. I need a security detachment to help them get things in order. Also, I was wondering what your opinion is of fighting a boarding operation on the remaining cruisers."

There was a long pause as the Major considered. "Sir, I'll need more people. Fighting aboard four ships... we haven't the manpower for it."

"From what I understand, the other crews are made up of conscripts, with a lot to hate about their officers." Lucius responded.

"That's another matter altogether then sir." The Marine officer answered. "I've boarded one of those cruisers once, any fighting will be rough, the Chxor won't go down without a fight. If you can give me enough time and the Marines aboard the *Gebneyr*, I think we can lead the crews to a successful mutiny. It will be bloody, but, if the crews are mutinous already, then things should fall into place."

"Make preparations then, Major." Lucius closed the connection and began his own preparations.

***

The cruisers didn't have the speed to escape, so the only real threat came from the vessels' guns, which could engage and destroy the shuttles as they transferred Marines aboard the ships. The light cruisers' only offensive weapons were six light lasers, designed more for missile interception than anything else. They could, unfortunately, engage and destroy a shuttle.

Lieutenant Naevius led his squadrons in close, to snipe at the turrets on one ship after the other.

Midway through disabling the vessels weapons, one of the other two ships lost all power and began to drift. It looked as if both power plants went offline at the same time, which suggested that a mutiny was already underway. Major Proscia agreed and rerouted the shuttles already dispatched to another vessel to that one. Lives might be saved in a quick resolution to that fight.

Lucius found the boarding operations much more strenuous to command than ship-to-ship engagements. He could hear all of the commands and reports, but he wasn't present. He couldn't see what his Marines saw. He couldn't help. He couldn't change the outcome, no matter what he did.

He was glad for Major Proscia's presence. The man possessed an almost frightening intensity. William Proscia had fought on many battlefields and it seemed that he could see exactly what his men saw as he directed their operations. He managed to speak calmly even as he directed the mutinous crews that rallied with the Marine boarding parties against the Chxor.

"Sir," Proscia spoke, midway into the operation. One vessel was entirely secured, the Chxor aboard had surrendered when faced with inevitable defeat.

"Yes, Major?" Lucius asked, his attention split between the battles aboard the enemy vessels and the two enemy dreadnoughts and their escorts.

"I don't think we can capture vessel two. Most of the crew is from Saragossa." William's said, his voice flat and unemotional.

Lucius winced. The Saragossa system lay not far from Nova Roma. They had had a dominant economy and heavy factories, which had made them a threat, especially since their colony's merchant cartels were in competition with those of Nova Roma. The short and brutal war that resulted culminated with the destruction of most of the system's infrastructure. Much of the system's population died from starvation before the Chxor arrived to take charge. "Offer to remove anyone who wants to leave, then evacuate your people. We'll destroy it." Lucius answered. He had nothing against the Saragossans, but if they fought on the side of the Chxor, they were the enemy.

The operation continued.

Lucius watched the Chxor forces on approach to Faraday. As expected, the planet offered no resistance. The Chxor took no chances, for they didn't trust humans. Besides that, Lucius added mentally, the Chxor commander had to be peeved about losing half his forces.

As the Chxor fleet assumed the high orbital position, it began to systematically target all other craft in orbit. Some ships tried to flee, then, but it was too late. Only ships on the far side of the planet had any realistic chance to elude that much firepower. One or two Faraday naval vessels attempted to return fire, but they survived only long enough to be engaged by the second salvo.

"Lieutenant Palmer, what is the status on the evacuation ships?"

"They're dropping into shadow now, Captain. They're headed for the rendezvous."

Lucius nodded, sadly. Sixteen thousand people saved. Nineteen million more and an entire world taken by the Chxor. At least the politicians who surrendered would be amongst the first to feel the lash of their new overlords.

***

Squadron Commander Kleigh finished the annotation of his notes as his flagship finished annihilation of all orbital traffic as a security measure. The standard operating procedure when beginning a planetary occupation, it also gave his gunners more needed practice. He sighed as he reviewed the notes on the engagement.

Obviously, these Humans behaved illogically again.

He acted impeccably, he approached the battle in the correct mentality, which left him blameless for the results, he knew. Who would have thought that the humans would sacrifice a world as a lure to destroy two dreadnoughts? Chxor high command would find their actions as puzzling as himself.

He looked up as one of the communications technicians attracted his attention. "High Commander, the planetary authorities have requested audience with you." Kleigh nodded and waited for the technician to rout the transmission to his command chair.

"What is the meaning of this!" an obese human demanded.

"We surrendered, you have no reason to fire on us!"

"Your orbital traffic was a potential threat to my vessels. It was dealt with." Kleigh answered, logically. "You will no longer question my actions. All military personnel on your world will assemble for their surrender and a facility will be prepared for their internment. All aircraft will be grounded and all ground transportation will be suspended. Any acts of aggression against my vessels or troops will be met with instant retaliation. Is that understood?"

The man stared at him in horror for a long moment. It was obvious now that he was too emotional, and would have to be replaced as soon as practical.

"In addition, you and your government will prepare to meet with our conditioning committee as to the new standards we expect of this world. Failure to meet our standards will result in retaliation for sedition." Kleigh informed the man. Without a doubt, some on the planet would act, foolishly, in the hopes that some minor terrorist actions would convince the Chxor to leave.

The Chxor would leave the planet uninhabitable before they'd leave it to their enemies. It was illogical and unthinkable to provide a potential haven to any enemies of order and structure.

Kleigh waved to the technician to disconnect the transmission and returned his attention to his notes. Obviously non-Chxor required further conditioning before serving as crew. Squadron Commander Kleigh scheduled further demonstrations on such sources of sedition as humans. All must know their place in the Chxor Empire. Mutiny was a threat most Chxor ships were capable of defending against. Every cruiser had a complement of one hundred soldiers, chosen for their loyalty and dedication. Unfortunately, they were trained to subdue a planetary populous and not for defensive fighting aboard their own ships. Especially not when such mutinies were led by trained soldiers proficient in shipboard fighting. It was an unfortunate gap in Chxor tactical doctrine, Kleigh saw now.

He added a suggestion for such training to the training regimen. Most of their regimen consisted of engaging civilians who lacked training and required lessons in obedience to the Chxor. Few units saw battle against any military under any conditions, much less those as unfavorable as aboard ship, against a mutinous crew and enemy boarders.

The most logical preventative measure would be self-destruct measures for each captain to undertake. No Chxor commander would hesitate to destroy their own vessel rather than let it fall into enemy hands, he knew. He'd ordered the commanders of the cruisers to attempt the same. Unfortunately, mutinous crew made the process difficult.

Chxor ships needed a quick means of self-destruction, he decided and made additional note of it. It would be a simple modification. He would, by necessity, avoid it aboard his own ship. His survival as the Squadron Commander was essential.

Kleigh nodded as a second of the cruisers disappeared off his screen. One disappeared earlier, which suggested that the commander had been quicker thinking than the others. This one was from the vessel that had signaled that the crew fought the boarders rather than their own officers. It was good that this ship too wouldn't fall to the enemy.

The other two, though, seemed to be under the control of the enemy. He made note that the two ships, along with the damaged one which had already mutinied. They would be treated as rogue and destroyed on sight.

Kleigh found it unfortunate that the enemy's forces had grown. Possibly the cruisers could function as screening units for the enemy. Possibly the differing accelerations would make that untenable. The enemy's firepower remained essentially unchanged, though Kleigh found the addition of other enemy vessels unfortunate. Obviously the enemy had planned this situation, planned to sacrifice this world for the destruction of the two dreadnoughts. An illogical move, one more sign that this enemy, the *War Shrike* and its commander, must be destroyed.

After the proper assimilation of this world, Squadron Commander Kleigh would attend to that.

***

After six hours of fighting, the last of the Chxor loyalists finally gave up.

It cost the lives of twenty three Marines and over two hundred crew who mutinied against the Chxor. No one counted the numbers of Chxor who'd fought and died.

It freed something over seven hundred people, most of them humans. And it gave Lucius four additional ships. The slow and unarmed cruisers made an interesting addition to his force.

The mutineers aboard one ship had cut power to the entire ship. At a distance, it may have looked like the ship was destroyed as its power icon disappeared. If that was true, the Chxor might not know he possessed the vessel, something which could come in handy later on.

Lucius' small fleet formed up now, for its jump to Shadow. As that thought triggered, he sighed.

"We failed again," he said, softly.

"Baron, we kicked the crap out of them," Lieutenant Beeson said.

Lucius snorted, "We're still running, and I'm abandoning another world to the Chxor." He felt the temptation, even now, to stay, to fight.

But that would have been foolish. He'd expended nearly all of his missiles. His supply freighter could have rearmed the fighters, but it would have taken most of the day to refill the *Gebneyr*'s external missile racks. During that time, they would be stationary, open to an attack

Without somehow repeating that devastating surprise strike, he had little chance of overwhelming the remaining dreadnoughts.

Besides that, the Chxor possessed ansibles, just as he himself did. To judge by previous actions, Chxor reinforcements would come all the sooner for a defeat here. It might take them months to arrive, but they would show up in force, with troop transports to spare.

Even if he won the fight today, it would leave the *War Shrike* a battered wreck and the Chxor reinforcements would sweep her aside when they arrived.

The only option that remained was to retreat.

"Baron, do we withdraw to the rally point?" Doko said, from aboard one of the captured cruisers.

Lucius nodded, "Lieutenant Palmer will send out the coordinates."

Lucius had spent many nights worrying over where to go from Faraday, should it prove indefensible. His limited choices shortened with availability by distance and his own vessels' fuel capacity. The Chxor cruisers had the longest legs of his vessels, which meant he might use them as fuel tankers. Otherwise, the *War Shrike* and the *Gebneyr* together had only twenty days of fuel for their fusion reactors.

Thankfully, the Chxor Shadow drive mirrored human designs, so the cruisers' FTL speeds were the same as his other ships. That meant he could travel thirty days with his on-board fuel supplies, before he needed to send out his refueling vessels.

Then, of course, there were the civilian refugee ships, which had the same speeds, but some had even less sustainable distance. He eyed the data on the motley assortment of vessels. The maximum distance of the least capable ship was twenty days. That ship was also the one which carried the most people, of course. That meant the maximum distance they could travel before they must refuel would be the same distance as that vessel.

To find one location where all of the vessels could meet after numerous jumps which had to be no more than twenty days total traveling distance was something of a headache.

Lucius Giovanni had received his commission because he was a landed Baron and when His Imperial Majesty determined that a general draft of the populous was necessary, those with titles were offered commissions, rather than being forced into the ranks of the enlisted.

Lucius had kept his commission and succeeded because he planned things thoroughly, even meticulously. He expected the unexpected and even his most optimistic plans took the unplanned into account. What had kept him and his ship alive for so long was that he considered even the worst of outcomes in the event that they did indeed come to pass.

Lucius had already planned for an initial rendezvous and had the travel routes for every refugee ship already prepared. It was one of his worst case scenario plans. The four additional warships would change the plan somewhat, but not significantly. He left some leeway in numbers of refugee vessels in his evacuation plan.

"Captain, all vessels are ready to jump to shadow," Doko was aboard one of the captured cruisers, Beeson aboard another. That left Lieutenant Palmer running three stations, and still talking with his irritating drawl. *Surely not all people from Earth talk that way,* Lucius thought.

"Order them to make the jump." Lucius's command was soft and regretful. He looked one last time at the star system which had, for a time, held so much promise. There would be other stars, other worlds, he knew, but he also felt a conviction growing within.

He stared at the central screen, with the image of the soft, blue world of Faraday. "I'll be back." As he said the words, the universe shifted and the *War Shrike* jumped to shadow.

***

CHAPTER IV

January 1, 2403 Earth Standard Time
Anvil System
Colonial Republic Space

The poorly lit spacer bar held only two or three drunks still in celebration of the new year. The only sober and conscious occupants consisted of a sour-looking bartender and a single man in the corner booth furthest from the door.

Both of them looked up as a woman stepped into the bar. She was tall, with short black hair and dark eyes, and she wore dark pants with a loose, dark gray blouse. She wore a large pistol slung at her hip. She looked too pretty, too naive to wear such a gun to the casual eye.

The bartender – a sharp judge of character – flinched, "I don't want any trouble."

"I'm not here for trouble," she answered as she stepped past him and headed straight for the corner booth.

The man in the booth lounged back as she approached. His left arm was held under the table, where he had already unholstered his own pistol. Anvil was a hard world, and like many in the Colonial Republic, a violent and bloody place often enough.

She sat down across from him.

"Rumor has it you saw something interesting in space not too long ago." She smiled.

The man pretended to relax, but his left hand remained under the table and clenched on his pistol. "Could be. I've seen a lot of interesting things."

"I might be willing to pay you for the information," the woman lay several bills of Colonial Republic Denari on the table.

The man smirked a bit, "Awful interested, huh?" His right hand swept the bills off the table. "Who might you be? Some kind of salvager?" He asked lightly.

"Information for information, Mr. McGann," Her response was cold.

The spacer frowned and rubbed at the black stubble on his chin, "Now the way I see it, there's only a few that could have heard what I offered. That is pirates, maybe some mercenaries, and then there are some shadier types than that." His voice was a slow drawl, very relaxed. It had taken him years to practice that drawl.

"Are you Mason McGann and do you have information or not?"

He sighed, leaned forward putting both elbows on the table. He spoke softly, looking into the woman's eyes. "I am Mason and I have the coordinates for the ship I saw."

"Excellent." Her answer showed actual relief. "I've been casing every bar in this Chxor-damned city for the past two days looking for you." Something of the way she spoke told him that she wasn't here to fight.

The man smiled and leaned back again as he holstered his pistol. His elbows rested on the back of the bench. "I've got reasons to be hard to find. But my information won't come cheap."

She nodded and extended one hand, "I'm Lauren Kelly."

He shook her hand and returned to his reclined position. He cocked his head as he studied her, "So what are you willing to pay?" He made mental note that she'd taken a seat to better watch the entrance.

Lauren smiled, "I understand you lost your ship."

His face went hard. Mason clenched his jaw. He took a deep swig of his beer. "If by lost, you mean port security seized it under false charges, you might be right." The irony that he'd run an honest cargo, for once, and lost his ship to it...

"I can give you enough payment that you could buy any ship on this rock."

He smirked, "Any ship, huh?"

She placed a handful of small, golden ingots on the table.

He frowned, picked one up. "These aren't what I think are they?"

"Gold, processed but not tagged. We got them on accident. They aren't stolen or reported missing. No one can track it and you could use it to buy whatever you want," Lauren said.

"Why not buy yourself a ship with this?" Mason asked, his eyes narrowed.

"We don't need freighters." It was more information than she really wanted to give.

He snorted, "You need these ships, apparently. And you're getting them cheap, if it's what you and I think it is."

"I can offer you transportation, to whatever world you want. A job even, from what I hear, you're a skilled pilot."

He shook his head, "I'm not in it for the money. And you're wrong about the payment, I can't use those stones to buy my ship back, which is the only one worth a damned thing on this planet."

Behind her, Lauren heard the door open, heard the bartender's voice.

"Friends of yours?" Mason asked.

Lauren's dark gaze flicked over at the door. Her back straightened. She turned to face Mason, "What's your price?" The six men in uniform moved towards them.

He leaned forward. "I want off this world. I want my ship back." He stared into her eyes. He added impulsively, "I want to know who you are and why you want *those* ships."

Lauren closed her eyes. "Done."

She stepped out of the booth and moved to stand in front of the six men.

They stopped. "You Lauren Kelly?" The one in the lead pushed back his visor to speak. His face was scarred and pitted. "We're Anvil Security. You need to come with us."

The woman didn't move for a long moment.

The door opened, several more people stepped inside.

The bartender gave a muttered curse. Mason watched him go into the back room and shut the door. He could hear the locks snap shut on the door.

The six uniformed men looked back at the newcomers. Three men and two women faced them, armed with assault weapons they'd hidden beneath heavy coats.

Lauren spoke coldly, "No, I don't think I'll be going with you." She drew her pistol but kept it pointed at the floor. "We can fight this out and all of you will die... or you can raise your hands and surrender. We already jammed your radios, so don't think about calling for help."

The leader cursed something under his breath. "You won't get out of this system, we don't know who you are, but we've seen your ships. There's a force lying in wait already."

"Let me worry about that." Lauren answered.

The leader glanced at his men, back at Lauren. No one moved for a long moment.

She moved so quickly that she'd fired before the leader had his pistol fully out of the holster. The shot sounded impossibly loud in the close bar. The rank smell of burning blood and voided bowels filled the air. The five remaining security men stood silent behind their visors as the sergeant dropped to the floor dead. They slowly raised their hands.

Lauren turned back to Mason. "We already got your ship out. The Baron said you'd want it as payment."

"Baron?" Mason asked, puzzled.

"You'll find out soon enough."

***

January 2, 2403 Earth Standard Time
Zeta Tau System
Unclaimed Space

Amalgamated Worlds' largest training facility off of Earth was once Alpha Seven. That ended when a passing ship spotted a lurking Provisional Colonial Republican Army force. Orders were sent, and the base shut down, its personnel boarded ships on a passing convoy where they displaced the intended cargo.

Unfortunately for those men and women, the PCRA targeted the convoy and its cargo. The ships of that convoy became the airless tombs for some thirty thousand people who died. The butchery of Alpha Seven became the first of many atrocities committed by both sides, all caused by one ship in the wrong place at the wrong time.

All of that had occurred nearly a century ago. It was the first significant defeat for the Amalgamated Worlds Fleet and it was soon followed by several others. The PCRA had been one of the bigger downfalls of Amalgamated Worlds, but the death of its enemy brought the fall of the colonial army, for without a common enemy, the worlds began to fear and fight each other. That had led to the squabble that enveloped the Colonial Republic in present times, Lucius knew.

The base shut down, its equipment mothballed, the corridors and chambers carefully cleaned, the entire facility eased into standby, waiting for the trainees that would never return.

When the *War Shrike* arrived, Lucius had found the moon base almost entirely intact.

It wasn't surprising. Amalgamated Worlds Fleet never left weapons or other sensitive items lying unguarded. That didn't stop people from looking. Numerous scavengers and salvagers previously prowled the base and the surrounding area. They'd looked for weapons caches, computer equipment, and the like. Someone had scavenged some of the environmental equipment. Some others had performed minor acts of vandalism and graffiti.

Even those events hardly marred the surface of the base. The main hub was designed for training up to forty thousand people at a time where they would have run raw recruits through basic training before they shifted them to Fleet or Marines or Army. The four external wings held quarters for another twenty thousand people each. The base was massive, a city in its own right.

It took a total of three weeks to get power, heating, and air restored to the northern wing. The fusion plants were buried deep beneath the surface, embedded in solid concrete and rock. Looters hadn't bothered to try and remove the huge reactors. It would have been far too much work for too little gain.

The base had lain abandoned for almost a century. Most people had forgotten it existed, with reason. No one needed the base. It contained nothing of worth, and was located in a relatively empty sector of space.

Lucius only knew about it because he had been part of a planning committee to use it as a base of operations against the Chxor, eight years previously.

The problem was the same then as it was now, why bother?

Baron Lucius Giovanni stood and moved around his desk to study the screen on the wall. It showed the moon, an overview of the base and its structures. Just over sixteen thousand refugees filled the north wing of the base. They had plenty of room, with ample, comfortable quarters. The furniture had been left behind, and while it was older and plain, it still made the quarters tolerable.

The base was everything they needed right now. It was an overlooked relic that no one would think to search any time soon. The odd scavenger who wondered in could be captured and held until they moved on. If they moved on.

Lucius shook his head. Thoughts like those would get him nowhere.

"Captain, the rest of the committee is assembled," a voice warned him over his intercom.

"Thank you," Lucius sighed and moved to the door. "Time for the difficult part."

***

Just after their rendezvous in the Zeta Tau system, home to Alpha Seven's airless moon, Lucius had asked the civilians to form some sort of temporary governance. He had seriously underestimated the mess that would result.

He quickly discovered three groups among his refugees. The smallest group was made up of Faraday military and their families, those who sided with the Contractor chose to leave while they could. Most of the military forces had stayed behind and chose to abide by the legal government.

Ordinary Faraday citizens made up a significant portion. These people had either panicked or had dealings with people in the know, and ran while they could. This group consisted of Faraday citizens of every stripe, from lady friends of the crew who'd been warned to flee, to businessmen and merchant captains.

The experienced refugees made up the majority. These people had fled before, either once, or several times. The displaced masses, those who knew how to survive. They'd lived for years, sometimes even decades on Faraday, but never considered it home. The hardiest, the toughest, they knew how to live on the run. Many had little liking for the citizens of Faraday who treated them like scum when they'd immigrated.

After a great deal of politicking, five chosen representatives came forward to meet with Lucius. Lucius told them where he stood right from the first. He would tolerate no commands, not now and not ever. He controlled the fleet, he controlled the crews. He would do his best to defend the refugees, to see them to a decent world, but he would do things his way.

The five councilors fought him over it. In this he hadn't budged. The experienced refugees understood the thin edge of survival. The Contractor, who the military refugees had selected, didn't like it, but accepted it. The fifth councilor Lucius replaced twice before the Faraday citizens came to accept that they lived on Lucius' conscience alone.

The five council members sat in the briefing room near the command section of Alpha Seven. The former Contractor, now using her actual name, Kate Bueller, sat to the right of Lucius' chair. The experienced refugees' three representatives were two men, Aaron Dallas and Max Nyguyen, and an Iodan, whose name involved limb movements that humans couldn't replicate. The Iodanians apparently made up a substantial part of the refugee populace, surprising since their worlds lay quite distant from Faraday. Lucius had yet to get the story out of them as to how three thousand of them had ended up in the back end of space.

The last representative was Matthew Nogita. The small man who ran the fighter facility on Faraday took the place of the last two representatives after Lucius refused to deal with them. How he managed to get elected, Lucius didn't know. He suspected Nogita to have spread about the fact that he worked with Lucius before. It didn't matter, Matthew was perfectly happy to make polite noises and go along with whatever Lucius said, as long as it didn't hurt his people.

All in all, the council worked because the other four had similar opinions.

They argued and fought with him when they disagreed, but when the matter was finished, they backed him and took his reasoning to their people. The council maintained a unified front, because they needed to.

Lucius had become a warlord, somehow, somewhere. He had lost his lands when he lost his homeworld, but he had gained followers. His ships' crews were startlingly loyal and they trusted him. Lucius had learned that the trust they gave him went both ways. He could no more abandon the refugees than he could cut off his own leg. They'd become his people –even the loudmouthed ones.

He shook off those thoughts as he took a seat. He looked around at the expectant faces, and the pile of writhing tentacles that was the Iodan. "Anything new?" he asked, informally. There was no reason for formalities. They didn't have the time or patience for it.

They all signaled negative. Each of them had taken over different tasks, Matthew Nogita managed salvage and repair operations around the base. Kate Bueller managed personnel, she found people with the necessary training to fill needed positions. Aaron Dallas and Max Nyguyen worked together to solve problems that involved resource management, everything from food acquisition, their most pressing problem, to the sale of items they'd salvaged, mined or made. The Iodan managed their medical and biological needs. The creatures had already stopped one viral outbreak and performed wonders on the environmental systems in the abandoned base. Their knowledge had brought the systems online far more rapidly than would have otherwise been possible.

"I may have found a buyer for the last of this gold." Max Nyguyen said, finally. "It's too early to say, but it looks like this guy will trade fair for it."

Lucius grinned wryly, "It will be nice not to have to discourage pirates from following our trading ships anymore." They'd found a damaged mining ship in the asteroids of the inner system. From the ship's log, it was evident that the miners had struck it rich when they discovered an almost pure lode of gold in one asteroid. The crew had celebrated with copious amounts of alcohol and thirty years later, Lucius' salvagers had discovered the ship, holed from a collision with a medium sized piece of space detritus.

Lesson learned: don't let a drunk pilot get behind the controls.

Trying to sell a large quantity of pure gold ingots, unfortunately, seemed to draw scavengers like flies. Burbeg intercepted five pirate craft and two mining vessels who had attempted to follow their trade ships.

Three of those pirate ships would never bother anyone again. The other two were taken intact. Lucius had both corvette-sized ships out to scout the local systems for any other potential salvage opportunities. The small vessels served well to scare off further mining ships without the need to reveal their larger vessels.

"I got a message from one of our agents. She's on her way back with the man who reported the sighting." As Lucius spoke, he brought up the recording up on the wall screen.

Everyone turned to look. The image was grainy. It was a copy off of a pirate's computer after the pirate ship in question got smashed to wreckage. The pirate's encoded copy came from the black market. Governments didn't pay individuals for that kind of information. They took it.

The vessel revealed was large, larger than a Chxor dreadnought, if the scaling was correct. It was a squashed cylinder, heavy armor formed an arc at top and bottom, to sandwich the vessel in the center. Massive doors and paneling along the side showed what might be hangar bays. Part of one engine was visible in the frame, a massive protrusion from the hull. All in all, the vessel was a ponderous seven kilometers long and one kilometer wide, perhaps half a kilometer thick at its deepest. Parts of the ship were masked in what looked like a dust or vapor cloud.

The visual feed zoomed in to focus on the stark lettering that had to be fifty meters tall. Between the grainy feed and whatever cloud enveloped it, it was hard to make out, but it appeared to say *AWS Patriot*.

"What is the purpose of finding this vessel?" The translation software the Iodan used was emotionless, it sounded like how a Chxor wanted to sound. Lucius realized that non-humans probably didn't have much human history spoon-fed to them.

"The *AWS Patriot* was said to have been Admiral Dreyfus' command ship..." Lucius began. He paused, thinking for a moment. "Eighty-four years ago, Amalgamated Worlds created a large fleet of very advanced warships. Those ships were far more advanced than anything they'd ever made before. The cost was incredible. The Fleet was named the Agathan Fleet, for the design of the command ship, a ship deemed so expensive it was never made."

Kate Bueller spoke, "And several million rogue psychics hijacked that fleet and escaped into shadow space with it. They went on the run, and they smashed every Amalgamated Worlds fleet that tried to follow."

The Iodan twitched its limbs, and the translation software spoke, "I thought Amalgamated Worlds was defeated by the Colonials."

Lucius nodded, "They were. The psychics fled persecution, they weren't out to overthrow the system." *Well, not that we know, in any case,* Lucius mentally added. "They still represented a tangible threat to Amalgamated Worlds, who... well, their general paranoia and specific hatred against ESP caused them to put a lot of resources towards exterminating that threat."

He typed in some commands, and the hologram put up an overlay showing six massive ships, surrounded by a haze of other vessels. "They constructed the Dreyfus fleet. It was designed with the sole purpose of hunting down and exterminating that threat." He shrugged, "Not a moment of human history of which to be particularly proud."

"This Admiral Dreyfus succeeded then?" The Iodan asked, "Was he a great warrior?"

Lucius stared off into the distance as he remembered books he had studied in his youth. "He was their best. Dreyfus was one of the rare Amalgamated Worlds Fleet officers who was outside their normal politics. He wasn't a political appointee or someone's nephew or son, he was the military figure they turned to when they needed to win. He defeated the Wrethe Incursion. He smashed the Tersal Pirates. He…" Lucius shook his head, "He was their best." Those words said it all, he decided.

"He came out of retirement and told Amalgamated Worlds Fleet what he'd need. They gave him everything he asked for." Lucius didn't need to look up the list to recite the numbers, "Half a million ship crew, selected from the best and brightest of the Fleet. Two hundred thousand Marines, again, the best and brightest." He shook his head, "Six ships, each of them larger than any human ship ever built, larger than any ship the human race had encountered. Those ships carried dozens of parasite frigates. They had a full escort of battlecruisers, cruisers, and destroyers. They had a dozen massive transports for equipment, supplies and personnel."

"Over a million personnel departed under Admiral Dreyfus, they set out from Earth on the Fourth of July, in a huge celebration." Lucius snorted, "Admiral Dreyfus broadcast a final message from Alpha Centauri on the Eleventh of July. They were never heard from again."

"What happened?"

"No one knows. No one ever found any sign of them." Mathew Nogita said, "There have been rumored sightings, ghost stories, legends…"

Lucius brought up the gritty picture, the battered lettering only just legible. "Until now."

***

**January 6, 2403 Earth Standard Time
Zeta Tau System
Unclaimed Space**

Mason frowned and shot a glare over at Lauren. "Never again."

She quirked an eyebrow at him as he kicked the organic detritus off of his boots.

"Never again." He repeated. "Once you get those, those..." McGann paused at a lack for words. "Once they're off, never again will something that foul board my ship."

The foul creatures in question mooed, as several people began to herd them off the ship.

"You got your ship back and we're paying you for carrying a cargo on top of that, which we loaded and unloaded ourselves, after we broke your ship out of a government impound," she answered. "Now, you're free, you're here, where without a doubt, someone will be glad to tell you our story as soon as you ask. I believe you owe me something."

"I'll take you there," he replied, "just as soon as you get my ship cleaned up."

She shook her head, "The deal was that you give us the coordinates."

"If Mr. McGann wants to take us there personally, he can do so," a calm, cultured voice said from behind.

Mason turned. He found himself looking at a short middle aged man in a crisp black military uniform. "Who are you? Dark Helmet?" Mason asked.

Surprisingly the man caught the reference, "You're hardly Lonestar, though you may look the part." He bowed politely, "I am Baron Lucius Giovanni, late of the Nova Roma Fleet, Captain of the battleship *War Shrike* and commander of several other vessels."

"Hmmm," Mason paused for a moment in thought. "Some kind of warlord?"

The man smiled politely, "Something like that." He turned to Lauren Kelly, "Excellent job, Lieutenant. I know you probably want a break, but could you get our guest up to the *War Shrike*?"

She nodded, "Yes, sir."

With that, Baron Giovanni turned and strode away. Mason

looked after him, "Interesting fellow." The man didn't look imposing, but he had a certain spark, one that even a cynic like Mason could feel. Men like that inspired from their own actions, Mason knew. They also tended to get themselves and a lot of other people killed, from his experience. *People with dedication like that don't know when to quit,* he thought.

"He's one of the sharpest minds I've ever known," the hero worship was almost painfully evident. "He's saved all of our lives at least once." The brown haired woman stared after the Captain with a look that mixed awe and dedication.

Mason sighed, "Any time you want to tell me what the hell is going on would be great."

Lauren Kelly looked over at him and smiled. Something had relaxed behind her brown eyes and it seemed like the first time that Mason had seen her drop her guard. "I'll tell you on the shuttle ride," she said.

***

"So after we withdrew from the Faraday system we came here, eventually," Lauren Kelly finished her explanation as the shuttle docked. The two stood and waited for the other passengers to disembark. Mason used the time to think... and a lot of his thoughts were confused, to say the least.

The two finally strode off the shuttle and aboard the battleship *War Shrike*. "You expect me to believe that story?" Mason asked, finally, his voice heavy with skepticism.

"I wouldn't believe it myself, Mr. McGann," Baron Giovanni stated from further down the corridor. He turned away from a meeting with several of his crew. "Now, we're all ready to go, so if you'll just come to the bridge and input the coordinates, we'll be on our way."

Mason straightened to his full height, "I just give you the coordinates and I go on my way?" He cocked an eyebrow at

There was an almost painful silence. "You did insist on coming here, on seeing this. You know our entire story, you know where we are, and probably can put together some easy guesses on our current armaments." The Baron's voice was slightly sad. "Would you want to put the lives of over sixteen thousand people in the hands of a mercenary you've only just met?"

"I'm also giving you what is potentially the most powerful fleet in the known universe." Mason said defensively. "It's not like I'd betray you anyway. It's not like there's any profit in it."

The Baron shook his head, "Now you're just being naïve. Those ships will be the most valuable items in known space. The information on where they are won't cease to be of value until they're fully recovered, refitted, and crewed. Do you think for an instant that a band of refugees can do that in any reasonable amount of time? Do you think that knowledge of who has them once they have been recovered won't be of value?"

Mason looked away. *I wouldn't tell anyone,* he thought angrily, *and with my ship, I don't have to worry about being cornered like on Anvil.* Still, some part of him knew that the officer was at least partially correct. Mercenaries, pirates and that ilk would still seek him out for that information. It would be valuable for months, if not years. *And yeah, I can draw some pretty detailed guesses as to their military strength, despite the abridged story that Lauren gave me,* Mason privately admitted.

"You understand, obviously, or else you wouldn't have asked. Had you simply given us the information, we would have taken the risk that we could recover at least some of the vessels before others arrived. But you wanted more information." The Baron's dark gaze caught Mason's and the smuggler could tell that the other man wanted him to understand. "We can't afford to let you leave now."

"Let me leave... or let me live?" Mason snapped. His hand dropped to the prayer beads that hung from his belt.

The warlord shrugged, "I hope it won't come to that, but there is an obvious answer. My people's lives are more important to me than your own. I promise you that you won't be a prisoner forever, merely until we are secure enough that your knowledge will not cause us undue harm. As you might notice, you've already received the payment we've given you, thus far."

"As much good as that will do me," Mason said bitterly. He valued his freedom far more than any payment, no matter how rich.

"Bitterness aside, do we have an understanding?" The shorter man stared up at him with an intensity that set Mason on edge. He had dealt with all kinds, psychics, warlords, psychotic pirates, even renegade Colonial Republic military commanders. There was something about Baron Giovanni's stare that pierced him.

"Yes." Mason nodded, "I won't try to leverage my freedom from the coordinates, either." He quirked a lopsided grin, "I'm a man of my word, in that, at least."

From the corner of his eye Mason saw Lauren Kelly relax slightly. Several things clicked together in his mind. For all that they had come to appreciate one another and that Mason felt that Lauren actually liked him, she had another reason to hang around him. She'd been ordered to keep an eye on him, yes. *But that's not all,* he realized, *no, she'd be less nervous if she merely was to restrain me.* Mason McGann realized that if he should betray them or attempt to escape, she was to be his executioner.

The Baron gave him a grave nod, "Good, then let's get up to the bridge then, shall we?"

***

Lucius had to give the man credit, he kept any fascination with the size of the bridge and the equipment displayed well concealed. His image of self-assurance slipped when he began to interface with the navigation systems, however. He looked up, an expression of hunger on his face, "Do you know what I could do with a system like this?"

Lucius answered without hesitation. "Probably elude every customs frigate in existence. It's just as well it wouldn't fit aboard anything smaller than a cruiser."

"A cruiser…" the smuggler's eyes went unfocused for a moment. "It'd be hard to hide after landing, but…"

"Leave it for later. The coordinates please."

Mason McGann muttered something and, after a suspicious glance at Lucius, began to type in a string of numbers. A moment later, the screens displayed a map, with the highlighted coordinates. Overlayed on the map of space were blobs of light that showed territory claimed by the major powers.

Lucius bit back a curse and heard others on the bridge less restrained.

"The universe has a cruel sense of humor," Mason McGann commented. "That's why I thought you were telling a tall one with your story. It just seems unbelievable that after you being so close, you have to pay me for the information."

The blinking light that represented the *AWS Patriot* lay in the very same star system that they had fled not so long ago.

It seemed the Faraday system was home to more secrets than Lucius had ever suspected.

***

Lucius convened a military council not much later. It consisted of Colonel Proscia, Captain Doko, Captain Naevius, Captain Burbeg, and Lucius's new head of Intelligence, Captain Reed.

"Sir, this has to be some kind of sick joke." This came from Cato Naevius, now the commander of a wing of fighters. They had hit a wall as far as production of further fighters and qualified personnel to pilot them, so for now, they had ceased expansion of their fighter force.

"A joke?" Burbeg asked, puzzled, "This doesn't seem humorous to me, perhaps it is a human type of humor?"

"No, Burbeg," Lucius answered, "No one here finds this of the slightest amusement. This is not a joke... this is a very unfortunate reality."

"How in the hell could those massive ships have lain in that system for almost a century undiscovered!" Naevius snapped. "Are we certain this mercenary didn't just tell us a story to dissuade us from finding out if the information was true?"

"It doesn't fit his profile." Lucius responded. "Besides, unless he's a computer he couldn't have spit out those coordinates without calculating them first, unless he just happened to have memorized coordinates for the Faraday system. The coordinates indicate that the ships are in the upper atmosphere of one of the gas giants, where they'd be screened from visual, electromagnetic, and even mass detectors. No, it's far more likely to be true, as unlikely as that seems."

Captain Nix Reed spoke, her voice calm, "It makes sense. Faraday has always been isolationist, even in our own star system." She'd been Faraday's Intelligence Chief before the exodus from the planet. "We didn't even have an outpost on the other inhabitable world in the system. We had little commerce with other worlds and fewer still once Fey Darran went into quarantine. We charted the system's main astral bodies and focused on our own society."

"However they got there and however they remained undiscovered, they are there. And with the Chxor in power, the system will receive much more traffic. Odds are: the ships will not remain undiscovered," Lucius made the statement with a calm that belied his own internal frustration. "Therefore, we need to eliminate the Chxor as a threat and recapture the system as soon as possible."

"Sir, I just don't see how it's possible." Naevius said. He buried his head in his hands. "By now they'll have a garrison fleet there, plus they'll have reinforced the force we mauled earlier. Within a year they'll have fortified the planet. On top of that, they've got the entire populace hostage. If it looks like they may lose the system…"

"I was at Lanei." Lucius' voice was flat. "I know what they'll do to worlds they don't want to lose."

"I don't really have enough information on the Chxor to guess what they'll do even if they find the fleet." Nix Reed said, her voice hesitant. "I'm not sure I understand how they think."

"No one understands how the Chxor think, least of all the Chxor." Lucius smiled grimly. Then he sighed. "They're extremely methodical. As soon as they think they've secured the planet, probably just after they've got the planetary defenses online, they'll begin a thorough scan of the entire star system."

"But, will they even use the ships?" her voice was hesitant.

Lucius blinked, "That's a question that is more complicated than any of us were thinking. Good job Nix."

She flushed, despite being decades older than him, "Thank you, sir."

"We can't assume they'll activate the ships or even use them. They might simply destroy the vessels, or scavenge parts off them." Lucius tapped the table in thought. "Then again, we can't assume they won't use them. The *Patriot* herself could very well wipe out one of their defense fleets."

"Baron Giovanni?"

"Yes, Colonel?" Lucius responded.

"Shouldn't we wonder why those ships are there and what happened to their crews? For all we know some plague killed them off and those ships are deathtraps. I'm sure I don't have to repeat any of the… theories about what might have happened."

Colonel Proscia's voice was filled with distaste.

"Ghost stories more like." Naevius said. "I'm sure there's a reasonable explanation." His voice lacked confidence though. Rumors and stories abounded about the fate of both the Agathan and Dreyfus fleets. Stories of madness and plague mostly, but also stories of mutiny and betrayal, and stories of worse things. Things like the Shadow Lords.

"I've always enjoyed a good story," Burbeg spoke, "but perhaps this is one best left unknown?"

"No. We need those ships." Lucius sighed. "And we'll need to keep them out of the hands of the Chxor. That means we need to return to Faraday." He looked around at his circle of advisers. "What that means is we need a cohesive plan of attack. We've got around one year to prepare, mount our attack, and somehow convince the Chxor to leave us alone afterward."

Nix Reed frowned. "Sir, what about the populace of Faraday, we didn't exactly make many friends with their government. Do you think they'll even want us back?"

Lucius grimaced. "After eighteen months of occupation by the Chxor, I think if Thomas Kaid himself showed up to liberate them they'd welcome him with open arms."

***

Kleigh watched with mild disinterest as the last of the planet's original government officials died twitching. The nerve gas was harmless to Chxor, so he'd worn no protective gear upon entering the chamber. It was unfortunate that he'd been forced to keep them alive so long. They'd been rebellious from the start, from when they made ridiculous demands from first occupation right up until their deaths. They had proven necessary, until now, to keep the populace in line. Finally, however, sufficient forces were available to control the populace without any illusion of their self rule.

The planet's military forces and their families had long ago been quietly exterminated, of course. Those were the first to go, followed quickly by the planet's teachers, doctors, and engineers. Other highly educated humans acted as threats to the Chxor Empire. It was best if the humans only functioned as manual labor.

Masses of the populous had begun work on the planetary fortifications that would secure the world for the Chxor once and for all. With time, population control measures would go into effect, and the human numbers would dwindle to make more room for superior Chxor colonists. Within a century, even the prolific humans would be gone.

Gradual transitions met with far less resistance, after all.

Kleigh was somewhat tempted to simply exterminate the populace right now, but they were too useful a labor source at the moment. Perhaps later, after the planet was more secure.

His promotion to planetary governor for his capture of the world was quite logical. If he were subject to emotions, he might have felt regret that his pursuit of the rogue warships was at an end. But he was above such emotions, of course.

He stepped out of the chamber and nodded for the cleaning crew to move in and collect the bodies. "Announce the termination of the government to the populace. And prepare the riot control units," he said to his aide. Some intransigents would riot, of course. It was the inevitable human response, to act with unthinking emotion to what was simply a logical progression. It was yet another unfortunate reminder of their inferiority.

The riot control units would use more nerve gas to contain the violence. That tended to eradicate most of the troublemakers before they tried to hide.

"As soon as the riots are dispersed, send out a broadcast extolling the virtues of serving the Chxor Empire," Kleigh stated as he strode down the corridors to his offices. He must update his notes on the course of events on this new Chxor colony.

***

January 9, 2403 Earth Standard Time
Zeta Tau System
Unclaimed Space

"Sir, no matter what we think of, we can't find a way to prevent the Chxor from wiping out the populace of Faraday," Captain Doko's voice was weary. His eyes were hollow, and his skin pale. Lucius knew that his friend had spent days with the simulators. "If we hit them with overwhelming forces, they annihilate the planet and then withdraw. If we don't, we get annihilated. Colonel Proscia doesn't have the equipment or the ground forces to take the planet quickly enough to establish defenses against orbital bombardment. We don't even really have the forces to take on eight or twelve dreadnoughts."

Baron Lucius Giovanni patted Doko's shoulder. "We have a tendency of doing the impossible, we'll find a way." He put both hands on the edge of the simulation tank. They both stared down at the battles played out in high speed, time after time.

"We need more information, first, I think." Lucius grimaced, "We're going to have to dispatch one of the corvettes." It was a risk, especially since neither had probe bays and they would have to draw dangerously close to the planet to get solid readings. Then again, both were former pirate vessels and they had better than average sensors.

After all, pirates who couldn't find their prey were rarely successful.

The battles in the sim tank continued to play out. Most ended with alarming suddenness. The simulation was run by the next best thing to artificial intelligence. The best Nova Roma could produce, in any case. The computer played through the most probable outcomes of a dozen different input plans.

Unfortunately, Doko's summation was brutally correct. They could hit the Chxor with overwhelming force, virtually impossible at the moment, and watch helplessly as the Chxor exterminated the populace and fled. Their other option to attack with a weaker force led to their own annihilation. If they jumped in close to utilize surprise, the battle became one of attrition, a slugging match that the Chxor's superior numbers would win.

"Baron, the problem is, we just can't get them away from Faraday, not without a massive threat." Captain Reed said, her voice filled with frustration. "Which causes them to massacre the civilians on the planet before they leave."

Lucius nodded. "If it was a battle of maneuver... we've the ships to pick apart a formation now, especially with our fighter strength." He stared at the sim tank and then began to type in commands for another simulation. "If we can get them to come away from the planet and fight…"

"But what would make them want to do that?"

Lucius began to smile, one corner of his mouth drawn up wryly. "Have you ever heard that Chxor seem to get slightly obsessive about certain things?"

"Sir?"

Lucius looked up from the tank and met the gazes of his officers. "I'm fairly certain the Chxor would recognize the *War Shrike*. If she were to come in system, what do you think their response would be?"

Cato Naevius began to smile, "They'd probably come out and do their best to squash us." The plural Cato used in spite of the fact that his fighter wing launched primarily from a freighter rigged as a carrier now. Once a crewman of the *War Shrike*... always a crewman of the *War Shrike*.

Lucius nodded, "And while they chasing the *War Shrike*, we take over the planet, and get a defense force in place."

"Uh, isn't that a little dangerous?" Nix asked.

Lucius laughed, "Those slugs couldn't catch the *War Shrike* unless I wanted them to. Their best tactic would be to split up into a lot of small groups and attempt to box me in, and hope I didn't jump to shadow space before they could get in some solid hits."

Naevius's smile was truly vicious now, "And if they split up, I'll cut them into dogmeat."

Lucius nodded, "This can work... this can definitely work."

They watched as the computer worked through a dozen different combinations of the tactic.

"We need more ships." Doko's voice was dull. Lucius could tell that the other man was frustrated that their idea still wouldn't work, not without more ships.

Lucius nodded slowly, "Not many more, but we need to be able to hit the Chxor simultaneously. And we need some *very* fancy flying." He paused a moment in thought, "If we insert Marines before we stage our attack, we can get the populace involved. If they can seize the planetary defenses, it will make things a lot easier."

"We can do it, I'm sure of it!" Burbeg said. "When do we launch our attack?"

"This is going to be very tight. We're definitely going to need some help," Doko said dubiously.

Colonel Proscia frowned, "I've got a lot of personnel out and about. If I'm going to be inserting troops covertly, I'm going to need time to prepare them. That means I need some of the excess duties clamped down on."

"What do you suggest?" Nix asked, "I've got a few teams I can help out with. Some of them, especially Lieutenant Kelly's team, will want to be in on the insert."

Colonel Proscia nodded, "Glad to have her. But I was thinking of things like the Chxor prisoners we've got and the handful of pirates we didn't space."

"We didn't space those pirates because they've proven useful." Lucius said. "But I agree the time has come to deal with them and with the Chxor. I think I have a solution that will free up your Marines."

"The planetary defenses are going to be heavily defended on the ground," Colonel Proscia said. "Casualties in the assault will be heavy, especially on the civilians helping our teams."

Lucius nodded, "The alternative is that the Chxor use those planetary defense centers against our ships. We'll insert as many people as we can, but we aren't going to have enough Marines to take all of the centers."

William Proscia nodded, "I understand, sir. From what my Marines who used to live under Chxor rule say... we'll have lots of volunteers amongst the populace."

"Yes, I have little doubt of that," Lucius grimaced. "Get me an outline of what you want, and what your plan of attack is for the centers. We can firm up the details with the information from the scouting expedition." Lucius stroked his chin for a moment, "As for more ships, I think our best option is putting out a general notice. There's mercenary and pirate groups that would sell their mothers for a piece of the Dreyfus fleet."

"They'd also cut our throats for a chance at the whole thing," Anthony Doko said.

Lucius nodded, "We'll cross that bridge when we come to it, I'm afraid."

***

CHAPTER V

January 12, 2403 Earth Standard Time
Zeta Tau System
Unclaimed Space

Lucius stepped into the prison bay with a brisk pace, hands clasped behind him. He looked left and right with a studious, thoughtful gaze. He wore his normal uniform, and the black leather boots shone with bright polish, his silver buttons and epaulets gleamed in the monochromatic lighting. The two Marines behind him were a stark contrast, clad in full body armor, rifles at the low ready, as they waited for any hostile move. Their faces, behind their masks, were contorted with worry.

The fifty-three Chxor in the long, high-ceilinged room turned to face their captors with bland, emotionless faces. The startling similarity of appearance between the two races made the situation surreal. Bland, gray-skinned faces, rubbery flesh, and wax-like features, made a caricature of a human face. Their faces looked like someone knew exactly how things should measure, what features should go where, but had no idea how the whole fit together. Bowl-cut tan hair and pale yellow eyes, faces hairless and misshapen, and box-like ears rounded out the Chxor's head. That conglomeration sat almost flush with broad, powerful shoulders, far wider than any Humans. To a Human, the Chxor were ugly, identical, and repulsive.

Chxor, naturally, didn't care what humans looked like.

The Chxor prisoners stared at the leader of their captors. What thoughts lurked behind their pale yellow eyes were unknown.

Lucius strode forward and the Chxor parted around him until he reached the one he sought. He stopped before this one, and cocked his head slightly, "You are Kral, the commander of these others?"

The Chxor stared down at the small human for a moment of consideration. "I am Kral, I did command these others."

"Walk with me." Lucius spun on his heel and headed for the door he'd entered. The lone Chxor followed after a moment's pause.

The Marines waited for the Chxor to pass, then backed from the room, eyes wary.

A dozen more Marines waited in the hallway beyond, they eyed the open door with narrow eyes and some of them had clenched jaws. The Marines had recruited heavily from the mutineers from the Chxor cruisers, Lucius knew.

Lucius strode past and calmly nodded to the sergeant who commanded the squad. "Carry on."

Kral stepped up beside the smaller man as he continued his brisk walk down the hall. They walked without speaking for a long while. Lucius listened to the clop of his boots and the shuffle of the Chxor and thought. He gave the Chxor some time to think, as well, and to wonder what this might be about. Lucius finally broke the silence, "The leader of your force was a Chxor known as Kleigh." Kral didn't say anything and Lucius continued after a brief pause. "He's a Logan, part of the dominant genetic line of the Chxor."

Lucius turned a corner and stepped into an elevator. He held the door open as the Chxor stepped inside. The two trailing Marines also stepped aboard and moved to the back. "The Logans are dominant because they're bureaucrats. They follow the strict rules of the Chxor Empire and rarely, if ever, violate those rules. As administrators they typically make excellent strategic decisions. Their long term plans are often extremely successful. That and their absolute obedience to the law has made them the dominant line. They purge the handful of transgressors, correct?"

Kral didn't need to consider the question, "Yes."

"But the Logans are notoriously inept at tactical decisions." One corner of Lucius's mouth turned up in a grin, "Kleigh is a perfect example. He's lost, to date, nine dreadnoughts and over thirty cruisers in the three times I've engaged him. Often those losses were at severe disadvantages in strength leading into the battles."

"One might say that a proper Chxor does not understand the emotion-driven insanity that drives many humans," Kral spoke in a dull monotone.

"Or one might say that Kleigh lacks any kind of ability in regard to application of resources beyond his limited knowledge base. Kleigh is a bureaucrat, not a tactician, and he should never have been given charge of a ship, much less a squadron," Lucius responded.

There was a long moment of silence. "One might," the Chxor

admitted.

"There is another genetic line," Lucius said as the elevator doors opened on another featureless corridor, "known as the Abaner." He stepped forward, and Kral matched his stride, "That line is remarkably... unmentioned by the other, more common lines. It has, however, been the force behind many of the successes for the Chxor. The researcher who reverse engineered the shadow space drive was an Abaner. The best Chxor admirals, with the most dramatic victories have often been Abaners."

"But the Abaners are known for sometimes crossing the line of Chxor law." Lucius stopped and turned. "Many Chxor, especially the Logan line, feel the Abaners are... tainted. Flawed, even. Therefore, victories gained by the Abaner are often poorly rewarded. Abaner receive the lowest reproduction quota of any Chxor genetic line."

"That is so." Kral's voice was as emotionless as ever.

"I was interested, when I heard that on one cruiser, the Chxor crew surrendered as a whole." Lucius stopped outside a plain, unmarked door. "I was even more interested to discover that they were ordered to do so by their Captain. What might happen to any offspring of such a Captain?"

"His genetic line would be purged," Kral spoke the words slowly. "Were he to have any offspring."

"As a question, what would have happened should the ship fallen anyway?" Lucius said, studying the Chxor's lumpy and ugly features.

"The same. Failure is a sign of inferiority."

"Even if that failure lay with another... more senior, Chxor? Perhaps one of the dominant Logan genetic line?" Lucius asked.

"By a certain logic," Kral said with the slightest trace of sarcasm, "especially then."

"To the other Chxor, there would be no repercussions?" Lucius asked.

"No. For them, they would be outcasts, of course, for surrender to an inferior species. However, the alternative being death, logically, surrender is the optimal choice. That is why many Chxor officers chose to do so. Those that were allowed by their crews, at least."

"Yes, repercussions for some brutalities are inevitable," Lucius nodded. "Another fact that surprised me was that one cruiser had no such repercussions. One ship's mutineers didn't execute the Chxor who surrendered. That might mean that on one ship, there were no brutalities."

"It would be illogical to treat those in one's service in an inferior manner. Beatings, executions, and threats incite mutiny and treachery, rather than the opposite. It would be foolish in the extreme to expect brutality to bring loyalty, especially in races such as Humans."

"So, you are an Abaner." Lucius smiled, "I thought so."

The Chxor shrugged. "I will yield no offspring. There will be no future for my genes. Therefore, my line doesn't matter."

Lucius opened the door and stepped out into a vast expanse of stars. They gleamed coldly in the vacuum above the moon and they were the only light in the domed chamber. A handful of tables clustered around a café. Some industrious refugees had assembled the place after arrival and Lucius had encouraged that kind of initiative where he could. A faint melody carried, just on the edge of hearing. The handful of people at the café watched the procession with interest.

Lucius moved over to take his normal seat, and waved for the Chxor to sit facing him.

The Marines remained to the alien's rear.

Lucius stared at the alien for a long while. He nodded politely to the woman who set a cup of tea in front of him. They knew his preference by now and he sipped at it, then turned his eyes up to the dome, so transparent it seemed they stood in space. "As I understand it, Karis is a world shrouded in clouds. The Chxor never even knew that other stars existed, not until they were first visited by aliens?"

"Yes."

"Yet they'd developed an advanced level of technology. Your population grew to the point that you established rigorous population control measures so you wouldn't exceed the limits of Karis. This was after a brutal war between several factions over dwindling resources. You'd developed all the keys to space travel, but you'd never even known it was an option."

Lucius stared at the stars as he spoke softly. "Humans, on the other hand… we've stared up at the stars since our creation. We gave them names and even evolved elaborate stories about them. Our drive to explore eventually led us there. It was our curiosity that brought us to Karis, and showed you the possibilities."

"Yes, Humans did have an advantage."

"How many centuries did the Chxor have fusion generators before my race had mastered the steam engine?" Lucius asked and turned his eyes on the Chxor. "Your race is old, your society is ancient, the Empire ruled Karis for millennia, after they exterminated their competition." Lucius shook his head, "They eradicated every trace of their former foes."

"Nostalgia is seen as a weakness and we had no need for trophies."

"Among some civilizations --the better ones, I've found-- there is a tradition of clemency by the victors to the defeated." Lucius sipped at his tea, eyes locked on the Chxor's emotionless face.

"Chxor have not exterminated all humans on all worlds." The Chxor didn't meet Lucius's eyes. "Not at first." He bit out the admission.

"No, but within a few generations, the last of them are either rounded up, or simply gassed in their ghettos." Lucius's lips formed a hard line, "I've read the intercepted messages, the congratulations for efficiency. Fifty human worlds have fallen to the Chxor. Four alien races and another fifteen worlds in addition to that. Human losses have been in the billions. I'm not sure how the other races have fared, but I doubt you've shown much more leniency to them."

"No... less with the Ghornath. What was done there has made the world uninhabitable."

Lucius sighed, "Humans owe significant blame in that case, unfortunately." He pushed his tea aside, "What has this gained the Chxor? Is your race better? Has your technology advanced? Have you learned new things?"

The prisoner spoke slowly, considering each word, "We have grown stronger. We are more numerous."

"All Chxor?" Lucius asked, "I had heard that some lines had dwindled, while others grew far beyond the original allotments."

The Chxor nodded slowly, "Yes." His yellow eyes met Lucius's. "Abaner, Wroth, and other lines. We are nearly extinct. The Logan are very successful."

"So why are these other lines loyal to a society that looks to make them as extinct as the humans they conquer?" The Chxor stared down at the tabletop. Lucius gave him a moment, but then he snapped, "Kral, I asked you a question. Answer me, why do some genetic lines allow their own destruction?"

"They control our reproduction." Kral's words were soft. "They control our continued existence. Only the Logan doctors know the secret anymore. Once we've reproduced, our offspring are hostage to our continued loyalty and are raised in the Empire schools, far away from those who might wish to… change things."

"I thought so." Lucius said. "Did you have any offspring, Kral?"

"One." Kral's voice was dead. "It will have been terminated."

"I'm sorry, Kral," Lucius said. He genuinely felt sadness, the loss of a child was something he didn't want to ever experience.

"It was one life against many. Logic said that he—" Kral broke off, eyes closed for a moment, then spoke again. "Logically, I could not put the lives of my crew against my offspring."

Lucius nodded, "I understand, Kral. I hope, if I am ever faced with such a situation, I can be as selfless." Lucius turned his eyes up to the stars again. "One of the races you haven't yet encountered is the Iodan. They never developed star travel on their own, but they've gained passage on many races' vessels. I don't know where they come from, but they've spread out to many worlds. They're notoriously good with chemistry, chemical engineering, and biology." Lucius returned his eyes to Kral. "I didn't want to broach this before they confirmed it, but they've found the manipulated genes that make Chxor sterile. They know how to allow you to reproduce naturally."

Kral stared at Lucius for a long moment, "We would have to do so without growth tanks and incubators?"

"Yes, you would have to reproduce as you did thousands of years ago, before the Empire." Lucius shrugged, "It was good enough for your ancestors, apparently, seeing as you are here."

Kral spoke slowly, "I was told this is inefficient and very… unsanitary."

"Humans have developed incubators, but they're designed for a different chemistry than the Chxor." Lucius shrugged, "Most humans prefer it the natural way, anyway. And it's not as if the

Empire will loan us the equipment."

Kral nodded, "That is most unlikely." He sat in silence for a moment, "What price must we pay?"

Lucius shook his head, "You misunderstand me. This, I will do without payment. It seems... evil to hold a race's future as a price. I won't do that. I will have the Iodans treat any Chxor who wish it with the retrovirus." Lucius tapped a finger on the table, "What I brought you here to ask, Kral, is what future you wish for your people."

"I am confused." Kral spoke as if in a daze.

"I'm about to go to war, Kral. I have to feed sixteen thousand refugees and prepare warships and their crews at the same time. I've limited resources, and generosity that costs me nothing cannot hurt me. The Iodans figured out how to cure Chxor infertility as an interesting puzzle. They can produce the retrovirus with ease compared to Human or Chxor scientists." Lucius shrugged, "There was no point to *not* give you that. I can't spend the resources on three hundred prisoners. What I want to know is if you'd work with me, or if you'd prefer to be dropped on an unoccupied inhabitable world."

"You would let us go? We know much of your resources, and I can guess what world you will attack," Lucius definitely picked up a note of surprise. Kral's voice had gained inflections, almost as if he had dropped his guard somewhat and allowed his emotions some leeway.

"Yes. Don't get me wrong, I'm going to leave you on an empty world, with the bare minimum you'll need to survive. We barely have the resources for that, as it is. The world is cold and there's little there to survive on, but it would be possible, with work, to expand, and grow. We'd give you all of the Chxor rations we have left, enough to keep you for several years."

"The alternative is to work with you?" Kral said, his ugly face expressionless.

"Yes, that is the alternative. You would be given positions in our forces. I would need you to vouch for those who are trustworthy, and who are not." Lucius spoke confidently.

"Were I strongly loyal to the Empire, it would be logical for me to lie and betray you in an opportune time," Kral said, his voice wooden.

"Something Abaner are known for, as well, is their strict, almost religious tradition of honesty," Lucius said.

Kral nodded, "This is unfortunately true."

"To be clear, I'm not offering vital positions and few positions of any authority. We need fueler crews, we need basic maintenance work, we'll need people to help keep this base operational. There are a thousand unwanted tasks, but they need to be done, and we can always use the help." Lucius met the alien's eyes.

"I will need to think on this." Kral said, his voice hesitant. "I know some will choose exile."

"I understand. When you have an answer for me, tell the Marines."

***

Mason McGann studied the face of his jailer. He saw suspicion there, along with distrust. He quirked an eyebrow at her, "Well?"

Lieutenant Lauren Kelly stared at him for a long moment. She glanced around at the others in the room and slowly he saw the resolution on her face crumble. She finally threw her cards down in disgust. "I fold." The others at the table groaned as well. Mason swept the chips from the center of the table into his pile.

Mason gave her a lopsided grin, "Well... look at that, I guess I win again."

"Funny, that," the navy Lieutenant to Mason's right said. "That's, what, four hands in a row?" Her nametag read Toria. Mason had heard Lauren Kelly call her Jessi.

"Five," the Marine on Mason's left said. He wasn't wearing his uniform top, but Mason had heard the others call him Tom. "He had the straight flush, a royal flush, a straight, four aces, and whatever we all just folded on."

Mason gave them all an innocent look, "I'm a lucky guy, what can I say?"

"Right..." Tom the Marine shook his head. "Glad we're playing for Republic scrip, or I'd be out most of my paycheck."

"What do you folks get paid in?" Mason asked.

"Right now, whatever currency we happen to have," Lieutenant Toria answered with a shrug. "The Baron tries to make it all balance out."

"Swell guy," Mason muttered.

"Better than some," Tom the Marine said with a grimace.

"Oh?" Mason asked.

"Yeah," He shot a glance at the others, "I did some time as a merc, not an official one, mind you, just hired security really, back on this tiny rock called Hotel Seven..." He shook his head, "We show up and the bastard who signed us on paid us in company notes. Says we can exchange it at the company store. Company store says we can buy goods and services there, but they don't have any cash for trade at the moment. Took me ten years to buy my way off that rock."

Mason nodded, "There's a few like that."

"The 'citizens' on Faraday for example," Toria grimaced. "I hope the bastards get what they deserve from the Chxor."

"I wouldn't wish the Chxor on anyone," Lauren Kelly said, her voice tight. "There's plenty of good folks that will suffer along with the bad. My experience, the good folks suffer a lot worse."

Mason gave her a nod, "That's how misfortune always works. The scum always rises to the top." He finished stacking his chips. "So... another hand?"

Tom the Marine grimace, "Not for me, I'm out."

Lieutenant Toria shook her head too and stood from the table, "Nope, I'm headed up to my ship." The pride in her voice was obvious.

"Ship?" Mason asked.

The female lieutenant stood a little straighter, "Yep, I've got my own command, it's a Terro Class corvette, the *Mongoose*. We captured her from some pirates and the Baron appointed me as the commanding officer."

"Well," Mason gave her a nod, "Congratulations."

"I've had command for a month now," she smiled. "But thanks, it's a good feeling."   Mason sat back as the two left, then quirked an eyebrow at Lauren. "Well, what to do now?"

She smiled at him, "Well, there's always the cafe."

Mason grimaced. "I'd rather use the bar down on G level." The cafe was too... clean for him, and they didn't serve alcohol. Down in G level some enterprising soul had put together a bar out of an old storage space. It had dim lighting, a low ceiling, and it felt like a fire trap. Mason loved it.

"You were asked to stay out, remember?" Lauren smirked.

Mason grimaced. "Yeah, I know." He shook his head. "A misunderstanding... and you saw it, that roughneck threw the first punch."

"Right..." She nodded, "Was that before or after you threw your drink in his face?"

Mason shrugged, "I don't really remember." He didn't, which bothered him. The truth was, though, that he was going more than a little stir crazy. He longed for freedom, of the sort that involved him and his ship alone in space. Too many people around him made it too hard for him to remember his restraint.

His hand dropped again to the prayer beads on his hip. *I have to remember my restraint,* he thought. He rolled up the winnings and tucked them inside his jacket on the inside pocket. It wasn't much, especially since it was small bills of Colonial Republic scrip. Most of the single notes cost more to print than they were worth.

Still, a little extra currency never hurt. And the good thing about playing officers, especially *dedicated* officers like those in Baron Giovanni's employ... they were terrible at poker and they didn't have the first clue how to cheat. Not that Mason really needed to, either, but he at least knew how to bluff. When his luck was up, like tonight, he almost couldn't lose.

"You play grav-ball?" Lauren asked.

Mason frowned, "Not in..." He shook his head at the memories that brought up, "... not in a *very* long time."

"They've got a small court, knocked together down by the reactors," she said. "We could go one on one." Mason could see the challenge in her smile and the confidence of someone who worked and trained in zero gravity on a regular basis.

That's right, she's super commando Chxor killer, Mason thought, *when she's not playing baby-sitter to me.* Some part of him winced away from the idea of awakening some of his old skills. He'd let them go rusty for a reason. Still... another part of him awakened at the challenge in her voice. What would it hurt to blow off a little steam... just this once?

"Sure," he said and his smile matched hers, "Let's play."

***

Lucius had just stepped back into the command center when

Nix Reed and Anthony Doko showed up at his shoulder, "We just got our first real offer."

"Really?" Lucius quirked an eyebrow. "I was beginning to worry we'd made the situation outline too vague to appeal to anyone."

"I don't like it." Doko's voice was flat.

"I doubt you'll like any of them. Tell me."

Doko shook his head, his dark eyes serious, "It's Admiral Mannetti, it's Lady Kale."

Lucius winced.

"She's got a lot of ships," Nix said, looking back and forth between the two. "What, do you two know her?"

"We have some... history," Lucius admitted. "It gets a little complicated."

"She stabbed him," Doko threw up his hands.

"Stabbed you?" Nix said, puzzled.

"Right in the chest." Doko said, his voice rising. "She missed his heart by half a centimeter."

"I was about to arrest her for treason against the Nova Roma Empire at the time." Lucius shrugged, "I'm sure she didn't mean anything personally by it."

"She stabbed you?" Nix said, still confused.

Colonel Proscia approached, "Sir, tell me you're not going to make any agreements with Lady Kale."

"Let's just see what she has to offer," Lucius raised a hand.

"She stabbed you?" Nix asked again.

Lucius turned to her, "Yes, she stabbed me." He moved over to the communications section. Operating from the base opened considerably more space, though they'd had to patch in all the equipment to the older antenna and power connections. "Dial her back." They'd patched the *War Shrike*'s ansible through a laser relay they installed in the base, otherwise Lucius would have had to go back aboard to make the call.

The wait would have been easier if Lucius didn't hear Nix and Tony in quiet conversation behind him.

"We've got an answer, sir." Lieutenant Palmer's drawl was never more welcome.

Lucius took a deep breath, "We need whatever help we can get. Patch her through."

"Lady Kale," Lucius greeted. He met her dark eyes. He looked into those still depths for a long moment until she finally gave him a friendly nod.

"You're looking good Lucius," her sultry voice spoke, "How is my ship?"

Out of the corner of his eye, Lucius saw Nix mouth 'her ship' in question to Anthony Doko. "You're looking good too, Lady Kale. The *War Shrike*'s seen a lot of action, but she's still in good shape."

"I understand you're looking for allies. You've got something big planned, with a *very* big reward." She wore a caricature of the uniform Lucius wore, the neck cut absurdly low, and she leaned forward as she spoke. Lucius was suddenly reminded of just how well she filled out that uniform.

"Yes I do." Lucius answered, keeping his eyes locked on her face. "Do you want me to forward you the outline?"

"No, I think I can trust it will be as brilliant as ever, coming from you, Lucius." She thrust her lower lip out in a pout, "I just hope you won't let our past… unpleasantness get in the way."

"The scars have all faded nicely. You play even with me and I'll do the same." Lucius smiled politely. "What do you bring to the table?"

"Good." Lady Kale smiled, "I always liked you, Lucius. There was never anything personal about our unpleasantness before and I'm glad you understand." She toggled something off the screen, "I've just forwarded my ship strength. I've got the *Peregrine* still and added a couple Republic cruisers along with some scouting units. Now, how are we going to divide the spoils?" She cocked her head as she awaited his response.

Lucius spoke briskly, "The planet we hit is a charity case." Lucius continued to speak over her fluttering laughter, "But ships captured, munitions, salvage, all that is split into shares determined by what each party brings to the fight."

"That includes the Dreyfus fleet?" She asked, "You wouldn't lie about that just to get more support, now would you?"

Lucius met her eyes, "No lies. Equal share on the Dreyfus fleet, so long as we can take it." He tried not to remember the brilliant officer he had nearly fallen in love with and tried to focus on the dangerous pirate she had become. If not for the fact that she had trusted him, who knew how far her treason might have progressed? From what he knew of her, she might have pulled it off. *Then again, she might have destroyed the Nova Roma Empire*, Lucius thought.

She finally nodded, a half smile on her face, "I love it, darling. I think both of us will be very happy with how this goes. Perhaps we could make this into a more... long term relationship afterward? Hmmm?" Her voice suggested all sorts of interesting interpretations.

Lucius smiled, "Perhaps."

"Well, I've got some preparations made, see you soon, darling." She cut the transmission.

"She's got to get her knives sharpened." Doko stage whispered.

Lucius rubbed a spot on his chest in rememberance, "They're sharp enough, trust me."

***

It was several days before the next serious offer.

Captain Doko called him to the command center just after breakfast, "Baron, we've got an... interesting offer." He shrugged, "I'm for it, but Captain Reed doesn't like it."

"I'm on my way."

There were times that Lucius wished he could run all the operations from aboard the *War Shrike*. Those times included when rushing across the base to the command center. The battleship, for all her size, was tiny compared to the base, and he'd never been more than five or ten minutes away from the bridge.

"What's the news?" Lucius asked, after finally stepping through the hatch.

"We've got a message from a Republic officer," Anthony said.

Nix Reed shook her head, "Oh, God, next you're going to say he's a patriot and a legend."

"Well... he is... on some worlds in the Republic." Doko shrugged, "It is Admiral Collae."

"He's a leader of a rebel faction that's tried to seize power on several worlds!" Nix said, "Not only that, but our smuggler friend ran across him once before, not too long ago. He allied with a Tommy King wannabe, and Mistress Blanc."

"Mistress Blanc?" Lucius asked as he moved over to the

communications section again.

"Yeah, she's supposed to be a psychic and very talented. She's also a pirate and a very nasty one. Not nearly the same league as the Shadow Lords, but pretty nasty stuff."

"We've confirmed it wasn't the actual Tommy King?" Lucius asked.

"Well, apparently the smuggler and the fake got in a firefight. The real Tommy King would have left the smuggler dead. I guess it went the other way." Nix's voice was dubious, "Either Mason McGann is the luckiest man alive or that wasn't really Tommy King.

"Or Mason McGann is as good as Tommy King," Lucius said, his lips quirked in a smile.

"Doubt that," Nix said. "Mercenary and pirate work is a lot more lucrative than smuggling. Anyway, if 'Admiral' Collae is willing to work with scum like that, we'd be better off making a deal with Thomas Kaid himself."

Lucius shook his head, "We've already dealt with the devil. We might get lucky and they'll back-stab each other before they get around to us." He pressed a button, "Go ahead and connect us."

The man who appeared on the screen stared at Lucius with cold, calculating, blue eyes.

"It seems you had more luck with Mason McGann than I did," Admiral Collae said. "I trust you've verified his information and we're not all dancing to his tune?" His gruff voice immediately put Lucius on edge.

"We're taking precautions. The system is currently in enemy hands. We'll need to defeat them—"

"I read your message." Collae interrupted. "I was surprised the avenue you chose to take with this. You're risking a lot letting every pirate and would-be warlord know what you're planning on doing."

"I'm giving them enough information so they know what they're getting into. We can always turn away anyone we don't feel we can trust."

"True." The rebel Admiral stared at Lucius for a long time, "So, here is what I bring. I have two Forerunner destroyers, a Liberator carrier, and my own ship the *Rubicon*. All told, I've got twenty four fighters, four squadrons, almost a wing."

"And what about your allies? Do you speak for Mistress Blanc and the fake Tommy King, as well?" Lucius smiled.

"You have some excellent sources," Admiral Collae's eyes narrowed, "Tommy King, if it was him, seems to have made himself scarce. Mistress Blanc will, graciously, accompany me. She'll bring her ship."

"Good. Too bad we won't have the *Revenge* along, the firepower would have helped." Lucius matched the other man's cold gaze.

"Yes, the Tommy King of my acquaintance never got around to bringing it, said his crew had it someplace safe. I think that, unfortunately, he lied." Admiral Collae moved his square shoulders in what might be a shrug, "A pity."

"Yes, true that." Lucius nodded, "Care to discuss the distribution of spoils?"

"No, it can wait until I get there. I trust you'll forward coordinates for link up soon?"

"Yes, as soon as we've got sufficient forces, you'll receive coordinates for rendezvous." Lucius smiled, "Neutral space, safely away from well-traveled space."

The other man smiled slightly, it looked painful. "I get the feeling you're concerned for the refugees you shelter. You needn't. I have no interest in them or in Faraday, after we liberate it from the Chxor."

Lucius felt his stomach flutter. He returned the other man's words, "You have some excellent sources."

"I've got spies everywhere, Baron Giovanni." Admiral Collae smirked, "Really, I just had to put things together. I honestly felt tempted make my own move to secure the system, once I figured out the details, but I think that having the exact coordinates for the fleet will speed things up."

"I see," Lucius answered.

"I trust I am now indispensable to your efforts."

"Yes, we'll definitely be bringing you along." Lucius said. "We'll contact you soon."

"My, god, sir, what do we do?" Nix Reed looked devastated. "He must have infiltrated my people, somehow. I don't even know how…"

"No." Lucius shook his head. "I think it's far more likely that he's just a very, very smart man and we've got too many clues out there." He paused a moment in thought, "By now, information must have hit half the Republic that the Chxor found and seized a planet out there. You were isolationist, but there were still the occasional trading ships coming through, correct?" Nix nodded slowly. "Put that together with a little bit of intelligence on myself, the rumor of refugees on the move, and the offer I put out there and we were bound to have someone guess at least very close to the truth."

"Baron, there's no way in hell we can trust him, you have to realize that!" Nix Reed said.

"I don't think we'll be able to trust *any* of the allies we make," Lucius said. "But no, I think more importantly we can't underestimate this man. If we don't bring him with us, he'll follow and strike us from behind after we've destroyed the Chxor. Better to know he's there with us, where we can watch him."

***

Lieutenant Palmer chimed Lucius' desk later that night. "Sir, we got another one that Captain Nix and Doko have signed off on. Some o' them no-mad people."

"Nomads?" Lucius asked, frowning.

"Yes, sir, them as live on ships." Lieutenant Palmer confirmed. "Captain Doko's talking to them now, they's apparently got several ships fixin' to fight."

"Thank you, Lieutenant." Lucius said, "Let Captain Doko know I'll be there soon."

"Yes, sir."

Lucius closed out at his desk, and then murmured to himself, "Fixin' to." He shook his head. He wasn't sure whether to be horrified or amused anymore at the butchery of the English language performed by his communications officer.

He stepped into a different atmosphere in the control room. This time, Captain Doko and Captain Nix were both had smiles on their faces. "I take it this is one you both agree on for once?" Lucius asked.

"Yes, sir." Captain Reed said, her voice confident. "I know we can trust them."

"Well, we can trust them in a way, sir." Captain Doko said,

slightly less certain. "It's the Garu. Several of their captains are offering to assist for an equal share for their clan."

Lucius stroked his chin, "I honestly don't know much about the Garu."

"They're... well they're a bit like Gypsies from the stories, sir." Doko said. "They travel from system to system, sell their goods, buy what they need, and move on." He shrugged, "There's stories of them stealing kids and they definitely are known for taking anything that ain't welded down, but they're good for their word."

Lucius raised an eyebrow at Nix, who smiled, "Baron, I can vouch for them. We've dealt with the Garu before, back on Faraday. They've always dealt fairly with us. They keep to themselves a lot. And, they hate pirates, so they'll help us to keep an eye on our other allies."

"How are their ships armed?" Lucius asked, frowning.

Both of them shrugged.

He nodded, "Okay, let's give this a try."

The connection was established with a man wearing a deep purple scarf and several bright gold earrings. "You be the Baron, then?"

"Yes, I'm Lucius—"

"We got six caravans willing to fight. Lots of crew skilled in boarding." The man spoke in a rapid staccato. "Want our fair share, we can haggle when we get there."

"Right." Lucius said, "If you can forward me your ship specs—"

"We're armed with energy torpedoes, two heavy and four light. Turret mounted. Also some missiles. Each caravan's got an energy screen." The man paused, "Ships are fast, not as fast as your ship, but as fast as that Ghornath battlecruiser you got."

"I see..." Lucius said. He felt totally off balance.

"Forward us the rendezvous point when you're ready." The Garu man cut the connection.

"That was... odd." Lucius said.

"They're a bit different, but they're fair traders." Nix shrugged. "I'm not sure about the armament—"

"Oh, energy torpedoes are pretty effective. They lack in accuracy, but they pack a hell of a punch." Anthony Doko said, voice eager. "I don't know how they've got them mounted, but those ships could do a lot of damage."

Lucius nodded. "They're our best so far." He somehow couldn't stop the ache of worry in his chest. He longed suddenly for a proper Nova Roma squadron. "If we get any other—"

"Sir, we gots a message, it's fer you, and it's got a priority code." Lieutenant Palmer interrupted.

The code started to blink on the screen and Lucius felt the blood drain from his face.

Behind him, he heard Doko's awed voice, "That code's reserved for the Emperor himself."

Lucius cleared his throat, slightly, "The Emperor is dead."

"But who else knows the commands to enter it?" Anthony said. Lucius could hear the shock in the other man's voice along with a note of hope. Lucius wondered how much of that hope was for the Empire... and how much for the woman Tony secretly loved.

Lucius shook his head, "I—"

"Sir, you gonna answer it, or should I tell 'im to stuff—"

Lucius pressed the stud as much to cut off the Lieutenant's drawl as to answer his own questions. "This is Baron Lucius Giovanni."

The young man who appeared on the screen was instantly recognizable, "This is Emperor Romulus IV." He wore the stark black uniform of the Empire, but the epaulets were unadorned.

Lucius bowed slightly, "Your Highness, I heard about your father, I'm sorry." Behind him, he heard muttered conversations as old hands from the *War Shrike*'s crew filled the newer people on who this young man was. He ignored it as best he could.

The young man nodded. "They made it a requirement of the surrender that he and my older brother be there." The man, little more than a boy, looked away. "He… he wasn't the best Emperor, but he didn't hesitate in the end." He grimaced, "They had to drag my older brother kicking and screaming.

"And you?" Lucius asked. "Last I heard you were still at the Academy."

The boy shrugged, "There was a lot of confusion just after the Chxor landed. The Chxor didn't think of the Academy as a real threat, so they… overlooked us at first. I took the opportunity to escape and to try and get as many out with me as possible."

Lucius stared. Part of him wondered if the young man was a

well-spoken coward or a quick thinking hero. The poor kid probably wondered that himself, Lucius decided. "That's a noble action, Your Highness. How may I help you?"

"You can help me retake Nova Roma, and liberate it from the Chxor!" His voice rose at the end.

"Ah... Your Highness, the problem is... I've only a couple of ships." Lucius couldn't meet the boy's eyes. This was the man, by honor, by law, to whom he owed his allegiance. "I don't have the forces and I've sworn to help some refugees here. I can offer you refuge--"

"Baron, I'm not an idiot." The boy-emperor shook his head, "I'm not asking you to throw your life away, or to forsake your duties. I didn't run away with nothing. I couldn't do that. We... stole just about every ship in the yards. I'm aboard the *Emperor Romulus* now. We have a small fleet, and I've read your message."

Lucius blinked, "That's excellent news, Your Highness—"

"Oh let him finish, Lucius!" A familiar voice spoke from out of the view screen and Lucius felt his heart stop and then start beating again. "You always were so stuffy!"

"Alanis?" He asked, jaw open in disbelief. "My God, I thought—"

She opened a second window and from the background she was at the communications station. His sister spoke with the exasperation that only a younger sister could impart, "I did make it out, Lucius. Now where is Reese?"

Lucius's face betrayed him, "We thought you were dead. He stayed behind on Faraday."

Her face fell, "Oh."

"I'm sorry. I—"

The Emperor took charge of the conversation again, his young voice brisk, "Look, Baron, we've got a dozen ships, a large number of sailors and Marines. With you in charge, we can take the Chxor, whatever world they're on and then we can take the Dreyfus fleet. With that—"

Lucius nodded slowly, "With that, we could retake Nova Roma. It won't be easy, Your Highness. We'll need to crew the Dreyfus fleet, we'll need to repair and refit those ships, without a doubt. But we could do it."

"See?" The youthful voice was exuberant. "Now, give me the coordinates for your location and we can link up immediately."

"Of course, Your Highness, link me through to your navigation department—"

"Ah, yes, that's Cadet Fleming."

"Uh, Your Highness, you have a Cadet in charge of navigation?"

"We're... a little short on trained personnel here, Baron."

"You have someone with experience at the helm, at least?" Lucius asked.

"Oh, yes, we've got Tug-Master Keeting at the helm."

"A, um, civilian tug-master?" Lucius asked, his heart fall.

"Oh, no, he's a retired master petty officer, eighty years of service."

Lucius had a sudden mental image of a dozen cadets and a handful of elderly retirees handling the most advanced and expensive Imperial warship ever made and worse yet, with his little sister aboard. "I see. Please put me through to Cadet Fleming then, Your Highness."

***

January 25, 2403 Earth Standard Time
Zeta Tau System
Unclaimed Space

Lieutenant Lauren Kelly stepped into Lucius's office almost hesitantly, "Baron, you wished to see McGann?"

Lucius looked up from the figures he studied. "Yes, I did. Please send him in." He paused, "We may be a while, so feel free to take the rest of the afternoon off."

She smiled, "Thanks, sir. He's not much of a hassle to watch, but it's nice to get some free time. I haven't been down to the range in ages."

Lucius frowned, "He doesn't practice with his pistol? I thought that pretty standard for those on the... shadier side of things."

Lauren shrugged, "I don't really know, Baron, but I've never seen him draw the thing, except once to clean it."

Lucius nodded, digesting the fact. "Thank you, Lauren, go ahead and send him in."

Mason McGann stepped into the room with his normal arrogant strut and seated himself in the most comfortable chair before Lucius could offer. "What's up?"

Lucius cocked a head, staring at the smuggler. "You still strike me as somewhat familiar. Are you certain we haven't met before?"

The smuggler's eyes darted about the room, "No. Pretty sure. I've got a thing for faces."

"Ah, very well then." Lucius stroked his chin, "Actually, I'm slightly surprised you're still here. I'm sure someone as… resourceful as yourself has found at least a couple ways to escape from our little refuge."

Mason shrugged, "Found a few. Your security is so focused outwards and on those prisoners of yours, really, you leave some pretty big gaps." He shrugged, "I'm good for my word, though, so long as you keep yours. Just keeping my options open."

Lucius nodded, "I understand."

"So what's with the prisoners you've got anyway?" Mason asked, "Most warlord types I've met would have spaced the lot of them, without much thought. I mean, especially the pirates. As for those Chxor… well, I'm sure it can't be a popular decision to keep them alive."

"Popular or not, I believe it's the right thing to do. The Chxor, actually, have taken my offer to join us. They'll soon be productive, though I consider them more of an investment in the future. The pirates in question… well they provided useful information, and for that I spared them. The ones not guilty of a dozen other capital crimes, anyway." Lucius shrugged, "Mercy is something I believe strongly in, McGann, but so is justice. Some of those men and women showed pride in the crimes they committed. One of the ships claimed to be the *Revenge*, and that the captain was none other than Tommy King."

The smuggler's eyebrows shot up, "I take it he wasn't?"

"No. I encountered Tommy King once." Lucius shook his head, "Chased him around a system for several days. I've seen the *Revenge*, seen her weapons close up. The pirates of this ship were… not so fearsome. They had their own list of heinous crimes, however. Those pirates received a fair trial and a quick execution."

"I see." Mason McGann looked away, "I'd heard of Tommy King being bested only a couple of times. What star system was it you faced him in?"

"Trinity." Lucius said, thinking back, "Though who bested who is debatable. I will say he lives up to his legend, he's tactically brilliant and he kept total control over his core force, even after we broke the majority of his allies."

"Trinity was a rough one, so I hear." Mason McGann shrugged, "What exactly did you want to see me about, besides reminiscing on dead pirates?"

"Oh, I'm very certain that Tommy King's not dead, not yet anyway." Lucius smiled slightly, "But what I wanted to speak to you about was a job offer."

Mason raised his eyebrows, "Talk, I'm getting stir crazy here."

Lucius's smile widened, "We need a cargo delivered quietly to a Chxor planet, no witnesses, no flashy exits. The cargo needs time to hide itself before the Chxor ever realize it was placed. Probably we'll need multiple deliveries."

Mason stared at him for a long moment, "You're going to drop infiltration teams on Faraday?" He shook his head, "That's nuts! Chxor will pick up outsiders in a day, maybe two!"

"That's why we're inserting people who know how to behave in Chxor controlled areas." Lucius said, "And this is not open for discussion. All personnel are volunteers and all of them know exactly what they'll be going into."

"You-- you're going to send Lauren in there aren't you!" Mason shook his head, "Go stuff yourself."

Lucius sighed, "McGann, we have to do this. Either you and your ship will help us, or we try to use one of our captured pirate craft. It'll be a lot harder to get a corvette—"

"Try impossible. The first thing the Chxor do is heavily seed the planet with scanners. They'll pick up the corvette as it enters the atmosphere." He shook his head, "There's a reason that you pretty much can't get any smugglers to take jobs in the Chxor Empire, you know. Once they get their sensor network established, it's damned near impossible."

Lucius nodded, "Unless we time it with entry of some cometary debris. Faraday gets a lot of those, and the additional thermal mess might hide its entry."

Mason frowned, "It might." His eyes narrowed, "Getting out would still be impossible."

Lucius nodded, "It's a one way trip for the crew. They're all volunteers too." He leaned back, "As I said, it's not the best option... just our only other one."

Mason grimaced, "You sure know how to talk." He rubbed one hand across the stubble on his chin, he seemed to find comfort in the soft rasp. "Okay, here's how it's gotta be." His brown eyes met Lucius's. "I'll take them in. One trip, to minimize chances of detection. The Chxor will look for rebels anyway, from what Lauren... that is, Lieutenant Kelly, said. They'll stir up like ants if they think someone snuck in." He paused in thought, "I don't normally run human cargo, but I can fit… maybe a hundred."

"We have fifty volunteers and two hundred fifty metric tons of equipment."

"That's… you're arming an insurrection though…" the smuggler muttered to himself for a moment, "Okay, I can do it. They'll be crammed in the passenger quarters. I hope they're friendly."

"Friendly or not, they'll do it. Most of them leapt at the opportunity."

Mason grimaced again, "Yeah, like me?"

"No, McGann, not like you. Some of them have family on Faraday, some of them lost their entire families on worlds controlled by the Chxor." Lucius shook his head, "They'd exterminate us if they could. Methodically wipe out every sign of our existence. Doesn't that make you want to stop them?"

The smuggler shrugged, rubbing at his pistol grip with is right hand. His left hand massaged a necklace of wooden beads that hung from his belt. "Sometimes I gotta wonder what we did for this universe that deserves us sticking around."

Lucius smiled sadly, "Sometimes I'd agree with you." He shrugged, "On the other hand, one thing I don't doubt is my duty to my people. I will not fail in that. I will not let the Chxor exterminate the human race without a fight."

"Duty," the smuggler said, "is a funny thing. It can make you do the worst things of all, you know?"

Lucius nodded and his thoughts went to Ghornath Prime. "Yes, yes it can."

Mason cleared his throat, "If you're taking Admiral Collae's help, do you have any psychics to counter Mistress Blanc?"

Lucius shook his head, "Unfortunately not, I'd want someone like that for the help in navigation if nothing else." Nova Roma had few psychics in general, but he'd been along on a raid where the commander had a psychic navigator once. They had cut days off their shadow space jumps and arrived with far greater precision than a computer could calculate.

"I know someone who could help." Mason cleared his throat, "I'm surprised she hasn't contacted you yet."

Lucius leaned back in his chair, "And who would that be?"

Mason shrugged, "Her name's Kandergain. I dunno if that's her first name, last name, or even her real name, but that's what she gave me." He paused for a moment, "She's powerful, and she avoided the Plagues." He made casual reference to the Plagues that had wiped out well over ninety percent of human psychics. Lucius had lost his own grandmother to them.

"How do I know I can trust her?" Lucius said, disturbed by how uneasy the smuggler looked. "From the way you're talking, I'm not sure I *want* her help."

"Oh, you want her help." Mason nodded, "Sometimes the price is a bit high, but you want her help." He shrugged uncomfortably, "She doesn't deal in currency, only in favors. She'll offer you what seems like a bargain, but is in the end a lot more effort and more involvement than you ever suspected."

"Really?" Lucius frowned. "That's vague enough."

Mason smiled, "As an example, last time she helped me, she gave me some information, and told me I couldn't use it unless I sold it to buy my ship back."

"You got the location of the Dreyfus Fleet from her?" Lucius stared. He felt his stomach clench, "So you haven't—"

The smuggler raised his hand, "Oh I checked, I definitely checked. The ships are there, I didn't believe it myself, but they *are* there."

Lucius leaned back in his chair, brow furrowed, "How do I contact her?"

"Well, as I said, I'm really shocked she hasn't—"

"Morning, sir, we got a call for you," Lieutenant Palmer's drawl interrupted on speaker.

Lucius frowned, "Another answer to our message? I thought we'd made it clear we have sufficient forces."

"Ah, no, Baron. It's, well, a ship just arrived in-system. The captain called us right off, and said she's wantin' to talk with you, personal-like." Lieutenant Palmer seemed disconcerted. "It's a small ship, looks like one of 'em Achaean scouts. Not much of a threat by itself."

Lucius had an unsettled feeling in the pit of his stomach, "Did she say how she found us?"

"Naw, sir, she just said she had to speak with you in person, and gave her name."

Lucius closed his eyes, "Her name is Kandergain, correct?"

Palmer didn't answer for what seemed like a long time, "Why, yes, sir, it sure is."

"Well, her timing is impeccable. Direct her to land at the south pad. Tell Colonel Proscia I want an honor guard, I'll meet them there." Lucius closed the link, "Well, Mr. McGann, it looks like she wanted you to introduce her."

The smuggler shook his head, "Like I said, she's… she's just spooky."

"I'm beginning to feel that way myself," Lucius sighed.

***

The ship settled on the south pad smoothly, "She knows how to handle a ship, that's for certain," Lucius said softly. Lucius waited in his best black uniform, with its silver buttons and epaulets. Twenty Marines stood by, dressed in their full battle harness. It might be excessive, but then again, it might not be enough.

"I'd love to add that ship to our forces," Lucius murmured. Ruggedly built scout ships, the Achaeans mounted the best scanning equipment and computers to match. That single ship probably had better systems than the *War Shrike* mounted. Of course, the handful of Achaeans that survived dated to just before the fall of Amalgamated Worlds.

The woman that stepped down the ramp didn't look like a psychic. With simple, rugged clothing and her blonde hair pulled back into a pony-tail, she looked like the normal prospector or surveyor that would crew an Achaean. She smiled as she surveyed the arrayed Marines, "Thank you for the honor guard, Baron

Giovanni. I swear to you that I will be on my very best behavior."

Lucius stepped forward, offering his hand, "Pleased to make your acquaintance." He took her hand, and made a slight half-bow over it. "Though, I must apologize that I'm not so certain I can take you at your word."

She smiled, "Sweetheart, if I wanted to kill you, there's nothing you could do to stop me." She sighed, "Though I suppose you'll need further demonstration." She released his hand and stepped back. The lights dimmed slightly. The air chilled suddenly and a crackle of static electricity rippled through the air.

Suddenly there were shouts of surprise from behind him. Before Lucius could turn, the rifles and sidearms of his escort flashed past him, to spin in the air around the psychic. They spun faster and faster, as she raised her arms.

She dropped her arms. The weapons settled into neat piles, just as if the Marines had stacked them prior to undertaking some work. The lights returned to their normal brightness, and warmth slowly returned to the air. She smiled wryly, "My best behavior, Lucius. I promise."

Lucius let out a breath that steamed, "Well, then. Perhaps we can dispense with the honor guard." He cleared his throat, "Would you care for some refreshments? We've prepared some in the observatory, it's my favorite place to eat."

She nodded, "I'd love to. Lead the way."

Lucius turned and started out of the landing bay. "As it would happen, by the way, Mr. McGann and I were just discussing you, prior to your arrival."

"Ah... how fortuitous."

"One might wonder at the timing." Lucius said

She gave a slight smile, "One might."

They walked in silence for a while, and Lucius took the time to study her more. She stood taller than him. She didn't appear much older than her early twenties, though life-prolonging treatments could make her much older than him, depending on which ones she'd taken. As they walked, her brown eyes roved over the activity of the base. She smiled, every now and then, as a child ran past.

They reached the observation level after only a short walk. Lucius seated himself at the same chair he'd taken when he spoke with Kral the Chxor. He hoped this conversation would prove as helpful. "So, what brings you to our delightful slice of the universe?"

Her face settled into a serious cast, "I'm here to help you and to warn you, Lucius." She sipped at a cup of coffee. "Your battles at Faraday may well decide the fate of the human race."

Lucius cleared his throat, "Oh... delightful. No pressure, then?"

She smiled, "Quite the opposite, I'm afraid." She shook her head and her face returned to solemnity, "I'm certain you see the Chxor as the greater threat, right now, but there are other things far worse. The Balor continue to rip through the Republic. The Shadow Lords continue to raid and loot entire worlds." She sighed, her brown eyes focused on something distant, "Shadow Lord Invictus just sacked the Haid system."

"Isn't that a Republic military world?" Lucius asked.

"It was. There weren't... there isn't much left there now," the way she said it, Lucius wondered if Invictus had left any survivors.

"Why?" Lucius shook his head, "Why would they do that, aren't they human, don't they care what happens to the human race?" He had no personal encounters with the Shadow Lords or their minions and for that he was grateful. He knew that Colonel Proscia had barely escaped from one of their raids. The Nova Roma Empire had fought off a serious raid by Shadow Lord Gargant shortly after the fall of Amalgamated Worlds... a battle Lucius's own father had been involved in.

"They're arrogant, and they're powerful." Kandergain shook her head, "Invictus did it to stop Imperious from taking the world, to tell the truth. They worry more about each other's machinations than the very real threat our race faces."

"You seem to know a great deal about them." Lucius said, having sudden dark suspicions. It wasn't unknown for them to send emissaries to manipulate those they saw as pawns.

"I'm not one of them." Kandergain rolled her eyes, "As powerful, definitely, but I lack their ambition, and the dark bitterness that drives them."

"And modest too," Lucius said dryly.

She shrugged, "The longer a psychic lives, the more she goes through, the stronger she becomes." She held out a hand, "The Shadow Lords have amassed armies and fleets to do their bidding, they don't exert themselves as much as some others do."

"So you're old and experienced then?" Lucius asked doubtfully. The Shadow Lords predated the fall of Amalgamated Worlds. *Hell, they helped to loot Earth and finish off Amalgamated Worlds,* Lucius thought. He somehow doubted that they had amassed a fleet to do so in any short period of time.

"I knew your grandmother, Lucius. I knew her when she was a child and *her* mother turned down the offer to escape with the Agathan Fleet. I helped to train her. When she turned twenty, I told her to go to Nova Roma and save the life of the young Emperor."

Lucius stared at her.

"Once a psychic hits a certain level, it's very, very hard to die." She shrugged, "I'm not invulnerable. There's a number of ways to kill psychics, as you must know."

Lucius timed his statement for when she took her next sip, "Poison is the preferred method." Not that he had, but he wanted some measure of her by her response.

She didn't so much as sputter, "Yes, that can work, so long as the psychic doesn't have full control of her body." She shrugged, "Brute violence does the trick, preferably done from far away. Bombs, large explosions, kinetic strikes, those are the most effective. Rather hard to dodge a nuclear airburst."

Lucius couldn't help but snort, "Probably true."

"In any case, while the Shadow Lords have fought amongst each other over the bones of Amalgamated Worlds, I've fought to keep humanity alive." She shrugged, "It's a hard enough task, especially when so many people can't see beyond their own ambitions."

"So you're the lone protector of humanity?"

"I'm not alone," She spoke almost defensively. "I get help from many people." The distant look came into her eyes. "There's another, like me. He's a lot more... direct, though."

"And where is he?" Lucius asked.

"He's fighting the Balor." She shrugged, "I'm not as good as him at the brute force aspects, so I leave that to him. He and his wife are *quite* proficient at direct war."

"Ah, so he's not your distant love?" Lucius smiled.

"No, he's definitely not. More of an older brother." She shook her head. "He's fighting a losing battle though. The Republic is too disorganized, too shot through with infighting." She sighed, "Which brings me back to my warnings and my offer of help."

Lucius sighed, "Feel free to explain."

"I'm not omnipotent, nor am I omniscient. The reason it took me so long to come here directly involved scouting out your allies." She frowned. "You really couldn't have picked much worse than Collae and Mannetti, you know?"

"I hadn't much choice with Collae," Lucius shrugged. He thought for a moment and felt grateful that Tony wasn't around to overhear. "Accepting Mannetti might have been a mistake," he admitted.

"Yes, yes it was." She shook her head. "Both of them are going to betray you as soon as they see a clear advantage. Despite what she may have told you, Mannetti has a serious grudge against you, though I'm not clear on the details."

Lucius shrugged, "I was her XO when she commanded the *War Shrike*. She was involved in a coup attempt, I turned her in. When we went to turn her over to Imperial Security, she stabbed me and some of her fellow conspirators aboard the *Peregrine* helped her to escape."

She cocked her head, "Very succinctly put, but I feel there's more involved." She shrugged, "With both of them, the knives will come out as soon as they feel safe. Expect Admiral Collae to try and use Mistress Blanc to throw some surprises your way."

"You won't be there?" Lucius asked, surprised.

"I will, if you'll take my help," She shrugged, "But you haven't heard my conditions yet. My warnings are always free. My help always comes with a price, as I'm sure McGann told you."

"Yes, yes he did. I wonder how much of events you've manipulated."

"Not as much as I'd like, or we'd be in far different straits, I assure you," Her smile was sardonic. "I've worked with the Garu before, you can take their help, though when it comes time to bargain, prepare to be fleeced." She shook her head, "They've a handful of moderately talented psychics in their families, so they'll be useful to watch your back."

"And what of my Emperor?" Lucius asked.

He waited some time before she spoke and when she did, he

could tell she picked her words with caution, "That's going to be a prickly thing." Kandergain took a deep breath. "I don't know what loyalties you have to him, but he's going to want a return to the status quo."

"Yes, I'd realized that."

She nodded, "All the same... The Nova Roma Empire caused almost as much damage as benefit to the human race. I don't see that changing, not even with you at the hand of the Emperor, giving advice. The idea that Nova Roma is paramount is too dangerous, led to too many poor decisions."

"I don't see many other choices." Lucius said, "The shipyards there are still the largest in human space. The population, whatever survives the Chxor occupation, will oppose the Chxor."

"And as I said before, the Chxor are not even the greatest threat." She shook her head, "There are factions among the Chxor that even now are looking for ways to stop their expansion. The threat of the Nova Roma Empire has kept the Chxor Empire together."

"You think if I help the Nova Roma Empire return I'll sustain the Chxor?" Lucius asked.

"I think so, yes." She shrugged, "The first Emperor Romulus wanted to set up a protective cushion around his world. He didn't conquer, save those worlds that strictly posed a threat, places that were, at the time, pirate havens." Her eyes went distant again, "The second Emperor was different. He was his mother's child... and he set out to conquer, to expand his empire. The third was, as you know, weak. He let his advisers guide him, and they wanted power and further expansion. I think that the legacy of Nova Roma has been poisoned by those men and their actions."

Lucius thought back to the invasion of Ghornath Prime and the attack on Saragossa. "You might be right."

"Of course I am, I'm psychic," Kandergain said with humor. Her face turned solemn again, "In many ways, the Colonial Republic has been poisoned as well. Ever since they betrayed Thomas Kaid... well you've dealt with some of their warlords. The best of their worlds are in trouble and the worst are pits like Anvil or Neverrun. The infighting and politicking has become a way of life for their rulers. No one will ever take full power there, not without breaking the Republic and rebuilding it."

"So, that leaves what?" Lucius smiled, "I know of a couple of warlords who control one or two systems. The Centauri Confederation is dissolved into a civil war, with Centauri and Tau Ceti merely as the largest fractions. Without manpower and resources, I can't use the Dreyfus Fleet. I need an actual nation for that kind of effort, and I won't get it without giving my loyalty."

Kandergain nodded, "All I'm asking, Lucius, is that you keep an open mind. I think that when the time comes, an opportunity will present itself."

Lucius nodded, "I *try* to do that anyway."

"I figured so. Now to the bargaining," she smiled. "I offer you my full help and cooperation, to share any information necessary to the defeat of the Chxor in Faraday, and for the liberation of that star system and in the recovery of the Dreyfus fleet." She shrugged, "All I ask in return is three favors, to be disclosed at the time I ask it. You'll have the opportunity to decline and remain in my debt."

Lucius asked. "Do I have to sign in blood?"

"No, your agreement is sufficient." She smiled, "For some reason I can't think of, few people feel safe going back on a bargain made with me."

"I can't understand why," Lucius shook his head. Even so, he made a note to see what he could do to improve the security of his base. He had not expected to deal with psychic threats, but there were some precautions that the Nova Roma Empire had figured out over the years. "Done then, and glad to have you with me."

"Glad to be with you, Lucius," She nodded. "So, when do we leave for the rendezvous?"

***

CHAPTER VI

January 29, 2403 Earth Standard Time
Zeta Tau System
Unclaimed Space

"Your Highness, welcome to Alpha Seven." Lucius said.

"Baron, I'm glad we made it in one piece." The boy stood from the command chair. Across the massive bridge a curious mixture of youth, elderly and even a couple average crewmen manned the vital stations. "We've run on a skeleton crew, and we've run into a number of issues with all of our ships, especially the *Emperor*."

"Frankly, Your Highness, I'm truly astounded the *Emperor* wasn't destroyed by the Chxor." Lucius frowned, "When did the *Emperor Romulus* leave the slip? I thought it wasn't complete prior to the Chxor arrival?"

The Emperor cleared his throat, "It... didn't." He shrugged. "The ship's systems were still locked down when we came aboard. I had to use the Imperial override codes to activate it."

"This ship hasn't even had a test cruise?" Lucius said incredulously, "How did you even know it could make shadow?"

The boy shrugged, "We didn't." He gestured at the command screen, "We managed to take this and those other ships because they were those tagged as damaged, undergoing refit, or not yet finished. The Chxor pulled all the fully operational vessels out of the yard and moved them to a secure location. They didn't think anyone would try to take them and they didn't want to destroy the shipyards that they might find useful." A dark look haunted the youth's eyes for a moment, "We... lost a few. Some ships didn't make shadow space and some others didn't survive to make it here."

Lucius nodded, "It was a brave endeavor, your Highness. An effort any man could be proud of, to get so many ships out."

The boy shrugged, "It was mostly due to the help I had." He glanced around the bridge. "I evacuated those personnel in the shipyards I could, as well as some others on the planet."

"Which, I might add, he had some help, in the doing," his sister's voice said from behind him.

Lucius turned with a smile, "Alanis!"

She smiled and embraced him, "Lucius, I missed you." Her hands clenched tight behind him and Lucius felt his heart melt at the thought that her husband wasn't here to greet her.

"I don't think I ever expected to hear that from you." He felt certain that his sister had probably played a bigger role than he really wanted to know. Though, he knew, she would undoubtedly tell him anyway. Lucius turned back to his Emperor. "Your Highness... thank you."

The boy shrugged, uncomfortably. "Honestly, Baron, I wish I could take credit. Your sister helped to rescue a number of younger sons and daughters of the nobility, many of them just children, that the Chxor planned to execute." He smiled slightly, "She even saved my own sister."

Lucius felt a shock and he glanced over at Commander Doko and saw the man had gone pale, "Princess Lizmadi is still alive?" He had a look on his face that mingled suddenly renewed hope and the agony that his duty put him in. Lucius silently cursed, not for the Princess's survival, but for the complications and pain that would result. *And that is assuming that Doko can remain strong...* Lucius thought.

The Emperor did not seem to notice Tony's expression. "Indeed and I am in Lady Alanis Giovanni's debt for that." He took a deep breath, "As far as military ships and personnel, the staff at the Academy was the most help. They organized us and got us moving. Really, Admiral Mund was the most help."

"Admiral David Mund?" Lucius said, surprise evident in his voice, "I thought he'd retired. He must be..."

"Not quite dead, yet, son." A dry voice rasped. "Not that I take much credit in this."

Lucius straightened and saluted, "Sir, it's a pleasure to see you."

The old man returned the salute, "And you. I'm glad you got past the troubles that... took you away from the Academy."

Lucius winced a bit, "I think that is in the past now, though it's been an issue with some officers since."

Alanis spoke and the bitterness in her voice told everyone in earshot exactly what she thought, "Those bastards kept you from rising in rank for the past ten years, Lucius."

"Past is past." Lucius said. He had no desire to speak ill of the dead.

"It is... Baron." The Emperor spoke, "As the senior remaining officer, I'm promoting you to Admiral, effective immediately."

Lucius shook his head, "Thank you, your Highness, but... I feel that might be premature." There was a moment of stunned silence.

"You are rejecting promotion from your Emperor?" The young man said, clearly shocked.

"No, Your Highness, I just feel..." Lucius paused to compose his thoughts. "When ordered to return to Nova Roma, I chose to disobey."

"You couldn't have obeyed that order," Emperor Romulus said, "Your ship was heavily damaged."

"Even so, your Highness..." Lucius cleared his throat, "When my ship was repaired, I made the choice not to return."

"By then, Nova Roma had already fallen."

Lucius nodded, "But perhaps we might have done *some* good. I chose to become a mercenary, then, your Highness. I chose to use a ship given to me by the Empire for my own ends."

"Your ends made a strong force out of a handful of crew, and you dealt the Chxor a strong blow at Faraday," the Emperor answered. "All of this is justifiable, all of this can be accepted."

Lucius sighed, thinking of the discussion he'd had with Kandergain. He met the Emperor's eyes, "But this, I think will not be for you." He took a deep breath, "I refuse to use the Dreyfus Fleet to reinstate the Empire, your Highness."

"What?!"

"Your Highness, in the Fleet, I have defended Nova Roma. I have done great things... and I have done terrible things." Lucius shook his head, "I was there when we sacked Ghornath Prime, your Highness. I was the XO of the *War Shrike* when we attacked the Saragossa Republic. I've participated in conquests, in raids, and in defense of our worlds. I've done many things I'm proud of, and far too many things I know will haunt my dreams for the rest of my life." Lucius met the eyes of the man he was sworn to serve... even as he told him that he could do so no longer, "When I made my choice to turn away from the Empire, your Highness, I made it for good. I cannot help return the Empire to power." Lucius stared at the youth, hoping the man could understand.

"The Empire is dead, your Highness," the rasping voice of Admiral Mund said. "The glory of it died years ago, only the shell of it died when the Chxor took Nova Roma."

The young Emperor looked around, "So where does that leave me?"

Lucius sighed, "Your Highness, your great grandfather established a place of security for his people, it was a noble endeavor." He shrugged, "Your grandfather was expansionist; he wanted the Empire to expand. He was impatient, and he betrayed alliances and treaties to further his ambitions."

"And my father?"

"Your father was a man, your Highness," Admiral Mund rasped, "a man advised by men with ambition."

The Emperor looked between the two, "So where does that leave me?"

"Your Highness, with the power of my ships and with the Dreyfus Fleet, I will fight the Chxor, I will liberate what worlds I can." Lucius sighed. "I may, indeed, found a new nation." He looked away, "I won't help you to reinstate the Empire. That dream is dead and it died for many a long time ago. I'll give you Nova Roma back, but I'll not conquer other worlds for you."

The boy closed his eyes, "So, history will remember my father as a failure and me as what, exactly? A footnote? Will Nova Roma become a backwater in your new Empire, Lucius?"

"No, your Highness." Lucius shook his head. "Nova Roma will always be great. I have confidence that you will lead it into prosperity." He smiled, "And the fact that the Chxor have not destroyed the shipyards means Nova Roma will remain a powerful place."

"So, Lucius, what then, is your plan?" Admiral Mund said.

Lucius pulled a data crystal out, "With Collae, Manetti, and the Garu, I'll have sufficient forces to take the system." He put the crystal into the computer. "I'll leave for the rendezvous site tomorrow."

"You trust these other allies more than us?" The Emperor asked.

"No, I don't trust them at all, which is why I've... modified my plans to include your ships. I've also assembled personnel to back up the crews you already have in place, and maintenance teams to begin any repairs your ships need."

"I've got a rather long list." Emperor Romulus IV said sardonically. "We don't even have functional weapons right now."

Lucius winced. "Well, nearly sixteen thousand people will be swarming over these ships, trying to get them ready. I need you ready in less than a week, your Highness. I need this ship, and as many others as you can get combat ready."

"Who do we fight?"

"If everything goes right, your Highness... no one."

***

January 29, 2403 Earth Standard Time
Faraday System
Chxor Empire

Mason McGann kept up a litany of constant, monotone curses as he settled the *Second Chance* towards the surface of Faraday.

"What's with you, anyway?" Lauren asked.

"There are more sensors here than there should be." Mason snapped.

"Have we been detected?"

Mason gave her an incredulous glance, "Are you seriously asking that?"

"I'm a commando and before that I was a missile tech, not a pilot."

Mason gave an exasperated sigh, "Well, if they'd seen us, we'd be dead. They're bad shots, but even a miss in atmosphere, with *those* weapons… yeah."

"Okay, so they don't see us, what's the problem?"

"The problem, honey, is this just became a one way trip."

"What?" Lauren said. "Why?"

"My stealth systems can't compensate for the amount of power my engines will draw, going out." He gave a particularly savage curse as yet another sensor satellite appeared on his monitor, "It's a damned good thing you didn't try getting a corvette down, you'd have been taken out well before hitting the surface."

She shrugged, "Worth the risk."

He gave her a nasty glance, "What's with you and death wishes, huh?"

Lauren stared out the window, "I grew up under the Chxor, Mason. They executed my brother because he asked a question in school. He was seven. They killed my mother when she started screaming obscenities at his executor. My father killed himself making a bomb in our kitchen when I was fifteen."

Mason cleared his throat. "Sorry."

"My world had less than a hundred thousand humans left. Before I was conscripted, they were marching people to execution pits, a thousand a day."

Mason shut his mouth and focused on his flying. His left hand stroked the prayer beads on his belt. "We'll reach the landing site in five minutes."

Lauren nodded, "I'll tell the troops to get ready."

After she left, Mason let out a deep breath and rubbed at his eyes, "Fuck."

***

The *Second Chance* settled towards a huge waterfall, and then slowly pushed through and into the large cave beyond. Mason relaxed, "We're here. As long as no one tells the Chxor, we should be good."

"Right. Well, we got company, already." Lauren said, pointing at a group of ragged people that approached from out of the shadows.

"Did the Baron set this up with the locals?" Mason asked.

"No, but from what the natives said, this cave's always been a site for hiding and smuggling." Lauren shrugged, "I'm going out."

Mason listened to the sounds of his passengers as they moved around and shifted the cargo of weapons and ammo. He stroked the prayer beads at his waist and watched the patterns of light cast on the cave walls by the waterfall. He spoke slowly and quietly, "Do you need help?"

Lauren popped her head in, "What's that?"

Mason cleared his voice, "Do you need help? I've… got some experience when it comes to killing."

Lauren smiled. It was a feral smile, like that of a predatory cat, "I'll never turn down help in killing Chxor." She nodded at the group, "Come on, let's meet the neighbors."

Mason followed her through the ship and down the ramp.

They walked across the damp stone floor toward the ragged group of rebels. There were a handful of weapons evident, none of them military grade, except for an assault rifle carried by the leader. The leader of the group that sheltered in the cave was a tall, blond man, with cold, hard eyes. "Who are you?"

Lauren stepped forward and held out a hand, "I'm Lieutenant Lauren Kelly. I'm here to kill Chxor."

The man smiled and took her hand, "Well, what do you know? So am I."

***

February 2, 2403 Earth Standard Time
Zeta Proxima System
Colonial Republic Space

"You're either a historian with a sense of irony or a tactical genius." Kandergain muttered over Lucius' shoulder as arrived on the bridge.

He looked up at her, "Excuse me?"

"You just happened to pick Zeta Tau and Alpha Seven as your base, which has rapid transit to Zeta Proxima," Kandergain said. "Which in turn has quick transit through shadow space to Faraday. Either that, or you were thinking of the PCRA attack on the convoy from Alpha Seven. They just happened to stage that here, as well, I believe. First successful strike against the might of Amalgamated Worlds. Seeking a bit of that luck? Or was it just the opportune transit time?"

"Can't I do both?" Lucius smiled slightly, "Though I'd hardly consider the butchery of that convoy a victory, I do feel that launching our first strike from here may be slightly auspicious." He shrugged, "I'll take what advantages I can."

Kandergain only nodded, then took her new seat there on the bridge. She'd suggested a spot at navigation and Lucius made room for her there. She looked odd, dressed in her rugged civilian dress amongst the uniforms of the crew.

Lucius rapped his fingers on the arm of his chair. He mentally ticked away the seconds. The *War Shrike* and the *Gebneyr* along with the converted fighter carrier *Success* sat with weapons, engines, and shields online and active. He didn't really expect any of his allies to pounce in and attack directly.

He just couldn't trust that they wouldn't.

"I'm surprised no one was here waiting for us yesterday, sir,"

Anthony Doko said.

Lucius nodded, "I honestly expected it."

"Well, just as well—"

"Multiple contacts, Baron!" Lieutenant Palmer cried, "A lot of 'em too!" There was a long pause, "Looks like a Desperado battleship and a couple Independence-class light cruisers."

Lucius let out a sigh, "Admiral Mannetti then... and that would be the *Peregrine*."

Captain Doko grimaced, "I wish there'd been some way to stop her."

Lucius shook his head, "If we had, we wouldn't have her support now. We need the *Peregrine* and otherwise the Chxor probably would have destroyed her by now." It felt good, somehow, to know that the *War Shrike* still had a sister ship left, even if it was in the dubious hands of a traitorous pirate.

Lucius opened a link to the other ship, "Lady Kale, I'm glad you accepted my invitation."

"It was so graciously offered, I could do nothing but accept, darling. When do we leave?" Kandergain rolled her eyes and Captain Doko made a gagging gesture.

"I'll do a briefing once we have all our companions. We should be expecting Admiral Collae as well as some Garu vessels soon."

"Oh, marvelous, I do so love working with… experienced partners."

Lucius managed to say something gracious before he cut the link. "Is she just out of practice, or has she always been that annoying?"

Captain Doko frowned, "She's pretty nasty to those she doesn't need to suck up to, trust me sir."

"Oh, I believe you." Lucius said. He fingered the scar on his chest.

"Sir, I got 'nother bunch emerging from shadow." Lieutenant Palmer said. "Looks like them no-mads." A half dozen ships appeared on the screens. They were all cruiser sized, but Lucius knew that much of their hulls consisted of cargo and living space. The Garu ships would be formidable, but not as dangerous as true warships their size.

Before Lucius could open a link, Lieutenant Palmer forwarded him one from the Garu. "Baron Lucius, I see that your other allies have arrived. When do we discuss terms?" The dark haired man still wore his purple scarf, and the same bright gold hoop earrings.

"As soon as Admiral Collae gets here, I'll brief everyone, and we can discuss division of spoils." Lucius answered.

"Understood. Garu out."

They waited several hours before the last group of contacts emerged. Admiral Collae's force emerged in tight formation, two destroyers flanking the light cruiser, with the carrier positioned to the rear. "Looks like an Independence cruiser for Collae's flagship, sir. She's pretty heavily modified, though." Lieutenant Palmer paused a moment, "He's definitely changed out the weapons systems at least."

"Admiral Collae," Lucius began, "Glad—"

"Save the greetings for someone who cares," Collae's voice was gruff. "Looks like everyone else is here. Let's hear your plan, and haggle on the price."

Lucius smiled slightly, "Of course, Admiral. Give me a moment to set up a conference call, and we'll begin." He paused a moment, "I'm not seeing Mistress Blanc."

"She arrived earlier."

"Sir, I've got a new contact." Lieutenant Palmer said, "It's, well, she's..." He broke off and brought up the icon. The previously stealthed battlecruiser lay only three thousand kilometers behind the *War Shrike*, easily in striking distance.

He shot a dark glance at Kandergain.

She shrugged, "I'm not omniscient."

"Obviously," Lucius said. "Lets hope our insurance policy works out."

***

"...consists of the plan." Lucius said.

"That's it?" Admiral Collae shook his head, his dark eyes cold. "At least you won't be around afterward to take the blame for failure."

"It does lack... options." Admiral Mannetti said. "If one part of the plan fails—"

"Then the entire plan will fail." Lucius said, "Yes, I know. But we've limited resources, and I'm sure, none of you want to split the rewards with any more partners."

"Speaking of which… Lucius, we haven't yet agreed on appropriate division of wealth." Admiral Mannetti said, her voice sultry. "I believe the most fair—"

"The only way to do it is equal shares for all involved parties," the Garu leader said. "Each of us gets a quarter of the vessels."

Admiral Mannetti made a grimace of distaste, "That is hardly equitable, considering the firepower some people have brought. My own force is considerably—"

"Equal shares is acceptable." Admiral Collae growled. "All four of us will take similar risks." A slight flicker of annoyance crossed Admiral Mannetti's face, "If we argue over relative worth of ships, my crews are better trained than your own and Mistress Blanc's ship, which I bring, will perform a task that no one else can match."

"My proposal is that there be five equal shares," Lucius began. "One for each of us, and one for the Faraday colony, since—"

"I don't think so," Admiral Collae snapped, "You're going to control that planet when we finish here and that would mean you get two fifths of the Dreyfus Fleet."

Lucius let out a breath, "That's not my intention at all—"

"I'm sure it isn't darling." Admiral Mannetti said, "But perhaps cutting them in for part of the fleet is a bit generous. After all, what have they done so far without our help?"

Lucius stared at her. He wondered at her callous nature, if she felt nothing for the thousands dying even now under Chxor rule. "They're going to be seizing the planetary defenses—"

"And they'll be rewarded with their freedom from the Chxor," Admiral Collae said, his gravelly voice stern, "This is not a charity case, Baron. None of us are naïve. Let us get on with the bargaining."

"The Garu people have little interest in warships, but we want first pick of the transports and cargo ships," the spokesman for the nomads said.

"First pick?" Admiral Mannetti's eyes narrowed, "I thought we were going with equal shares, split down the middle."

"We forgo any rights to warships, we only want ships with cargo capacity or construction capabilities." The Garu leader said, "You three may divide the warships equally, but we must receive three quarters of all transport craft in return."

"Sounds reasonable enough," Lucius said. Neither of the others argued. He wasn't sure if that was a good or bad sign.

"What about any Chxor ships we capture?" Collae asked, "How do we divide those?"

"More straightforward with that," Lucius said, "Whatever group receives the surrender, or whose troops seize a vessel retains it. They can then trade or bargain with those ships as they see fit." He scanned the faces, "Lady Kale, you don't like that?"

Admiral Mannetti frowned, "That's… not going to work well for those of us without Marines available."

"I thought you were heavy on boarding crews?" Lucius asked, eyes narrowing.

"Yes, quite." She smiled, "But still, I think you will have the advantage, certainly with the course of your plan." She shot a glance over at Admiral Collae, who maintained a stone-faced silence. "You will be in position to deploy your own boarding parties better than us. And you've given the Garu a tasking that specifically will aide them the capture of ships."

"I think I'll be a bit busy dodging the Chxor to capitalize on ships I damage," Lucius said, "And as for the Garu…"

"We have little interest in warships, especially crippled warships. We'll trade those we capture at a premium for transport and cargo vessels."

"Still…" Mannetti frowned.

"Unless you have a better alternative, one we can agree on, then we move on," Admiral Collae snapped. "We all know what the real prize is anyway."

Lucius nodded, "Then there are no further discussions on strategy and payment?"

"When do we confirm the presence of the Dreyfus Fleet?" Collae said.

"What?" Lucius asked.

"For all we know, Baron, this is all a story dressed up by that smuggler to enable you to capture Faraday." Collae gave Lucius a basilisk stare. "When do you give us the coordinates, and how do we confirm the fleet is there?"

"That, I'm afraid, is going to be a matter of trust." Lucius said. Admiral Manneti burst into light, mocking laughter in response. He spoke over the laughter of Mannetti, "We have no way to enter the system and scan that section of space without alerting the Chxor to our presence and interest." He shrugged, "My insertion force discovered the Chxor already seeded the planet and a good portion of the surrounding space with sensor satellites. We don't have much time, I fear, before the Chxor discover the fleet themselves, we certainly don't have time to covertly arrive, verify the Dreyfus Fleet's position, and then covertly leave."

Admiral Collae remained silent for a long time, "What happens if you die? Does the secret of the Dreyfus Fleet die with you?"

"Admiral, the Faraday system is quite large. I am sure, however, that someone with sufficient patience and tenacity can scan the entire system. You know it's there, I can't very well hide the entire star system from you." Lucius shrugged, "In this, as I said, I think you just have to trust me."

"I think we can take Lucius at his word, on this." Admiral Mannetti said with a tolerant smile.

"Thank you, Lady Kale."

"Don't mention it, darling."

"How long does our partnership last then?" the Garu leader asked. "How long until I must watch my back for the knife?"

Admiral Mannetti smiled slightly, "Oh, I think you're quite safe from that, dear."

"It lasts until the job is complete, the Dreyfus Fleet is ours and we go our separate ways," Lucius said, "Or until one partner betrays the others and voids their share of the profit."

"Sounds fair," Collae said, "If you betray us, we cut you out." The unspoken part was that only worked if the betrayal failed. Obviously, neither Mannetti nor Collae expected their plots to fail.

The silence grew long, and Lucius could hear the knives scraped across the whetstones. He smiled slightly, "Well, gentlemen and lady, do we have an agreement?"

The others responded with nods and polite laughter from Mannetti.

"Very well. Synchronize your clocks, the *War Shrike* will depart in thirty minutes."

***

"Unfortunately," the rebel leader spoke bitterly, "the government of Faraday had quite accurate census records." He grunted as they eased another crate of weapons into position on the back of a truck. "They knew exactly who had weapons, how many, and what types. They collected them within the first couple days. Any weapons missing and they killed everyone in the house."

"Yeah, that's one of their first moves, using the previous government against its people." Lauren grunted. "On my world, they used the tax records to seize all assets. They knew who to turn, who to execute... they knew everything."

"Yeah, they used the employment records to round up all the military, all the teachers, and anyone else with authority." Reese shook his head, "Wasn't pretty."

"Uh, have you heard anything about a Captain Beeson?" Lieutenant Beeson asked. Despite his normal slot on the *War Shrike*, he had volunteered for ground action.

"Yeah!" A scruffy looking rebel said as he settled his crate in the back of the truck, "The Captain led the prison break, got me an' twenty others out of a death camp!"

"He's my father, I was hoping—"

The other man shook his head, "Ah, sorry, sir, no, he died." The rebel shook his head, "He took a round when we broke fence, bled out before we even made the tree-line." The rebel spat, "Only three of us left from that escape."

Lauren nodded, "Insurgencies against the Chxor tend to be bloody. Chxor won't hesitate to use lethal force up to and including nukes."

Reese nodded, "We lost a couple of small cities, till we learned they'll accept any civilian casualties. They really don't care-- even about their own colonists."

Mason McGann flipped a tarp over the crates in the back of the truck. "What have you been able to do so far?"

Reese shrugged, "We've bombed a couple barracks, assassinated a few Chxor officers. Their military is really only an extension of their civilian bureaucracy, so we've been killing them off too." He shrugged, "Mostly, we've been dying."

The driver of the truck spat, then jerked his door open before climbing in. "We had a population of nineteen million before they came. Sometimes I wonder if anyone will be left by the time we beat the Chxor."

"They're killing hundreds, maybe thousands, every day," said the scruffy rebel, who'd spoken of his prison break. "They finished with the teachers, the military, the doctors, they started on the old, the sick, the retarded." He shook his head, eyes haunted. "Rumor is, they've emptied all the hospitals."

"Any time there's a protest, or riot, they'll gas them," Lauren said, "That's what they do everywhere."

Reese nodded, "Most of us avoid crowds. Sometimes, it'll just be a random group of people, and the Chxor will sweep overhead. The Planetary Governor is a Chxor named Kleigh."

"I've heard of him," Lauren said, her eyes dark.

"We lost a team, not long ago, that tried to get to him." One of the rebels said, "The Chxor nuked Fredericksburg, up north, in retribution."

The driver ground the ignition until the truck coughed into life, then ground the gears until it lurched out of the cave. The group of rebels stood and watched it go. Lauren drew a folded map from inside her uniform tunic. "Tell me about the defense centers."

Reese nodded, "Follow me."

They strode deeper into the caves, winding through several dark tunnels before emerging in a long, low room with entrances draped with heavy blankets. "They're using slave labor for most of the basic construction. They don't let the slaves get into the technical aspects, but we've got some people with knowledge on the inside who can make educated guesses." Reese moved to a table, taking the map from Lauren and spreading it out. He pointed at two locations, and waited as she marked them on her map. "They've got these two sites operational. The Flattop Mountain facility is the closest, there's a larger garrison there, since we've been active in the area. The facility near Grey Coast is the other, not as heavily defended, but it doesn't look like the guns are fully operational. On both sites they're more worried about space than ground attack, so they finished those weapons emplacements first." He shrugged, "We've had our people slow things as much as they can on the ground defenses."

"You planned on storming the defense centers?" Lieutenant Beeson asked.

"Yeah, I figured, if things looked bleak enough," Reese shrugged, "we'd take a center, blast what we could in orbit and at least go out with a bang."

"I understand the feeling." Lauren said, her voice distant. "You already have teams in place, then?"

"Yeah," Reese said, "Our last stand was approaching. Without weapons, it was a pretty weak hope, but…"

"With weapons, we can take them and hold them." Lauren said, turning to Beeson, "You can turn the guns on any ships in orbit, as well."

He nodded. In his mind, he saw the stern face of his father. "Be glad to."

***

CHAPTER VII

February 9, 2403 Earth Standard Time
Faraday System
Chxor Empire

"Baron, we got an update from our corvette on station," Lieutenant Palmer drawled, "The Chxor haven't moved much. Nothin' new came in neither." The ansibles worked, even through shadow space, though once they engaged the drive on the plotted course, it was far too late to turn back.

Lucius looked at Kandergain, "You are certain that we'll..."

"I guarantee we'll be spot on." She said. Her brown eyes showed amusement and confidence.

Lucius nodded, "Now I only hope everyone else positions themselves correctly."

Captain Doko spoke, "Sir, I've updated our firing solutions from the data we received. That one force in orbit above Faraday is still setting idle, engines cold." There were three Chxor squadrons in the system, two elements of four dreadnoughts and sixteen screening cruisers, which they had labeled Alpha and Bravo, and a third element, Force Charlie, of six dreadnoughts and twenty four cruisers.

Lucius stroked his jaw, "Timing's going to be close. We don't want to kick this off early." Timing was everything with this plan. "Lieutenant Palmer, cut a message to the corvette, have them relay to our insertion teams that they should commence their attack preparations." He felt a cold lump settle in his stomach at the thought of those brave men and women on the planet, about to put their lives on the line in the hope that he could pull the Chxor away.

Kandergain appeared at his shoulder, "It will be alright, Lucius. I promise."

He gave her a sardonic grin, "I thought you weren't omniscient."

She smiled back, "I'm not... but I know a good plan when I see one. Trust me, I've had to execute of off plenty of bad plans, I can tell the difference."

He let out a deep breath and then checked the screens again.

His plan counted on Chxor arrogance, their lack of long range sensor platforms, and their tactical inflexibility. If everything worked out, the Chxor would essentially defeat themselves. Not all Chxor were stupid, however. He looked over at his assistant weapons officer, the newly promoted Lieutenant Kral. "It still seems strange with a Chxor on the bridge."

Kandergain grunted, "Trust me, stranger things have happened." She locked eyes with him, "Remember, Lucius, the real enemy isn't the Chxor."

He gave a nod, then raised his voice, "Navigation, start the countdown. Plan Alpha is in effect." He looked at Kandergain. "You are certain we'll hit our target precisely?"

She laughed, "Lucius, I bet you a favor I'll get us within five hundred meters."

"That's less than a ship's length."

She nodded and held out a hand to shake.

Lucius hesitated, and she raised an eyebrow, "Come now, surely you aren't afraid?"

He let out a sigh, "Even the best nav computers can't hit a jump within five hundred *kilometers*. I'd be satisfied with that." He hesitated again, "Why do I get the feeling I'm being fleeced?"

She smiled, "Because it's a sucker bet. All psychics are naturals at shadow space navigation. I'm not the best, not by far, but I'm pretty good."

"How about this, I bet you a fine dinner that you aren't within five hundred meters." Lucius said.

She grinned at him, "Deal." They shook and she walked briskly over to her station. He watched the countdown. She had under a minute before they emerged.

Lucius opened the ship's intercom. "People, today, we return to Faraday. Today, we'll meet the Chxor in battle once again." He paused. "Today, we'll kick their sorry asses out of this system." He heard cheers, and he waited a moment. "It's going to be dangerous. Some of us may not live to see tomorrow." He knew that more faces would join the many that lurked in his nightmares. "But today we begin a fight that will become legend. Today, we halt the decline of humanity. Today, we fight back!"

Even the crew on the bridge had begun to cheer now and Lucius felt some of the fire return to his belly. "I want you all to know, I could never ask for a better crew. Baron Lucius Giovanni, out."

He cut the intercom and sagged back into his chair.

A timer appeared on the edge of his monitor. Lucius watched it tick down.

They emerged from Shadow barely three thousand kilometers from the planet Faraday. A part of Lucius' mind noted they were within three hundred meters of their targeted location. He owed Kandergain dinner.

"Targets are acquired, Baron, ready to fire." Anthony Doko's voice was cheerful, excited. Their target was one of the three Chxor task forces, the one that sat, engines cold, shields and weapons powered down, in high orbit over Faraday.

"Launch the fighters," Lucius grinned, "and commence fire."

The *War Shrike* emerged without warning. The dreadnoughts, without active defense screens or engines to maneuver, lay open to any inbound fire.

The other two forces of Chxor warships lay twenty thousand kilometers away, to either side, positioned to interdict any force that might move towards the planet. They were in no position to prevent Lucius' attack.

Lucius felt the thrum of the EPCs firing. He watched on the screen as the first missiles shot away. He snarled at the first ripple of explosions from the EPCs. The first set of four missiles bracketed the most distant dreadnought. Before the explosions faded, the missiles launched by the fighters erupted against the unshielded, defenseless warships.

Kral raked the secondary battery across the nearest dreadnought. Further explosions and clouds of debris erupted. At less than three thousand kilometers, they were at knife range. Every shot hit. Each hit smashed weapons and gutted engine pods.

The first dreadnought exploded, a colossal flash as at least one fusion plant lost containment. The explosion and cloud of debris ripped two of the nearest cruisers apart and sent two others spinning from impacts. A second dreadnought shattered, large secondary explosions and internal fires lit space around the dying hulk.

"Baron, Chxor forces Beta and Charlie just went to full power, both of them are on least-time intercepts." Lieutenant Palmer highlighted both forces.

Lucius nodded, the fighters had already begun docking, their missile racks expended. "As soon as the fighters are aboard, begin withdrawal plan Alpha."

Both Doko and Kral continued to rake the two remaining dreadnoughts. Force Alpha ceased to be a coherent threat. As Lucius watched, one cruiser lit off its engines. Perhaps it was an attempt to interdict fire at a dreadnought. It looked to Lucius like an attempt to escape. Either way, the cruiser's unplanned thrust shoved it into Faraday's atmosphere. Without its screens up, the atmospheric friction ripped portions of the hull away. The cruiser began an uncontrolled decent towards the planet's surface.

Hopefully it lands someplace empty, Lucius thought.

Lucius shook his head, all the fighters were aboard. "Cease fire with missile tubes. Continue turret fire on Alpha until we leave weapons range." The *War Shrike* rolled up and away from Faraday. The powerful engines thrust it away from the gutted task force.

He studied the distances, calculated the angles. "Time until Strike Point Bravo?"

"One hour sir."

Lucius nodded. He watched the icons of the two other Chxor forces. For the moment, both attempted least time intercepts. Neither had the acceleration to catch him. "Any sign of missile separation from Charlie or Bravo?"

"Negative, sir. For now, it looks like they're still trying to get organized."

Lucius nodded. Soon enough it would become evident that they couldn't catch him in outright pursuit.

"Force Charlie just altered course, looks like they're closing with what's left of Alpha, sir," Lieutenant Palmer drawled. "Force Bravo's changin' course, they're maintainin' current separation."

Lucius nodded sharply. Someone, probably the Planetary Governor, had finally given orders. "Excellent. Anything from Naevius?"

"The corvette relays that Captain Naevius has launched, he says he'll be in position."

Lucius let out a deep breath. "Very well, maintain our current course, we're going with Plan Alpha. Keep monitoring Charlie, let me know of any changes there." Charlie was the largest Chxor force with six dreadnoughts. Lucius figured that to be the command element.

Lucius sat back and adjusted his chair restraints. The game had begun... now he could only wait.

***

Planetary Governor Kleigh sighed at the extravagant waste of resources inflicted upon him by the humans. It wasn't enough that this world's populace felt the need to oppose rightful Chxor rule. It wasn't enough that they had slowed progress of total control. Now, his old opponent returned and with his suicidal attack, destroyed two dreadnoughts outright!

The time had come to end this annoyance, once and for all, "Prepare my shuttle, I will take charge of this battle." He stood from his desk and walked briskly towards his private shuttle pad. His aides scurried along behind him. "Have Captain Klun prepare my flag bridge, I'll join him momentarily."

"Planetary Governor, should I make addendum to standing orders that all vessels retain shields and engines at standby?"

Kleigh looked at the aide, slightly surprised, "Why? Such suicidal attacks by the humans are unpredictable. Wear and tear on equipment on standby will cut deeply into our profit margins. No, once this threat is dealt with, there will be no further attacks such as this." Kleigh stared at the Chxor aide, "You are an Abaner line, aren't you?"

"Yes, Planetary Governor. I am Tactical Planning Officer Krath."

Kleigh nodded, "Place yourself on half-rations for your ignorant assumption."

"Yes, Planetary Governor."

"Also, I will not need your assistance for the upcoming battle, take charge of personnel recovery and salvage operations from the damaged vessels in orbit. Priority is, of course, Chxor officers. Other crew can be retrieved during salvage operations."

***

Mason McGann had not expected to run out of guns.

Just over five thousand rebels gathered in the narrow canyon short of Flattop Mountain. They stood silent, the morning mountain mist pooling around them. Half of them bore weapons, either stolen from the Chxor, home-built from scratch, or the weapons from the Baron.

Mason wore just his gun belt with his second pistol slung on his other hip, right below his prayer beads. He had pulled on his black shirt and pants, both lined with fiber weaves designed to stop bullets or shrapnel. He hadn't worn either in years... yet they felt as comfortable as the embrace of an old friend.

Lieutenant Lauren Kelly looked over, "You look good in black."

Mason tugged self-consciously at his black shirt, "Just something I had lying around."

She snorted, "Well, if you did fly with Tommy King, Right? He must have taken his clothes sense from you." She shook her head and her eyes swiveled to the sky as a series of bright flashes signaled the use of nuclear weapons dangerously near the planet. "Time to go kill some Chxor."

He wished she didn't sound so cheerful when she said that.

The rebels began movement. They walked silently through the brush and rocks of the canyon floor. Mason eyed the canyon walls for any signs of security sensors or sentries, "How far can we take this?"

"Locals say the canyon runs right up to the edge of the perimeter. They have a bunker that overlooks the canyon. Rebels on the inside are going to take it," Lauren answered. "That'll be our entrance into the tunnels."

"We didn't try to smuggle weapons *inside*, did we?" Mason asked, horrified.

"Oh, no." Lauren waved a hand. "Chxor security is too good for that. They'll be using their tools and some improvised explosives. The Chxor are still mining tunnels there, I imagine there's equipment they can use."

"Mining tools against automatic weapons?" Mason winced.

"Oh yes." Lauren's eyes went cold, "Mason, just so you understand the hatred here... There will be women throwing their bodies into the Chxor bullets to buy their husbands long enough time to avenge their dead children." She paused, "That's what I saw in my mutiny anyway."

Mason looked away, "Hate... it isn't good to cling to it."

She reached out a hand and caught his chin and turned it to face her, "It's all I have, Mason. Look into my eyes and tell me you could turn away from a hate like mine."

He gently removed her hand from his chin and grasped her head in both his hands, "I would, and I have, and I wish you would." He released her and continued to follow the file of rebels. "The Chxor aren't the only horrible things out there, Lauren Kelly. Us humans can be pretty bad ourselves, trust me."

She stood silently, watching him move further up the line. Then she wiped at her eyes. "Lieutenant, you okay?" She turned to find the rebel leader Reese stopped nearby.

"Today there are Chxor to kill, of course I'm okay."

***

"Looks like Charlie just decided they're coming out as well." Lucius murmured.

"Got a lot of traffic between them and planet-side," Lieutenant Palmer said, "Look's like they had some visitors before they broke orbit."

Lucius nodded, "My bet is that Commander Kleigh decided to take personal command." He stared at the screens for a while. "Time until Strike Point Bravo?"

"Thirty minutes, sir. Captain Naevius says he's ready, and Bravo is right where we want 'em." Lieutenant Palmer drawled, "Looks like Force Charlie isn't going to reach the battle in time."

Lucius nodded, letting out a deep breath, "Start deceleration."

***

Planetary Governor Kleigh stared at the fuzzy images transmitted by his lead element. The enemy battleship still lay outside his sensor range. If he felt emotion, he might have felt mild regret that the Empire made no use of reconnaissance units or drones.

"Enemy vessel adjusted course, they've begun deceleration, Planetary Governor."

"Acknowledged. System Defense Task Force Two adjust your course to compensate. Close and engage the enemy at optimum range." Kleigh said, his voice bored.

"Planetary Governor, the enemy will close with our forces at the edge of that debris cloud." Ship Commander Klun said. "Might it be possible that the humans have additional vessels concealed there?"

Kleigh turned a cold eye on the officer, notionally his second in command. "It is possible, however unlikely." Kleigh shrugged, "Direct Defense Task Force Two to commence active scanning of that debris cloud before they enter."

"Yes, Planetary Governor."

***

The *War Shrike* lay, almost at rest, in the debris cloud.

Lucius looked over at Doko's chuckle. "Something amusing Captain?"

The younger man shook his head, "Just find it appropriate that we're using the debris from the last force we faced here to shield us in our next attack.

Lucius smiled, "Yes, I do find that appropriate." He checked the flight monitor, and noted the *War Shrike*'s two fighter squadrons had already rearmed and launched.

The Chxor force still lay twenty-five thousand kilometers out, just outside of battery range, though well within missile range.

"Sir, they've gone to active sensors!" Lieutenant Palmer said.

Lucius nodded, "Our luck could only hold so long." He opened a channel, "Captain Naevius, initiate Strike Bravo."

As the Chxor sensors swept the debris cloud, they picked up the lurking fighter squadrons that had used it to cover their approach.

Lucius' converted carrier carried three squadrons of six fighters. Those three squadrons, backed up by the two from the *War Shrike*, gave him five squadrons, thirty fighter craft.

Those thirty fighters launched ninety ship-killer Pilum missiles.

The four five-class dreadnoughts had their sixteen ten-class cruisers to screen their approach. The Chxor commander acted swiftly. He altered course and took his ships on a perpendicular course, up and away from the ambush.

Force Bravo had almost two minutes to watch the incoming fire. The dreadnoughts launched their own missiles against the *War Shrike*. Lucius watched as Kral directed fire against the inbound missiles.

None of the enemy missiles drew closer than two thousand

kilometers.

The outbound missiles caught up to the fleeing Chxor force only seconds later. The light weapons on the cruisers shot down twelve missiles. Eighteen more impacted on the lighter cruisers. The remaining sixty fusion warheads detonated in close proximity to the Chxor dreadnoughts.

Two dreadnoughts and three cruisers emerged from that cataclysm of explosions. Those five bleeding wrecks staggered away from Lucius' forces. The ships were broken, crews slaughtered. A wide band of debris and irradiated gas mushroomed in the area where fifteen warships once cruised.

"Force Bravo is continuing to withdraw. Acceleration at constant speed, it looks like they're headed right where we want 'em." Lieutenant Palmer said. "Force Charlie went to full acceleration. Looks like they want to hit us before the fighters rearm."

Lucius nodded sharply, "Move us to Strike Point Charlie."

***

Something snapped in Kleigh. "Maximum acceleration. Match their course and close with them. We will destroy this threat."

"Planetary Governor, might it not be more advantageous to withdraw to orbit above the planet? We will have the planetary defense centers to provide additional firepower, and the—"

"Commander Klun, give me your sidearm." The Commander stared at Kleigh for a long moment. "Do so now."

The Commander drew his pistol and handed it to the Planetary Governor. Kleigh lifted it, cocked it, and fired. He blasted fragments of the Commander's skull across the bridge. "The Chxor Empire does not accept cowardice in battle. The Chxor Empire does not accept defeat. We will close with the enemy and destroy them. We must close before they have time to rearm their fighters."

Kleigh tossed the pistol to the deck. "Someone clean this mess." For some reason, his breath came fast and his heart beat rapidly. Perhaps he was ill.

He noted the enemy changed course, "Where will their new course take them?" He snapped.

"Planetary Governor," the sensor officer said, voice low, "the enemy has adjusted course to take them into the gas giant's shadow. We will lose sensor contact briefly with our current heading, but we will regain it and close with them only three juhn afterward."

The Planetary Governor nodded. "I see that the fighter squadrons flee ahead of the enemy warship. No doubt, the humans have panicked. Today, we prove once again, the superiority of the Chxor! For the glory of the Chxor!"

***

"Move, move, move!" Lauren shouted. A continuous rattle of gunfire came from ahead. "We fight and win... or we all die! *Move!*"

She staggered over a tangle of bodies, humans and Chxor. Mason caught her arm, "Watch your step."

She jerked her arm out of his grasp, "No time to be coddled." She turned to where a group of rebels stood. They gaped at the carnage. "Let's go! These people died that we could avenge them and their families! Let's go!"

She shoved them ahead of her into the tunnels. She felt Mason follow behind her.

The rattle of gunfire grew louder. Two rebels ahead of her dropped, either wounded or killed. Lauren lifted her submachine gun and fired a burst at the dimly seen Chxor who had just emerged from a side corridor. Two sprawled out, the third raised his weapon to return fire when two pistol shots from beside her put him down.

She smiled over at Mason, anger suddenly gone, "See, wasn't that fun!"

He just shook his head. "He had a grenade launcher. If he'd fired that, we'd all be dead."

Lauren shrugged and moved deeper into the tunnels. Total chaos ruled, as Chxor and human killed each other in dimly lit darkness. Lauren just moved toward the sounds of gunfire. She picked up more people as they moved. She chopped off bursts of fire with her weapon at any Chxor they encountered. Mason's single pistol shots punctuated her controlled bursts.

After what seemed like hours, they broke into a main corridor. Mason tapped her on the shoulder. "Command center should be that way."

She nodded, "This way people. You two, guard our rear. You six secure those side corridors. The rest of you, follow me." Not until they'd reached an open area did she realize how many people followed her.

Twenty rebels moved with her down the corridor. Ahead, a group of Chxor fired from behind a barricade. Three rebels fell, the others charged. Lauren fell back, an impact knocked the breath out of her lungs. She shook her head, dazed. Mason stood over her, and fired precise shots at the Chxor. He had an almost serpent-like combination of smooth control and speed, she noticed. He moved his pistol in line with a Chxor with viper like speed, fired, and moved to the next.

Mason reached down and grabbed her by the shoulder to pull her to her feet. Lauren groaned as he quickly patted her down. "You're okay, your weapon took the hit. Don't scare me like that."

She disentangled herself from the shattered gun and stooped to pick up a pistol from a dead Chxor officer. Her ribs ached, "Let's go."

They continued on, through the smoke and dust.

***

The fighters swept ahead of the *War Shrike* in an organized withdrawal to the carrier to rearm. Lucius grunted as he checked the time estimates of Force Charlie and his own forces. Things would be tight.

"Well, Lucius, are you going to pull it off?" Kandergain asked.

"I think so." He shrugged. "At this point, we've destroyed or disabled half the enemy forces." He stared at the timer, "It all comes down to this last part though. If we can beat them here…"

"Then the rest is easy."

They watched as Force Charlie continued to accelerate. The Chxor commander seemed desperate to close and Lucius felt certain the arrogant Kleigh still retained command.

The *War Shrike* and the five squadrons of fighters retreated to the shelter of a gas giant planet. The positioning allowed the remaining Chxor force to cut the corner. The Chxor continued to pile on speed and Lucius half wished for a convenient accident.

"Isn't now when their acceleration dampers fail or they run into a convenient mine field?" Doko asked in a mirror to his thoughts.

"Yes, that's how it happens in the movies." Lucius smiled, "We should only be so lucky."

The Chxor continued to accelerate.

Lucius frowned, he started to type up calculations, "Bring acceleration to full. Fighter squadrons as well." He forwarded the new course corrections to navigation. "Load that into our course plot." He looked over at Kandergain, "I did not expect them to pile on speed like that."

The Chxor acceleration was up, at their current velocity, they'd flash past Lucius' forces before either side could fire a shot, though Lucius would still beat them to the gas giant.

The two forces continued to close, and finally, the Chxor began to decelerate. Lucius nodded. With that deceleration, the two forces would be at a high rate of closure on intercept. Obviously the enemy believed one quick pass would be enough.

He studied the screens and noted that the remnants of Force Bravo would be pass through the Garu ambush position in minutes. On the planet, Lieutenant Kelly hopefully had control of the defense centers. No matter the outcome here, the Chxor would reel from the blow.

Lucius stroked his jaw, thinking. The absurdity of the wait never failed to irritate him. He hated the wait, the inactivity while ships converged. "Not long now."

***

"Not long now." Kleigh stated, "Soon we will show the superiority of the Chxor once and for all."

No one on the bridge spoke. Kleigh frowned down at his screen as he puzzled over what the enemy had hoped to accomplish by his actions. The humans had accomplished a horrifying amount of damage. As Planetary Governor, *he* would have to explain the ship losses to the Benevolence Council. Still, the humans could not hope to defeat his force, not with the fighters missile racks expended. He would not give them time to reload and rearm.

"Can we see beyond the gas giant yet?" Kleigh demanded, "The enemy's carrier must be there."

"No, Planetary Governor, our approach angle doesn't allow us to see. If you wish, I could alter course, take us around the other side of the planet—"

Kleigh shook his head, "No, it's essential we catch their fighters in the carriers as they rearm. The humans might have some screening force for the carrier, tell our ships to be prepared for some additional forces there."

"Yes, Planetary Governor."

Kleigh stared at the screens. He frowned as a new set of icons appeared. "What are those?" The new icons rapidly approached the wounded remains of Defense Force Two.

"Planetary Governor, it appears to be a force of cruisers. They hid behind that small moon and they went active when Defense Force Two approached." The sensor officer looked up, "They don't match any ship-type we've encountered before."

Kleigh shook his head, "Order Defense Force Two to destroy those ships." Further waste of lives and resources. Why did the humans continue their resistance?

He turned his attention back to the forces that fled before him. They obviously saw their end approach. From what he knew of humans and their pathetic emotional ways, it would only be a matter of time before they broke and scattered.

"Uh, Planetary Governor?"

"Yes?" Kleigh turned his attention back to the sensor officer. He couldn't remember this one's name, but he'd already decided to demote the Chxor.

"The cruisers have opened fire on Defense Force Two. They're using high-power, short range weapons, more powerful than Commander Kleiss expected. Commander Kleiss is requesting assistance and doesn't think that he will be able to escape them."

Kleigh spoke slowly, as if to a child, "Tell Commander Kleiss he is relieved of command, and his second is to take charge and destroy the enemy."

"Planetary Governor, Commander Kleiss' vessel just lost power. The other ships of his force have lost engines or power or both, and some are reporting they are being boarded."

Kleigh stared at the officer for a long moment, "Tell them to fight to the last, for the Chxor Empire."

"Yes, Planetary Governor."

***

A tangle of human and Chxor bodies all but blocked the doorway to the command center. A dozen men and women were dragging them out of the way. Lauren stepped inside, trying to ignore the charnel house reek. Blood and bits spattered control panels. The Chxor commander and a handful of Chxor officers might have tried to surrender, from the looks of things. She doubted any rebels had noticed, not after the carnage of the past months of Chxor rule.

"Get Lieutenant Beeson in here," She called.

"He's on the way." Reese stood over a panel and frowned. "This is the fire control station. I don't read Chxor though."

"I do." Lauren said. She moved over to stare down at it. "I was a tech aboard a cruiser for a time." She frowned, "Everything is online, power plants are up, weapons are charged."

"Where's the communications systems? We stopped jamming as soon as we took the command center. I'd like to let the Baron know we've taken over down here."

Lauren looked around, and pointed at a console, "There, that one. I can help you—"

"No, I'll figure it out. Here's Beeson." Reese nodded as the breathless lieutenant hurried in. They'd told him to hang in the rear, for his knowledge of the weapons systems would be essential. Evidently, he'd disregarded those orders. A bandage wrapped the side of his head. Scorch marks and blood stained his uniform.

"Oh, crap, it's in Chxor." He stared at the console.

"Already ahead of you," Lauren laughed. "What do you need to know?"

"I need the sensor repeater, targeting data…" She pointed out the things he required.

"This won't work, we need two people trained in weapons systems to handle the main guns. And with how they've got it set up, neither of them will be able to operate the air defense systems. We'll need those up to deal with the Chxor combat shuttles that will come as soon as we open fire."

"I can operate ship's guns," Mason said. "I just need someone to read Chxor."

Both looked over at the smuggler. He was just as dirty and blood spattered as them, but there was a new vitality to his face.

Lauren nodded, "I'll show you. Just show me how to operate the air defenses."

He gave a sharp nod.

The three settled at different consoles. Lauren moved from one to the other, now and again directing individual rebels to push toggles or buttons at various areas around the room.

"How are we getting targeting data?" Lauren asked.

Reese smiled from the communications console. "Live feed from the Chxor. They're forwarding us their positions, for now."

"Seems fitting." Mason said. He looked over at Beeson. "I'm ready here."

"Me too."

The entire base vibrated slightly as the massive lasers began to fire.

***

"Planetary Governor, one of the planetary defense centers just opened fire."

Kleigh peered down at his screens. "What is their target? There can't be anything in their range."

"They're firing on our own ships."

Kleigh jerked his head up, at a loss for words.

"Dreadnought 05848 reports severe damage, they are evacuating ship. Officer Krath reports that enemy fire has destroyed two cruisers and that he has ordered troops to attack the facility from the ground."

"No, order the first assault to be by air. It will be more rapid that way." Kleigh said instantly. He knew that he must correct his officer in at least one way to show that he was in charge.

"Tactical Planning Officer Krath respectfully responds that he believes the air defenses will knock out at least half of such an assault."

"Casualties are irrelevant, only victory matters." Kleigh snapped. "Have—"

"Planetary Governor, Tactical Planning Officer Krath reports that a new warship has begun firing on his forces. He reports it possesses sophisticated stealth systems and their sensors are unable to target it."

Kleigh shook his head. He looked first at the retreating human force, then at the ongoing battle near the moon, and lastly at the battle which had erupted at Faraday. "Order the other planetary defense center to open fire on the intruder. Tell Officer Krath that we will return to Faraday as soon as these other humans are crushed."

"Sir, the other planetary defense center is not responding to communications. Krath believes that a rebel force has attacked both sites. He—"

"Cut all further communications from Faraday, we must focus on the task at hand." Kleigh typed in several notes. First, he would insure that both planetary defense commanders and their officer cadre received demotions. Next, he typed up a request for reinforcement and a detailed list of the failures of his officers that led to the current losses He attached his expectations of the next battle. This one he forwarded immediately to the Sector Commander, his superior at the Melcer system.

Chxor High Command would act best on the most relevant information.

***

Lucius tightened his restraining straps one last time. His gaze roved the bridge.

"Thirty seconds fer' the Chxor comin' around the gas giant."

"Thank you Lieutenant Palmer," Lucius said. He contemplated the forces he'd mustered. The two squadrons of fighters launched from the *War Shrike* and the three from his makeshift carrier *Success* hung in a halo around the gathered warships. They'd rearmed in record time, due to Captain Naevius's ritual of constant drill.

Those fighters were joined by another squadron launched from the *Gebneyr*, and brought the total to thirty six Harassers.

The fighters of Admiral Mannetti joined his own. The smaller Interceptor-class fighters carried a lighter payload and two lighter guns. She was able to bring more of them for their size, though. The *Peregrine* carried three squadrons rather than two..

Admiral Collae's carrier carried another three squadrons.

Her two cruisers and the added bulk of the *Peregrine* herself made up one flank of Lucius' force. The *War Shrike* and the *Gebneyr* made up the other. Admiral Collae and his heavily armed destroyers and the modified cruiser *Rubicon* lay in the middle.

"Here they come."

The Chxor force crested the horizon of the moon. They finally received solid sensor readings of the force they faced.

At that moment, every fighter and ship launched their missiles.

Over two hundred and twenty missiles stabbed out. Most of those came from the halo of fighters. The *Gebneyr* launched forty from its external racks. Most of the other ships mounted only a couple or more missile tubes.

The Chxor commander didn't have time to gain sensor lock on the numerous ships. Lucius wanted it that way. The Chxor might claim to be above emotion, but he knew even they knew panic.

The Chxor force split, half went to full deceleration in a vain attempt to avoid the battle. The other half continued their course, too stunned to take action. Sporadic fire lashed out at the inbound missiles as all the Chxor ships attempted evasive maneuvers. One of the dreadnoughts, and Lucius had a suspicion it was Kleigh's, rolled behind the others. That ship couldn't lend its firepower to support its fellows, only hide behind them.

Lucius marked that icon, "I want this ship. If it survives, we go after it."

The Chxor had almost a minute before impact. Lucius' ships began to match their course. The two fleets lay separated by twenty thousand kilometers on launch. By the time the missiles began to impact, they had closed to fifteen thousand kilometers, just at the edge of range for the heavier ships.

The two hundred missiles slammed into the Chxor force. Explosions blossomed and ships died. The screening cruisers did their job, this time, for every one of those lighter ships took two, sometimes three ship-killer missiles that otherwise would have hit a dreadnought.

Even so, cruisers could only take so much damage. Over a hundred missiles made it through to target the larger dreadnoughts. The six dreadnoughts shuddered in the grasp of that firepower. Two of them vanished, wreathed in nuclear fire. Two more came through as gutted hulks, lifeless irradiated tombs.

One dreadnought, streamed air and water but still managed sporadic fire at the human forces. The other, relatively untouched, heeled over in an attempt to evade the enemy forces.

"Close the range. Don't let them withdraw." Lucius said. "That one! Target that ship."

Admirals Collae and Manetti swarmed over the damaged dreadnought. They fired their lighter weapons into the massive ship from point blank range. Their lighter ships dodged and wove as they closed the distance and fired everything they had. The *War Shrike* and the *Gebneyr* closed on the relatively undamaged flagship. The cloud of fighters swarmed around them to strafe the damaged and crippled cruisers that sought to intercept.

"Target his engines, he'll try to jump to Shadow," Lucius snapped. Commander Kleigh had a knack for surviving defeats.

Fire snapped out. The dreadnought, as if it finally realized that its pursuers would not allow its escape, returned fire. The *War Shrike* shuddered as it took a grazing hit.

"We just lost forward hangar rails and missile tubes three and four."

The ship thrummed as the EPCs cycled. Explosions and debris marked the effectiveness of Kral and Doko's fire.

Lucius spared a moment's attention to look at the rest of the battle. One of Mannetti's cruisers spun, powerless, a shattered wreck ripped lengthwise by fire. A squadron of Naevius' fighters had strayed into the path of a Chxor broadside. Twelve more bunks would be empty tonight.

Lucius jerked against the seat restraints. The *War Shrike* lurched and then heaved again from a second hit. A third and fourth hit signaled they'd received the love of a full battery. "Major hits, Baron. We lost our port fuel tank, the hangar, and environmental in sections—"

Another hit cut off the list, and the forward bulkhead exploded. A fireball cut through the compartment. Lieutenant Palmer vanished, along with half his department.

***

Planetary Governor Kleigh forgot about his legacy. He forgot about his duty. As his squadron died around him and his ship reeled from impact after impact, everything ceased to have meaning beyond his own survival.

"Plot us a course, now!" His throat felt raw and he couldn't seem to get enough air. "Jump as soon as you have a course plotted through shadow space!"

***

The fire died and a vortex of air ripped through the bridge. Pressure doors slammed down. Lucius slammed his visor. "First responders to the bridge. Medic team to the bridge." He looked over, Doko and Kral still typed in firing orders. Chief Winslow seemingly teleported from his console to the helm and managed to replace the wounded helmsman and put the *War Shrike* through a dizzying evasive maneuver at the same time.

When he looked back at his screens, Lucius saw the fleeing dreadnought had finally turned at bay. As he watched, sections of the ship's defensive screen flickered. A haze of escaped gas and water vapor boiled around the damaged ship.

One of the engine pods exploded. Another series of hits stippled the flank.

Half the enemy's batteries still fired. The *War Shrike* lurched again at another glancing hit. Lucius tuned out the damage description, "Focus fire on his rear quarter. We've weakened him there, time to finish him off." Later he could think about faces and names, people he'd known who would never have a future.

Sustained fire finally hit something vital and the dreadnought's defense screen went down. The *Gebneyr* swept by, underneath, and raked the larger ship from point-blank. A series of explosions nearly engulfed the smaller ship.

A squadron of Interceptors swept over the top of the larger ship and fired their light guns. One of the tertiary batteries swatted two of them in return. Atmosphere and hydrogen fuel leaked from the dreadnought. Only one main battery still fired. Kral hammered that one till it too went silent.

The dreadnought finally lay still.

The fight ended so suddenly that Lucius looked around in shock. He saw the crew busy at damage controls and that the immediate battle seemed completed. Lucius turned his attention to the battle reports and responded with a voice raw from shouted commands. The Garu secured the remnants of Force Bravo. Mistress Blanc and her stealthy battlecruiser along with the captured planetary defense centers had Faraday secure. The remaining Chxor ships of Charlie were either gutted hulks or wreckage.

Lucius let out a deep breath. "Message to all elements, commence clean up operations. Rendezvous at Faraday in eight hours."

***

The hammer-blows on Planetary Governor Kleigh's flagship had stopped. Sparking electronics and dim emergency lights left most of his bridge in the shadows.

Kleigh wiped a smear of green Chxor blood off his visor and his hands worked at the straps of his command chair. His previous emotional detachment felt as hollow and empty as all his previous declarations of emotionless rationality.

Kleigh realized now that Chxor *could* feel emotion. The hit that had shattered his bridge left him totally unharmed, an untouched center in a whirlwind of destruction.

Kleigh stared at the empty shattered, airless abattoir around him and felt total terror.

The indicator lights on his suit began to blink red.

Two hours later, the Marine boarding party found him, vacuum frozen to his command chair.

Kleigh had neglected to check his suit seals.

***

Lieutenant Jessi Toria rubbed at tired eyes as she monitored her screen. She loved her ship and crew, but there were times where the long watches grew exhausting.

In particular, she wished her ship was the one chosen to scout out Faraday. She wanted a chance to prove herself, to test herself.

She knew that the *Mongoose* wasn't up to a full engagement with the Chxor. For that matter, it was an elderly corvette, built for raids or scouting, not for full combat with warships. Still, she wanted to make a difference... and to show that her ship could serve as good as any.

"Ma'am," Ensign Miller spoke up from the sensor station "Got something on our sensors."

Jessi straightened in her chair, "Oh?" She wondered if it were another mining ship to scare off... or maybe another ambitious pirate.

She gazed at the reading for a moment. "That's... odd." It looked like a drifting asteroid. But it was hotter than it should be... and it wasn't one of the ones they had already mapped in the system. For that matter, it had come in way off the elliptic plane, it was lucky they noticed it at all.

"Yeah," Ensign Miller said. "That's what I thought. So I used one of the sensor platforms to hit it with active radar. The 'asteroid' knocked out the sensor with a missile."

"Shit," Jessi said. "What did you get?"

"Looks like its a ship, trying to run cold and avoid notice. I'm getting some kind of weird doppler effect, I think it might have some stealth systems but they're not at a hundred percent."

"Right," Jessi nodded. "Estimate on class?"

"Looks like a destroyer," he shrugged, "When it goes active, we'll know more."

She nodded. They didn't have the capability to launch probes themselves, and the enemy ship had tagged their one sensor platform in that area. That left her in a jam, though. The enemy knew they'd been discovered. They continued on their current course despite that, which suggested that they were either very brave or that they had some other kind of backup.

"I want you to sweep this entire sector," Jessi said as she highlighted the region. "Passive sensors only."

She watched her own tactical screen as the ship coasted closer. Her own vessel mounted only a single spinal laser and eight missiles on external racks. The Baron, thankfully, had authorized her to draw two Pilums, in case something truly nasty came calling. Still, the other six missiles were the light ones they had captured with the ship. They would be marginally effective against a destroyer... but would barely scratch the paint on anything larger or better armored.

Finally, a second blip appeared on the screen. "Got them, it is cruiser-sized, ma'am." He paused, "I've plotted their course."

Jessi nodded. It was pretty much what she had both expected and feared. Both ships were en route to Alpha Seven. They had gone engines cold and powered most of their systems down, but they could bring them online with a few moments notice.

Her corvette had no business engaging a cruiser. She was positioned as a tripwire... yet her corvette had been chosen to remain behind because they couldn't mount an ansible on it, the ship was too small and there wasn't enough room. The *only* way that she could warn the Baron was to go back and tell him.

At the same time, if she did so, these unknown enemies would have days, possibly weeks, of control over the base. True, they had already moved the refugees as a precaution, and reduced the base to a caretaker staff.

Still, those people down there needed protection. The base hadn't been sanitized and still held information on their operations, supplies, and other resources that a pirate might utilize.

Her orders had left her leeway in her response. She knew that no one would second guess her if she withdrew from the system without a shot fired...

But she also knew that she'd never forgive herself if she abandoned the people down below. "Alright, here's what we're going to do."

***

The *Mongoose* coasted still and silent as the two enemy ships continued their own silent approach. Jessi tapped updated commands on her console even as she made a mental estimation on the enemy course of action.

She had accelerated her ship below the horizon of the airless moon and made use of the gravity well to bring her ship on line with the enemy vessels. Neither ship had lit off their drives yet, and Jessi wondered if they somehow hoped to sneak into orbit unnoticed.

Regardless, she wouldn't give them that option.

Her optics had identified the larger ship as a Liberator-class cruiser, a standard Colonial Republic class. It wasn't uncommon for a Colonial Republic officer to go renegade or for their crew to mutiny and turn pirate, she knew. The ugly, boxy vessel packed far more firepower than Jessi wanted to engage, but she had the advantage with her two missiles... if she got to use them.

The other destroyer continued to elude her tactical section. She couldn't blame them, plenty of pirates conducted extensive modifications to their ships. They still had the odd, doppler effect, which Jessi had come to agree must be some kind of stealth system.

"They will reach initiation point in three minutes," Ensign Miller said softly.

"Right," Jessi took a deep breath. In theory, the two ships would have to light off their drives and engines at that point in order to take up an orbit. If they did so, there would be a brief moment when their reactors and drives lit off that their other systems, to include sensors, would operate at reduced efficiency. Most smaller vessels couldn't operate their defense screens for up to a couple of minutes after they brought their reactors online.

In that window, they would be vulnerable... and that was when Lieutenant Jessi Toria would order her ship to fire.

As the timer wound down, Jessi had a strange moment of disjunction. Only a year ago, she never would have dreamed that she would be in command of her own warhip... or that she would risk her life for people she had never met.

"I'm picking up a thermal spike," Ensign Miller said. "They're bringing their reactors online!"

Jessi already had both ships bracketed. She and her weapons officer launched the eight missiles before the last word left the Ensign's mouth. Two Pilum missiles lanced out towards the Liberator-class cruiser, while the eight lighter warheads sped toward the destroyer.

There was a long moment before the two ships noticed the attack. "Their weapons are going hot, I'm picking up active radar from both ships!" Ensign Miller said.

Jessi saw that her engineer had begun the start-up process aboard the *Mongoose*. For a moment, their own sensors lost track. *Just two minutes until our defense screen comes up...* she thought.

Her sensors cleared to show the missiles on final acquisition. The enemy destroyer had gone into evasive Maneuvers and the cruiser began to do the same.

A moment later, two pinpricks of light signified that both Pilums had detonated. The electromagnetic hash that filled the sensors cleared to show only a spreading cloud of debris. Jessi's eyes went to the sensors that showed the destroyer. It too was enveloped in detonations, and its hulk streamed air as it drifted out a moment later.

Jessi heard a gasp a moment later, "Ma'am, the doppler, it was a second destroyer!"

Head snapped around, ready to give the order for evasive maneuvers... but it was too late.

The second destroyer's volley arrived only seconds behind its emission and struck the *Mongoose* a full minute before the defense screen could come up.

There were no survivors.

***

Lucius's alliance gathered in orbit above Faraday. The *War Shrike, Peregrine, Gebneyr*, and the *Rubicon* lay in similar orbits. All four ships had taken heavy fire, though Lucius had no doubt the others had managed to avoid his extent of damage.

"We've managed to capture two dreadnoughts." Admiral Collae said. "I've got engines operational on both of them. They'll need some yard time, but my men will take them to one of my bases."

"We captured two dreadnoughts as well," the Garu leader said. Lucius still didn't know the man's name. "Admiral Collae has graciously offered a number of cargo ships he's acquired in exchange. We will keep the captured cruisers."

"I received a message from an Officer Krath stating he surrenders all remaining Chxor forces on the planet." Lucius nodded, "Now, I think, we need to—"

"Now, Baron Giovanni, I think we need to discuss the distribution of the Dreyfus Fleet." Admiral Mannetti said. Her voice had gone sharp. A glance at her showed a look of thinly veiled hate.

"Excuse me, Lady Kale?" Lucius asked.

She smiled. "I tolerated your arrogance and the uneven distribution of the wealth before. I could even tolerate the amusing notion that these nomadic vagabonds deserved a share." Her face was flushed. "What I will not tolerate is the losses my ships have taken, the drastic losses in my fighter squadrons, for your gain. I will not accept a third of the Dreyfus Fleet. Not, at least, when I can have half."

"What exactly, do you mean by that?" Lucius asked, his voice cold.

Admiral Collae shot her a cold look. "What she means, I'm afraid, is that we're renegotiating." His craggy face showed nothing, "Though, I think, she spoke sooner than we'd previously discussed."

"Baron, Admiral Mannetti's ships just went active. They're targeting us." Anthony Doko's level voice held a note of tension.

Lucius didn't look away from the conference screen. "Both of you, then, are voiding our contract?"

Admiral Collae nodded to someone off screen. Lucius noted, on his own screen that Collae's ships, too went active. "It's nothing personal. I actually thought that this went very well, Baron. It's just that fifty-fifty is a much better division."

"And all of it is better than that?" Lucius asked, eyes going from Mannetti to Collae.

Neither of them so much as twitched, but Lucius could see both had a plan for the other. "I'll let you leave, Lucius, and you can keep the cruisers and the dreadnought you've captured even. You fought for and earned those."

"And Faraday?" Lucius asked. He typed in a command into his chair's arm.

"It's a well-positioned world. We're just off the axis of the Balor advance. From here I can accomplish much. I think it will make a good base of operations." Collae smiled.

"Admiral Collae, I think letting him go might be overly generous." Mannetti said, "He's betrayed me once before and he's certainly shown a determination to return here. Besides, the *War Shrike* was mine and I want it back."

Admiral Collae stared at Lucius, "Perhaps you're right."

Lucius nodded, "I see. I wish that things could be otherwise." He nodded to Doko, and the *War Shrike*'s defense screens came active, along with those of the *Gebneyr* .

"Surely you don't want to fight this out?" Collae said. "You won't cost your crew's lives for nothing will you?"

Lucius waited.

"You know things can get quite painful for those civilians on the planet, don't you?" Collae said. "A weapons exchange in orbit can have shots hitting planet-side."

"Let's just get this over with." Admiral Mannetti said. "We've got—" She broke off and her mouth hung open as she stared at her screen.

A new fleet crested the horizon of Faraday. It came around from the far side of the planet. Led by a screen of destroyers and cruisers came a massive superdreadnought. The first, and only, of its class, the *Emperor Romulus* swept forward menacingly, a massive, black wedge.

"Attention pirate craft. This is Emperor Romulus IV of the Nova Roma Empire. You have voided our treaty and insulted the honor of our military. You are trespassing on my sovereign territory." The young man's voice could sound quite stern when backed by that firepower, Lucius decided. "I offer you this chance to surrender."

Admiral Mannetti stared at the screen, totally speechless.

"To the crew of the traitor to the Empire, Admiral Mannetti, I offer leniency for your crimes should she be apprehended alive and turned over for Imperial Justice." There was a slight pause.

Admiral Mannetti looked around rapidly. "Don't you—" Her transmission cut off.

"Admiral Collae, what do you have to say about this?" Lucius couldn't, quite, withhold a smile.

"It appears you planned to betray us, in turn." Admiral Collae said, his face as emotionless as a stone bust. "I suppose it's only foresight that I took my own precautions."

"That's absurd." Lucius snapped. "I would have split the fleet—"

"Whatever you say is irrelevant." A relayed tactical screen replaced Collae's image. It took Lucius a moment to recognize the Zeta Tau system, and Alpha Seven. He immediately recognized the Forerunner-class destroyer that rested in high orbit above the moon. "I interpolated that your base of operations would have to be a system receiving little traffic, and still retain a place to keep several thousand refugees in relative comfort. Few places manage to meet those requirements." Admiral Collae's gruff voice said, "Unfortunately, my men had to destroy the corvette you had on station. They fought valiantly, I'm told."

"What is the meaning of this, Admiral?" Lucius said.

"Simple enough. That destroyer can kill everyone in the base on Alpha Seven. They can finish the job that the PCRA never did. It might even be lauded as a victory." Admiral Collae's gruff voice cut through the silence of the bridge. "But I've no taste for that. My offer is that you withdraw. Leave this planet and the Dreyfus Fleet. I'll leave your people alive."

Lucius let out a sigh, "No deal. You've shown you can't be trusted. I'm not going to let you have an entire planet's population to use as pawns. I'm not going to let a callous bastard like you have the Dreyfus Fleet. I'll let you leave, alive, and that's all you get."

"I don't think you understand the gravity of the situation, Baron." Collae said. "Perhaps I didn't make it clear?" On the screen one of the destroyers fired, once. A blossom of gas vented from the hit on the base. "How many people just died, a hundred, a thousand?"

Lucius shook his head and cut the connection. He broadcast out to all of the ships, "All units who surrender will be treated favorably. I gave Collae a chance to leave, he didn't take it."

They waited almost a full minute, "Collae is trying to reach you, sir."

Lucius shook his head. "Open fire."

Weapons went hot. The ship thrummed as weapons prepared to fire on the Republic officer's ships. An instant later, Collae's ships vanished. "They jumped to shadow, sir," Doko said. "It had to be an emergency jump."

Lucius shook his head, looking over at Kandergain. "He had Mistress Blanc plot the course, didn't he?"

She nodded, "She'd be able to plot a course in under thirty seconds, she could have transmitted that to the other ships."

Lucius sighed, he opened a channel to the Emperor's flagship, "Well, your Highness, I hope the evacuation went as planned?"

The younger man nodded, "We left a small caretaker force. Hopefully they got into the deeper bunkers in time."

Lucius nodded, but he thought of Lieutenant Jessi Toria and her crew. Only the latest of the ghosts on his conscience. "Can you dispatch some ships to look into it? I don't think Collae is the vengeful type…"

"But he'd kill every man woman and child on Faraday or any other world to accomplish his goals." The Emperor nodded. "I understand, Baron."

Lucius nodded. "I believe we'd better get some Marines aboard Mannetti's ships before some enterprising person decides to emulate Admiral Collae. Thank you for your help. Excellent timing, your Highness.

"Do you think I'd let him be late, brother mine?" Alanis said as she jutted her head into the screen. There was a slight pause, "Let me know as soon as you hear anything about Reese."

Lucius nodded. He did not mention the fact he'd specifically told her *not* to be anywhere near a ship that might be involved in the fight. He had a terrible suspicion that she'd ignore any such orders from him or any other person. He cut the link, "Thank god she hasn't joined the military, she'd be impossible."

Kandergain smiled at him, "I can't imagine."

Lucius shook his head, "She's too smart for her own good. She'd never follow orders, she'd always be haring off on her own missions, she'd probably have some kind of cult of personality of followers…" He trailed off, then gave her a suspicious glance as the psychic giggled.

"What?"

She burst out into full laughter.

"Lets just get down there and see what kind of mess the Chxor made."

***

The first shuttles to land on Faraday contained medics and their supplies.

Lieutenant Lauren Kelly was very, very glad of that.

Just over five thousand rebels had attacked Flattop Mountain. After the Chxor surrender, less than two thousand remained. She heard of substantially more casualties at Grey Coast.

She didn't want to know about civilian casualties in the cities. Some people always took the chaos to heart, and aerial footage still showed riots in progress. She looked over at Mason, who stood cold and silent nearby. "It shouldn't be like this. We won."

He turned dead eyes towards her, "This is a victory. Defeat is worse." He shook his head and pushed his own dark memories aside. "Was it worth it?"

"I hope so."

***

CHAPTER VIII

February 15, 2403 Earth Standard Time
Faraday System
(status unknown)

A week of frenzied activity later, Lucius finally set foot on Faraday again. The tiny customs station remained, bullet pocked and windows smashed. The tower of the space port, gutted by fires from the riots, lay empty. The handful of cargo ships left by the Chxor lay abandoned as well.

The celebration underway had a muted quality. The men and women that survived Chxor occupation possessed a dark attitude. It was as if the Chxor had leached away their ability to experience joy.

The once-refugees return had not been a thing of welcome. Though the populace hated the conservatives who'd ousted the Contractor, there remained a core of resentment to those who had left. Part of that seemed to be a sense of abandonment, part was simply a sense that the refugees had not suffered to their extent.

Lucius learned, as evidenced by the riots and collapse of Chxor surrender, that the occupation had destroyed the society of Faraday. Many of the educated and knowledgeable people fled with the refugees. Most of the rest went to the Chxor death camps. The Chxor killed the military, teachers, doctors, judges and police. They hadn't killed the lawyers. Perhaps they possessed a professional courtesy.

Lucius met a crowd of self-appointed officials and leaders who'd filled the power vacuum. "How many of them will I have to shoot for corruption or outright treason?" he asked rhetorically.

"At least three of them were Chxor supporters," Kandergain said. "Five others spent the whole occupation reporting on their neighbors. Two more of them used the riots and witch-hunts to kill off political opponents. One of them is a child murder-rapist." She frowned distastefully.

"There's two leaders of organized crime, they actually think of themselves as patriots, though and they did help to fight the Chxor. They, by the way, have plenty of evidence on the others in this deputation. I'm sure it is enough for trials and executions."

Lucius stared at her for a long moment. "You're certain of all that?"

She nodded, "I'm surprised half of them aren't screaming about their guilt. The worst part about being a psychic is that sometimes you can't shut people's thoughts out... not when they are this worked up."

"Point out the two we can use," Lucius turned to Colonel Proscia. "Take those men into custody, minus the two she points out."

"With pleasure, Baron."

The Marine Colonel spoke into a hand communicator, and a moment later, a dozen Marines started to move forward.

Lucius smiled coldly, "The one advantage in putting down riots with Marines is that the law-abiding citizens know to stay down when they start moving forward."

"There's something odd, though." Kandergain said, "Something about— Get down!" She moved impossibly fast and shoved Lucius to the ground. Something hot and bright cut through the air above him.

Someone screamed. Shouts and gunfire erupted. Lucius got his head up and saw something blur across his vision. Dark shapes moved rapidly among the humans. A shape collided with a Marine. The Marine screamed and flew backwards twenty or more feet to sprawl out. Another Marine disappeared as a beam of energy cut through him.

Another blur, that moved too fast to register, intersected two dark blurs. For a moment, Kandergain stood still over two dark alien forms. Then she lurched into motion again.

Marines fired and one of alien attackers fell to the ground and bled dark blood. Another flew away from Kandergain and smashed into a wall to lie still. Another beam lashed out from the remaining alien, to cut down two more Marines. The return fire wounded the last and Kandergain caught the creature and finished it off.

Lucius stood. He felt a sense of horrified detachment at the carnage. At least a dozen Marines were down, many of the civilians lay dead as well. Colonel Proscia snapped out commands at the dozens that had swarmed to the sounds of fighting.

Lucius walked over to stand next to Kandergain where she

looked down at the dead alien. A hairless, eyeless, dark purple head surmounted a slender body. It looked vaguely insectoid, though Lucius could not tell if it had some kind of exoskeleton or body armor. "God, that's ugly. What is it?"

She looked up, her eyes dark, "This is a Balor drone."

The hairless creature looked totally alien in a way that made Lucius want to vomit. A small pistol lay near its outstretched limb.

"So this is the enemy?" Lucius asked.

"This is the enemy."

***

Lucius and Colonel Proscia spoke quietly, as Kandergain paced nearby. She looked uneasy and Lucius wasn't sure whether that should make him more worried.

"My men have established a perimeter, and—"

Distantly, they heard a scream.

Around them, the light seemed to dim.

Lucius let out a startled gasp and noticed his breath fogged. The warm spring day turned suddenly cold. He looked over at Kandergain, who stared across the pavement.

The ground began to tremble. "What the hell?"

Lucius fell to his hands and knees, unable to stand against the shaking earth.

He didn't see the figure cross the landing strip. Suddenly, it was there, only a dozen meters from Kandergain. The ground continued to rumble.

Lucius heard screams and shouts from around him. The shaking earth threw everyone to the ground. Everyone except the insectoid figure in glossy gray armor, and Kandergain. The two stood silent and motionless. A gust of wind buffeted Lucius. He saw the wind stir Kandergain's ponytail, and ruffle her clothes. She didn't move.

"What's happening?" Colonel Proscia shouted.

An arc of lightning crashed out from the armored figure to Kandergain and bounced back. The roar of thunder deafened Lucius. The wind strengthened and spiraled around Kandergain and the mysterious figure. Shards of broken pavement, bits of trash, and pieces of equipment spun in the hurricane.

Another arc of lighting crashed out. The noise assaulted

Lucius's ears.

The ground's shaking rose to greater heights.

A boulder-sized square of pavement flew up suddenly and swatted the gray armored figure like a bug.

The wind died. The earth stilled.

Lucius stood, hesitantly, to his feet. "What was that?"

Kandergain turned, for a second, her eyes seemed to glow. The second passed, and she returned to normal. "That was their leader. He decided to try his luck. He failed." A faint sheen of sweat beaded her forehead. She turned to Colonel Proscia, "I need you and your men. We have to cleanse the Balor infection."

"There are more?" Colonel Proscia asked.

"They'll have a base. We need to move now." She turned back to Lucius, "Get back aboard your ship. Ready your weapons. I'll relay a target for you soon."

***

"Lucius, this is Colonel Proscia. The psychic woman wants you to fire at the coordinates we've highlighted."

"What's there?" Lucius asked.

He heard a muffled conversation, and what sounded like shouting.

"She, uh, says to fire as soon as possible, using your main weapons. Apparently, there's a Balor base hidden inside the abandoned hospital." Colonel Proscia sounded discomfited. "She believes there's an enemy ship hidden beneath the building."

"Are you clear of the area?" Lucius asked.

"My men are clear. There may be civilians in the area." Colonel Proscia paused, "Kandergain says that the Balor are about to send some kind of message. She says to fire now."

Lucius looked over at Doko. "Do it."

"Firing." The deck plates vibrated.

The ship lay close enough to the planet that they could see the results. A shockwave of compressed air blasted out from the target and smashed buildings in the vicinity. Lucius winced at the collateral damage.

Something inside the building or beneath it detonated. The flash temporarily blinded their visual sensors.

"What was that?" Lucius demanded.

"Looks like a one kiloton explosion, Baron. If there was something under the building, it just blew up."

Lucius nodded. He thought of the number of dead civilians now on his conscience. "Colonel Proscia, are you still there?"

"Yes sir. Kandergain says you hit the ship, that was the secondary."

"Threat neutralized?" Lucius asked.

"Roger, sir."

"Thank you," Lucius cut the connection. He turned sad eyes to Anthony Doko. "I'll be in my quarters. I don't want to be disturbed. Get some assets down there to help out the civilians."

***

"So. Where do we stand?" Lucius asked. His eyes roamed the council room. The government center used by the Chxor occupiers had too much damage, and too many bad memories for use. Today, they met in a board room for a defunct corporation.

"We still don't have a full picture of civilian casualties from the occupation." Kate Bueller said. "I honestly don't think we ever will. There are just under fourteen million people, that we can track, anyway." She shook her head, "Best estimates are something over five million dead between the occupation and liberation."

Lucius knew the estimates on the deaths from his attack on the Balor base to be upwards of three thousand.

"Civilian infrastructure damage will be nominally repaired in many areas in two weeks." Mathew Nogita said. "Power and water supplies didn't take much damage, we've found enough people to keep those systems up in the major cities. Garbage collection is going to be an issue. Between the riots, damage from the Chxor, and just normal use… there's a lot of trash that needs removal. Issues also exist with body removal and disposal. The Chxor overwhelmed even their mass burial sites. They've got thousands of bodies stacked in trenches. "

"Disease prevention issues with so many corpses will rapidly become a problem." The Iodan spoke through his translator. "We recommend incineration of remains to prevent outbreaks of serious levels of pestilence."

"Have we identified…" Lucius sighed, "Can we identify the

dead?"

No one wanted to speak, finally, Kate did, "Baron, I've spoken with a lot of the people here. Many of them… they just want to put this in the past. They know anyone missing, anyone taken by the Chxor… they went to the death camps." She looked up, "Over one quarter of the population is dead, Baron. If they held services for them all, they'd never have time to do anything else."

Lucius nodded. "Very well, start collection of the bodies. We can use our Chxor prisoners for that." Lucius gritted his teeth as he thought of the culpability of those same Chxor in the massacres of the Faraday populace.

"What about restoring order?" He asked, turning to Colonel Proscia, "I know we don't have enough Marines, and I know Marines aren't a police force. What's the best way to do this?"

"I've contacted some of the rebel leaders who our insertion team worked with. They've begun a neighborhood watch program. It's got some bad sides, there's a lot of familial favoritism and patronage, but it's getting the job done." He shrugged, "Once the system is in place, I think things will calm down a lot." He shrugged, "The riots ended, the remaining violence, some of that is leftovers from the Chxor occupation, I think a lot of it originates from the previous government, both under the Shareholders and even under the Contractor. There are a lot of people who never qualified for citizenship getting even."

Lucius nodded, "That brings us to the structure of the new government here." His eyes ranged the table. "I did not liberate this planet for it to return to the status quo." He paused. "I personally think the previous Contract of the colony became abusive and distorted, especially by the wealthy of the colony. It had a number of laws drawn up in its basic premise that allowed such favoritism. The new Contract will not contain such flaws, is that understood?"

The civilians nodded their agreement, and Lucius sat back. "What is the plan for drawing up a new system of laws?"

Max Nyguyen spoke, "It's something a few of us did back at Alpha Seven, Baron. We drew up several plans, most of them based on a democratic republic." He paused. "Something the entire thing depended on, sir, was whether or not you'd remain in charge."

"Excuse me?" Lucius asked.

"Baron, I think I speak for all of the refugees, and a good portion of Faraday when I say that we'd prefer to leave you in charge." Kate said. "You're an outsider, you have none of the contamination of the old government. You saved the planet from the Chxor. You've got a significant military force, which will only grow larger with the Dreyfus Fleet. Our only other option, as I see it, is to petition to join the Republic, or to bow down to the Nova Roma Empire."

Lucius frowned, "I'm... I'm not in this to make my own kingdom."

"Baron, that's probably one of the best reasons to make you our leader, permanently." Kate laughed. "God, I'm a politician and I *know*, the people who want power shouldn't have it!"

Lucius shook his head, "I have no experience with civilian power. Order of law and civilian bureaucracy... I think I'd be worse for this place than the Chxor!"

"Just... just think on it." Max Nyguyen said.

"I will. In the meantime, draw up your drafts. I'm not sure even what kind of means of ratification we can get from the populace. Work on that as well. Let me know what you need." Lucius stretched and stood, "Do we have anything else?"

"No, Baron, I think that's it."

He nodded, "I'll see you tomorrow, pending any crises."

They'd only begun to file out when Kandergain stepped in. She wore her normal rugged civilian clothing, her blonde hair pulled back in a ponytail. Strapped to her leg she carried a stub-barreled riot gun.

He waited for the others to clear the room before he spoke. Lucius stared at her with haunted eyes, "Now explain to me why I killed three thousand civilians yesterday."

"You fired on that building because I told you to," Kandergain said, her own voice sad. She sat in the nearest chair, putting her feet up. "We had a Balor infiltrator cell."

"Which means what?"

She took a deep breath, "Think of the Balor... like a virus. You know how a virus works? It invades a normal cell, scrambles its DNA, and produces a bunch of viruses out of the corrupted cell." Lucius nodded and waved a hand for her to continue. "The Balor infiltrators, they work like that. They... convert a local. They use him to turn others. They use those infiltrators to gather information on new worlds, and to sow confusion and discord among their enemies. "

"So... why were they here?" Lucius asked.

"Balor love Chxor worlds. They can subvert the top Chxor, and take over entire worlds, no Chxor will question the commands of his superior. The ones here probably came with the occupation forces."

"How?" Lucius asked. "How could one of those purple-skinned aliens hide? They don't look remotely like Chxor, much less Humans."

Kandergain set her feet on the floor looking out the window for a moment. "We're getting near things I can't talk about."

"Seventeen of my Marines are dead and over three thousand civilians, and you won't tell me what I need to know?"

"Not won't, I *can't*." She shook her head. "There's some things, I simply *can't* tell you, and there's others you won't understand." She took a deep breath, "Part of why the Balor are so dangerous is that they are all psychics."

"All of them?" Lucius asked, startled. "I thought that was intrinsically rare."

"Among humans, yes." Kandergain said, "But other races are different. The Chxor have none, at all. The Balor are all psychics." She shrugged, uncomfortably, "The... powers of individuals is determined solely by birth, though. The abilities of each are useful in their jobs. The workers can communicate and cooperate more effectively, their soldiers are faster and stronger."

Lucius frowned, "What you're describing sounds like an ant hill, or a hive of bees."

"That's a close enough approximation. I'm giving you an approximation, only," Kandergain said. "Don't make too many assumptions on that analogy."

"Okay... more information would—"

"Make things more confused at this time." Kandergain said. "Some of what I know, you can't understand. Some other things... some things you won't want to know."

"I may need to know them to make an educated decision."

"Trust me, some things you just, really don't want to know."

Kandergain said and she finally met his eyes. "A lot of things about the Balor make the Chxor's actions here seem... civil."

"Fine, then," Lucius said, "What do we do about the Balor here?"

"This infestation was recent. They probably came with the Chxor." Kandergain said, "The warriors who ambushed you were young and inexperienced. It meant we had a cell here, and we needed to neutralize that cell before they reported."

"Why, what would the Balor care that the Chxor lost this world?"

"The Balor are psychic, remember?" She said, standing. "They'll be able to take secrets out of any normal human's mind. They knew about the Dreyfus Fleet. They're having their way with the Republic right now. They will not allow you to get a strong power base here, not when they can prevent it."

"What do we do?" Lucius asked.

"I'm not sure." She sighed. "They were sending a message."

Lucius nodded, "How long do we have?"

"I'm not sure. You destroyed their ship, so you might have stopped the message."

"Their ship?" Lucius asked.

"They secondary explosion, I'm pretty certain. Their Patriarch—" she cut off. "Their leader will always have a means to escape."

"I see. Will we need to prepare for a battle in space?"

She shook her head, "I don't know if they'll attack directly."

Lucius frowned, "I don't like being kept in the dark about this. I understand what you're saying, but, I think I've earned the right to know what I'm killing people for."

She sighed, "You have nightmares, Lucius?"

"Yes."

"Have you ever had a nightmare where you woke, screaming? Have you ever had a nightmare so real, you clawed at your face to wake yourself?" Kandergain's eyes were dark. "This is that kind of horror, Lucius. These are thoughts and ideas that you don't want to pollute yourself with."

Lucius sighed, "Kandergain, I've seen terrible things. I've done terrible things." He paused, "The only nightmares I ever have are when I see the faces of the people I've lost. The only dreams that haunt me are the ghosts of the dead, and I can't face them without knowing that I sent them to their deaths for good reason."

Kandergain nodded, "Think on this then, Lucius, and tell me if it's a good enough reason." She swallowed slightly, "Those Balor who ambushed you incubated in a Human host. Somewhere, some poor bastard screamed and twitched while those things ate their way to the outside when they hatched. Then they fed on what was left. Is that a good enough reason to want to kill the Balor?"

***

Lucius returned to his office to find Reese waiting. "I see you returned, Lucius, though I don't know why you'd fight for this world and not for our home."

"Reese, you don't know how glad I was to hear you're still alive," Lucius began.

"What, you forget so quickly why I left?" Reese snarled, "You left my wife to die on Nova Roma. I saw what happened here, Lucius. I saw what Chxor rule is like. If we'd gone back—"

"Can I get a word in—"

"No!" Reese snarled, "You left Alanis to die!" Lucius typed something into his keyboard as Reese rounded the desk, "I don't know why you—"

He broke off as the door opened. His head snapped around, an angry expression on his face that vanished into shock at the person who had arrived. "Alanis?" he asked.

"You idiot!" She shouted. "I told you to stay with Lucius, and when I catch up to him, what do I hear? You decided to stay and fight the Chxor? Are you insane!?"

"Alanis?" Reese asked again, totally confused.

Lucius shook his head, "I'll let you two be alone for this joyous occasion."

"What in God's name possessed you to get off the *War Shrike*! I told you to stay with Lucius, no matter what, I told you—"

Lucius firmly shut the door behind him, shook his head and decided he would finish his work the office down the hall. The building had many unoccupied offices, thankfully.

He heard the muted sound as something glass broke. He thought he heard a couple of thumps. He shook his head again, "I don't want to know."

***

A few hours later, a bewildered looking Colonel Proscia found him. "Your office..." He shook his head, "Was that your sister?"

"I don't want to know," Lucius said.

"There were clothes on the floor and Commander Leone..."

"I don't want to know," Lucius said, more firmly.

"And—"

"There are things I don't want to know." Lucius asked, "This is one of those things. I love my sister dearly, and Reese is—was—a friend. I don't want to know."

Colonel Proscia shook his head, "It certainly was... confusing. I take it you relocated?"

"Yes." Lucius let out a breath, "Why'd you come looking for me?"

"I wanted to ask you about earlier, when you fired on the building." The Marine Colonel looked tired, almost haggard.

Lucius sighed, "What do you want to know?"

"Did it have to be done?" Colonel Proscia asked, his voice calm. Lucius could see the other man's ghosts bothered him.

He thought back to Kandergain's descriptions and of the terrifying battle between her and the psychic Balor. "Yes." He sighed, "I wish there was another way. But yes, it had to be done."

The other man nodded. "Thank you."

Then he left Lucius to face his own ghosts

***

CHAPTER IX

February 19, 2403 Earth Standard Time
Faraday System
(status unknown)

"Lucius, darling, so glad you could take the time to see me." Lucretta Mannetti said, either with total sincerity or total sarcasm.

Lucius bowed slightly and decided some sarcasm of his own in order, "Lady Kale, looking as splendid as ever."

She smiled, "What do I need to do to get out, Lucius?"

Lucius cocked his head, "That… might take a lot on your part." He shrugged, "Something about an attempted coup d'etat, piracy, and several counts of murder."

"Surely you can put a good word in for me?"

"Let's see…" Lucius looked to the ceiling, as if for inspiration. "I could put in a word about how you… stabbed me. Or… there's also the fact that you betrayed me a second time."

"You wouldn't hold that against me, would you Lucius?" she pouted.

"Lucretta, you tried to kill me. Twice." Lucius snapped, finally sick of the pretense. "I respect your ability, I respect your persistence." He let out a deep breath, "You're an attractive woman and you've got some amazing attributes. That doesn't mean you're not a traitorous snake."

"Well, if we want to get down to it, Lucius, you betrayed me first." A gust of wind off a glacier held more warmth than her voice. "You foiled a plan ten years in the making when you betrayed me and you didn't even get rewarded for it. How long was it before you finally received command of the *War Shrike*?"

Lucius looked away, "Ten years."

"Ah, yes, ten years shackled to a series of bungling captains. I might have fled in exile, but I heard." She laughed darkly, "Oh, I heard about brave Captain Stravatti, who received a rapid promotion from his ship's valiant actions at Resev Beta. And there was Duke Penn, who amazingly cornered the Privateers of Saratoga. What happened to him after his promotion? Ah, yes, he led five thousand men to their deaths in a vain attack against the

Chxor."

"I stayed loyal to a belief," Lucius said.

"A belief that you still follow, apparently, if you serve the puppy-Emperor who wants me hung for treason." The pirate admiral seated herself, treating the prison stool as a throne, "Did you ever ask yourself what rewards you could have held with me? Did you ever wonder whose orders I followed in my bid for power? Did you ever think I had loyalties beyond my own ambitions?"

Lucius turned away, "I doubt, very much, you looked beyond your own gains."

"Then you're wrong!" She surged forward, face pressed against the bars. "My gains... those significant rewards, I earned those, and you know it. Didn't we fight off the infamous Thomas Kaid, together at Port Fel? Name another *admiral* to match that. Didn't we bring down Saragossa's defenses, despite the knowledge it would buy us little time?" She spat, "Those corrupt bastards at Fleet hated our successes and you know that. They hated that I was a woman, that a woman could do what so many of their cronies couldn't. They hated you, because of your father, a man whose only crime was to ask for what should have been his in the first place."

"And why does my father always come up?" Lucius asked, his voice tired. "I made peace with my father's failures long ago."

"Your father, that's the center of all this, don't you realize?"

Lucius turned, startled by the raw emotion in her voice.

"He made me see, Lucius. He made me see clearly, for the first time, what had to be done. What still can be done." She pushed back from the bars, shaking her head. "That coup attempt you foiled, the mastermind behind it that no one ever uncovered... that was your father, Lucius."

"My father is dead," Lucius said, his voice suddenly tight. "They executed him for treason three days before my fifth birthday."

She cocked her head, an image of false surprise on her face, "Did they, Lucius? Or is that just what they told you?" She chuckled at the look on his face. "Think about loyalties, Lucius. You stopped the very plot that would have made you heir to the Empire."

Lucius stared at her, unable to look away.

"How different would things be, Lucius, were your father Emperor. Would he have accepted the corruption? Would he have burned with the ambition that caused the sacking of allies? Would he have been the puppet that this last Emperor was?"

"You lie." Lucius whispered.

"Think about loyalties, Lucius. Think about all the questions you never asked." She sagged back onto her stool. "Then, when you've thought about all the loyalties they never gave you in return, and then come tell me I'm a traitor and deserve to hang."

***

Lucius stepped into the tight office without knocking. "I need to know—" He broke off, startled to see Kandergain and Admiral Mund in close conversation.

The two shot each other looks that spoke volumes and Kandergain stood. "Lucius," she nodded. "I was about to leave anyway."

Before he could say anything, she squeezed past him and stepped out of the office.

"What was that about?" Lucius asked, hiking a thumb over his shoulder.

The old man smiled slightly, "Oh, she had some questions for me."

"About?" Lucius asked, suddenly suspicious. He wondered how much manipulation by people he'd trusted had shaped his life.

"Something personal to her," Admiral Mund said, his voice suddenly flat.

"I see." Lucius answered. He took a breath, "Tell me about my father."

Mund sat down in a chair. He pulled a bottle from behind it and poured himself a drink. "Hmmm." He stared at Lucius for a long moment.

"That's not an answer."

"That wasn't a question," the Admiral said.

Lucius snorted, despite himself, and took a seat across from his former mentor. "When I went to the Academy, you told me you'd served with my father." Lucius took a deep breath. "I've heard..." He looked away, staring at the walls of the office. Somehow, the old man still had his sword collection. He stared at the blades for a long moment, searching for the words. "I know my father attempted to put himself on the throne. I know that he was the bastard son of Emperor Romulus I, older by a year than the Emperor he served."

Lucius met Mund's blue eyes. "Tell me the truth. Did my father rebel from ambition for the throne? Did Romulus II have my father executed for treason?"

Mund took a long sip. "Marius Giovanni was a complex man, Lucius." The old man turned his gaze on the swords of his collection. "He had ambition, in plenty. He had a sense of justice, and a knowledge of men. He held loyalty to those he served and to those who served him." Mund turned his gaze back to Lucius again, "When we served together, he was a good friend. I can't say what drove him to betray his half-brother, his Emperor." Admiral Mund shrugged, "I've wondered about that for a long time myself, Lucius."

"Did you ask him?"

Admiral Mund laughed, "Of course! God, I asked him a dozen times! He'd spoken of the Empire for so long like it was some holy thing and then did his best to tear it down." He shook his head, "The answers he gave, when he gave any answers, were cryptic at best."

"Cryptic?" Lucius frowned. He remembered his father only as a warm presence, a deep voice. He'd heard Marius Giovanni described as a raving madman, an ambitious schemer, and as a brave warrior. Cryptic did not match with any of those impressions.

"When he…" Admiral Mund tossed back the drink and set the glass aside. "When he led his ships against the Emperor, I was the Admiral who fought him. When Marines dragged him before the Emperor, I commanded them. Your father… he changed, Lucius. He saw something, or heard something, and it changed everything for him. He never shared that knowledge, but it lurked in every word he said, every move he made."

Mund reached out and grabbed Lucius' hands, and held them and stared into his eyes. "When I asked him why he went rogue, he said it needed to happen. When I asked him why he led ten ships against twenty, he said it needed to happen." The old man let

Lucius' hands go and sat back, his rasping voice little more than a whisper, "When I asked him why he surrendered, knowing he'd face death, he said it needed to happen."

Admiral Mund shook his head, "He was brave and noble then too, for his surrender meant the men under him received lenience. He and his officers, though..." Mund shook his head. "There's only one penalty for treason, you know that."

"Lucretta Mannetti told me that my father lived." Lucius said, suddenly bitter that he'd listened.

"What would she know—" the old man suddenly broke off. "No..."

"What?" Lucius asked.

"There were rumors." Admiral Mund said, "There always are. I thought nothing of them. But, sometimes the truth can lie in a rumor."

"Could my father still live?" Lucius asked, incredulously.

"I doubt it." Mund said. "The bitterness of his betrayal... I very much doubt it."

Lucius nodded, "Thank you."

The old man shrugged. "The past is the past, Lucius. It hurts to remember, sometimes, but it lies behind us." He sighed, "I'm old, Lucius. Truth to tell, I'm afraid if you don't take the Emperor's job as fleet commander, he'll drop it on me."

"You've served before." Lucius said.

"And left in disgust." The response came immediately. Mund gave a rasping laugh. "I'm too old for that nonsense now. Half the life extension treatments won't work on me at this point, and the ones I've already had don't help much anymore. It will be worse if you choose to... do whatever you've planned."

"Do you..." Lucius cleared his throat, "Do you think I betrayed the Empire by not accepting his offer?"

"Yes."

Lucius winced.

"But I also think you would doom humanity if you took it."

Lucius looked up sharply.

"I served the glorious Nova Roma Empire for fifty three years, Lucius. I watched it change from the hope for humanity to the cancerous sore it died as." He shrugged. "Nations rise and wane, Lucius. I think that the legacy of the Empire is too tainted to rise again."

"What about the Emperor?"

"I don't know." The old man shrugged. "Were he not burdened with his father's legacy, he'd serve as a fine leader. As it is, even many on Nova Roma had come to hate the Empire."

"So what's the future, then?" Lucius said, "The Republic, rotted from the center? I know of a dozen minor warlords, a handful of pirate kings. Who else stands for humanity?"

"Well, Lucius," the old man smiled, "there is you."

"Ah," Lucius sighed, "Baron Lucius Giovanni, champion of the doomed?"

"Has a nice ring to it."

***

"Hello?"

Lucius stood up from his chair and moved to the door. He opened it, "Yes?"

Kandergain stood outside. "Hi, Lucius, got a sec?"

He nodded, reluctantly. "Certainly." He wanted more time to think about the day's stunning revelations, but…

He stepped aside and she stepped into his living quarters. He could have taken something bigger, but the apartment building served as the officer quarters for his fleet. He didn't even need the two rooms of the apartment. His handful of possessions still sat in two chests tucked neatly against the wall.

She stared around at the bare apartment, "Getting moved in?"

Lucius shrugged, "Not much to move. Most of my possessions are still on Nova Roma."

She winced, "Oh, yeah, sorry."

"Alanis said the Chxor didn't seem in much of a hurry to loot the estates, so it might still be there when we eventually retake it."

"So eager to rebuild the Nova Roma Empire, then?" She asked, her voice sharp.

Lucius felt his shoulders sag, he didn't want a fight, "No, but it's my home. I don't want to see it ravaged by the Chxor."

"Ah." She said, "So you haven't…"

"No, I haven't decided to take the Emperor up on his offer," Lucius answered. "I don't see a lot of options… but I haven't made the decision yet."

"Anyway..." Kandergain said, throwing her ponytail over her shoulder, "I thought you might like this," she said and held out a picture frame.

"What is it?" Lucius asked, taking it. He stared at the picture for a moment. A woman and a girl stood near a lake or perhaps the ocean. The faces looked familiar, but he couldn't place them.

"The girl is Sera, your grandmother." Kandergain said, taking a seat on his couch. "The woman is her mother, Kaylee."

Lucius sat down slowly, staring at the picture. "I... I don't have many pictures of my grandmother." He looked up, "Thank you."

Kandergain shrugged, uncomfortably, "I thought you'd like it. Sera had turned eleven in that picture, they still lived in Australia then."

Lucius blinked, "My grandmother lived in Australia?" He frowned slightly, "That's on Earth, right?"

Kandergain laughed, "Yes, it's in the southern hemisphere." She smiled, "You didn't know?"

"She didn't talk much about... the past. From what she said, unpleasant things happened on Earth." Lucius shrugged. "She raised me, but she never spoke much about her past."

"It... wasn't a good time to be a psychic, and not a good place for it either." Kandergain said, her voice sad. "Kaylee decided to stay on Earth, to hide, rather than go with the Agatha Fleet." She shrugged, "Those of us who stayed had years of hiding and prejudice to deal with. Before they broke out, ESPSec locked people like Kaylee up in camps. Afterward... Amalgamated Worlds issued shoot-on-sight orders for any psychic."

Lucius shivered, "That's barbaric."

"Terribly," Kandergain said grimly. "Kaylee... she knew how to hide, how to blend with a crowd. She and Sera stayed out of the camps, living in Australia. But someone bungled, someone who knew her got caught, and spilled the info to save himself."

Kandergain's eyes went distant, "An ESPSec agent put a bullet in Kaylee's head when she answered the door. They dragged Sera out, put her in a cell. When I heard, I got her out, then I tracked down the agent."

"Did you kill him?" Lucius asked, eyes alight.

"No." Kandergain shook her head. "He... well, he deserved it. He wanted it, too, I think. But I didn't kill him, as much as I wanted to. Sometimes, I wish I had killed him."

"Why didn't you?" Lucius asked.

Kandergain sighed, "We drifted off subject a bit, I suppose. I just wanted to give you something good, and I think I've ruined it."

Lucius shook his head, "No. You've given me knowledge of my grandmother. Thank you for that."

Kandergain nodded, "You're welcome, Lucius." She stood to leave.

"Wait," Lucius said, as she stood in the doorway. "What was the name of the agent?"

Kandergain looked away, "The ESPSec agent's name was Tommy King. He became a pirate after Amalgamated Worlds fell."

***

CHAPTER X

February 20, 2403 Earth Standard Time
Faraday System
(status unknown)

The slight differences between the bridge of the *War Shrike* and the *Peregrine* stood out in stark contrast when seated in the captain's chair.

"This seat's too damned comfortable," Lucius muttered.

"What's that?" Kandergain asked. Since returning from her Balor-hunt, she seemed distracted.

"Nothing," Lucius said. It strained his manpower to crew the *Peregrine*, but he hated to have a ship and not put it to use. Rather than burden another with the command of a mostly-green crew, he had taken the ship himself. "What have we got so far?" He asked.

"Uh, we lost two probes so far, sir, uh, Baron." Ensign Brunneti said.

Lucius quirked an eyebrow, and the newly-made Ensign flushed. "Look, sir, that grid is actually in-atmosphere for the gas giant. The pressures at those levels are significantly higher than our probes can take. The only way we can get anything from there is to go in ourselves."

Lucius stared at the screens. The blue-green gas giant lay at the edge of the Faraday system. Alone of the other twenty-four planets, this one had no moons. The smallest of the gas giants, it still massed twenty or thirty times the planet Faraday. Lucius turned his gaze to Kandergain, who said nothing. "You know what's in there, don't you?"

"Yes, but I'm not going to hold your hand, Lucius."

"Thanks," Lucius grimaced. "Ok, people, we're going in, but we do this by the book." He took a deep breath. "Captain Naevius, I want a fighter screen, but if we start hitting pressures your ships can't take, pull out. Strike-Leader Burbeg, I'd like you on my flank." Lucius paused, deciding on some polite phrasing, "Emperor Romulus, if you would remain in overwatch, prepared to fire on any hostiles we detect—"

"I'll stay out of your way, Baron." The young Emperor said.

Lucius smiled slightly. He thought that some of his sister must have rubbed off on the boy. "Alright, let's see what's down there."

The *Peregrine* descended towards the gas giant. As the ship entered the atmosphere, arcs of lightning surged from the clouds around them. The ship shuddered slightly and Lucius noted several warning lights. "Damage control reports electrical discharges throughout the ship. Mostly in engineering spaces. No injuries."

Lucius nodded. He'd hoped the defense screen would provide some shielding, but apparently not. "All crew, strap into combat positions." The chairs should protect the crew from further strikes.

They descended. "External pressure approaching three hundred atmospheres."

Lucius only nodded. Warships seldom descended into atmosphere. Even so, most ships had some limited atmospheric capabilities. Armor and bulkheads designed to fend off enemy weapons and vacuum worked just fine against crushing pressure in a supergiant.

The ship groaned.

"Nearing the specified grid, Baron."

Lucius nodded, "Anything on scanners?"

"Our mass detector and EM detectors are overwhelmed," Brunnetti snapped, "There's too much interference from the clouds. I'd have to go active."

"Do it."

The active phased radar came up. A second later, a dozen ships came up on the sensors. Lucius let out a breath as he registered the size of three of the contacts. "It's here, it's the Dreyfus fleet."

"Sir, we're getting hit by active sensors!" Brunnetti snapped. "They've got firing solutions!"

"Open a channel!" Lucius snapped. Any kind of fight with those ships would be… disastrous. Especially at this close range. Most of the ships still lay well within minimal safe distance for a warhead in atmosphere. "Attention vessels, this is Baron Lucius Giovanni, I come in peace!"

The pause seemed to last an eternity.

A voice spoke, distorted by interference. They did not send any video, "Your ship has Ghornath technology and you've a Ghornath vessel with you, but a human speaks for you. What nation do you serve?"

Lucius sighed, it was a question he didn't really know how to answer. Best to stick with the truth, "I once served the Nova Roma Empire. Now I defend the Faraday colony. I no longer serve any nation."

"You are a warlord."

"I saved the colony here from the Chxor. I plan to liberate Nova Roma from them as well, and turn it over to the rightful ruler." Lucius answered.

"Then you are a warlord with principles." Lucius caught the sarcasm despite the distortion of the voice. "How did you come here?"

"I met a smuggler named Mason McGann." Lucius said. "And then a woman, a psychic named Kandergain."

The other voice didn't answer.

Lucius let the silence linger for a long time, "Hello?"

"Return to orbit, Baron Lucius Giovanni," a different voice spoke. "We will meet you there."

Lucius looked over at Kandergain. She met his gaze with an emotionless mask.

"Take us back into high orbit."

***

"I knew, intellectually, how big those ships were, but…" Lucius shook his head.

"Very impressive how much effort we put into the destruction of the things we fear," Kandergain said, her face impassive.

Lucius stared at the screen. He felt… lost. The recovery of the Dreyfus Fleet contained too many variables, too many unknowns for him to plan. *I wasn't sure what I expected, but this certainly wasn't it,* he thought. Half formed mental pictures of drifting hulks or plague-filled tombs, mental daydreams of mothballed vessels… All that evaporated as he stared at the screens.

The six super-capital ships of the Dreyfus Fleet formed a battle front. Dozens of cruisers and destroyers, and hundreds of fighters, hung in space, formed up in a battle formation. Thirty or more transport vessels hung behind the formation, some massive, some small. Every ship, fully active, apparently fully crewed.

"We're getting a message for you, Baron," Brunnetti said.

"Put it through."

"To the commander of the vessels who came here, welcome. We've waited a long time. We've trained and prepared over the past eighty years, and we're ready to take up the fight. Please come aboard the *Patriot*, we have much to discuss." The eager voice cut off, and Lucius found himself speechless. He took a deep breath.

"Have a shuttle prepped. Inform Colonel Proscia I'll need a Marine escort." He thought for a moment and then opened another link, "Emperor Romulus, would you—"

"I'll be there, Baron."

"Thank you, Your Highness," Lucius said dryly.

***

Lucius stepped out of the shuttle into a massive chamber. Hundreds of Marines, dressed in the archaic uniforms of Amalgamated Worlds, came to attention.

The sight of who stood at the end of the shuttle ramp to greet him caused Lucius to miss a step. Kandergain shot out a steadying hand. Lucius flashed her a grin of thanks, and immediately turned his attention back to the Admiral awaiting him. He looked, startlingly, similar to the pictures in the history books. In fact, he looked younger than the last pictures, taken as he led his fleet out. *Finally someone who can take charge of this mess.*

He came to the end of the ramp and saluted, "Admiral Dreyfus, I have to admit I'm rather surprised to meet you face-to-face."

"You would be Baron Lucius Giovanni then?" He asked, giving a warm smile, then holding out a hand for a shake. Lucius noted the man had a firm, but not overpowering grip. "Thank God there's finally someone here who can take charge of this mess."

Lucius felt his jaw drop at the echo of his own thoughts, and at the idea that *he* was expected to know what to do. "I… think we need to talk, Admiral."

"Yes, Admiral, we need to discuss the use your fleet is put to, and address many crises that have to be dealt with." The young Emperor spoke, stepping past Lucius to take the venerable Admiral's hand. "I'm Emperor Romulus IV, of the Nova Roma Empire."

Admiral Dreyfus' eyes narrowed slightly, "Yes, I'm certain we have much to discuss." He released the Emperor's hand and nodded in recognition, "Kandergain, I see you've got your finger in things again. I take it that you believe our time has come to surface as well."

Both the Emperor and Lucius turned inquisitive expressions her way.

Kandergain merely smiled mysteriously, "Well, I suppose, seeing as I'm here, and they're here, you could take things that way."

"Ah, how I did miss these stimulating one-sided conversations." Admiral Dreyfus smiled, "But, gentlemen and lady, please step this way."

***

Lucius had a suspicion that he could have landed his shuttle on the briefing room table.

He felt a slight surprise as they stepped around it and then into what had to be Admiral Dreyfus's private quarters. Lucius felt an almost church-like reverence for the room. As he looked around, it seemed much like any decent officer's office. A handful of plaques from former commands, a few pictures of family, a desk, couch, and several comfortable chairs.

Admiral Dreyfus seated himself behind the desk and sighed, "I gather from your near-tumble, and the surprise evident even now, that Kandergain didn't tell you much."

Lucius snorted, taking a seat, "She didn't tell me anything, save to keep an open mind."

"Yes, that *is* like her." Dreyfus said, casting a scowl towards the woman. "In any case, if you haven't guessed, my fleet is fully manned, fully armed, and fully operational. We've used a combination of longevity drugs and hibernation sleep to wait these past eighty years, hiding in the clouds of Sanctuary."

"But... why?" the young Emperor asked. "Why did you hide here? Wasn't your mission to track down the Agathan Fleet?"

Admiral Dreyfus sighed, "Yes... to the knowledge of most of Amalgamated Worlds, our mission involved the destruction of the Agathan Fleet. My orders, the orders of every man and woman in my force, were to find and kill every man, woman, and child who left in that fleet, and to recover the ships or destroy them." He lifted a sheet of paper, and passed it over to Lucius. "I received this from a friend. A short time later, Kandergain contacted me, with a similar story. You can see where this leads."

Lucius glanced over the document. The memo outlined the collapse of Amalgamated Worlds with startling accuracy. The date at the top posted only a month after the departure of the Agathan Fleet. "So... you believed that Amalgamated Worlds lay on the brink of collapse, and you... ran away?" he asked, confused.

"No." Admiral Dreyfus shook his head. "I chose to help lay the groundwork for the survival of the human race." He sighed, "there are a dozen dead civilizations we've found so far. I didn't want humanity to be the next. I hand picked every sailor and Marine in my fleet. When Amalgamated Worlds gathered their families as hostages, I arranged for them to be put on ships. We gathered everything we needed to start, or restart, a civilization." Dreyfus pulled up a hologram on his desk, displaying numbers and data, "We recruited civilian scientists, doctors, teachers, and engineers. Behind the show of a force set on vengeance, we created a force designed to defend humanity."

"And then you hid?" Lucius asked incredulously.

"Yes, we hid. I had no all-seeing glimpse of the future. All I had was the word of a rogue psychic, and a pencil-pusher's analysis. For all I knew, Amalgamated Worlds would survive a thousand years."

"But it collapsed seven years later, instead," Emperor Romulus said.

"Yes, it did. And we waited." The old Admiral let out a long sigh, "A handful of people knew our location, and they knew that when right time came, we could be called on to come forth, to begin rebuilding."

"You didn't have any contact with the outside?" Lucius asked.

"Little. Every now and then someone came. Kandergain dropped in every decade or so." Admiral Dreyfus shrugged, "Mostly we trained, stockpiled weapons and ammunition. The eggheads talked about government and laws. The scientists played with their toys."

"So now, what?" Lucius asked.

"Now, we turn things over to you." Dreyfus answered. "You're the man who found us. You're the man in charge now."

"You don't even know me," Lucius said.

"Trust me," Dreyfus said, "If Kandergain says you're the one... then you're it."

"I—"

"I think we're ranging a little away from the important thing, right now," the Emperor said. "Now that we have the Dreyfus Fleet, we need to use it. Nova Roma is currently under the control of the Chxor. Admiral, you once defended my world from the Wrethe, when they attacked human space almost ninety years ago—"

"We have other issues besides that." Kandergain said.

"My people are dying. Every day we wait thousands—"

"I know exactly how bad it is on Nova Roma right now, trust me." Kandergain's impassivity disappeared, replaced by something dark and angry. "And I know something that everyone else seems to forget. The Chxor are not the main threat. The Balor will exterminate humanity. They will eat or enslave every last man woman and child."

"The Balor aren't on Nova Roma, they aren't butchering my people!"

Kandergain sighed, "No, they're not. Currently, a significant force of them are headed here, though."

Into that silence, Lucius spoke, "The Balor are coming here?"

"Yes."

Lucius stared at her. He realized suddenly that some of the darkness, some of the anger in the psychic woman lay in another emotion.

Kandergain felt fear.

Even in the midst of battle against the Chxor, when the *War Shrike* heaved around them, he hadn't seen fear in her face. Lucius hadn't thought the woman knew *how* to fear.

But she feared the Balor or, at least, feared what they might do.

"How long do we have?" Lucius' voice felt weak.

"Two months, more or less."

"Why even defend this—"

Lucius' head snapped around, "I did not fight a battle to save this system from the Chxor, did not lose many good men in battle, just to abandon it and its people to the Balor." He stared at the boy Emperor, wondering if the time had finally come to sever ties with his home.

He stared at the boy and something told him that the time had not yet come.

But it would soon.

He turned his gaze back to Kandergain, "Can we defeat them?"

"Balor ships are faster than most of this fleet. Also, their weapons outrange even the heaviest gun batteries aboard these ships." She shrugged, "Their missiles are smaller and faster, and carry heavier payloads. The *War Shrike* has more acceleration than anything but their fighters, but one of their battlecruisers carries a heavier armament. All of their ships mount shields, actual shields, not defense screens, that you need to hammer before you can even damage the ship beneath."

Lucius met Dreyfus' eyes. "We're going to need a battle plan."

***

CHAPTER XI

March 3, 2403 Earth Standard Time
Faraday System
(status unknown)

"You promised *what* to the Garu?" Admiral Dreyfus demanded.

"The terms of our original alliance stated that they would receive all of the transport vessels of the Dreyfus Fleet, after we recovered it," Lucius said, massaging his head.

"That's thirty four ships!"

"Thirty seven ships," the Garu spokesman corrected. "Your ammunition ships are transport vessels as well."

"How are we supposed to fight a war without transport ships?" Admiral Dreyfus snapped.

"The Garu people, of course, would be willing to lease some vessels back to you, at a reasonable price, considering the current situation." The Garu leader spoke in a polite tone.

"At the time, I thought that warships would be more important than the logistical chain." Lucius said, with a shrug. "As it is, I still believe so."

"I see." Dreyfus turned his gaze to the Garu leader. "What kind of reasonable price are we talking?"

"We are not unreasonable." The man smiled, and Lucius winced. "We wish duty- and tax-free trade with any world that comes under your protection."

"That seems pretty reasonable..." Dreyfus frowned.

Lucius held up a hand, "Any world?" He asked, eyes narrowing. "You're essentially stating that we'd be blackmailing worlds to open their trade to you. If they didn't, they'd lose our protection."

The Garu man's eyebrows went up in mock surprise, "Why, I do suppose it could be seen that way. Certainly a suspicious government, not... fully appreciative of the benefits of free trade, might come to believe so."

"If you deal tax-free with a dozen worlds, you could undercut the prices of any other merchant." Lucius said, "You'd have a monopoly on trade within a decade."

The Garu man shrugged, "There are many families and clans within the Garu. We would still have competition. A healthy economy requires such."

"I see." Lucius frowned. "We'll talk more on this later. In the meantime, 'recovery' of the Fleet is not yet complete. The crews, their cargoes, and their passengers must still be offloaded."

"Under some interpretations of the law, a ship's cargo—"

"Under my interpretation, Admiral Dreyfus owns those ships and that cargo until they're offloaded." Lucius snapped. "You're already getting far more than you or I planned for, don't get greedy."

The Garu man smirked slightly, and bowed. "Understood, Baron. We will have to discuss the exact terms of the lease at your earliest convenience."

"Agreed." Lucius growled. He waited for the trader to depart, then turned to face Admiral Dreyfus, "How long do you think, for your people to off-load?"

"It'll take time." Dreyfus shrugged, "Families have lived on those ships for eighty years. Most of that for many of them was in hibernation sleep, but even so, they'll have to pack and unpack their private possessions." He frowned, "All of the manufacturing equipment we can offload in a couple weeks. The scientists and their labs… some of that we'll need to build facilities for. Some of those facilities need to be in space or on an uninhabited world, just for safety."

"Some of their projects are dangerous?" Lucius asked.

"Some of those *scientists* are dangerous," Dreyfus shrugged, "I took a couple of them out of mental institutions. One of them…" He chuckled, "Well, he means well, but I honestly feel uncomfortable being in the same *star* system as his experiments."

Lucius winced. "There's plenty of uninhabited systems in the vicinity. If all else fails, there's Alpha Seven at Zeta Tau."

"Yes, I think an out-of-the-way spot is best for some of them."

Lucius spent a moment in thought, "My staff is meeting tonight to discuss the defense of this system. Can you have your—"

"We'll be there, Baron"

***

"We need to talk." Lucius said as he stepped into Kandergain's quarters.

Kandergain, seated in a chair already, gestured to a chair across from her. Lucius had a sneaking suspicion she expected him. "Yes, Lucius, we do need to talk."

Lucius again felt the same sense of bitterness. He clenched his jaw, "Why didn't you tell me that the Dreyfus Fleet lay manned and armed, just waiting?"

She cocked her head, "Do you want the truth?"

Lucius threw his head up, "Of course I want the truth."

"Then here it is, Lucius. You didn't need to know."

"Of course I needed to know!" Hands clenched, Lucius shot to his feet, "I lost one hundred and seventy two people taking this system! I still don't know how many millions of civilians died! All that time, that entire force lay there waiting!"

"Are you done?" She asked, her voice cold.

Lucius let out a short angry breath, forcing himself to calm. He really didn't want to. "Yes. I'm done."

"Then sit." Her sharp words startled him into his chair.

She stared at him for a long while, and Lucius realized she, too, had grown angry. "First, Lucius, the universe doesn't revolve around you." She shook her head, "I didn't know the Chxor came here, I didn't know you fought a retreat against them before you went to Alpha Seven. I'm not omniscient. I couldn't have told you the fleet lay hidden at Sanctuary without knowing that."

"But—"

"Second," She cut over his words, "What good would the fleet have done you? You couldn't have reached it without drawing the Chxor's attention. If it came out of the clouds of Sanctuary to fight, the Chxor would have seen it coming. What would they have done, seeing an overwhelming force bearing down on them?" She demanded.

Lucius knew, he looked away.

"Say it Lucius."

"They would have gassed the entire population, rather than let it fall."

"Exactly." Her icy voice continued, "Third, the success against the Chxor by you made you a hero, Lucius. You saved a planet, you saved the colony of Faraday. I don't think you realize how much that means right now."

"I lost—"

"And third," Kandergain spoke over him again, "The few

million people who died on Faraday are only a drop in the bucket, Lucius." She shook her head, "I've watched billions die, so far, killed systematically by the Chxor and slaughtered by the Balor. I've fought, as hard as I can, to save individual lives, but we're in a war for species survival." She clenched her eyes shut and shook her head, "When it comes to it, I'd have let you lose here at Faraday, I'd have let the entire populace die, if I thought giving you the Dreyfus Fleet would ruin humanity's last chance."

She stood from her chair and went to the window to stare out at the battle-scarred city. "Lucius, the human race is doomed." He could hear the despair in her voice. "We've garnered the attention of two powerful races and neither has any problem slaughtering us to the last babe. This is a war of survival." She let out a long sigh, "Part of what makes you a great leader, Lucius, is your compassion. You care about your people."

She turned to face him, "Right now, you feel used. You feel manipulated. You think I let your people die for no reason." She met his gaze with her chocolate brown eyes, "It's understandable, admirable, even, in a way." She shrugged, "But if you can't realize that I'm doing my best to help you, to help the human race, then I think it's time we go our separate ways."

"I..." Lucius put a hand over his face. "I just want to know *why*. Why have I been manipulated? Why did you tell Dreyfus to hide in the first place... What are you trying to accomplish? What makes you think you can judge things so accurately?"

Kandergain took her chair again in silence, she stared at Lucius for a long time. "Now we get to the hard questions." She closed her eyes, as if she hoped to find inspiration behind her eyelids. "You know what a precognitive is?"

Lucius frowned, "A psychic who can see the future, right?"

She shrugged, "In a manner of speaking. Most can't do much more than catch glimpses of the near future. Some can get fleeting impressions of events to come. Every now and again, there's the occasional precog that can see more than that, sometimes much more."

"So... what, you're a precog too?"

Kandergain snorted with laughter, "Oh, God, no!" She shook her head. "Most precogs are a little crazy—" She scowled at Lucius' sudden smile, "Not a little odd, I really mean a little crazy.

They hear voices from conversations that never happened or might still happen. The future is just as real to some of them as the present."

"So there are people that can see a little into the future. Is one of them whispering in your ear all the time?" Lucius asked, he felt as if she only waited to spring the punch line.

"No." She cocked her head, tossing her blonde ponytail back over her shoulder, "Well, not quite." She shrugged, "There are the occasional precogs who go a long way beyond most. Most of them… when they looked far enough ahead, they saw something that scared the shit out of them."

"The death of humanity?" Lucius asked.

"Or close enough to make no difference." Kandergain shrugged, "When I say occasional, you have to know how rare I'm talking." She closed her eyes, "There are, give or take, fifty billion humans alive right now."

"Okay."

"There's only one precog alive right now that has the abilities I'm describing." She caught his eyes, "And he's… not nearly as accurate as we'd like."

"You're not exactly filling me with confidence here."

"Trust me, try living like this for eighty-six years," she smiled, "And no, before you ask, I'm a little older than that. That's just when I started on this little quest." She suddenly looked tired, "Almost a hundred and fifteen years ago, a man named John Mirra was born."

"Weren't we talking about precogs?"

"He was a precog."

"Why didn't you say so?" Lucius asked.

"I just did," She scowled. "Do you want to tell this story or should I?"

"Go ahead."

"*Thanks*," Kandergain snapped and then let out a deep breath, "As far as the talent of precognition goes, John Mirra went off the chart. As a child, he could see the result of every decision he could ever make, throughout the rest of his life."

"That sounds… impressive." Lucius said, thinking of how useful an Admiral with that ability would be.

"Think terrifying." She responded, "I'd be paralyzed. Most

people would be. I mean, what if you come to a situation with no good choice? What if, no matter what you did, people died? And remember, I said that the more a psychic practices his powers, the more powerful he gets?"

Lucius frowned, "There was a science-fiction book, wasn't there, about a man predicting the future with mathematical calculations—"

"Foundation, yes, I read it. It's long since been disproved, you can't predict random things. It's the butterfly effect: a butterfly flapping its wings in China causes a hurricane in Florida. The thing is: John could."

"You're saying he was omniscient."

She shrugged, "I'm saying that either he had the ability to subconsciously alter random events, everything from dice rolls to the movement of electrons, or he tapped into something big, or else, yes, John Mirra was omniscient."

"So John Mirra tells you—"

"I never met him. When he was twenty five, he gave his life to alter the future."

Lucius winced. "He could see every possible outcome and the only way to change the future was to kill himself? That's..."

"Horrible? Twisted? Yes, it's a tragedy. The good news is: he left clues, puzzles. He left notes in places no one would ever look. Sometimes it's been damned odd." She shook her head. "I once found a note from him in a roll of toilet paper..."

"So, if I understand this right..." Lucius frowned, "An omniscient suicidal riddler left you clues that guide you in making decisions that the survival of the human race depends on?"

"A simplified but relatively accurate statement."

Lucius felt a headache coming on. "Do me a favor, please? Next time I ask 'why' just tell me I don't want to know."

***

"Sir, could I... have a moment of your time?"

Lucius looked up to see Captain Doko in the doorway, "Tony, absolutely, what's the problem?" Lucius felt like a juggler or circus performer at the moment, but anything that brought his longtime friend to him so nervously suggested he should help out at one more task.

"Well, sir..." Captain Doko trailed off. His posture was slumped and his gaze went to the door. Lucius felt his heart sink as he realized just what had brought the other man to his quarters so late at night.

"It's about the Princess?" Lucius asked softly.

Anthony Doko looked up in surprise, but he met Lucius's eyes. "Yes, sir. It is." He took a deep breath. "After... after she helped us to bring down that nasty bunch of pirates.... Well, when it came out as far as who she was... I could resign myself. I knew that low-born trash like me–"

"You aren't trash, Tony. You're worth more than a dozen noblemen, both to me and to the Empire." Lucius interrupted, "And her mother was a commoner just like you."

"But her father was the Emperor," Anthony said. "And that makes the difference." He sighed. "Bastard or not, she's a Princess and I'm..." He shrugged. "So I resigned myself. And then we got the news that the Chxor executed the nobles and the entire Imperial Family." He took a deep breath. "That was hard, especially because I thought she'd have a long life, and maybe, just maybe, I could prove myself, get a knighthood or something."

Lucius shrugged, "You'd have had better chances of that if you'd cut off on your own. Being around me wasn't good for your prospects."

"Sir, I'd rather serve under you than any other officer," Anthony answered. He quirked a bit of a smile, "But I suspect you're right as far as my prospects. I never told you, but I had more than one senior officer pull me aside and warn me that serving with you would slow my career, especially if you gave me good evaluations."

Lucius grimaced, "I can't say I'm surprised."

Anthony finally went over to take a seat. He slumped a bit again. "But all that has changed, yet again. She's alive. She's here." He looked up and a look of agony went over his face. "Lucius, I could take this if she didn't love me back, but we've spoken a dozen times since she arrived here with your sister and the Emperor. There's no question how she feels about me... God, what do I do?"

Lucius walked over and put his hand on the other man's shoulder, "My friend... I don't know. With anyone else, I would say that you should do what makes you happy and damn the consequences. I know that your sense of duty and responsibility pulls you one way and your affection another. I can't make that decision for you, Tony... only you can."

"I know," Anthony took a deep breath. "But I needed to talk with you about it."

"Whatever your choice and whatever *her* choice, I'll back the pair of you," Lucius said. "She saved my life too, you know."

"I know," Anthony responded. He stood. "Thanks for the talk, sir."

***

Lucius never imagined that the shuttle-bay-sized conference table aboard the *Patriot* wouldn't suffice for a meeting.

He had not taken into account his staff, the staff of the Dreyfus Fleet, and the Nova Roma contingent. "This isn't going to work."

"What?" Admiral Dreyfus asked. A dozen captains and commanders looked between the two. Several voices began to speak.

Lucius shook his head. "We need to organize this." He gazed around the table. Thankfully, staff officers, department heads, and ship captains had illuminated titles at each seat around the table. "You, you and you, you're on a committee to organize all of us into one cohesive chain of command, get with Captain Doko over there and talk it out." Anthony Doko took his sudden assignment with a blink and a quick nod.

"You three," Lucius pointed, "Please speak with Captain Naevius regarding fighter organization and specs. We'll need to arm, fly and pilot at least three different types of fighters, and I'll want an integrated fighter doctrine nailed out ASAP." Better to promote all his key personnel, else their experience in current warfare might get drowned by rank. Doubtful with Admiral Dreyfus hand-picking his crews, but even so...

"You three, I need a logistical analysis of munitions, spare parts, and all the engineering essentials. I need to know what we can cross-load, what we can adapt, and what we cannot allow aboard the same vessels," Lucius paused and his eyes narrowed, "Professor Harbach is currently aboard the *War Shrike* overseeing some repairs, but he'll speak with you. He's thoroughly familiar with all aspects of my ship's hardware." He hesitated to saddle any of them with the arrogant 'Jimmy Wiggles,' but… the man did know everything about the equipment.

"Captain Nix, you and… Lieutenant Kelly should get with these two ladies from the Admiral's Intel department. I'm sure you'll have a lot to discuss." Lucius wondered suddenly why all four Intel officers were female. He had a sneaking suspicion that a number of Machiavellian machinations might lay behind those attractive, attentive faces.

"Captain Reese Leone-Giovanni, if you can get with the Admiral's communications heads and hash out common frequencies we can use, that should be the last area of importance."

"Admiral Dreyfus, am I missing any other essential areas that need to be analyzed?" Lucius asked, suddenly realize he'd taken charge without thinking.

The Admiral's mouth twitched, as if he suppressed a wry grin, "No, I believe that the essential areas are covered. I think myself and my second in command are good for the initial briefing."

"Yes…" Lucius looked around at the other expectant faces, "I'll want Captain Kral as a Chxor expert… and Captain Beeson, as the Faraday representative." He saw the young man wince at the title. Lucius silently cursed himself for forgetting the boy's father, also Captain Beeson, killed by the Chxor.

"Emperor Romulus?" Lucius asked, politely. The young man could either bring along much of his entourage, and look a fool, or select a couple important people.

Evidently, the young man figured much the same, "Admiral Mund and I will be sufficient."

"Well, now that that's done?" Kandergain said, from the doorway. "The conference room down the hall is quite sufficient for the eight of us."

Lucius looked over at her, not sure whether she'd read his mind, found some clue, or just logically realized that a mob like this would be a terrible way to cover information quickly.

She smiled at him as he stepped past her, "I am psychic, you know."

Lucius raised an eyebrow, but continued down the corridor.

The much smaller group seated themselves around a table in the other conference room. She moved to stand next to a holographic projector. An image of a sleek, almost organic ship formed in the air next to her. "This, gentlemen, is a Dagger-class destroyer. Any Balor force we face will have at least a dozen of these at its core."

A bar appeared next to her; it showed a number of estimates on its abilities. "Its acceleration is roughly equal to that of the *War Shrike* at around a hundred thirty kilometers per second per second. The maneuverability exceeds that of any human ships, except maybe some of the Republic Forerunner class destroyers. It is encapsulated by an energy field that absorbs enemy kinetic and energy attacks."

Kral the Chxor spoke, "How is this possible? The Chxor scientists have assured many in the military of the impossibility of this feat."

Admiral Dreyfus spoke, though he seemed slightly uncomfortable with the alien. Lucius couldn't blame him, he still felt some uncertainty about Kral's presence. "Some of Amalgamated Worlds scientists got close to duplicating it. They did something similar with the Agathan Fleet, anyway. I know it's possible."

"Something to keep in mind is that a lot of the Balor tech is centuries, perhaps millennia, ahead of our own." Kandergain said. "Their destroyers are the least of our worries, gentlemen, trust me." She took a deep breath, "It mounts one bank of capital-strength weapons, three banks of anti-fighter energy batteries, and between thirty and fifty anti-ship missiles, of either sixty or two hundred megaton equivalence, which can launch in one salvo."

"This is a destroyer?" Emperor Romulus asked incredulously.

She nodded, "It's only a hundred twenty meters long, and has a crew of roughly one hundred Balor."

"What else?" Lucius asked.

"This is a Ravager-class heavy cruiser. It is designed primarily for engaging ships of similar size. Again, one capital-class weapons battery. Additionally two cruiser-class batteries, and heavier anti-fighter batteries." She shrugged, "It has less acceleration, only a hundred kilometers per second squared. Even so, it has heavier shields, heavier armor, and it carries two platoons of... I guess you could call them Marines."

"I see." Admiral Dreyfus said. "How many can we expect?"

"In the force that they'll send... I'd estimate a half dozen of them." She sighed and brought up a swollen, seed-like vessel. The holographic image showed dozens of open ports down its flanks. "This, gentlemen, is a Wrath-class carrier. It is still slower than their cruisers, at sixty KPS squared acceleration. It has heavy shielding, heavier armor, and it carries twelve squadrons of twelve fighters."

"That ship carries a hundred and forty-four fighters?" Lucius asked, "How? It's barely bigger than the *War Shrike*."

"Part of that answer is that the ship is designed purely as a carrier. The other part..." She shrugged, bringing up another hologram. "This is the Bane Sidhe fighter. It's half the size of one of Admiral Dreyfus' Raptor fighters, a third the size of one of your Harassers. It carries a full payload of anti-ship and anti-fighter missiles, and mounts a powerful close-in energy weapon."

The Emperor spoke, his voice calm. "Once again, I say, why defend this system? We have the transport capacity now to evacuate the colony. We could seize Nova Roma from the Chxor with the aid of the Dreyfus Fleet, we could evacuate the entire populace there. The Balor would arrive to find nothing to fight."

Lucius cleared his throat, "I... actually brought that idea up to some of the civilians. Most of them would rather stand and fight than leave."

"So we force them to go," the Emperor shrugged. "It's not like it isn't for their own good."

"We're entering dangerous territory there, your Highness," Admiral Mund rasped. "How are they going to see it? We'd be abandoning their world to save yours. That's not going to win anyone any points with them. They've just finished an insurgency against the Chxor. Do you think they'd hesitate to fight one against another 'oppressor,' however well intentioned?"

Kandergain let the young man stew on that idea before speaking herself, "It doesn't matter, anyway, the Balor have agents sewn throughout most of the Chxor Empire by now. As soon as we arrived at Nova Roma, they would alter course."

She shrugged, "Kral, how would the Chxor respond to the resurgence of the Nova Roma Empire, with a new, more powerful fleet?"

The Chxor shrugged, "They would amass whatever forces necessary to defeat such a threat. Even the dumbest Chxor bureaucrat knows that the Nova Roma Empire would immediately seek to expand again and all Chxor worlds and colonies would be at risk."

The words had all the more effect on the young Emperor from the obvious fact that Kral had spoken truthfully.

"Alright, then. We can't run." Lucius said into that pregnant silence. "Which means we're back to fighting. What else do they have?"

"Probably, you'll only face one carrier. The Balor fleets typically form around one carrier, and one battlecruiser. Occasionally, they have a super-dreadnought." She pulled up an image of a large warship, "This is their battlecruiser, Terror-class. Very heavy shields, very heavy armor, just as fast as the *War Shrike*. It carries twelve fighters, a company of their warrior drones and shuttles to land them and their forces." She shrugged, "Three capital-class energy batteries and one super-capital energy battery."

"Super-capital?" Lucius asked.

"Heavy tachyon cannon, faster than light particle beam. The battery mounts four of them in a bank with a hundred eighty degree arc of fire." Kandergain shrugged. "One of those beams could gut a cruiser."

Lucius nodded, even as he thought dark thoughts.

"They only have two other classes of combative ships. That includes the Leviathan super-dreadnought class, roughly the size of the *Emperor Romulus*. If one of those shows up, start thinking about last stands." She shrugged. "There's also a ship we've called *Colossus*. It's bigger than the *Patriot*, far more heavily armed, and frankly, it's only been seen with several Leviathans in escort."

"I think we're heading into 'we're dead if it happens' territory." Lucius said. "Let's keep in mind the... worst case scenarios, but focus on what we can handle." He rubbed his face, he suddenly felt old. "What are their tactics?"

"If you're hoping they cripple themselves like the Chxor do, without using screening forces, you're hoping in vain." Kandergain said. "They use their destroyers to scout ahead. Ambushing them is nearly impossible."

"Sensors can be fooled," Admiral Mund said. "Screens can be

avoided. A ship setting silent—"

"Is a ship that will die before it can power up." Kandergain said. "The Balor don't rely just on normal sensors, they also have mechanical augmentations for their psychic abilities. It is damn near impossible to hide from them. I might, *might*, be able to hide a ship the size of the *War Shrike*." She shook her head. "It takes a psychic to screen from them and that still leaves their normal sensors."

"So our tactics against the Chxor won't work." Lucius shrugged. "We'll think of something. Their weapons range, is it comparable?"

She looked down at the data, "I'm not a weapons tech," she apologized. "Their capital and super-capital batteries range twenty four thousand kilometers maximum effective range. I can say for certain they fire with extreme accuracy."

Lucius looked over at Dreyfus, "The Nova Roma ships use Ghornath exotic particle beams. Max range is twenty thousand klicks."

Dreyfus winced, "Then in that respect, you've got my own vessels beat. Our guns are heavier, I'll wager that, but they only effectively range fifteen thousand." He shrugged, "To be honest, all of those ships will be able to run rings around my fleet."

"They can outmaneuver us, out range us, and have a sensor sphere we can't fool." Lucius said. "They've got heavy shields, swarms of high-tech fighters, and amazing missiles." He looked around the gathered group, "So... how do we beat them?"

"That's the big question," Kandergain said, her voice weary. "Remember what I told you about the extinction of the human race?"

Lucius nodded.

"Well... best guess from the people in the know, if you fail here, against this attack, then there's no stopping it." Kandergain said.

"Oh," Lucius said, "Good... no pressure, then."

***

"So, you've got your end of the agreement, am I free to go now?" Mason McGann stood in the doorway.

Lucius looked up, "Honestly, I figured you'd have come

earlier." He shrugged, "I've no reason not to allow the smuggler Mason McGann to go his way."

Mason's eyes narrowed, "I don't know that I like the way you said that."

"I'm interested in another ship." Lucius said. "Perhaps you might know who I could talk to about it."

"Well... I know some people—"

"It's a very specific ship. Infamous, well known, and instantly recognizable." Lucius smiled slightly, "The pirate ship *Revenge*, she's a battlecruiser, as I remember."

Mason stiffened, "I wouldn't know about that. I try to avoid pirates."

"Hmmm, true." Lucius raised his glass, looking into its depths for a moment. "I told you I fought the *Revenge*, once, right?"

"I think you mentioned you met it at Trinity."

Lucius nodded, "I can't remember how long Tommy King and I hunted each other in that star system. A couple of weeks, at least." Lucius shook his head, putting his glass aside. "I do know that in the end, I couldn't tell you who won."

"Some might count it a victory." Mason said neutrally.

"Some might," Lucius shrugged, "At the time, I felt only frustration that the infamous pirate got away. God knows, he caused enough misery and death in his time. I thought then, that finally I could put an end to that." Lucius sighed again, "Did I ever tell you I actually met Tommy King? When Admiral Fontaine parlayed with him at Kestrel, I was the junior officer in the delegation."

"Oh really?" Mason asked. Lucius saw one hand go down to clutch at wooden prayer beads hanging from his belt.

"Yes. I pride myself in my ability to remember faces. I'll remember that one for a long time." Lucius sighed, "Maybe truth lies in the rumors of Tommy King's death. Maybe the hate that drove him finally consumed him."

Mason relaxed slightly, "Hate's a powerful thing."

"Or maybe, somehow, he's alive, working at redeeming himself. Maybe he's putting his skills to use doing something good." Lucius said.

"That's... not beyond the realm of possibility." The smuggler said.

"Do you think so many years of villainy can be forgiven?" Lucius asked.

"Never." The smuggler spoke with instant sincerity.

"Hm." Lucius said. "Yesterday, I received a letter of resignation from an officer I wouldn't have expected it from."

"Oh?"

"Yes, Lieutenant Kelly has requested I give her permission to leave." Lucius lifted the paper out of his desk, looking at it, "She said she didn't think she could fight the Chxor, not without succumbing to her hatred."

Mason blinked at that, "Did she say what she planned to do?"

Lucius gave a half smile, "I think she mentioned signing on with a freighter pilot she knew. I told her I understood, and wished her my best."

"Thank you." Mason barely breathed the words. He turned to leave.

"One last thing, Mason."

The smuggler turned, slowly, as if he feared the loss of a reprieve.

"Tommy King and his evils need to stay dead." Lucius stared at the man across from him.

"Yes, they do." Mason nodded. At the doorway, he paused, "It was really you and the *War Shrike* at Trinity?" He asked.

Lucius nodded slowly.

Mason gave a small grin, "Those were seventeen educating days, Baron."

Lucius smiled slightly as the door closed.

***

Lucius stared at the amber liquid in his glass and sighed.

He wondered how the fierce woman who raised him would have taken the release of her mother's killer. He knew her feelings on capital punishment, shared them really. He also knew she had possessed a strong belief in redemption. It might have sprung from her belief in God, or maybe from her telepathy that let her see the sincerity of a person's thoughts.

Lucius didn't possess that ability. He had only his own intellect and gut instinct to go by.

He hoped he hadn't misjudged Mason McGann.

Lucius sighed and set the glass aside. The upcoming problems of the Balor attack, of the inevitable confrontation with the Chxor, and the possible depredations of the pirate Tommy King should have bothered him more than they did.

He couldn't focus on those, not any more. A vortex of problems he'd thought long past swept through his mind. What did Lucretta Mannetti know about his father that he didn't? Had his father, long thought the traitor—even by his own son—been motivated by ambition or by something else?

Lucius wondered about that, and if he could have prevented the crumble of the Nova Roma Empire if he had turned a blind eye to the Mannetti Coup. Had he doomed millions to their deaths, in a struggle against the Chxor... in a war that the right leaders could have won?

God knows I've enough deaths on my conscience, he thought mordantly. His command of the *War Shrike* had left many ghosts to haunt him at night. His only defense, the only thing that let him sleep, was the knowledge that he'd always done his best. He'd never sacrificed his people like pawns in chess. *Is that enough?* He wasn't sure anymore.

At least he'd got Reese back alive and reunited with Alanis. He doubted Reese had forgiven his decision not to return to Nova Roma. He doubted the man would ever forget it or allow Lucius to do so. Even so, the sight of the affection and love they shared, gave Lucius some hope for the future.

He envied them that, in a way. He felt selfish for it, but he saw what his little sister and her husband had and wished, somehow, he'd been so blessed.

Granted, a number of Faraday's well-to-do had begun to introduce their daughters. A particularly ambitious widow had cornered him at the last government meeting he attended.

That kind of arranged marriage made him feel physically ill. The same situation prevented his grandmother from marriage to the man she loved. It made his father a bastard, and possibly set into motion the collapse of the Empire.

Lucius knew the pressures of nobility. He understood the pressures Emperor Romulus I faced. That didn't mean he agreed with the actions the old man took. Nor could he forgive him for the consequences. *One more reason for me to avoid the dynasty everyone seems set on me creating*, he thought. Many people had the capabilities to do as good, if not better, a job. By accident as much as skill, Lucius led them. That authority and responsibility he would gladly forsake. He thought of a cottage on Nova Roma, a small plot of land, a beautiful wife...

For a moment, he could almost see her, as she looked back at him from the nebulous future. Her chocolate eyes and blonde hair, pulled back in a ponytail...

Lucius shook his head and pushed the daydream away. He had recognized the infatuation he had. The idea was so preposterous as to be comical. If his own age wasn't a factor then her own certainly came into account.

Lucius grunted to himself and stood. He poured the rest of his drink down the sink. It did no good for him to drink when he already felt depressed; it only made him worse.

Better to focus on the things he could do. Better for him to keep his mind on the problems he could face. Loneliness wouldn't kill him, nor would it hurt him to smother a childish infatuation. He decided it better to focus on other issues, rather than give into foolish daydreams.

Lucius knew from experience it hurt less in the long run.

***

CHAPTER XII

March 15, 2403 Earth Standard Time
Faraday System
(status unknown)

The conference room with the shuttle-pad-sized table had not changed. The people around it had. Their faces held purpose, their murmured side conversations held confidence.

Lucius hoped it would be enough.

He welcomed the change, but after Kandergain's information, and after reading over the specifics himself, he wondered if all their preparations represented the height of folly.

"Alright people, we've got a little under two months to prepare, what will we have?" Captain Franks, Admiral Dreyfus's Chief of Staff, spoke. Lucius privately believed the man too tightly wound. If he could choreograph a meeting this size, Lucius supposed he deserved some leeway in his eccentricities.

"Starting with the Fleet, we've got five Crusaders and the *Patriot*. They each can launch five hundred and twenty eight of our Raptor fighter-bombers, and carry forty-four parasite Partisan-class frigates. We've got a screen of forty-eight destroyers of four different classes. Another twenty-four light cruisers, sixteen heavy cruisers, and eight of the Nagyr-class battlecruisers make up our rapid forces." Captain Cruz said, her voice bland.

Anthony Doko spoke next, "Recently captured, we have three Chxor five-class dreadnoughts. They're slower than everything except the super-capitals, so they'll probably work best in concert with them. We have two Desperado-class battleships, for those who don't know... think in terms of scaled-up battlecruisers." He shrugged, "Then there's the *Gebneyr*, she's a Danak-class Ghornath battlecruiser, currently on an extended loan to us."

Lucius smiled slightly, he certainly hoped Strike Leader Maygar didn't call in that loan any time soon. Then again, given the mystery of his departure, Lucius wasn't really sure that he wanted to know what payment the Ghornath would want... and how much it might cost Lucius.

Captain Doko continued, "Additionally we have one converted fighter carrier, ten captured ten-class Chxor cruisers, and one

Republic Independence-class cruiser." He paused, "All told, we have forty-eight Harasser fighter-bombers, and have the facilities and pilots to prepare another two squadrons of six which can be planet-based. We're short on trained personnel, especially for the newly captured ships."

Admiral David Mund spoke for the Nova Roma forces assembled. "We've got the *Emperor Romulus*, the first and only of the Imperial-class super-dreadnoughts. Along with it, we've four Hammer-class heavy cruisers, three Patrol-class light cruisers, seven Knight-class destroyers, and a single Prime-class carrier. We've room for fifty-four fighters, though we only have two squadrons of fighters." He shrugged, "All of our ships are short on trained personnel, some of our ships still require significant maintenance work."

The silence lasted a short time. Most of the gathered officers looked over the ship specs for vessels they had never encountered before.

Captain Naevius spoke into the silence, "The majority of fighters we'll have are the Raptors. They have a smaller payload than the Harassers, but they're lighter and more maneuverable as well. We have one squadron of Interceptors, captured from Admiral Mannetti, which are roughly similar to the Raptors, though with inferior avionics, sensors, and a smaller maneuverabily advantage compared to Harassers. Raptor and Harasser doctrine have a few differences. This is mainly because fighter support has grown more important over the past eighty years, especially because so few places have the shipyards for capital ships."

He shrugged, "We've plenty of volunteers from Faraday for pilot slots. Which class of fighter we stick with depends on what type of fight we face long term. Probably a decision for someone higher than me to decide. Either way, we've set it up so we can coordinate our fighter elements as necessary."

Captain Franks prompted, "Logistics?"

Commander Magnani gave a poisonous smile, "Yes, well, I think we'll need some more time to really organize things."

Admiral Dreyfus raised an eyebrow. "You've had several days, all I need are preliminary estimates."

She grimaced, "Yes, sir." She took a deep breath, "At this time, we've stockpiled well over five million metric tons of Mark V missiles and Mark II interceptor missiles. Unfortunately, the missile racks and tube bores are different between our own ships and our... allies." She made a moue of distaste. "I really don't see any way we can equip them."

Lucius coughed slightly, "Your Mark V missiles mount hundred megaton antimatter warheads, correct?"

"Yes."

"We're using sixty megaton fusion warheads." Lucius said, frowning. "I think the difference in firepower is significant enough that it merits some looking into modification."

"Well, we could alter individual missiles, but keeping track of which missiles are modified, and then making sure the right missiles go to the right ships, that's going to be an awful lot of work." Commander Magnani said.

Lucius looked between her and Admiral Dreyfus. He wondered if this were some sort of joke. The Admiral looked like he'd swallowed a frog. "Commander Magnani, your people will begin on the modifications immediately."

"But, Admiral—"

"We'll talk about this later." Admiral Dreyfus nodded to Captain Franks.

"Personnel and maintenance issues will be a significant factor." Captain Heshim said. The swarthy captain scowled slightly. "Honestly, the Chxor dreadnoughts are the biggest issue. Frankly, they're crap. They're obviously designed for mass production, and the builders cut a lot of corners. They're also very manpower intensive to operate at full capacity. We can get all three up in two months, but it'll take a lot of our attention away from other repairs."

Lucius nodded, "For now, focus on other repairs. The Chxor ships don't fit well in any formation."

Captain Franks spoke again, "That covers the important material for today, gentlemen."

The group rose, and most of the officers filed out. Lucius waited for the room to clear somewhat and then signaled Kral to approach. "Were you able to send the message?"

The Chxor nodded slowly. "It was received. I do not know what the response will be, if there will be any."

Lucius nodded. He figured it would require significant trauma for the Chxor Empire to fragment. He hoped he'd added a bit more tension to it, however. "Thank you. Have you visited the prisoners from Faraday yet?"

The Chxor shrugged. "I have spoken with some of them. Some show reception to the offer of positions in your new empire. Some prefer the option of the penal colony on this system's ice moon."

"A polite way of saying it will be a cold day in hell." Admiral Dreyfus said from nearby.

The Chxor nodded, "Perhaps."

Lucius snorted, "Thank you Captain Kral. Tell me when you feel that you can vouch for any who wish to join us truthfully."

The Chxor recognized a dismissal, "I will do so, Baron."

"What was that about?" Kandergain asked from behind him.

Lucius turned, startled, she hadn't said a word through the entire meeting. He'd almost forgotten she'd attended. "The Chxor control their population through limits on reproduction. It requires service to the Empire to produce offspring. The Iodans cracked their biology. I'm offering them a way to cheat the system. Kral tried to contact someone to spread the secret."

"For what?" Kandergain asked. "I imagine you'll get some to betray—"

"No cost." Lucius smiled. "I'm giving it to them for free."

"That's... very devious." Kandergain frowned in thought. "That could have a lot of unpredictable results."

Lucius shrugged, "True, but I think an important one is to show the Chxor just how wrong they are in their philosophy. Their society is artificial and hypocritical. I can't imagine them particularly liking their noses rubbed in that."

She shrugged, "Your call. I was wondering if either of you have any viable plans."

Lucius looked at Admiral Dreyfus. "Why don't we discuss that in the Admiral's office."

Dreyfus gestured them ahead of him and they stepped into his office. Lucius took a seat and sighed slightly, "Honestly, I'm seeing only a few options. The main one, and the one with most chances of success, is to fight our way close and engage the enemy at close range." He shrugged, "How we do that is debatable."

Admiral Dreyfus spoke, "We could push their screen back with our faster elements, give them less time to react. Granted, even so, we'll face a pounding as we close, especially with their higher accelerations and greater range."

"We can build up speed and make high velocity passes." Lucius shrugged, "Provided they don't alter course to avoid us, that's an option."

Kandergain looked between them, "I don't have to be psychic to realize you don't like either option."

"No," Lucius said, "We don't like either option. Both plans rely on the Balor allowing us to do something they won't want us to do."

"Either way, we'll have to run a gauntlet of missiles, fighters, and enemy fire before we can close," Admiral Dreyfus growled. "It's the height of irony that the stockpile of advanced warships we put in reserve aren't advanced enough."

"I... might be able to help you with that." Kandergain spoke almost reluctantly.

"What, you can lead me to the Agathan Fleet now?" Lucius joked.

Kandergain didn't say anything.

Lucius blinked at her, "Wait a second, do you know the location of the Agathan Fleet?"

"I can't help you with that," Kandergain said. "But I can put you in touch with a couple people who have advanced ships—and maybe—the desire to help you fight the Balor."

"Who would these philanthropists be?" Lucius asked.

"One of them is a Shadow Lord," Kandergain said.

"That doesn't exactly fill me with confidence." Lucius said. "I think I'd be safer asking Thomas Kaid to tea."

"I didn't say I was eager to seek their help," Kandergain said. "I've fought the Shadow Lords since before you were born." She shrugged, "And I didn't say she was my first option. I know someone else who might be able to help, if he can."

"And who is he?" Admiral Dreyfus asked.

"He's the most powerful psychic I know and he's been fighting the Balor for a long time now. He knows more about fighting them than anyone else," She shrugged, "I honestly don't know if he can pull any ships free." She caught Lucius' eyes, "There's also the whole issue of what I told you about before."

"The ah… timing issues?" Lucius asked.

She nodded.

"So you can take representatives to meet with him, and if that doesn't work, then with the humanitarian Shadow Lord?" Admiral Dreyfus asked.

"No." She sighed, "The man I talked about won't leave at the summons of an emissary or diplomat. He'll want to meet Lucius in person. And the Shadow Lord… she'd take anything less as an insult." Something in the tone of her voice suggested that such a perceived insult would only make things worse.

Come to think of it, Lucius thought, *I've never heard of anyone who has insulted one of the Shadow Lords and survived.*

"That's out of the question," Dreyfus said, "We can't spare a ship and we definitely can't spare him for any period of time—"

"I'll go." Lucius said. He rubbed his face, then turned to Admiral Dreyfus, "We can't spare a warship, I agree, but she's got her scout. And as for me… I lack the experience to be making a lot of the calls. For god's sake, you've got well over a century in uniform!"

Dreyfus sagged, "And I feel every year of it!" He shook his head, "Trust me, Lucius, you underestimate yourself."

Lucius looked to Kandergain, "How long will this take?"

"With me piloting, we can reach my friend in a couple days. It might take a little longer to track down the Shadow Lord I'm thinking of and return." Kandergain shrugged and a look of worry flashed over her face *"If* we return."

"You're dead set on this?" Admiral Dreyfus asked.

"Yes." Lucius said. "It sounds like our best chance to change the equation."

The other man sighed. "I know for a fact that a commander leaving in the middle of battle preparations isn't a good thing. I'll trust your judgment though." He took a deep breath, "Before you go, however, there are some things you have to do."

Lucius raised an eyebrow, "What's that?"

"First off, you need to hammer the civilians into forming a government and adopting a constitution, or contract, or whatever the hell they want to call it." Admiral Dreyfus said. "Second, you need to accept overall command." He raised a hand, "Everyone has heard your arguments, and when it comes down to it, no one really cares. Anyone who wants the job *shouldn't* have it, that's a given. This whole thing is your brainchild. Every human left knows someone needs to take a stand, to fight for Humanity itself, and you're the only one to do so."

"Fighting to defend one colony—"

"Please, Lucius, I've listened to the stories of your men, the ones who served with you before Faraday. I've heard enough to judge you've a better soul than most. Take the position. Take command, now or I guarantee whoever does will have a civil war in ten years."

Lucius looked away, but Kandergain caught his eyes, "You're the best for the job, Lucius."

Lucius sighed and closed his eyes. When he spoke, it seemed to take all of his determination to force the words out. Yet, he knew he would abide by them... no matter what it cost him. "Okay, I'll do it. God knows how I'll manage, but I'll do it."

"Thank you." Dreyfus said. "Last, we need to deal with Emperor Romulus."

Lucius frowned, "What's that supposed to mean?"

"He doesn't like that you haven't returned to Nova Roma. He doesn't trust you any more and he has tried to pressure me, a lot, to take this fleet there, now."

"I thought our arguments about the Chxor—"

"Have only made him rethink means of attack. He's already assembled a guerrilla strike force you know? They've got a lot of recruits from former insurgents of Faraday."

"I hadn't heard." Lucius said. He realized he'd focused too much on other issues.

"You have to reach some kind of agreement with him, as soon as possible, before he decides to take matters into his own hands."

"I don't like the sound of that." Lucius admitted.

"I didn't think you would. Right now, I know, he's had a lot of his people in and around the captured Chxor dreadnoughts and cruisers. I'm not sure what his goals are there..."

"I can think of a few unpleasant ideas," Lucius said. "I'll have a talk with him, and with Admiral Mund."

Admiral Dreyfus nodded. "Thank you. Now, since you seem ready to shoulder me with the majority of the work regarding preparations for this battle, I think you'll need to excuse me." The man shook his head as Lucius stood, "Meeting with a Shadow Lord, really? Some people will do *anything* to get out of work."

***

Lucius' first stop after the meeting was a secure com where he could contact Kate Bueller. "What's the status of the interim government?"

She smiled and Lucius realized immediately that he had been set up. "Why, Baron, I'm glad you asked." She chuckled at his sour expression, "I can't imagine why you might suddenly have taken an interest in such a minor matter. Did something come up? Perhaps a discussion with a certain military man? Did he wax eloquent on the necessity of a strong leader?"

"Okay," he growled, "I repeat, what's the status—"

"Oh, *fine*, don't let me gloat." She sighed, "Right now, we've got three types of people at these meetings. The first group are the reformers. They're in the majority, since they saw how bad things went earlier. Then we've got the remnants of the conservative party, who want a return to the status quo. The third group is the ambitious people who want cushy jobs for themselves and their families."

"Can we just hang those other two groups?" Lucius asked.

"Just say the word, Baron." Her words were light... but something in her voice suggested that she wouldn't mind the opportunity, if it came up.

Lucius shook his head, "What happened to the elections? I thought you organized a mass vote?"

"We tried that. We had ninety three proposed constitutions, thirty seven proposed contracts, fifty three proposed—"

"I get it." Lucius said. "So now you've got a group of politicians hammering over a compromise?"

"Yes. And it's going painfully slow, there's a lot of horse trading, and we're getting a system that's going to be extremely flawed."

"Great," Lucius sighed, "What do you want me to do?"

"Show up, smile at the right people, and when the time comes for the popular vote, endorse the people responsible." Kate shrugged, "Essentially, the only important thing I need from you is a decision."

"What would that be?" Lucius all but growled.

"Are you going to be in this for the long term?" She asked, her face suddenly serious. "Will you pledge yourself to the fate of this world and to any others you liberate?"

Lucius swallowed. He felt suddenly self conscious. He realized how selfish he'd been when he saw the fear in her eyes. If even Kate, hardened politician and practical through and through feared he'd abandon Faraday, how must all the others feel? "I will, for as long as there's a need."

"Good." She took a deep breath. "We'll go with my proposal then."

"Your proposal?" Lucius asked.

"With your support, we won't need the compromises and horse-trading. I can get this one pushed through in… oh, say a week." She smiled at his expression. "You don't quite realize the effect you've got here. You're kind of like a mixture between George Washington and Dwight Eisenhower with most of the people down here."

Lucius frowned, "George Washington didn't really know tactics very well, and Eisenhower—"

"They were both military figures who became Presidents of the United States." Kate said. "And both of them had a huge base of popular support because they did what other people said was impossible. That's the important thing and that's the thing that's going to hold this thing together."

"What exactly is 'this thing'?" Lucius asked.

"It's a representative democracy." Kate shrugged, "It'll have a built-in non-elected legislative branch made up of successful people in various areas, a meritocracy of sorts, as well as an elected lower house with over-turning powers. It'll have a separate judicial branch, partially selected by vote, and partially by the executive branch."

"Executive branch?" Lucius asked.

"That's where you come in." Kate shrugged, "Most democracies don't have the… speed to react to rapid changes, such as a war or a catastrophe. The other problem is many develop a short-term focus, an election-cycle memory where…" Lucius' eyes had begun to glaze over and he cleared his throat. She shook her head with a bemused smile, "Anyway, I'm going to try to short-circuit that by appointing a monarch."

"Wait!" Lucius shook his head, "I'm not going to be a king!"

"Oh, no, far too pretentious... for the time being." She shrugged, "Right now, you'll retain your current title, though I've left provisions for you to be 'promoted' should the populous feel your rank not equivalent to the size of the realm."

"You're kidding."

"Not at all."

Lucius winced, "This is *not* what I expected."

"Of course it isn't, then again, that's probably for the best." Kate laughed, "I haven't even gotten near the enfranchisement of voters and the bill of rights. I'll say this, I've done my best to neuter the government regarding the rights of the people." She smiled, "I've had my best weasels, one of them your favorite lawyer, do his best to find loopholes for the government to follow. Short of actually breaking the system, or a very long-term subversion, I think I've protected the people from the government." She paused, "Then again, I've had a few thousand years of governments to plagiarize from."

Lucius sighed, "Fine, send me a copy—"

"Oh, no, I'm not going to let an amateur muddle with it." Kate snapped. "You may be in charge, but you're no more going to muck with it than any of these wanna-be's at this interim government. Most of them will find themselves out on their asses anyway once this gets ratified by a popular vote."

"You expect me to back a constitution I haven't even read?" Lucius asked incredulously.

"Lucius, you know me, would I do any less than the best?"

"No, but everyone makes—"

"If you finish that, I'll make sure your title is '*Princess.*'" Kate snapped.

"Ah." Lucius cleared his throat. "And what exactly, is your position going to be?"

"I have no idea. Either I'll try for an upper house seat, or I'll run for office with the other schlubs," She shook her head and Lucius saw with surprise that her blonde hair had gray streaks in it, "Maybe I'll take a break for a few years. God knows, I've had a busy year with you."

Lucius nodded in response. Part of him wondered at how the

stress had affected her. She'd seemed so energetic when he first arrived at Faraday, but now he noticed the weariness in her posture and the exhaustion behind her eyes. "When do you want me?"

She frowned, "Today's what, March fifteenth?" She cocked her head in thought. "Show up tomorrow morning for my presentation. I guarantee I'll have the current constitution thrown out before lunch and my own proposal ratified before dinner." She tapped her teeth. "Give me a couple of speeches on the twenty eighth, and then... hmmm. I think I can push for ratification by the second of April.

"Not the first?" Lucius smiled.

"No. April Fools Day is *not* the day to ratify a constitution. I can just foresee the legal implications." She shook her head. "The vote will be on the second."

"Good. I'll be departing on the third then."

"You... but... *what*???"

"I've got some important business to attend to." Lucius said. "It shouldn't take more than a week, maybe two. I assure you it is vital to the survival of the human race, though I can't say much more than that." He shrugged, "I'll be out of contact the entire time, I'm afraid."

It was several minutes before Kate could speak. When she did, she glared, "You're really batting for that *Princess* title, aren't you?"

***

Private Frank Lopez snapped to attention as the door to the corridor opened. He felt a nervous tremble as he recognized the officer's face. "Good morning, sir!" He mentally cataloged his uniform and he really hoped he hadn't scuffed his boot's shine.

"Good morning, Private, how are the prisoners?"

Lopez grimaced, "Some of them are... disturbing. I do my best to just ignore what they say, as per the standing orders, sir."

"Don't let them get to you, Lopez." The officer sighed, "Go ahead and open it up, I've some questions to ask Admiral Mannetti."

Lopez frowned, "Shouldn't I wait for the Sergeant of the Guard, sir?" On the standing orders, it had said that the prisoner's door was to remain locked unless an officer and the NCO of the Guard were present.

"Private, I've dealt with prisoners worse than this before. Do you know how long I've served with Baron Giovanni?"

"Sorry, sir, right away." Lopez turned around and hunched over to fumble with the lock. As the door opened with a click, he heard the snap of the friction release of a holstered pistol.

Lopez straightened up, just as the man he had trusted put two bullets in the back of his head. The officer stepped over the body and the spreading pool of blood and into the cell block. He walked down the corridor to the cell he wanted. He typed in the code to open the lock. It had been simple enough for him to get those, even if he had no direct authority over the prison.

"Ah, darling, so *glad* you could make it. I'd wondered if you… rethought our previous relationship," Lady Kale stood from her cot and strolled over to stand before him.

The officer gritted his teeth, "I just killed five good men to get you out of here."

She stroked one finger down the side of his face, "Yes…and I've killed a lot more to preserve our little secret." She brushed past him and strode past the other cells. She paused over the corpse of the guard as she lifted his sidearm free, "Pity… he was such a *cute* boy."

***

"Hello, Baron." The young Emperor greeted him with a politely bland face.

"Your Highness." Lucius bowed politely.

"I hear you've entered politics."

Lucius winced, "I had my arm bent, but I finally agreed."

"I'm sure." The Emperor didn't hide his bitterness.

Lucius sighed. "I think we need to discuss the future, your Highness."

The young man clenched his jaw, "Are you now deigning to tell me my place in the universe? Now do you finally acquiesce to lend me the aid to save our home world?"

Lucius looked over to Admiral Mund for support. The old man shrugged. Lucius spoke slowly, "Your Highness, it comes down to this… I can't fight multiple wars at a time. Tactically, we can smash the Chxor at Nova Roma. Strategically… if we take it, we're screwed."

Lucius went to the holograph stand and brought up a map of space. "The Chxor have mastery of logistics and general strategy. They invested every system around Nova Roma before they took it. We'd have a month-long journey to the nearest inhabitable system we could use as a base. Once we took the planet, we would face waves of succeeding forces deployed from every system in vicinity to Nova Roma. The Chxor could coordinate those forces, with a little bit of effort on their part, we could face as many as a hundred dreadnoughts at a time. That's just their available forces, they could mass a much larger force given a couple months to prepare."

The Emperor grimaced, "So... what? We wait, while they butcher the populace of Nova Roma? Do I set here in exile while my people, *your* people, die in the millions?"

"Yes." Lucius said and for once he didn't try to hide the anguish he felt. "Right now, I do think we can launch some raids on the nearby systems, probably draw some Chxor forces away from Nova Roma. That might make things easier on the population." Lucius shrugged, "If I knew a way to make things better for them, I'd do it, I swear." He met the young man's dark eyes and tried to make him see his sincerity.

The Emperor of Nova Roma stared at him for a long moment in silence. His face went from angry to thoughtful. Finally, when he spoke, his voice was calmer, "So what are you suggesting?"

"Right now?" Lucius sighed, "I'll have to discuss it with Admiral Dreyfus, but I think we've got time to launch a raid, maybe two before we face the Balor. I think blooding our pilots would be good, if nothing else."

"I think a raid by the *War Shrike*, the *Peregrine*, with some battlecruiser and fighter support could do a lot of damage, and certainly cause the Chxor some confusion." Admiral Mund said. "I can think of a couple of targets that might relieve pressure on Nova Roma."

Lucius nodded, "God knows, I've longed for another battleship to work with the *War Shrike* for years and with a proper escort..."

The Emperor frowned, "What then?"

"Then we'll defend this system from the Balor." Lucius shrugged, "Kandergain says, if we can stop this onslaught, the

Balor are likely to leave us alone for the time being." Lucius didn't mention the origins of that belief. He believed in God, he just didn't want to think a suicidal omniscient precognitive might *be* God.

"Oh, of course *you* trust Kandergain," the Emperor snapped.

"What does that mean?" Lucius asked levelly.

"She's a *psychic*, Baron. It wasn't all that long ago that psychics were universally hated. It wasn't until they were nearly wiped out by the Plagues that—"

"My grandmother was a psychic, and she died in the Plagues." Lucius said, and he kept his voice level.

"Yes, and Kandergain isn't your grandmother. We don't know we can trust her. She's got her own agenda, and that agenda doesn't include Nova Roma." The younger man rubbed his face, "Don't you see? She has influenced your mind against me this entire time!"

Lucius shook his head, "I've thought a lot of this through before I ever met her, your Highness. Our best options…"

"We'll go with your plan, for now, Lucius." The Emperor said. "But I don't have infinite patience. If you won't help me, I'll find those who will. Make sure you know who your friends are, that's all I'm saying." His voice seemed distant and he looked suddenly distracted

Lucius nodded slowly.

"Very well, then, Baron, you may go." The boy waved his hand.

Lucius bit his tongue and departed. His stomach rolled and he felt slightly sick.

He wasn't terribly surprised to meet Kandergain in the corridor. "Well?" she asked.

He looked at the Marine guards, stationed to either side of the door. "Walk with me."

She followed him out of the building and into the garden outside. The Emperor of Nova Roma had chosen an abandoned estate for his living quarters. Lucius thought it a bit pretentious, but he doubted the former owners cared much. The Chxor had exterminated that entire family.

He stopped next to a fountain. Dead leaves choked it and only the slightest dribble of water trickled out. "Have you influenced my thoughts?" he asked.

"No!" Kandergain said, startled.

"What about the Emperor's?"

She was silent.

"So you have?" Lucius demanded.

"Yes." Kandergain said, quietly. "I've been doing my best to keep him calm."

"Calm?" Lucius asked, "He's... well, I wouldn't call him calm."

"No. I'm trying to influence him without taking away his free will." She shrugged slightly, "Basically, I'm treading my own knife edge of morality. I hate to do what I've done, but..." She shrugged, "Lucius, he's a kid, and he got dumped with a title he never expected to have. His older brother should have inherited, though thank God he didn't. On top of that, his homeworld is in enemy hands and his people are being massacred. It's a little much pressure for a boy of eighteen years to handle."

"So, what are you doing?" Lucius asked.

"I've... eased the coping process." Kandergain shrugged uncomfortably. "Frankly, I hate to do what I've done without his permission. What he needs is a therapist. I actually recommended that to Admiral Mund."

"So he's cracking under the stress?" Lucius asked, horrified.

"Not yet, but he's close. I think your talk with him will help." Kandergain shrugged. "Honestly, he's a good kid. I think he'd be great in any other position. Now, though... I just don't know."

"Okay." Lucius sighed. "Anyone else you're tampering with?"

"Now, Lucius, you got to leave a girl her secrets!" Kandergain dimpled.

"Isn't there some kind of code or something, for you psychics?" Lucius asked.

"Well... it's not polite to intrude without saying something. Like I said, I'm bending the rules with the kid, but... I've bent a lot of rules in my line of work." She looked away, "I've done a lot of things I'm not proud of, Lucius, but I'd do them again, when it comes to it."

"I'm not going to condemn you for it. Does Admiral Mund know?" At her nod, he continued, "I have a question for you, by the way."

"Why do I get the feeling I'm not going to like it?"

"Hm, maybe because you're psychic," Lucius said with a sarcastic tone. He frowned though, "But seriously, I'm trying to find information on something that happened fifty three years ago."

"You want to know about your father," Kandergain said. The flat tone of her voice suggested that she didn't like the line of questioning.

Lucius stared at her, he hoped that he wouldn't strain their working relationship. Still... he had to have *some* answers. "I thought you might know something."

She took a seat on the lip of the fountain, one hand flicked the surface of the stagnant water. "Why do you want to know, Lucius?"

Lucius paced back and forth, hands clenched behind him. He chose his words with caution, yet he knew the words sounded rushed as he spoke them, "Someone told me something, recently. Apparently, my father wasn't executed. And—"

"Digging into that isn't going to do you any good, Lucius," She sighed. "That whole thing damn near broke your grandmother." Her gaze went distant, "In some ways, I think that it did... she probably could have recovered from the Plague, part of me thinks that she just didn't want to go on living."

Lucius tucked that knowledge away even as he tried not to think about it too much. The sudden loss of his grandmother had been part of what caused his own downward spiral when he was younger. "So... were you involved?" Lucius stared at her intently.

She caught his eyes, "I swear to you, Lucius, I had no part in your father's actions." She sighed, "Trust me Lucius, if I could have stopped that whole affair, I would have."

"I'm sensing a 'but' in there." Lucius said.

"I've told you before, Lucius, that I've fought the Shadow Lords, predominantly."

Lucius cocked his head, "Yes."

Her lips pressed into a firm line. She raised her head and met his gaze, "Sometimes I don't do as good a job as I'd like."

Lucius narrowed his eyes, "So... what, my father got caught in a Shadow Lord's plot?"

She looked away, "Trust me, Lucius, we *don't* want to go into that right now."

Lucius opened his mouth, suddenly angry. His communication unit rang and interrupted him. He cursed as he answered it. "What?"

"Baron, this is Colonel Proscia. We've got a problem."

"What?" Lucius snapped.

The Marine's voice was filled with barely controlled anger, "Apparently someone broke Lucretta Mannetti out of her cell. I've set up a cordon of the area, but I thought I'd let you know immediately."

Lucius cursed again, "Thank you, Colonel." He took a moment to think, "Are there any ships landed at the spaceport?"

"Yes, sir, we've got a couple of transports as well as our corvette and a couple of parasite frigates."

"I think we can rule out the frigates as her way out, but make sure we get some people stationed around those transports and our corvette." Lucius thought rapidly, "Also, warn the watch crews aboard the *War Shrike* and the *Peregrine*. She's... rather possessive. She'll want either or both of those ships."

"Yes, sir."

Lucius looked at Kandergain. "You aren't going to tell me any more, are you?"

"Some things should stay buried."

"Is my father dead?" Lucius asked.

She looked at him, and then her brown eyes went wide with surprise, "I—"

"Lucretta Mannetti told me he wasn't executed."

She stood up, eyes narrowed, "What *exactly* did she say?"

Lucius took a deep breath, "She said the conspiracy she was part of had its origins in my father. She said it would have placed him on the throne."

Kandergain began to curse. "We need to find that woman, right now."

***

"I'm sorry, sir." Colonel Proscia said, as Lucius came through the door.

"Was that a ship taking off?" Lucius snapped.

"Yes, sir." Colonel Proscia shrugged. "Whoever broke her out had our uniforms. They showed up at the corvette a half hour ago. The team I had in place was told they had orders to get the ship off the ground."

Lucius shook his head. "Did you contact our ships in orbit?"

Colonel Proscia nodded, "We're tracking it on the screen, as well, sir."

Kandergain stood near the window, staring out. "Too late."

A tech rushed in, "Colonel, it's—she—the corvette--just made a jump to shadow!"

"I'm sorry, sir." Colonel Proscia had an exhausted tone in his voice. Clearly, he blamed himself, Lucius thought.

Lucius shook his head, "Not your fault, Colonel. Find out how she did it, that's the important thing." He looked at Kandergain, "Anything break loose that you think you can tell me now?"

She shook her head, "Nothing that will help."

"Great."

***

The council room of the interim government possessed the bland, nondescript construction of many Chxor-built buildings. From what Lucius understood, they had chosen it as a reminder of the Chxor occupation.

The room held the fifty men and women who had stepped forward with ideas on how things 'should be.' Of them all, only the original five from his council had any type of experience in governance. None of the original government of Faraday had survived the Chxor occupation.

Lucius waited, politely for the introduction by Kate Bueller. When she nodded for him to step up to the podium, he did so. As he stood there, under the lights, he suddenly wondered if anyone recorded these sessions. He rather hoped they didn't.

Lucius realized, then, that he didn't have it in him to endorse a constitution he hadn't read. Nor, knowing how much he would gain, however little he wanted that gain, could he stand there and read the speech Kate wrote for him.

Even so, the wrangling and delays of the interim government needed to stop.

"Thank you for your time, ladies and gentlemen." Lucius

looked around the chamber. He wondered how many of them did this from an actual desire to make the world better. He hoped, for humanity's sake that more did than Kate believed. "I'm speaking to you, today, because right now, we're in the middle of a crisis."

He didn't wait for the babble of confusion to die down. "In a short time, we'll be fighting for our lives once more. We've driven the Chxor back, but now, we face the Balor." Lucius shrugged, "I can't say that a real government will help us to stop them. I can say that it will do your defenders much good to know they fight for a country and to know their country feels their sacrifice worthwhile."

Lucius looked down, "Right now, this 'interim government' is a joke. You've met for the past two weeks, and you still haven't come up with a name?" Lucius swept his gaze around the chamber and few of the men and women gathered could meet his eyes. "You've argued over this or that pet projects. You've traded political favors while portions of this very city are still without food, power, and water."

"Your people, *my* people, deserve better."

Lucius nodded once, "I hope this has come as a wake-up call. I hope you'll focus on what's *really* important now. Thank you for your time."

Lucius stepped away from the podium. On his way down the steps, Kate pulled up next to him, a small smile on her face. "Excellent speech, Baron."

"I couldn't just read—"

"All the better that you didn't read words of the page. Much better coming from the heart." She turned, about to retake the podium, "I'll have to change strategy a bit, but I think this will work even better than I planned."

Lucius shrugged, "Whatever. Just make sure these people do something good."

"Oh, they'll look good for the cameras and they'll have some good sound clips, but really, they're just here for window-dressing. The real vote just happened with you, just now. They're pudding in my hands, Lucius."

Lucius looked over the faces full of consternation, fear, anger, and the handful that showed actual thought. "We'll see."

***

"Please repeat after me," Lucius said as he held up his right hand.

"I, Lucius Giovanni, do solemnly swear," he waited for the rumble to die away, "my loyalty to the United Colonies Fleet." He looked over the sea of uniformed men and women. "I swear to support and defend the Constitution of the United Colonies," Ten thousand men and women stood in the formation, right hands raised. They wore their new gray uniforms with pride, "against any enemies, foreign and domestic. I swear that I take this oath without coercion or personal reservation, so help me God." He finished his much paused repetition, the fifth ceremony today. There would be two more.

"Today, people, you are no longer deserters or mercenaries or anything else less than defenders of a nation." Lucius spoke without a written speech. Each speech he'd given came from within and he hoped each word meant as much to those listening as they did to him as he said them. "Yesterday, the interim government signed the Constitution. A month ago, we welcomed our new brothers and sisters in arms from the Dreyfus Fleet."

Lucius looked over the brave faces, "Today we begin a new tradition. Today, we start a navy that will bring down the tyranny of the despots and the terror of the alien. If they knew what we've done, they'd do everything they could to stop us." He gave a broad smile, "When the time comes, we'll let them know that they should have when they had the chance."

The formation cheered and Lucius nodded once. "Thank you, I could not ask for better people to serve with."

He stepped away from the podium and watched as non-commissioned officers and petty-officers marched the different formations away. When he had stated his intentions to pull every man and woman in uniform planet-side, he had heard grumbles. Certainly, the chore to shuttle them down in shifts and to coordinate the watches so that everyone had their opportunity to give their oath in that formation made things difficult.

Lucius knew, from the beginning, it would be worth it. All those who had doubted it need only look upon the shining faces of the new Fleet.

All of the ships of the Dreyfus Fleet, as well as the vessels

Lucius captured, had received new papers. All of those ships would undergo a rechristening ceremony as darkness fell on Faraday's capital city. No more a ragtag group, no longer the hidden weapon of the human race, Lucius wanted to make a statement. Something new came into the universe on Faraday. Something bright, something conceived in hope that would change the human race, or die trying.

Lucius looked up at the brilliant blue sky, beyond which lurked so many dangers.

"All enemies," he murmured, "bring it on you bastards, we'll be waiting."

***

Lucius ran a hand over the hull of the Achaean scout as he stood near the airlock. A ship carried a log of its history in the surface of a hull. The scarred hull of the *Daedulus* showed the pitting of many atmospheric entries. Battle damaged sections, replaced by repairs, showed as smoother patches against the worn hull. Occasional seams and creases marked where stress and time deformed the hull.

All in all, the *Daedulus* showed her years.

"Like what you see?" Kandergain asked as she came to stand across from him.

Lucius smiled, "Yes."

They waited and Lucius waved Kandergain to lead the way onto the ship. "How did you manage to find an Achaean, by the way?" Lucius asked, as he stepped in through the open airlock.

"With difficulty," She laughed. From the tone of amusement in her voice, she preferred to keep him in the dark.

"Is it a hard ship to keep going, just by yourself?" Lucius asked.

"Who said I'm by myself?" Kandergain asked, over her shoulder.

"Oh, I just assumed it was you alone," Lucius followed her down the corridor.

"Kitchen's to the left, so is the mess. There's an entertainment unit against the wall," Kandergain pointed. "Living quarters are to the right. I've got the closest one. You can have one of the other five."

"Okay," Lucius glanced down either corridor. Neither went

more than a couple meters.

"We've got a science lab on board, really more for prospecting than anything serious. I doubt you'll need to use it, but it doubles as the sickbay, just in case anything happens."

"If we need it, I think my lack of medical knowledge might be a problem."

"Noted." Lucius could hear the smile in her voice.

"Cockpit is up here. Two seats, in case you want to watch," Kandergain said, as she keyed open the door. "Are we clear with control?"

Lucius glanced in at the narrow cockpit. The two jump seats were one right behind the other, but the array of screens and controls seemed far in excess to what two people could handle. "Yes, you probably should verify, though. They've been touchy since Mannetti broke out."

She looked over her shoulder at him, "Probably a good bet she'll turn up again, Lucius."

"Oh, I know." He sighed, "Frankly, with everything going on, I'm beginning to regret the decision to leave."

"We haven't even made it off the ground yet, Lucius. Trust me, if this pays off, it will be worth the investment of time." She shrugged, "It's not like Admiral Dreyfus doesn't know what he's doing militarily, either."

Lucius nodded.

"Anyway, let's get going."

She climbed into the cockpit, and Lucius trailed her. Unlike most ships, the *Daedulus* had an actual canopy that the pilot could look out. Even most fighters had armored cockpits with nothing but sensors and screens to show the outside.

It was another reminder that the *Daedulus* came from a more peaceful time. It was a ship from a time when unarmed scouts pushed out into the distant reaches, with few fears of hostile aliens, human pirates, or military interdiction.

Lucius seated himself. He pulled the seat restraints tight and felt the seat adjust to his body. Even though he saw Kandergain go through a complete preflight sequence, his eyes flickered over the co-pilot systems.

"You've got the nav-computer disconnected?" he asked with consternation.

"It gets annoying," Kandergain said, irritation plain in her voice. "Damn thing thinks it knows better than me where we are, where we're going, and how to get there."

Lucius bit his tongue. He knew Kandergain had a skill for navigation, but even so, she'd disconnected the navigation computer?

"Alright, control says we're good to go." She brought the light vessel up and kept their ascent subsonic, if only barely. Lucius suddenly felt vertigo as he saw the stars through the crystal-clear canopy. He fought the feeling back and then swallowed his stomach as Kandergain threw the ship through several gyrations. "Ah, it feels good to be at the controls again!"

"Oh?" Lucius asked nervously. He could feel the thrum of the ship's engine even through the padding of the seat. The small scout massed only twice one of his fighters.

"You never spent time as a fighter jock?"

Lucius shook his head, then realized she couldn't see him, "No."

"Ah, that's right, you were expelled from the Nova Roma Academy," she said, "Sorry."

"Nothing to be sorry about." Lucius answered. "I went through a stage where I felt bitter about it, but that passed. I was more bitter when I got drafted back in, but at least they gave me a rank equivalent to my title."

"Well, I've got a thing for flying." Kandergain said, "And the *Daedulus* is… indescribably perfect for that." She paused, "Okay, I've got the jump calculated, here we go."

They entered shadow space. As always, the experience raised hairs on the back of Lucius' neck. He felt none of the physical discomfort that normally went with a transition. As if she had heard his thoughts, she spoke, "I know the harmonics of my drive and I compensate for it when I make a jump. You can program that into nav-computers, but they change over time. Most people don't bother."

Shadow space remained the same gray and black void. Lucius found the sight as discomforting as always. In a larger ship, he could avoid it, but with the *Daedulus*' canopy, the sight was unavoidable. "Sometimes I swear I see things moving out there."

"Then you're more observant than most." Kandergain said.

"Trust me, shadow space isn't nearly as empty as people think." She typed in commands to the vessel, "Hold on, this will feel odd."

The ship *turned*. Lucius couldn't describe the motion. They didn't turn up or down or left or right, but they still turned. "What—"

"There's more dimensions in Shadow than in the real universe. Normal humans can't perceive them, but most psychics can feel them. That's why we can plot better navigation courses than computers."

"More dimensions?" Lucius asked.

"Yes, there's more to shadow than meets the eye." Kandergain nodded, "Here we go."

Outside the canopy, the universe changed. The gray and black void altered and suddenly became a spiral of blues and greens.

"What the hell?"

Kandergain unstrapped herself and turned around and gave him a broad smile, "Most people only ever travel on the edge of shadow space. They only ever see the monochrome surface and never dive in." She shrugged, "Good enough for going from place to place, I suppose. But this," she waved a hand at the universe beyond the canopy, "is just one region. There are colors out here that have no name, that only exist in some parts of this realm."

"That's..." Lucius stared at her for a moment and watched the myriad colors reflecting off her face. "It's beautiful."

She looked up and out of the canopy and she smiled like a child, "Isn't it?" She sighed, "Sometimes, I sleep in here, if I'm passing through a portion I can afford to sleep in."

Something in her voice put a chill down Lucius's spine. "So this is dangerous?" Lucius asked.

Her smile faded, "Just knowing about this side of Shadow space is dangerous." She shrugged, "The Shadow Lords live in places like this, places only a psychic can reach."

"And the Balor are psychic?" Lucius said.

"Yes and so are some other things." She sighed, "As always, reality isn't as pretty when you look closely enough to see the pimples."

They sat in awkward silence for what seemed to last forever. Finally, Lucius cleared his throat. "Well... how long till we reach your friend?" Lucius asked.

"We'll reach Lithia in a little less than two days," Kandergain said briskly.

"Lithia?" Lucius frowned, "Isn't that on the far side of the Republic?"

"Yes, that piece of junk," she pointed at the nav-computer, "might get you there in two or three months, if you're lucky."

Lucius stared at her, "You're incredible."

She smiled wryly, "Thank you, Lucius. One thing I didn't mention is a lack of prepared meals. Since I'm so amazing and seeing as you owe me a 'fine dinner' anyway... you get to do the cooking."

***

"I don't believe it."

Kandergain stared down at the plate of pasta fettuccine. She looked up at Lucius incredulously. "You can cook?"

Lucius shrugged, "Everyone has talents."

"But *nobody* cooks anymore!" She protested and then she started digging in.

"My grandmother had a fascination with things Italian, as you can guess by the surname she chose," Lucius said. "I learned how to cook mostly to please her, then I found I liked it."

"Mmph mwr alph." Kandergain said around a mouthful.

"What was that?"

"I said," Kandergain swallowed, "It's not fair. You were supposed to fail miserably, that way you wouldn't complain when I couldn't cook a thing." She frowned, "Where the hell did you get pasta from anyway?"

"The recycler produces starches and proteins in requested quantities." Lucius shrugged, "I had it produce pasta."

"But... you'd have to know the chemical make-up of pasta!"

"For some, cooking is an art. I just cut corners a little and make it a scientific art." Lucius smiled as he poured her a small glass of wine.

"I knew you cheated somehow."

"Well, then I yield, you may cook—"

"Not so fast, buster, you cook, I fly, that's the deal, take it or leave it." Kandergain growled.

"I'm touched by your appreciation." Lucius gave a mock bow.

"Now, would you like to wager one of your favors on whether I can tickle some bread dough out of the recycler?"

***

Two days later, they sat in the cockpit, staring out at the gyrating colors of Shadow.

"I still don't believe it." Kandergain muttered as she gnawed at a roll.

"You didn't take my wager on the pie."

"I still say you're cheating." She tapped one of three chronometers mounted on her control panel. "Five minutes more and we reach Lithia."

Lucius looked at the clock. "Why do you have three? I could understand one to show relative time and another to show universal time... but three?"

"Harrumph." Kandergain said and then swallowed. "The first is a clock that showing ship's time at destination. The second is showing our ship's time, adjusted to match, more or less, with time at destination, the last is just a countdown timer."

"Wait... ship's time doesn't change." Lucius said, "It's calibrated off a ship's drives, it takes into account velocity, acceleration—"

"We're *inside* Shadow space. The rules are different here." She shrugged, "Time doesn't necessarily progress at the same rate here as in the real universe."

"But..." Lucius frowned, "I thought that was one thing constant about shadow space. Position might change, but time has to stay constant, or else..."

"Or else you get paradox." Kandergain finished. "If time flows at different speeds, you can go into the future, or more importantly, go into the past."

"Can we go into the past?"

"I wouldn't recommend it." Kandergain grinned.

Lucius frowned, "But... think of all the things that—"

"Butterfly effect, remember?" Kandergain said. "I may not like what we have, but no way in hell will I risk drastic changes to the present. Besides that, you'd be plotting the course through shadow space. All sorts of unpleasantness can happen from a normal course, from point A to point B. You would have to know exactly when and where you're leaving, and exactly when and where you're going." She shook her head, "Traveling A to B the way I do, I can play some games with how long something takes, but I've never even *tried* to go backwards."

Lucius nodded, then his eyes went dark, "A... unpleasant idea just occurred to me. What happens when people make emergency jumps?"

Kandergain turned around in her seat, "If you're suggesting it's possible to go back in time from an emergency jump..." She scowled, "I *really* don't like that idea."

Lucius nodded. It was often an act of desperation from a commander. Sometimes it offered the only chance of survival, though. Statistically, a ship only had a one in three chance of survival. Most of the time, the ship, or pieces of ship emerged relatively nearby. Sometimes, however, ships never emerged at all, that anyone could tell.

And sometimes, people found lifeless hulks. Ghost ships, mangled as often as not, but sometimes, they were ships with odd registries. Everyone heard stories, and Lucius wondered how many of those ships might come from outside of time.

Shadow space flickered around them, suddenly replaced by the welcome sight of stars.

"I let him know we were coming, but even so, I jumped us a ways out." Kandergain spoke as she swung the ship around and put it on a heading for a nearby moon. "I don't want a finger twitch to end my journey prematurely."

Lucius nodded. "I didn't see an ansible."

"I don't need one. Well... not to contact him."

"So he's a psychic."

"Duh." Kandergain brought up her microphone and spoke softly into it. She waited a moment, then nodded at something said into her headset. "We're good, Lucius. They authorized me to do a flyby. You're getting the five-dollar tour."

"Oh, great."

The *Daedulus* swept in, and they approached a cluster of ships. Most of them Lucius recognized as Republic ships. There weren't many warships. He noted two squadrons of fighters in a combat patrol of the area.

A larger vessel loomed over the other ships in the fleet. Lucius frowned at the alien, but still familiar shape. He blinked, "Is that?"

"Yes," Kandergain said. She brought her ship underneath the bulk of the warship. Along the smooth, almost organic lines, Lucius could see modifications done by a human hand. From close up, Lucius marveled at the sleek lines. No bulky turrets or blocky projections ruined the ship's predatory look.

"It's a captured Balor battlecruiser, their Terror-class, rechristened the *Defender*." She smirked, "There's an amusing story to its capture, if we have the time, you should hear it from Shaden himself."

"Shaden?" Lucius asked, distractedly. He stared at the ship, as they flashed past. His eyes picked out blackened sections of hull, pits and even the occasional hole in the armor. The ship had seen battle and seen it recently enough that repairs remained incomplete.

"My friend." She swung them up, coming into an awaiting hangar. "They ripped out the Balor shadow space drive and put in a human version, ours is actually about half the size of theirs, we do *some* things better. That left room for bigger hangars and some other goodies."

"Interesting," Lucius said as he looked around the man-made hangar bay. He squeezed out of the cockpit ahead of Kandergain and made his way to the airlock. She arrived just after him, gave him a quick smile and then opened both airlocks and stepped out.

Lucius followed her down the ramp. No party awaited them in the hangar. Two swearing petty officers dressed down a pair of spacers near a partially dismantled fighter. The ugly, box-like body of it looked ungainly. *Havoc-class, I hadn't realized anyone still used those,* Lucius thought.

Lucius looked forward in time to see Kandergain moving towards a hatch. "He'll meet us in the briefing room."

They stepped into a round corridor. Dull gray walls stretched away, fore and aft down the ship. A wire ran along the ceiling, tacked into place and bulbs hung from it to provide the only light. Kandergain caught his look, "The Balor don't have eyes, they don't need light. They don't see colors, either, so everything looks the same to us."

"Ah." He'd have to brief Colonel Proscia. It would certainly make a boarding operation more difficult. He didn't want to think about how nasty the Balor would be in the dark, especially with their weapons and speed advantages.

They made their way down the corridor, turned at an intersection, then at another. Lucius prided himself at his sense of direction, but even so, with no markings, no differentiation, he felt disoriented. He smiled as they came to the next corridor and he saw a slip of paper taped to the wall with 'bridge' written on it by hand, with a pointing arrow.

They stepped into a room off that corridor.

"...the Vizier know, we need a replacement draft as soon as possible." The man who spoke looked far too young for the rank he held. Light brown hair, cropped short to his head, of medium height, he looked almost boyish in the uniform. The four, five-pointed stars pinned to his collar seemed totally out of place. He looked no older than the young spacers who received their dressing-down from the petty officers in the hangar.

"Yes, General." The ensign he spoke to nodded, "Anything, else?"

The young-looking General looked up, and for a second, Lucius met his eyes. However young his face and body looked, Lucius saw age and weariness in those eyes. "I think that will be all."

As the woman left, the General stepped forward, hand held out. He had a firm, polite grip, Lucius noted. "Baron Giovanni, welcome. I'm Shaden Mira. I wish we met under better circumstances."

Lucius shrugged, looking around the room. A mess of papers lay across the conference room table. He recognized the clutter as that of a man with too much to do and too little time to worry over tidiness. "I'm glad you could make the time to meet me, though I'm guessing I'm not going to enjoy the answer I'll receive."

Shaden smiled grimly, "You're right. We just fought the Balor to a standstill over in Centauri Gamma Omicron. I've got about two weeks to repair and refit, before they hit here." The young/old man grimaced, "If I could spare anyone experienced, I'd send them, but..."

"You don't have anyone you can spare." Lucius nodded. "I understand."

The other man snorted, "You think you wasted the time coming, but not so. I've had my people assemble battle records as well as summaries from a dozen engagements. I spent the past couple days going over strategies that work for us. That, among other things," he shot a look at Kandergain, "should help you."

Lucius took the data chip. "Thank you." He felt a sort of calm resignation at the outcome. He should have expected this.

"Baron, I wish I had better news for you." Shaden shrugged, "But things are never the way we want them."

A pair of officers came in the door in a heated argument. They quieted at the sight of Lucius and Kandergain, but Lucius recognized the sight of a problem that required their leader. He bowed politely, "Hopefully, we'll meet again under less... pressured circumstances."

He and Kandergain moved back into the corridor, "Sorry Lucius."

He shrugged, "It—"

"Kandergain!" A redheaded torpedo barreled down the corridor.

"Moira!" Kandergain shouted.

The two collided and for a second, Lucius winced. He half expected combat at the force of the collision. Instead the two women hugged. The redhead pushed Kandergain at arms length and studied her critically, "You look good."

"You are too! What's it been, ten years?"

"Seventeen," Moira sniffed, "And you didn't write."

"Moira, I've been awfully busy..."

The short redhead turned and looked Lucius up and down, "This is him?" Lucius had never before felt so much like a piece of farm produce on display at market.

"Yes." Kandergain said. She too looked Lucius over and he wondered, absently, if he'd forgotten to shave or something similarly embarrassing.

"Baron Lucius Giovanni, this is Moira Kaid."

"Ah, pleased to meet you Mrs....*Kaid*?" He couldn't help but squeak the last.

Kandergain snickered and Moira guffawed. "A common enough reaction, trust me." Moira nodded, "You are now graciously introduced to the only surviving child of Thomas Kaid." She said it with the same relish as a midwife might relay the news of a child born with cleft hooves and horns.

"Oh," Lucius said. He'd had experience with being the child of a man considered a traitor to his own people. Even so, he wasn't certain he could ever be so cavalier about it.

"She's Shaden's wife," Kandergain said as if that explained everything.

"Ah."

Kandergain and Moira shared a look and then Kandergain shrugged, "He cooks."

***

"That was really one of Thomas Kaid's children?" Lucius asked, as they pulled clear of the hangar bay.

"Yes," Kandergain said. "She and Shaden have been together since the beginning or near enough." She sighed a bit, "I envy them for that. It's almost sickening how affectionate they can get."

"Ah." Lucius said. He felt like a blind man scouting a river. "You said the beginning, what did you mean?"

"You picked up on Shaden's last name?"

Lucius thought a second, "Mira. That's the same as the precog you mentioned, John Mira, right? Are they related?"

"Yes. In a manner of speaking." She shrugged. "The essential part, I think, is that John Mira gave his life to ensure that Shaden Mira lived."

"So, the omniscient suicidal riddler is Christ-like as well," Lucius said.

"Not funny," Kandergain said.

"Okay, sorry." They coasted away from the *Defender*. "Where to now?"

"Now… now we're going to see a Shadow Lord." Kandergain typed in a final command on her navigation console. "Are you ready?"

"Yes."

The ship hurtled into shadow space.

They lay in the outer layer of shadow for only a few seconds this time before the ship *turned* in a way that Lucius couldn't quite describe. Again, shadow space altered around them. Now, it crawled with browns and yellows, a putrid look that made Lucius slightly nauseous.

"How long to get there?"

Kandergain typed something in on her console, a second later, the sensors brought up a contact. "We're here."

"Already?" Lucius asked, stunned.

"I asked her to meet me here. The Shadow Lords hide their fleets away in pockets of Shadow, away from prying eyes. With Shaden's fleet here in real space, this is as close to neutral ground as we can get." Kandergain brought up her microphone again. Lucius watched the icons grow on the sensors.

He adjusted the passive sensors for the radiation and background mess of shadow space. Even so, he got an odd doppler effect on the screen. "This can't be right, I'm seeing hundreds of ships."

"Huh, I guess she didn't bring her entire fleet."

Lucius felt his stomach roil, "She's got several hundred warships?"

Kandergain nodded, "Lachesis has had a few centuries to plunder the space-ways. She's got a substantial armada."

That made some sense... but to support that force, she would need a vast logistical support structure, "Several hundred warships?"

"These are the Shadow Lords, Lucius. They loot entire star systems. Lachesis makes Tommy King look like a humanitarian, and she's motivated purely from self interest."

"Why are we asking her for help?" Lucius asked.

"She's not the most powerful of the Shadow Lords, either in ships or actual psychic power. So she occasionally makes a bargain which some of the others wouldn't comprehend." Kandergain said. "She's ruthless, cold and calculating, but even so, she's occasionally done the odd act of kindness. She helped Shaden fight the Balor at Celestia. She might help you."

"What did she get at Celestia?"

Kandergain didn't say anything. She didn't have to. As they approached, Lucius picked out the sleek lines of a Balor dreadnought. "So... Shaden got a battlecruiser and she got a superdreadnought? Did anyone think that maybe, giving her something like that was a bad idea?"

"They didn't have a whole lot of options." Kandergain said. "And weren't you going to give Admiral Dreyfus and the good Lady Kale two thirds of the Dreyfus Fleet?"

Lucius kept silent.

They came up on the flank of the dreadnought. Kandergain brought them into a waiting hangar bay. Lucius stared out the canopy, stunned at what he saw.

Lush carpeting lined the hangar deck. Potted plants and stacks of pillows made small islands amidst the brightly painted fighters crouched in their launch cradles. "You're kidding."

"You haven't seen her throne room yet."

"This is a *hangar bay*. Who puts carpeting and plants in a hangar bay?!?" Lucius demanded.

Kandergain led the way out again. This time, several people awaited them outside. Four of them were obvious muscle. The fifth was a youth with spiked red hair and several metal studs that pierced his face. "Kandergain."

"Aaron." Kandergain nodded. "Lead on."

He smirked and twirled his fingers for them to follow before he led the way.

Brightly painted murals covered the gray corridors of the captured Balor ship. Deep carpets lined the floor, and ornamental lamps hung along the corridor. The scent of incense floated down the corridor.

Lucius thought he heard orchestral music in the distance.

The group paused at an intersection and a line of children went by, collared at the neck. A cable ran from one collar to the next. Lucius felt his hands clench as he realized with horror the children were slaves.

"Lucius, don't violate the peace of the ship, she wants to goad us." Kandergain breathed in his ear. He nodded slowly. He glanced over in time to catch a smirk from their guide.

Several further atrocities paraded before them on their descent into the bowels of the ship. The contrast of riches and cruelty displayed turned Lucius' stomach. At every display, he found a smirk on the face of Aaron, as if he calculated how much more would be necessary to provoke a confrontation.

But finally, they stepped into the audience chamber of the Shadow Lord Lachesis.

It was a vast room, with a vaulted ceiling. Flags and banners of various types hung from the ceiling. Tapestries and artwork lined the walls. Men and woman, many scantily clad, stood in conversation in small clusters, though they left the central aisle open. A large throne stood on a raised platform against the far wall. It was formed of steel and wrought as if it were a rose bush in the shape of a throne. Steel roses bloomed in perpetuity all along the arms and back.

Aaron stepped forward, "Honorable Lachesis, I introduce to your presence the rogue psychic known as Kandergain, and her... vassal Lucius Giovanni."

"Kandergain, do come forward," the woman seated on the throne gestured. Like all the powerful psychics Lucius met, she had the same young, youthful body, though there were harsh lines around her eyes. Those cold gray eyes appraised Lucius as he and Kandergain stepped forward. He felt dirty after that evaluation, as if he needed to wash her dark thoughts away.

"Shadow Lord Lachesis, I'm here to ask for your help regarding—"

"You want me to help you fight the Balor at Faraday." Lachesis's cold voice said. "You offer me nothing in return."

"You haven't asked for anything, yet." Lucius said. "Obviously, there's something you want or you wouldn't have met us."

"Ah... it speaks." The woman stood from her throne. A babble of voices around the chamber suggested it was a rare sight. The Shadow Lord sashayed down the steps, her eyes ranged over Lucius as she walked a circle around him. "A little old in appearance to our tastes, though some do go for the gray at the temples look. Shorter than we normally enjoy, though perhaps he has skills we could enjoy to make up for that. His pride, oh, that is delicious, for he has the arrogance to believe that sentience begets rights." She stopped in front of Lucius, staring at him with thinly veiled hunger and lust. "Do you offer this one in exchange for our help?"

Kandergain stepped forward, putting herself between them. "His name is Lucius Giovanni. Perhaps—"

"We know the importance of a Giovanni and there are other precogs besides Mira." Lachesis spun, walking around the pair of them. "There are other Giovannis, and none of the prophesies specify which will be *the* Giovanni." She stalked around, head cocked to one side and then the other. "Hm, perhaps you make another offer, then? Would you offer yourself, instead of this one?" Lachesis's voice hummed, the words echoed peculiarly in the chamber. "Would you give yourself, Kandergain, for us to save this one at Faraday?"

Kandergain answered softly, "Yes."

Her laughter mocked Kandergain. It rang out from the Shadow Lord, echoed an instant later by the gathered court. Lachesis cut off her laughter and those of her followers with a sweep of her arm. "Foolish of you. Normals are common and easily replaced. We will not take your life, tempting as it is. We remember how you foiled us at Alpha Centauri. We will watch the Balor destroy what you have wrought at Faraday, we will watch your efforts come to nothing, and we will *laugh*. You may go."

***

CHAPTER XIII

April 7, 2403 Earth Standard Time
Lithia System
Colonial Republic Space

"Well… that went well." Lucius said as they left the armada behind them.

Kandergain shot him a look halfway between anger and humor.

"So what exactly happened?" Lucius said. "I gather she's not going to help us—"

"Yeah, that's accurate enough." Kandergain snapped.

"But what about the rest of it?" Lucius said. He watched her, cautious for any sign that he had asked too personal a question.

Kandergain stared out at the myriad colors of Shadow for a while. "Lachesis has a grudge against me. She wanted to… watch me squirm."

"Why didn't she just kill us both? It's not like we could have done much."

Kandergain looked over her shoulder, a comical look on her face, "Are you serious?"

"Normal human politics I can grasp. I don't exactly hold audience with Shadow Lords on a daily basis," Lucius snapped back. He felt suddenly tired of being treated like a child.

"Sorry." Kandergain said. She stood up, "Come on, I'll buy you a drink."

She led him back down towards her quarters. She ducked inside and came out a moment later with several dusty bottles of beer. Lucius caught a glimpse of a cluttered room, stacked with odd items. He saw at least a couple swords before the door closed.

"Have a sit," she pointed at the galley.

She popped the top off one of the bottles and passed it to Lucius, then opened one for herself. "What do you know about the Shadow Lords?"

"They're pirates." Lucius shrugged, "But on a scale above anything else. They loot entire worlds, when they want to. They can intercept ships or fleets in shadow space. They hide there, and apparently, they're psychic."

"All that's true enough. The core of their forces are psychic too. It allows them tactical flexibility in their attacks, and gives them shock troops with unique capabilities." Kandergain frowned. "Many of those psychics have become, over time, nearly as powerful as the Shadow Lords they serve. They're bound to their Lords with pledges and oaths, oaths that are only as valid as the word of the Shadow Lords they serve."

"Pirates with a code of honor?" Lucius asked.

"Not really a code," Kandergain said, "but close enough, I suppose."

Lucius sat in thought for a long moment. Finally, when he spoke, he chose his words with care. "So if Lachesis killed us, she'd have broken her word, and her people would abandon her?"

Kandergain took a long pull on her beer, "More likely that they would turn on her and the strongest would replace her. It's a survival thing, they live in a totally lawless society. If any of them doesn't behave in the expected manner, they put her down like a rabid dog."

Lucius shivered.

"Like I said, there are some nasty things out here in Shadow. The Shadow Lords, unfortunately, aren't the only ones."

Lucius kept quiet. He sipped at his beer and then looked at it in surprise, "Hey, this is good." The label was a black dog of some kind. He didn't normally drink beer, but there was a rich variety of flavors that impressed him.

"Yeah," Kandergain said. "Every now and then I slip into Alpha Centauri and buy a case or two." She leaned back in her chair and stared at the ceiling.

"So what now?" Lucius said. "As far as I can tell, I'm back to square one."

"No. You've got that chip, it'll help. You've met Shaden. That may prove useful in the future." Kandergain looked back down and met his eyes, "Also, you've seen the face of one of your enemies."

"One?" Lucius asked.

Kandergain shrugged, "The Balor and the Chxor are external threats. People like Lachesis and those like her are the internal threats. The Balor might wipe humanity out, but the Shadow Lords thrive in the current chaos. They love that no one is strong enough to oppose them. Right now, you're a small fish. In a few years, once your fledgling nation has had time to expand, you'll create stability they'll hate."

"And then I'll fight the Chxor, the Balor, *and* the Shadow Lords?"

"It's either that... or watch our race be exterminated."

Lucius snorted, "Well, when you put it like *that*..."

They sat in silence for a long moment. "So what got you started in the save the universe job?" Lucius asked. "Something you were born to?"

Kandergain set her beer down. "When I was fifteen, my mother turned me in to ESPSec."

"Ah." Lucius winced. "I'm sorry."

"I don't remember it." Kandergain spoke in a monotone, "I went to a special lab where they wiped my memories. They experimented with artificial means to increase psychic abilities. They succeeded with two patients, I was one. Eventually some psychics broke me out, and, like that, I joined the greater universe. Power brings responsibility and all that," she shrugged. "Really, Lucius, our lives aren't that different."

Lucius gave her a skeptical look.

"We both have power, Lucius. Yours is one of personality and skills. You've forged a fleet that's going to have a profound effect on the universe. Mine is more personal. You struggle to make things better, a fight I've carried for a long time."

"I bow to your wisdom," Lucius said. He stared at Kandergain for a moment, suddenly struck by her. The determined line of her jaw, the purpose in her dark eyes, they called to him. He looked away quickly, "Well... I'd better start getting dinner ready."

"Oh for God's sake, Lucius!" Kandergain threw up her hands. "You can lie to yourself, all you want. You can hide your feelings from other people, but stop trying to hide them from me! I wouldn't need to be a psychic to see some things."

Lucius flushed, "I'm not sure—"

Kandergain quirked an eyebrow, "I am a psychic, you know. I know what you want to say, and you know what you want to say. Just say it."

He moved past her and stood looking into the tiny kitchen, "If you know what, I'm going to say, then why do I have to say it?"

"Because some things need to be said aloud, Lucius."

Kandergain smiled, slyly, and maybe because I *want* to hear you say them."

Lucius turned, "You're the most amazing woman I've ever met. You're more alive, more in the moment than anyone I've ever known. You always speak your mind, you've dedicated your life to a cause, and I see in your eyes how much that has cost you. I love you, Kandergain," he said. "Is that what you wanted to hear?"

She stepped forward, and for a second they shared a kiss. She broke away slightly and smiled, "It's a start. Now go make dinner."

***

Later on, Lucius lay in his bed and felt her warmth pressed against him and smelled the herbal scent of her hair. "What are we?" He asked.

"What's that?" Kandergain asked, sleepily.

"What kind of future can we have?"

She craned her head to look at him, "Isn't this enough, for now?"

He smiled and kissed her, "This is more than enough, for now." He stared at her, "But tonight we reach Faraday. In less than a month the Balor arrive there."

She lay her head on his chest, her hair tickled his nose. "We'll deal with them."

"And then?" Lucius asked. "What then? I'll go on to fight the Chxor and the Balor, and the Shadow Lords. Are you going to stay with me or will you carry on your own war?" He stared at her and wondered at what secrets she hid away, at the barriers, the walls that lay between them, even now. Even in this, they'd come to his cabin, rather than hers. He felt, he knew, that for some reason, she could not let him inside those barriers.

She drummed her fingers on his chest, "Always asking the difficult questions."

Lucius closed his arms around her and kissed the top of her head. "I don't want to lose you."

They lay in silence for a while, then Kandergain spoke softly, "I know what it's been like, Lucius, I know your loneliness." She sighed and she pressed herself against him tightly, as if she wanted to be inside his skin. "It's... not easy for me, Lucius. I've been alone for so long, I've... played my war of shadows for so long..."

"I've never let anyone this close to me, Lucius. I've never... I've never allowed myself to care for those I worked with. It wasn't safe, for them, or for me. God knows, *this* isn't safe. I can't do it anymore, Lucius, I can't go on fighting and not have something to fight for. You won't be alone anymore, I swear."

"Well," Lucius said, "I suppose that's all the more reason to win, then, isn't it?"

***

As the *Daedulus* set down in one of the *Patriot's* hangars, Lucius felt an ache in his chest. He looked over at Kandergain and noticed her face set back into her normal mask. They both felt it then. Their brief vacation from reality aboard the small ship came to its end now.

As he stepped down the ramp, he saw that Admiral Dreyfus, Admiral Mund and Captain Doko awaited him. "Bad news?" Lucius asked, staring at the solemn faces.

"No, sir." Anthony Doko said, "But we've got a battle plan, and we need to get it in motion ASAP in order to make it work, before the intelligence is out of date."

"That pressing?" Lucius raised eyebrows.

"We should talk about it in a secure room." Admiral Dreyfus said.

Lucius looked around the abandoned hangar bay, "Aren't we a little small to start being paranoid?"

David Mund smiled, his wrinkled face pulled tight, "There appears to be a security issue. We can discuss it later. In the meantime, best for you and Miss Kandergain to be briefed on the new information."

Lucius nodded, "Lead the way."

As they stepped down the corridors, Admiral Dreyfus spoke, "Any good news from your end, Baron?"

"We got a data chip with suggested tactics, a promise of friendship, and a nice little notice from the Shadow Lord Lachesis that she hopes we die horrible deaths." Lucius said.

"Oh."

"Any good, non-confidential news?" Lucius asked.

"Captain Doko just got married." Admiral Mund said, his voice dry.

Lucius froze mid-step. He turned, surprised, "That was sudden!"

Doko shrugged, slightly embarrassed. "I, uh, well, Lizmadie and I didn't want to wait."

Lucius nodded, though he felt a spurt of panic as he realized the implications. That Tony and the Princess had gotten married was good news for them. And Lucius felt grateful that Emperor had given his approval. He just wondered what favors the Emperor would demand in return for that approval. He shot a brief glance at Kandergain, "Take what joy you can in this world." He cleared his throat. "Congratulations, Captain, and many fine children."

Anthony Doko flushed, "Thank you, sir."

Lucius continued down the corridor, "Though… I am disappointed I didn't receive an invitation."

"From what I understand, they married in private," Admiral Mund said. "Very private, you might even say secretive. We only just learned of it earlier today."

"*What!*" Lucius coughed. He actually stumbled this time.

He looked between Admiral Mund and Captain Doko, "Please tell me you got the Emperor's approval?"

"Baron, we're both tired of pretending. Given the dangers we all face, the idea that we needed his—"

"Captain Doko—" Lucius broke off, taking a deep breath, "Anthony, use your head, this is a matter of succession. Whether or not his approval means anything regarding the love you and the Princess may share, marrying without his approval has massive political ramifications."

Doko leaned close, "Baron, I'm the illegitimate son of a well-off corporate executive. What do you think the Emperor told me when I asked him?"

Lucius sighed, rubbing a hand across his face. "He refused to approve of the marriage?"

Admiral Mund spoke, his voice dry, "I think if the Emperor used such polite words, there might have been more delay before the wedding. I don't think I've ever heard of two people getting married in anger."

"Oh, God." Lucius looked between the two men, and finally he burst out in laughter. He waved a hand, "I expected all kinds of crisis, but this..." He continued to laugh, to the growing consternation of both Anthony Doko and Admiral Mund. "I'm sorry, I truly wish the best for you two."

He started down the corridor again, "Any more good news?"

They finally reached the conference room.

Admiral Dreyfus spoke as soon as the door closed, "The investigation into the escape of Lucretta Mannetti has finished." He pulled a folder from the conference room table, "That's the details. In summary, someone knew your codes, knew your watch schedules, and someone had some of your uniforms."

"One of my crew?" Lucius said, his voice filled with shock.

"One of the officers of the *War Shrike* had to provide the codes that they used to take your corvette. Either she infiltrated your crew from when you recruited from Faraday upon your initial arrival or she had a sympathizer aboard the *War Shrike* all along."

Admiral Mund spoke, "Going by what you said about Mannetti's political aims in Nova Roma, I'm drawn to feel it must be the latter."

Lucius looked between the two men, "You have just suggested one of my men, one of my *officers* must be responsible for the deaths of sixteen guards, the release of a pirate, and possibly knew about and assisted in acts of treason?"

"Baron, that's what it looks like." Anthony Doko said. "And that means even I am suspect, I realize. I didn't want to believe it, but I've had three days to look at the evidence."

"I understand." Lucius felt something hollow in his chest. He knew betrayal, but never by his own, never by people he'd trusted and served with.

"I trust Captain Nix is looking into this?"

"Negative, Baron," Admiral Dreyfus said, "We thought it best my people handle that investigation, as they're clear of any possible ties. They didn't have access to the information. We're keeping things as compartmentalized as possible right now."

"I put Captain Nix Reed to work interrogating Chxor prisoners who've decided to come over, along with Kral," Admiral Mund said. "That's where we got *this* intelligence, and that's why we have to act on it quickly. It's already a month out of date, and at this point... you can see how important it is we act soon."

"What's this battle plan?"

"The Chxor began construction of a shipyard at Melcer." Admiral Dreyfus said as he pulled up a hologram of the region. He highlighted the system, "Apparently it started as a repair base to support the attack on Nova Roma. They needed a lot of basic labor, so they brought in prisoners, mostly humans. After the final battle for Nova Roma, they had lots of damaged ships. They expanded the yards. Apparently, someone decided they should just expand the base there for construction purposes, since they already had a lot of assets in place."

He brought up a diagram of several stations and dock-yards. "They've brought in hundreds of thousands of human POW's to serve as slave labor. Mostly the bad jobs, zero gravity mining, working the refineries. Stuff they could use robots for, but the Chxor find expendable slave labor cheap."

Lucius felt his stomach turn, "What's the plan to save these people?"

David Mund smiled, "We've got three damaged Chxor dreadnoughts and a dozen Chxor cruisers in varying states of repair."

"We fly in there and play a Trojan Horse?" Lucius asked.

"That's the basic plan, yes." Anthony Doko spoke, "Most of it was my idea, Baron. I spoke with Kral, he and some Chxor turncoats can take our captured ships in, talk nice, and then take out the Chxor defenses from the inside while some fighter support comes in, mops up the survivors."

"Risky." Lucius said.

Admiral Dreyfus spoke, "The Chxor have a lot of assets there we can use. Raw materials, manufacturing machinery, hell, if we have time we can loot their orbital refineries and strip their shipyard to the bones. Failing that, we can nuke the yards after we get those people out."

"Glad you kept perspective." Lucius smiled, "The prisoners must be our number one priority. I approve of the plan, let's hash out the details." He looked over at Admiral Mund, "The Emperor, I hope, realizes that we'll be saving a lot of Nova Romans in this operation?"

"He sanctions it. I think his words were 'it's about damned time.'"

"Took the words out of my mouth," Lucius' smile turned hungry. "I hate playing defensive all the time. Gentlemen and lady," he nodded at Kandergain, "it's good to be back, now let's take the fight to the Chxor."

***

Lucius' enjoyment didn't last till nightfall, as Kandergain found later that night.

"Economics!" He threw up his hands, "I'm a ship commander, what the hell do I know about printing money?"

"You're actually printing paper money?" Kandergain asked.

"Well… some," Lucius said. "Bank notes, but most of the newly elected Lower House's hard currency would consist of cast precious metals." He shook his head, "It's the amounts. My advisers," by that, they both knew he meant Kate, who had become the President of the Lower House, "suggest scaling up currency production as the economy gets on its feet. On the other hand, half the people out there want money, to buy things they need *now*. And on the third hand, people on the streets are screaming that the currency they looted or hoarded is no longer worth anything."

She rested her hands on his shoulders and massaged at the tense muscles, "Sounds like a mess."

"It *is* a mess." Lucius leaned back. "And again, I'm going to do what Kate Bueller says, not because I understand... but because she's been correct before."

"You don't like making decisions when you don't know the answers yourself?"

"I'm a military man, I'm supposed to know the reasoning behind the orders I give and follow, even if I don't agree." Lucius snorted, "I don't understand the first thing about half of what she's advising me on."

"You know enough to keep people around who do understand the things you don't." Kandergain said, "Which is more important than understanding those things yourself. I've seen too many leaders —military and civilian— fall into the trap of believing they had all the answers, and putting people around them to nod their heads and agree."

Lucius spun his chair around, putting his arms around Kandergain's waist. He smiled, staring up at her, "What would I do without you?"

"Probably get yourself in a lot of trouble." Kandergain smiled and leaned down to kiss him.

His link buzzed, and Lucius bit back a curse as he answered it. "Yes?"

"Baron, the Nova Roma Emperor wishes to speak with you."

Lucius sighed, "Put him on."

"Uh, Baron, he's standing in your office."

Lucius sighed. He rose to his feet, "I'll be out in a moment."

He straightened his uniform and looked over at Kandergain. "Hold that thought."

Lucius stepped out of his bedroom into his office. His mood did not improve to see the Emperor seated behind his desk. "What can I do for you this evening, your Highness?"

"You can have Captain Anthony Doko stripped of rank and arrested."

"Excuse me?" Lucius asked.

"You heard me, Baron. Captain Doko has made a grave mistake, he disobeyed a lawful command from his Emperor, he committed an act of Treason, and he must pay the penalty for that," Emperor Romulus IV commanded.

Lucius stood, staring at the young man for a long time in silence. "Your Highness, Treason carries the penalty of death."

"A fact I think you should be quite aware of considering *your* father," the young man snapped. "I certainly have not forgotten that." The purposeful ambiguity of the statement was not lost on Lucius.

Lucius turned away in silence. He walked over to a cabinet near the desk and poured himself a small glass of scotch. He did not offer one to the Emperor. He knocked it back quickly, then turned.

"Have you ever been in love, Emperor Romulus?"

"Excuse me?" The young man scowled.

"Have you ever fallen in love before?" Lucius repeated.

"I've had infatuations a couple of times, if that's what you're asking."

"No, I'm asking if you've ever fallen in love, and that's quite a different thing, entirely." Lucius said. He thought of the curve of Kandergain's neck, of the way the sun shone on her hair.

He sighed, "There is a saying, an old saying, your Highness. 'Love will find a way.' It dates back to Earth." He held up a hand to forestall the Emperor from speaking, "The reason I say this, your Highness, is that there are some things that no mortal man can stop, no matter how hard he tries. Moreover, there are things he shouldn't."

"Your statement that Princess Lizmadie and your Captain Doko are in love is absurd. It's obvious he's using her inexperience as a means to leverage himself into—"

"Into what, Emperor?" Lucius snapped. "Into a dynasty in exile? I've known the man for over a decade, since he stepped aboard the *War Shrike* as an Ensign. I know his flaws, Emperor. I also know his virtues. He can't hide that he loves your older sister, and he hasn't tried. He gains more difficulty than advantages in this marriage."

"Whatever the cause, I am his Emperor and I denied him the hand of my sister. He disobeyed my command and married her in secret. That is an act of Treason I cannot tolerate." The young man spoke rapidly. "He is a Captain of one of my ships, an officer of the Nova Roma Imperial Fleet. He must stand trial for his betrayal of my trust."

Lucius stared at the young man, he spoke slowly, "In that, you are mistaken, Emperor." Lucius took a deep breath, "Captain Doko is in command of the *War Shrike*, which is a ship of the United Colonies, a ship under *my* command, which you are allied to."

"What kind of nonsense is that?" Emperor Romulus IV snapped. "The *War Shrike* was built in the Nova Roma system, in a Nova Roma shipyard. *Captain* Doko was born on Nova Roma, the bastard son of a corporate magnate and his mistress. He graduated from the Fleet Academy on Nova Roma, twelve years ago. *You* are an officer of the Nova Roma Fleet."

Lucius leaned forward, "If you check the records of my government, you will find the same stated there. All the crews of this fleet, including the *War Shrike* swore an oath the day the interim government signed the new Constitution."

The Emperor's eyes narrowed, "I don't care what some scruffy little colony in the back-ass of no-where says, the *War Shrike* is the property of the Empire. You and your crew are members of the Nova Roma military. Either you will do as I say—"

"Or what, Emperor?" Lucius whispered, "What do you have that you can hold over us?" He shook his head, "My men knew they committed desertion when we didn't return to Nova Roma's defense nearly ten months ago, when we made safe harbor here. Will you declare us traitors and pirate? Will you fire on us? Will you destroy any chance of us restoring you to your rightful throne because your older sister fell in love with a commoner and it makes you feel your heritage is polluted?"

The Emperor flushed, starting from the chair. "You can't talk to me that way."

"I just did. Now get out of my office," Lucius snapped.

***

"Alright people, we have one week before the task group departs." Lucius stared around at the small group of officers. "Captain Kral, do you feel your force will be ready to depart?"

"More time for the ships crews to drill would be beneficial." Kral answered. Almost half a million Chxor survived the liberation of the planet, and the riots that followed. Kral hadn't had time to interview more than sixteen thousand. He had, however, selected ten thousand he believed trustworthy enough for the mission. "However, I believe the crews will perform their duties acceptably."

Lucius looked over at Captain Doko, "How go the crews of the *War Shrike* and *Peregrine*?"

"The shuffling of personnel has left us weaker than I'd like," Captain Doko said. "We're not as proficient as I'd like in the lower enlisted ranks. We've got a lot of new people," he shrugged. Most of the new recruits from Faraday had gone to those ships and though they'd transferred over some personnel from the Dreyfus Fleet, the differences in equipment meant they lacked experience in those areas. "It's something that will be a more long-term problem, but it's likely to decrease as an issue as our crews gain proficiency with their departments."

"Understood." Lucius nodded. He looked back at Kral, "Do you think the damage to your ships will impair your part?"

"Dreadnought 50—that is, the *Retribution*'s damage is the worst," Kral said. "The missing main batteries cannot be replaced in time for the operation, leaving it with only three operational turrets." He shrugged, as if half a ship's primary weapons missing made for only a minor inconvenience. "The *Retaliation*'s damage primarily lies with its engines. Since most of the battle will be fought without maneuver, that will not be a problem. I do not feel that the damage to the *Justice* is much more than cosmetic."

Lucius grunted at the damage estimate. It looked a lot worse to him. Power plants damaged, weapons systems missing, defense screens at partial loads due to missing and still-damaged emitters. "You have no reservations?"

Kral spoke softly, "Most Chxor who receive suicidal orders have no recourse. They go to their deaths knowing the failure of their actions will lead to the murder of their offspring. I think the plan full of risks. Had I thought it suicidal, I would not have volunteered."

"Thank you, Kral." Lucius looked over at the two Admirals. "Any questions?"

Admiral Dreyfus shook his head, "We've sorted through this for the past six days, now. I think we've talked through every possibility already. There are a lot of ways this can go wrong, from more significant forces, to a talented Chxor commander. We need to get ship crews fully briefed, and get people moving."

Lucius nodded. "Very well, make it so."

***

"Miss Kelly, thank you for seeing me." Lucius said, later that afternoon.

"Well, sir, I was a little surprised to get a message, we take off this afternoon." She looked uncomfortable as she stood in the office in civilian dress.

"Take a seat, please." Lucius said as he pulled out a folder and passed it across to her. "I'm not sure, exactly, what your plans are. I'm not sure if you even have any plans, but I think this might help you."

She opened the folder, and stared at the illuminated certificate inside. She read over the decorous lettering twice, before she looked up, "Baron, is this what I think it is?"

"If you think it a letter of marque, you are correct," Lucius said.

"But… why?" She looked confused, and a little bit hurt, "Baron, I thought my letter explained it, I'm done with fighting.

I've seen too many people die—"

"I understand." Lucius said. He sighed, "Honestly, I hope you never have to use it. At the same time," he met her eyes, "I know you, Lauren Kelly. I know that you can't set idly by and watch bad things happen to good people. Hopefully, if you find yourself in a situation where you have to act, this will help you." He shrugged, "Honestly, there are systems that will hang you just for having that, so I wouldn't advertise it."

"Oh." She looked down at the certificate and he saw her rotate it to show the imbedded holograms and verification chips. "Then you aren't going to try to use me as some kind of secret agent?"

"I'm… not against you getting messages to us if you come across anything important. Captain Nix is putting together a military intelligence net, I'm sure she'd like to tie you in. I think that's a little out in the future. Mostly, just do whatever you and Mason were going to do anyway." He doubted either one would ever come into a situation where they'd need it, but still, it wouldn't hurt for them to have at least a *claim* of legitimacy.

"Thank you, Baron."

"For what its worth, I hope things work out for you, Lauren." Lucius said, "You were a hell of an officer, and I really didn't want to lose you."

She shrugged uncomfortably. "Thank you, sir."

Lucius stood, giving her a crisp salute. "Dismissed. Clear space and quick time."

She returned the salute, her eyes slightly misty. "You too sir." She spun on her heel and departed the office. A few minutes later, Captain Nix stepped in. "So, how'd she take it, Baron?"

"Fairly well." Lucius responded. "I hope I didn't just get them hung for piracy."

Captain Nix shrugged, "Nah, a lot of small colonies have privateers. Faraday had a couple, actually, a few decades ago. Didn't work out, then, though. They ran afoul of some Republic warlord," she shrugged.

"How goes the interrogations?" Lucius asked.

She made a grimace of distaste, "I'm so *sick* of looking at Chxor…" She shook her head, "You said before you were working on transferring them over to civil authorities for processing, how's that going?"

"A couple snags, I hope to get those fixed soon. How is everything else going?"

She frowned, "I need to expand my staff, Lucius. I need some intelligence analysts. I've borrowed a couple spooks from Admiral Dreyfus, but… they and I aren't really sure who reports to who, you know?" She shrugged, "On top of that, it seems like we're doing double the work half the time. We don't coordinate with each other, just because we've got two separate organizations. I've definitely got the lead in HumInt, but they're ahead with SigInt and they've got some great gadgets."

Lucius nodded, "Integration of units is going to take a while. There's some issues with seniority of rank, as well, especially since most of their date of ranks will be thirty or more years older."

She snorted, "I don't care about that, too much," she shrugged again, "I ran the intelligence for a planet before, all else fails, I know I have a job if I decide to quit here."

"I'm tempted to transfer you over to the civilian side," Lucius said, after a moment. "President Bueller has assembled heads for a lot of the civilian services, but the United Colonies Federal Investigation Bureau is lacking in experience."

She shuddered slightly, "You couldn't come up with a better acronym than 'FIB?'"

"I could move you over to the Director slot there." Lucius said. "Not a lot of work right now, but they'll be our primary counter-espionage force."

Captain Nix pursed her lips, "Director of the FIB? Where's the headquarters?"

"Well, I'm certain there are enough empty estates that you can appropriate for the time being."

She waved a hand, "Unnecessary. Actually, I'm pretty tempted by that offer, Lucius." She narrowed her eyes, "Wait a second, you said earlier, that you'd be transferring the Chxor prisoners over to civilian authorities…"

"Primary responsibility would fall to the FIB."

"Argh."

"I'm sorry?" Lucius said in such a way to suggest that he really wasn't. Alicia Nix was a capable woman, she would do a good job, and despite her complaints, she loved challenges.

"Do you have any idea how much of a headache processing half a million POWs is?"

"We're estimating between four hundred thousand and a million people rescued from this upcoming operation." Lucius said.

Captain Nix put her head in her hands. "Let me guess," her muffled voice said, "They'll all need to be processed too? And you'll want the Chxor finished before we start processing human POWs."

Lucius smiled, "No big rush, you know. Just two genocidal alien races to worry about."

"Did I ever thank you, Baron, for coming to Faraday and saving us?" Nix Reed said.

Lucius cocked his head, "No, I don't think you ever did."

"Good."

***

Captain Kral knew that tactical patience won many wars.

That kind of patience the Chxor excelled at. They had much practice as a race, he knew. Years of subjugation culled the Chxor to those who could either accept their lot in life or pretend to very well.

Kral had much practice in pretense. Now, his patience would finally pay off.

After months spent with humans, Kral had come to realize that Chxor too, felt emotions. Granted, those emotions did not approach the range of the human consciousness. Kral had no concept of regret. He had no idea of 'love.' Friendship too, he understood poorly, beyond the forging of alliances.

He found that, when he allowed himself to do so, a Chxor could experience human-like emotions. Obsession, he knew, might explain some of the wasteful actions of certain Chxor commanders, such as Kleigh. Selfishness certainly showed in the actions of the dominant Chxor gene-lines. Kral came to find that generosity, when applied to his fellow imprisoned Chxor could also breed loyalty. They found he could help them, and they reciprocated.

Loyalty had its strong points in the emotions that Kral discovered. But Kral found that ambition had its own draw. Ambition fed upon success, and Kral became very successful.

Ambition, however, like obsession, burned away at one's tactical patience.

He ran calm eyes over his all-Chxor bridge crew. More likely than not, the Chxor at the station would not search the entire ship. However, it would not do to take chances in something easily preventable. His crews aboard both the dreadnoughts and defense cruisers consisted entirely of Chxor.

And all those Chxor owed their freedom--and their loyalty--to him.

"We have established communications with the base defense forces, Squadron Commander." The communications technician spoke hesitantly, "There are more ships here than normal, a Chxor convoy arrived a few hours ago."

Kral nodded his head, he accepted the Chxor rank. It meant more to him than Baron Giovanni's granted title of 'Captain.' He keyed open a link to the System Commander, "System Commander, this is Squadron Commander Kral. I have important news, which will require immediate action."

"What news is that?" The monotone answer somehow carried overtones to Kral's emotion sensitive ears. He realized, suddenly, that other Chxor, even those in high positions, must feel emotions. This System Commander obviously felt despair at his lowly position. No doubt, a Chxor of high genetic rank, he felt his command over this repair base to be beneath his station. He saw it as a dead-end job.

A Chxor who won a great victory here, however, might receive rapid promotion, especially for the defeat of a known irritant. He might further reward the Chxor who warned him of such an opportunity.

"System Commander, until recently I and my crew were captives of humans." Kral spoke, "They captured these vessels in actions at the Faraday system. Knowing the glory of the Chxor would reign triumphant, I and my fellow prisoners lied to the humans. We professed loyalty to them. In their emotional foolishness, they believed us."

The monotonic voice might have gained the slightest hint of surprise, "That is an interesting story."

"There is more, System Commander. Knowing great rewards would be ours if we could defeat them, we made up a story to lure them here. They planned a two part attack, with us to slip inside and open the way for their forces." Kral kept his diction precise, his voice level. It would not do to show his excitement.

"Logically, then, your force becomes a threat."

"Logically, unless I can prove my own loyalty to the Chxor." Kral said, "The human force is scheduled to arrive in just under six hours. I will transfer to you a list of their forces. My own ships, as you see, have received heavy damages and are not yet repaired. System Commander, obviously, my force is no threat to your own. Indeed, the recapture of these vessels for the Chxor Empire would be a great boon."

"What good would knowledge of the human plans provide me?"

Kral wondered, absently, if stupidity could be considered an emotion. "With knowledge of their emergence point and their probable course of action, your forces could await them and catch them at close range. It is highly likely you could destroy those vessels to include the known pirate vessel *War Shrike*."

The slight pause, Kral interpreted, had to be the System Commander's need to listen to his personal ambition. "I had heard of this ship. If I win a victory over this ship, your assistance will not be forgotten."

"Understood, System Commander."

"Take your ships to station, you are not allowed to dock. Your ships will wait on station near the derelict yard until I defeat the human attack." The Chxor on the other end paused, "For the glory of the Chxor."

"For the glory of the Chxor, System Commander."

***

Forrest Perkins was not a hero.

He'd graduated from an academy with a degree in astralnavigation on Saragossa at twenty two. He could have joined the Navy, but at the time, he'd wanted to start a family. He did so and got a good, well-paying job on a merchant ship. He'd left Saragossa in July of 2393. Three months later, he had returned to find his homeworld ravaged by the Nova Roma Empire. He gave his spot on the ship to another man there to take his family off-world and went to find his own. His new wife vanished in the chaos, never to be seen again. With the system's infrastructure and defenses gutted, he saw his world plundered multiple times.

Over the next two years, millions of his fellows starved to

death. Forrest held on, till the Chxor came. Some saw them as saviors, for they brought stability. Forrest just saw them as one more step down the rung for his world.

It might have been a sullen look in his eye that got him assigned to slave labor. It might just have been his luck finally ran out. Either way, his knowledge of ships meant he got assigned to one of the Chxor 113 mining ships.

He started his sixteen hour shift as normal, shoved roughly out of his bunk by one of the other two men he split it with. With something more than a rudimentary knowledge of spacecraft, Forrest got the thankless job as commander of the mining craft.

The only Chxor on-board, the purser, controlled the rations. That was the real power.

Forrest just commanded the movements of the ship, and made sure they made quota at the end of the day.

"Any changes?" He asked as he stumbled into the cramped command deck. It really wasn't much more than a cockpit, he knew. He scratched at an itching spot behind his ear. They'd just gotten a batch of new guys. Probably one of them had fleas and brought them along for a ride.

Boris Timovich might be considered an XO, if an XO made moonshine out of the moldy grain mush they got twice a day. "Some new ships came in. Way they are moving, at least one of zem's damaged. Ve vill have increased quota, you vill see."

"Care to bet a bottle?" Forrest said with smile. He rubbed one hand across his shaved-bare scalp. Shit happened, he'd be damned if he let the Chxor take away his spirit.

"Nyet."

Forrest laughed, then frowned at the sensors. "Looks like most of the Chxor ships are moving." He pointed at the crude screen, which showed the ships' movement. They only had the most basic radar systems, just enough to show rough positions and to avoid collisions. "Maybe something's happening." He shot a glance at the other man. "Might be the opportunity we've been waiting for."

Boris stared at the screen suspiciously. When he spoke, the words came grudgingly, almost as if he resented the opportunity, "Da... might be."

***

Lucius rapped the fingers of his right hand against his thigh, then checked the tightness of his seat restraints again. He looked over at Kandergain again and then looked up at the clock that ticked away the seconds.

The bridge of the *Peregrine* sat silent and Lucius felt tempted to call over to the *War Shrike* to hear Captain Doko's voice. He half wished he had remained aboard his ship, and not transferred to the captured vessel.

"We'll emerge in thirty seconds, Baron." Commander Beeson said. The youth had aged prematurely from the events of the Chxor occupation. He'd lost his entire family, and Lucius wasn't sure the young man really knew how much he'd changed. He had lost a good deal of weight and his normally cheerful voice still sounded subdued. "If Captain Kral did his job, the base will be wide open."

"Hopefully, so." Lucius said to his XO. He glanced at his screen as he studied the formation of ships. They'd elected to make this attack a small one, to use their more rapid vessels and their fighter squadrons to chew apart the Chxor formations rather than overwhelm them with force.

The two battleships remained the largest vessels in the attack force. If things went badly wrong, they could find themselves massively out-gunned.

Lucius glanced up at the clock one last time, and caught a smile from Kandergain, seated over at navigation. As he watched the last seconds tick away, he hoped his instincts weren't wrong about Kral.

***

Kral watched with dispassion as six human ships appeared in the system. They came in ten thousand kilometers further out than he had specified. The System Commander immediately contacted him. "They are not where you said they would be, *Commander* Kral."

"System Commander," Kral said calmly, "Jumps can be off by several thousand kilometers. They are close to where I said they would be, and they came in when I said they would. You should still be able to force an engagement and at least drive them off with heavy damage."

He waited patiently, as he knew the System Commander would need longer than himself to calculate the velocities and engagement windows. "That is correct. Thank you for your assistance, Squadron Commander Kral. For the glory of the Chxor."

"For the glory of the Chxor."

Kral looked over at his bridge crew. They remained alert and ready. The ships' drives remained up, their weapons remained powered. Had the System Commander questioned such actions, he could honestly state that it was merely a precaution, so that his own force could move to support a defense of the repair base.

"The human force is fleeing, Ship Commander."

"Thank you, Sensor Officer Frel." Kral looked at the technician, again, and decided, should he have the opportunity, she would not be a bad option to continue his genetic line. She came from decent genetic stock herself, being a minor genetic line, but one known for professional behavior. Now that he and his crew were self-fertile, he thought the time had certainly come for the perpetuation of his own genetics.

He turned his attention to the sensors and watched the human withdrawal. The ships needed time to calculate a jump through shadow space, or risk an emergency jump. Their withdrawal, however, showed many signs of apparent panic. Several of the ships broadcast transmissions, one ship totally in the clear broadcast a blubbering female captain as she shouted for someone to save her.

He thought that a bit excessive.

The ships drove a course that weaved. They pushed themselves through corkscrews and curves along their withdrawal. Those gyrations drove their ships all across a massive area of space and spread the individual ships out greatly. At the same time, they fired out metallic chaff, thermal decoys and did their best to make themselves hard to see. Because of their gyrations, however, they left the clouds of chaff behind them. It littered the space behind them with a sensor fog. All the System Commander needed for a clear shot was to pass around or through that relatively small area of space.

To the System Commander, they must look like an optimal target. None of those ships could support the defense of the others with their broad formation and their gyrations slowed their acceleration. Furthermore, Kral knew the ships lay outside maximum engagement range by only five thousand kilometers. With their current velocity, the Chxor force would most likely overtake the fleeing human ships soon.

The Chxor System Commander clearly saw that some dispersal must be necessary and spread his ships out slightly to allow them to cover a wider spectrum of space and engage more of the human ships as they fled, just as the force crossed over the entry point of the humans.

A few seconds later, one of the Chxor cruisers disappeared in a bright flash.

***

Lucius Giovanni, despite his surname, had no real knowledge of acting or the theater arts.

He did think the blubbering Captain Deacon Martinez did lay it on a bit thick, however.

"Force Bravo has remained in covering position for the repair base, still thirty thousand klicks out. Force Alpha is closing on Point Hollywood, now," Reese said, from his station. It felt good to have him as his sensors and communications officer again.

Lucius stroked his chin, watching, "Any moment now."

The Mine, Area Denial, version II, also known as the MAD II, contained a number of useful features. The most important one, for this operation, was its ability to identify targets via IFF and mass. Also important, each mine had a two hundred megaton antimatter warhead.

Minelayer ships never played a huge roll in space battles. Space was big. Mines were static. Mine fields could never cover all of the possible approaches to a world, much less a star system. Even so, the Dreyfus Fleet had six minelayer ships, each roughly the size of a battlecruiser. Those minelayers carried two hundred of the large mines in their external racks, and their corkscrew maneuvers littered the area behind them with dense vertical minefields the pursuing Chxor commander couldn't hope to miss.

The first mine ignored the Chxor cruiser approaching right up until it physically collided with it. The two hundred megaton explosion erased the Chxor cruiser.

The other mines in that formation sensed the passing Chxor dreadnoughts only a few seconds later. Detonations in space did not propagate as well as those in atmosphere. Even so, the massive explosions wreaked terrible damage to the dreadnoughts. The screening cruisers, even out in front, also took damage.

Before the first chain of detonations finished, the Chxor hit the second.

"Orders to the strike force, move out from behind Melcer VII and engage Force Bravo." Lucius turned his attention to the other Chxor force and ignored the chain of explosions as the Chxor System Commander committed suicide in a very spectacular fashion.

His own force, led by the two battleships, swung out from behind Melcer VII and its dense debris cloud.

Most Chxor, Lucius knew, would be paralyzed by the loss of their commander. Many would hesitate, waiting to see if any orders would be forthcoming. A few, a small few, would realize what was had happened and do their best to take action to salvage a situation.

Unfortunately, it looked the commander of Force Bravo was one of the latter.

"He's moving towards the repair base."

***

Forrest Perkins knew an opportunity when he smelled one, and either Boris had actually used a water ration to bathe or the series of massive explosions stank of it.

The explosions had to be massive, they were visible to the human eye, hundreds of thousands of kilometers distant. The pinprick flashes of light signified some kind of battle, at least. The Chxor force out there wasn't even on their radar anymore, "Someone's sure as hell getting the shit kicked out of them," Forrest crowed.

"Da, is probably not Chxor." Boris cautioned.

"Either way, get on the net, call Chelsea and Bruno, have them get the others, we're blowing this turkey joint!" Forrest pumped his fists in the air. "Woohoo!"

Boris shook his head then growled into his handmike.

The Chxor used ten of the small, labor-intensive mining ships and they'd planned to use all of them for the break. The ships didn't have much for engines or anything for FTL. They didn't have any real weapons, either, just the mining lasers and the tractor beams. They had the handheld cutters for some people and just about everyone except the brand new guys had at least a shank.

Forrest seated himself in the pilot jump seat. "Tell the boys that Bren the Chxor can breathe vacuum." If nothing else, they'd kill the one Chxor. *Cruel bastard deserves it, too*, Forrest thought.

He spun the ship away from the hunk of rock they'd mined for the past week. The ship's fusion drive shoved them forward at a sluggish sixteen kilometers per second per second.. Behind him, his tractor cables drew the rock along with them.

The plan, such as it was, put a lot of hope into surprise of the Chxor and to somehow capture a transport or something.

Boris pointed at the screen, "The Chxor, that new force and the other one, they're headed for the station. They try to cut us off."

Forrest cursed, "No, they must realize the attackers are here to free the prisoners. Why else lure most of the ships away for the battle? Those Chxor are going to destroy the base, and kill the prisoners."

Boris stared at the screen, a fierce scowl on his face. "The human ships won't reach them before they can fire." His accent had gone thick with anger.

"We could be alright... if we waited here." Forrest said, even as he started to alter course to intercept the closest Chxor. "We don't have to be heroes."

Boris was too busy on the radio with the other mining ships.

"Buddy, this is when you say 'nyet, not vorth my life,' and tell me to turn around."

"Nyet. I think this might be." Boris sounded... almost happy.

Forrest looked over at the hairy face with its big broad smile and suddenly scowled, "You're kidding me right? Four years on this clinker, you don't smile once. You just mope and say we're doomed to die. We set on a suicidal course to throw away our best chance of survival, and you're suddenly mister sunshine?"

The other man gave a shrug, "How many Chxor we kill before today?"

"None," Forrest growled.

"How many we going to kill today?" Boris asked, as they drew within range of the Chxor ships. He coerced the pitiful radar to give them a firm lock on the large dreadnoughts.

Forrest suddenly smiled as target carats appeared on the nearest dreadnought, "A lot." He flipped on the ship's intercom, "Fire up them lasers boys, we're killing us some Chxor today!" He tweaked the tractors and juggled the ship's trajectory. He juked the Maneuvering thrusters at the same time as he cut the tractor cables and watched as the vessel-sized rock began to drift ahead of them. "Woohoo!"

***

Kral the Chxor stared at his screen, plotting the intercept with the four remaining dreadnoughts and their cruiser screen. The Squadron Commander had just sent a message for them to unite forces, to destroy the shipyard and then turn and fight the human forces.

They were followed the first part of that plan, though the enemy commander had figured things out sooner than planned.

"Squadron Commander," Technical Officer Frel said, "It appears that the mining ships are attempting to interpose themselves between Force Bravo and the station."

Kral nodded. To a normal Chxor, that suicidally brave action would be inexplicable. He thought he understood it, at least somewhat, now. "We shall give them, 'supporting fire,' I believe is the word. We must stop them from killing the human prisoners. Message to all ships, open fire, primary target is the enemy Ship Commander."

The three dreadnoughts of Force Trojan opened fire.

***

Lucius watched the battle unfold ahead and bit back a curse. His missiles had plenty of range to the enemy force. The chance that a single missile might impact the repair base kept his force from engaging. He watched, throat swelled in pride as ten small mining ships, obviously crewed by men who'd had enough, moved out of the debris field to interdict the oncoming Chxor.

"Get a message to them, tell them they only need hold a little while. And for God's sake, tell them Force Trojan is friendly!"

He watched as the first fire left the mining ships. The mining lasers fired from only a couple thousand kilometers, caused minor damage. The Chxor retaliated and fired their massive fusion lasers. One of the light ships vanished and a second spun away to leak air into the void. Lucius hoped those on board had vac-suits. Knowing the Chxor, the prisoners kept as slaves probably didn't.

"I think they'll realize that, Baron," Reese said, as Kral's force opened fire.

Force Bravo's screening cruisers lay to the rear of the formation, positioned to interdict fire from Lucius's force. The massed fire of three dreadnoughts targeted one ship. That dreadnought took hit after hit, before it finally vanished into a haze of debris.

"Plot the course of that debris, make sure it's not headed straight at the station." Lucius commanded.

"Should be clear, Baron, the Chxor angled for a firing pass."

A second dreadnought shuddered suddenly and then the forward end exploded. "What was that?" Lucius said.

"Looked like it hit something."

***

Forrest crowed as two hundred thousand tons of rock smacked head-on with one of the lead dreadnoughts. "I got me a dreadnought, I got me a—"

The ship lurched, and the engineering console exploded. Alarms blared. Forrest looked over at Boris. "Oh, bummer dude."

Something hit the mining ship. The whole ship shuddered and a scream of escaping air swirled through the cabin. Forrest flew out of his chair and slammed against the wall. Boris threw himself across the cockpit to wrestle with the heavy manual door where he finally threw it closed.

Forrest stared up through the canopy, "Is that what I think?"

Boris looked up, then looked at the dead lights across his panels. "Da."

They stared as the aft end of their ship drifted away.

"Well, shit." Forrest looked over at Boris. "I think we're done here. Got a bottle?"

"Da. Two."

***

With the loss of the second dreadnought and their commander, the squadron split its fire between the mining ships and the ships of Force Trojan. The screening cruisers of Trojan Force stayed in position to deflect that inbound fire. In this case, the standard Chxor formation worked perfectly. Two cruisers received moderate damage.

Both enemy Chxor dreadnoughts got badly mauled. One lost power after only a few minutes more. The other continued to fire right up until it exploded when one or more of its fusion reactors lost containment.

Lucius breathed a sigh of relief, "Contact the cruisers, order them to surrender or be destroyed." If those ships weren't already in the midst of mutiny, he figured they would surrender.

He looked up and his eyes ranged to Chxor Force Alpha. All eight dreadnoughts, and ten of the twenty four screening cruisers were gone. The remaining cruisers lay stretched out over thousands of kilometers of space. Some of them leaked atmosphere; others, unharmed, drifted without purpose.

"Launch the Marines to secure the repair base. Have the shuttles begin recovery operations as soon as they've dropped the Marines." Lucius said. "I want every one of those miners saved, every one that survived."

Only four of the mining ships remained under power. He didn't know how many people had just died, but he did know he wanted to be able to personally thank the people who had placed themselves between the other prisoners and the Chxor.

***

"We've finished loading the personnel transports, and begun salvaging the base. Best guess is around eight hundred thousand prisoners of war. Mostly human, but also some Ghornath, a few thousand Iodans, and even a couple hundred Wrethe," said Captain Urenski, the commander of the transports they used to evacuate the prisoners. "Colonel Proscia and Brigadier General Morris have handled security, they've got teams aboard all my ships. Most of the prisoners are too grateful to be out of Chxor hands to make any problems anyway."

"How many Chxor captives?" Lucius asked as he turned to Brigadier Morris. He'd offered Colonel Proscia another promotion, but the Marine argued he wanted to retain his battalion. Lucius let him win that battle for now, but soon, he knew, the Colonel might get a promotion from necessity.

"Looks like around seven thousand. We've got them secured in the cargo holds of a couple ships, under guard. We... uh, failed to capture the base command staff alive." The Brigadier looked slightly embarrassed, "Some of the prisoners got to them first."

Lucius nodded, "Understood. I'm not sure I want to dissuade people from rebelling against the Chxor. I'm also not sure I want a policy of killing the bad ones discouraged." Lucius shrugged, "Even so, I'd prefer some of them got a trial for their crimes, however apparent their guilt is."

"Understood, sir."

"What about the recovery of the miners?" Lucius asked.

"That's been rough, sir." Captain Doko spoke, "It's been pretty gruesome, so far. None of those ships were designed for battle. Most of the people aboard the ones that took damage are dead. We've found a handful of survivors off a couple, but... we're finding a lot of people who could have survived if the Chxor just gave a damn about basic safety."

Lucius nodded. "How many?"

Captain Doko sighed, "Each of those ships had between eighty and a hundred and twenty crew. Of the six that were destroyed, we've picked up thirty survivors. I don't think we're going to find any more at this point."

Lucius winced, "I see." He let out a ragged sigh. "Were you able to get names of the dead?"

Captain Doko nodded, "The Chxor kept extremely accurate records on these prisoners. I take it, they considered all of them troublemakers. We know exactly who manned what vessels, even if we don't know what position they held." He cleared his throat, "We, uh, also recovered the two men who claim they're responsible for leading the attack on the dreadnoughts. One of them claims he threw the asteroid that destroyed the Chxor dreadnought in a collision." He coughed slightly, "We found them drunk off home-made alcohol in the cockpit of one of the destroyed mining ships."

"That's..." Lucius found himself at a sudden loss of words. "Bring them in, I suppose."

"Yes, sir, I had them brought on-board already. I understand they've had some time to sober up."

Two Marines escorted the two men in. The lead man's scarecrow appearance startled Lucius. His gaunt face split in a wide grin and it looked like he did a lot of that. The man who followed looked like he should have had excess weight, his skin hung loosely off his frame. A fierce black beard carpeted most of his face.

Lucius held out a hand, "Gentlemen, you saved a lot of people's lives today. I want to personally thank you for your efforts, and to tell you that your companions' sacrifices will not be forgotten."

The lead man stared at Lucius as if he'd sprouted tentacles. "Aw bloody hell, all this time in a Chxor prison and a fecking Nova Roman's gotta be the one to rescue us?" He turned to his companion.

"Boris, tell me you still got that second bottle."

***

CHAPTER XIV

May 2, 2403 Earth Standard Time
Faraday System
United Colonies

"So we're down to two weeks," Lucius said.

"Plus or minus," Kandergain answered from where she sat at his desk. "It really depends on how many ships they put together, where they departed from, and a dozen other factors. And as you know, I'm not omniscient."

"I think you mentioned something like that before," Lucius said, as he stepped behind her and kissed the top of her head. He inhaled her scent and felt some of his tension leave him. Seven days after the fight at Melcer, he still had a lot of work to keep on top of. He also had too many new issues to worry about.

"How are things with the Saragossan prisoners?" She asked.

Lucius sighed as she mentioned the most painful problem, "Most of them still remain hostile. There's a couple, like the one who led those miners on their attack, who seem at least somewhat open to peace."

"But?"

"But that leaves thirteen thousand, many of them ex-military, who would love to start a war here. We've had to keep them secured in a separate processing facility and that hasn't exactly made them more friendly. We've had numerous escape attempts already." Lucius shrugged, "I'm tempted to ask the Garu to ship them off somewhere in the Republic."

"Might be your best option," Kandergain said, with a sigh. "Some bridges can never be repaired."

"I just wish I could get through to them that we're trying for a fresh start," said Lucius.

"Give them passage to a different world, and something to start their new life, that might help," Kandergain said.

"Yeah." He rested his hands on her shoulders and began massaging them.

She laughed, "You're the tense one, shouldn't I do that?"

"Just touching you relaxes me." Lucius said. It was true enough.

"Well, in that case—"

The com unit on the table chimed. Lucius bit back a curse. He hesitated before pressing the answer button. Somehow, he knew this would be bad news.

"Yes?"

"Lucius!" Admiral Mund spoke, "Not interrupting, am I?"

Lucius bit his inner lip, "No of course not."

"Well then, if you can disentangle yourself from Kandergain, we need you and her up here immediately."

"I am not entangled with Kandergain," Lucius growled. He heard her chuckle behind him.

She snagged the unit from him, "We didn't have time, you old goat!" She yelled.

He snagged the phone back, even as he started to prepare, "What's the crisis this time?"

He froze at Admiral Mund's next words, "We just detected a Balor force arriving at the edge of the star system."

"I'm on my way."

***

"Any ideas why they're here two weeks early?" Aboard the *Patriot,* Lucius and Kandergain stepped into the conference room. Admirals Mund and Dreyfus had a number of links open and both snapped out commands to officers and ships preparing for battle.

"They don't tell me their plans, Lucius. The two month mark was an estimate. If the Balor feel you're a real threat, they might have assembled more quickly than we expected. Also, they could have played games with their navigation, cut some time off their transit, though it's harder with their drives."

He nodded, then looked to the waiting Admirals. "What's the weight?" Lucius asked.

"They're pretty far out," Admiral Dreyfus hedged.

"How bad is it?" Lucius said, not liking that answer.

"Pretty bad." Admiral Mund admitted. "They are far out, almost at the system's Oort cloud. There's a lot of junk in this system, so that and the range has made our a mass estimate very rough," he warned, as Lucius stepped forward to the repeater screen.

"Six superdreadnoughts? Thirty capital ships?"

"We think around half of those are carriers." Admiral Dreyfus said. "They don't have as high a power signature."

Lucius closed his eyes, "That's over a thousand of their fighters. That's over two thousand two hundred megaton warheads and four thousand sixty megaton warheads, *just in their fighters alone!*"

"We know."

He felt Kandergain's hand on his shoulder, "Focus, Lucius."

He sighed, "That's more than we'd expected." He didn't have to say it was far more than their most pessimistic plans. "What are they doing, so far?"

"Right now, they're just waiting." Admiral Dreyfus said. "Best guess, from looking at the tactical chip you brought back, they're scanning the system. We know they're capable of doing inter-system jumps, though they don't undertake such actions normally due to difficulty with the calculations."

Lucius shook his head, still disturbed by that ability. Human ships couldn't make a jump through shadow space at any less than a light year without spending a massive time in calculations. Even then, the accuracy of the jump would be lousy. Tactically, most considered it impossible.

To the Balor, apparently, it was merely difficult.

"Very well, they're gathering data. I trust all our ships are on standby to minimize emissions?" At the nods, he relaxed some. They couldn't hide the presence of the colony, not if the Balor had the sensors to see it. They could make it difficult for them to judge the strength and disposition of the United Colonies forces.

"I'm glad we've got the majority of the fleet away from Faraday." Lying quiet and distant from the colony, the fleet would be almost invisible, especially in the cluttered star system.

The glaring exception, of course, would be the captured Chxor ships and Emperor Romulus's forces. Both forces sat in standby orbits over Faraday.

"OK, if they follow their normal course, then, they'll send a group of dispersed scouts in, looking for trouble." Lucius stared at the map. "They'll probably kick off sometime later tonight, maybe early tomorrow morning."

"Odds are, they'll see the Nova Roma forces in orbit." Lucius nodded at Admiral Mund. "Since they don't know for certain about the Dreyfus Fleet," he looked to Kandergain for confirmation, "we can reasonably expect they'll think that's the sum of our forces."

"What are you saying?" Admiral Mund said.

"I'd like to keep our full strength unknown for as long as possible." Lucius said. "We can probably clobber the hell out of their scout forces with our full strength, but then they gain the knowledge they want. If we conceal our full strength until the opportune moment…"

Admiral Dreyfus nodded slowly. "You want to keep the main body here?"

Lucius nodded, "Any additional forces we use we can move out with maneuvering thrusters, then light up a few thousand kilometers clear of the Fleet. The Balor will, hopefully, think it's just a detachment." The Fleet lay between the orbits of the unnamed gas giant Lucius had ambushed Kleigh at, and a barren, lifeless rocky planet. The Faraday colony lay inside the next orbit after, several million kilometers star-wards.

"So…" Lucius frowned, "We peel off our fast units, to deal with their scouts. They'll coalesce into a body to test our strength, and we clobber them… say here." He pointed at the gas giant. "That stops them well clear of the colony and won't give them reason to look here."

"You realize if they see us anyway, they can jump in on top of us and fire before we realize they're here." Admiral Dreyfus said.

"Yes."

"Oh, good, glad you took that into consideration," His light tone belied the worry on his face. Admiral Dreyfus frowned, "So, we're the backstop, I don't mind setting out the early fighting, but what's the overall plan should the worst happen?"

"The worst?" Lucius asked.

"He means what happens if you die," Admiral Mund said, dryly.

"Ah."

"Well, hopefully we drive the scouts back, and then let the main body come in. Try to pull them towards the main fleet at high speed." Lucius frowned, "Get them coming in chasing our faster ships and we might get them moving fast enough they can't avoid a head on close weapons pass with main body."

"That… might work." Admiral Dreyfus admitted. "Of course,

if they see us in time, they can just alter course and do a quick firing pass outside our range. Or they could volley all their missiles."

"Yeah." Lucius said.

"What do I tell the Emperor to do?" Admiral Mund said.

Lucius looked at him. Despite their best efforts, many of the Nova Roma ships still required significant repairs. Almost all of them were combat capable, but they were still low on personnel and many had systems in marginal shape at best. Finally, Lucius shrugged, "Pray."

***

The *War Shrike,* the *Peregrine*, the *Gebneyr*, and all eight of the Nagri-class battlecruisers, along with three squadrons of destroyers, coasted a hundred thousand kilometers before they lit off their drives and altered course to intercept the largest body of the scouting Balor.

The Balor altered course almost immediately.

Lucius chuckled slightly, "Somewhat arrogant, aren't they?" The enemy destroyers, rather than scatter, began to draw closer into a formation. Clearly they preferred hard data to estimates via sensors.

"They've only been defeated a handful of times. I've never heard of them in this kind of strength." Kandergain said. "They must believe it's impossible for them to lose."

"Well, it's the impossible I get paid for." Lucius said, then frowned, "Remind me to ask Kate if I actually do get paid." Oddly enough, it wasn't something he'd considered yet.

"Why don't we focus on the immediate problem rather than whether you'll be eating out of the garbage in a month or two?" Kandergain said.

"Hmmm, yes, definitely remind me to ask her." He rapped his fingers on his leg, "Message to all ships, keep the speed down. Let's not clue them into the fact we can match their speed with this force. Well, not until we chase down the survivors." Lucius grinned.

"They're not the only ones being a little over-confident?" Kandergain asked.

"Ah." Lucius shrugged, "That reminds me." He opened a

channel to broadcast to all of the United Colonies ships. "Defenders of the United Colonies, this is Baron Lucius Giovanni. Today, the tyrannical Balor invade our system. They think that their empire, their race, shall supplant humanity. They come to destroy our society and to consume our people as food."

"Today," Lucius said, "We take a stand. Today, we will drive them back. Today, the Balor will know defeat as never before."

"A century from now, your grandchildren will look back on this day and know that everything changed at this time. They will know that humanity, in its darkest hour, came together and said 'No!' They will know this day as the end of fear."

"I know of no other place I would rather be. I know of no other men and women I'd rather stand beside," Lucius said. "The Balor, the Chxor, they think we are a doomed race... a fallen race. Today we are the Champions of Humanity and we'll prove them wrong."

***

The two forces closed faster. Lucius watched the interception force closed up formation. Lucius put the squadron of Kris-class destroyers out front, with their anti-missile batteries. He hoped the two Archer destroyer squadrons would help to balance the missile capabilities of the enemy.

He knew his five squadrons of fighters would help some.

Even so, he angled to force the engagement near the gas giant and its moons. Should the destroyers launch a truly devastating missile launch, they could try to use the planet to cover a withdrawal.

"Launch the fighters," Lucius said.

The ship thrummed as the twelve fighters launched. The small craft formed up, to bolster the formation. A moment later the *War Shrike's* fighters launched as well. Lucius watched the sensor data on the enemy firm up, despite the heavy jamming.

"Looks like three of their Ravager cruisers, and an even dozen Daggers," Reese said as he massaged data out of the emissions. "I've got sensor lock on all of them."

Lucius just nodded. They neared the maximum enemy powered missile envelope at just under six hundred thousand kilometers, if the scout elements carried the heavier missiles.

"Nothing yet sir."

They waited, and Lucius finally sighed. He would have preferred the launch, for it would have meant the Balor had half of the larger missiles to throw his way.

The next possible engagement, unless they merely played with him, lay at two hundred fifty thousand kilometers. Even with the new missiles, Lucius's maximum range lay at only a hundred eighty thousand kilometers given their closing velocities.

Both forces kept their speeds low; their combined closure rate meant he'd be in range in just under fifty minutes. The Balor's destroyers could volley their external racks, potentially forty of their hundred megaton warheads for each of the twelve destroyers in twenty five minutes more.

He'd have to weather that storm just to fire in return.

The clock ticked away the time. Lucius's eyes returned to the icons of the ships in the outer system. This whole engagement set the ground for that battle. He knew, quite confidently, that he could defeat this force. He wasn't sure he wanted to pay the price it would cost.

He just didn't see any other way to win.

He looked up. The Balor launch approached.

"Missile launch, multiple launches." Reese reported, his voice calm. "I have excess of seven hundred enemy birds in the air."

Lucius bit back a curse. "Activate jammers, launch the decoys."

He felt the acid bite of anguish at the coming onslaught. His people were good. They would survive it, but it was going to cost them. They had three minutes to watch the wave of missiles approach.

As the inbound missiles drew closer, they launched counter-missiles. The *War Shrike* and the *Peregrine* had replaced their standard load-out with interceptor missiles. The eight Nagri battlecruisers mounted external racks of interceptor missiles. Even so, less than a hundred counter-missiles lanced out.

They took eighty of the inbound missiles.

Jamming burned out many more.

When the missiles swept into range, they traveled at seventy two thousand kilometers per second. The firing solutions gunners programmed into the defense guns and even the main batteries swept a cone of destruction through the space ahead of the formation. They angled the fire in coordinated, overlapping patterns.

That left nearly two hundred missiles that slipped through or around the defensive fire.

The ships, moving evasively, did their best to generate misses. Sometimes that wasn't enough.

The *Peregrine* heaved, struck at least one glancing blow that made it through the defensive screen. "Missile tubes three and four are destroyed. The refueler is destroyed. Loss of atmosphere on decks six through fourteen."

Lucius's eyes went to his other ships, seeing his own had survived.

Others in the formation had not been so lucky.

The Kriss-class destroyers *Fox* and *Vixen,* and battlecruisers *Royal Gorge* and *Yosemite Park* did not survive. Bands of gas and a haze of small debris signaled the futility of a search for survivors. The destroyer *Minx* barely coasted along, damage icons near it suggested that even if it survived the upcoming battle, it would be best to scuttle the ship. All of his other ships took damage to one degree or another, and two of his remaining battlecruisers boasted less than half their weapons systems operative.

"Nearing launch range." Commander Beeson said.

Lucius waited, a dark hunger growing in his belly. "All ships, fire."

"All ships firing, sir." Reese relayed.

Lucius gave a feral grin, "My turn, bastards."

Nearly seven hundred missiles went out. They were slower, they probably would be less accurate, but each of those missiles carried a kilogram of antimatter in a polarized matrix designed to maximize energy release.

"*Roosevelt Forest* reports damage to missile racks, they had to jettison their missiles."

"Understood." Lucius answered. His eyes remained intent.

The Balor had almost four minutes to watch the inbound missiles.

"I'm detecting no counter-missiles. I think they fired everything they had at us." Reese said.

Lucius nodded, it fit their standard of operations. They were used to facing lighter human ships. A Republic force of cruisers and destroyers would not have survived, he knew.

The Balor scout force began evasive maneuvers. They lay down their own cone of destructive fire. Three hundred missiles died. The jamming burned out another hundred.

Lucius waited.

Massive explosions blossomed in the midst of the Balor formation. The first destroyer died, then a cruiser, followed by another destroyer. The shields took a beating, but nothing the size of a destroyer could take more than a couple of hits from the massive warheads.

Lucius snarled in satisfaction as the last of the explosions faded. One cruiser and three destroyers remained. All lacked shields. All bled atmosphere from damage. The survivors altered course and moved to escape.

"Close with them, wipe them out."

Lucius ships went to full acceleration. "We've got them as long as—"

He broke off as the surviving ships split. Each ship's course took them on radically different paths. Lucius could divide his force to chase them down or watch them get away.

"Break off the pursuit." Lucius sighed. He was not about to throw away the victory by scattering his forces, not with how the main body lurked at the edge of the system. "Begin withdrawal towards Shadow Point, take it slow, let's see if we can sucker them in."

***

An hour later, the Balor fleet finally began its approach into the system. Lucius stared at their course, and he felt the stirrings of depression. They swept in slowly, on a course that would take them past the ice moon with its penal colony. They could alter course, they could speed up, but Lucius felt certain the Balor would take a cautious sweep of the system. They couldn't know what waited, but the enemy commander suspected something might.

"Why the long face?" Kandergain asked as she came up to stand near him.

"An aggressive commander, we could have trapped. A cautious one…" Lucius pursed his lips, "not good."

"Any hope?" Kandergain kept her face placid, but he heard the despair in her voice.

"We'll keep the speed down. With the damage we did take, they'll think we're worse off than we are. They might try to catch us short of the planet."

"But not likely?"

"No. Not with the course they're on, right now. It looks like they wanted the measure of us, and they got one." He sighed, "We're refining our data on their ships, as they get closer, but it looks pretty close to a nightmare case."

"They'll pass the ice moon in a couple hours. They won't be in engagement range for another six, maybe eight hours, depending."

"All ships, go to battle stand-by. Half-on watches, three hour rotations." Lucius said.

"Are you going to rest?" Kandergain asked.

Lucius shrugged, he didn't feel tired, but he knew even a few minutes rest could make all the difference between a poor decision and a good one. "A couple hours."

She clasped his hand, "You can do this, Lucius. I believe in you."

Lucius squeezed her hand, "I haven't given up." He snorted, "Though God knows, that's been a recurring problem for me."

***

Four hours later, Lucius stared at the screens and wished some kind of change. The Balor scout force and the main body had combined and they swept in towards Lucius's small force, and the as-yet concealed United Colonies Fleet. "Come on, I could use anything," he muttered.

"Sir, multiple new contacts, just emerged, vicinity the rocky planet." Reese snapped.

Lucius blinked in surprise, looking over at Kandergain, who shook her head, not her doing.

"Who are they?" Lucius asked.

Reese stared at his screen for a long time in silence. Finally he looked up. "Significant Chxor force. Looks like thirty dreadnoughts, around a hundred and twenty cruisers."

Lucius stared at the new contacts. He felt his heart sink. The Chxor, either through luck or coordination with the Balor, had put themselves in a position to squeeze his fleet between the Balor and their forces. He figured the UCF fleet could engage and destroy the Chxor force. Doing so would compromise the position of his forces to the Balor. The added damage might also tip the balance even more against him.

He stared at the screen, suddenly out of ideas.

He looked up to find Kandergain's eyes.

Lucius just shook his head.

***

CHAPTER XV

May 2, 2403 Earth Standard Time
Faraday System
United Colonies

With the majority of the fleet in emissions control, Lucius couldn't talk to Admiral Drefyus without possibly giving away his position. That meant he could contact Admiral Mund and Emperor Romulus. "I'm not seeing any viable options." He said. He sat in the conference room aboard the *Peregrine*, away from the eyes of his crew.

"Perhaps it's time we withdraw," the Emperor said. "It might be too late to evacuate most of the planet, but we can still save millions."

Lucius felt the temptation, but he just shook his head, "No, if we run now, the Balor will smell our defeat, they'll hunt us." He looked over at Kandergain and she nodded slightly. "Besides, I won't abandon millions to their deaths, not when we have a chance at stopping them."

"We don't, you said it yourself," the younger man said angrily. "With the Balor and the Chxor working together to bring us down—"

"Wait," Admiral Mund said, "Why would the Chxor and Balor work together?"

Lucius frowned, "Can it be anything else? They arrived at the same time, I don't see how they coordinated this but..."

David Mund shook his head, "This doesn't fit with the mentality of the Balor or the Chxor. Does it?" His question went to Kandergain.

She frowned, "No... No, the Balor might use the Chxor, provoke them into attacking us, but they don't have any kind of alliance. The Balor don't negotiate with anyone."

"So, you're saying the Chxor just happened to attack us at the same time as the Balor?" Lucius frowned, "That doesn't make any sense. Not unless they're reacting to something."

"Like our attack at Melcer?" The Emperor asked.

Lucius's eyes went wide, "That's it, your Highness! The Chxor aren't here to smash us against the Balor, they're here to retaliate against the attack at Melcer!"

"How does that change anything?" Kandergain frowned.

"It changes everything!" Lucius slammed his hand down on the table in excitement. Then he pulled up a map of the system, and the course of the Balor Fleet. "Right now, they're approaching the gas giant. They'll be in the shadow of that, probably as they launch their fighters and shake down into their final formations. Their psychic sensors or whatever won't have range on us, and their longer range sensors will be blocked by the gas giant."

"So they won't be able to see us do what?"

Lucius stroked his chin in thought, "I'm not sure."

Admiral Mund spoke, "Alright, what are the Chxor here for?"

"To engage and destroy a threat to the Chxor Empire."

"So… we give them that threat?" the Emperor asked. "My ship's can advance to meet them. That will give your forces time to deal with the Balor." For a moment, he looked almost eager to throw his massively outnumbered force against the Chxor.

"No…" Lucius stared at the map, thinking. There had to be a way. "If we could get the Chxor turned, headed for us, we might get them to engage the Balor." He checked the movement of the Chxor versus the position of his own fleet and the powered-down ships of Dreyfus's command. "Now… if we bring our fleet's drives up in... thirty-three minutes, the Chxor will see them, and alter course to engage. At the same time, the Balor will be behind the gas giant and they won't be able to see my force. When the Balor come from behind the gas giant, the Chxor will see them, and move to engage the new threat."

"Is that before or after they shoot their way through your fleet to get there?" Admiral Mund asked dryly.

Lucius turned to Kandergain, "The Balor can do intrasystem jumps because they're psychics, right?"

She frowned, "Yes."

"Can you plot me a near-real-time jump to take all our ships? It doesn't have to be quick, we can afford a couple hours transit time, but I need that jump to happen in the next forty five minutes," He licked his lips, "and it would be best if we jumped behind a planetary body."

She frowned in thought, "I'll need the ship's nav computer. And, as soon as Admiral Dreyfus's ships go active, I'll need access to the *Patriot*'s nav computer."

"Go."

She was out of the room before he messaged the bridge, "Kandergain will need full access to the navigation computer."

"Yes, sir, uh, how—" there was a shout.

"Lucius, this is Kandergain, I'm plugged in. Make sure Dreyfus is ready to give me access as soon as his ships go active." The line went dead.

Lucius hurried up to the bridge. His navigation officer stood, looking somewhat dazed, "Uh, Baron, she—" He shook his head, "She just threw me across the compartment."

"She was in a hurry." Lucius said.

***

The strike force and the rest of the fleet merged twenty five minutes later.

The Chxor, with their limited sensor range, couldn't see them well enough to target. They would have to be blind as well as deaf not to see them coming.

The drives of the five Crusader-class ships threw off enough background radiation to give someone sunburn. The drive of the *Patriot* at full acceleration threw off a larger signature than all thirty of the Chxor dreadnoughts.

"Come on, you bastards," Lucius muttered, starting at his screen.

"Surely they're not that blind?" he heard someone say.

Lucius glanced at the timer displayed in the corner of his screen. They had just under twenty minutes to change the course of the Chxor, and then to jump. If they passed that window, then the Balor would see his entire force. Lucius didn't know what their course of action would be then, but he doubted it would favor him.

"Chxor force is altering course, they're swinging around, sir." Reese said. "Looks like they're going for a least-time closure rate."

Lucius let out a sigh of relief, "Kandergain, we ready yet?"

"Did I mention I *hate* being pressured when I work?" She snapped. "I need thirty more minutes."

"You've got..." Lucius checked the timer, "eighteen minutes

and thirty seconds."

"Sir, I can link the Fleet's processing power if that—"

"Do it." He and Kandergain spoke simultaneously.

That took five minutes.

"Transferring the calculations," Kandergain said.

Lucius's screen flickered. He looked up, "What was that?"

"She's sucking up all the processing power from our computers, sir." Reese said. It took Lucius a moment to recognize the emotion of awe in Reece's voice. "Sir, I've never seen anything like this. If she put those computations in wrong, she could shut our computers down, crash every system in the fleet." He looked over at Lucius, "We'd have to go over to manual controls for everything." That would doom them.

"Can you pull the plug?"

"Don't," Kandergain snapped, "I'm nearly done. Five minutes."

Lucius looked at his flickering screen and watched Chxor ships as they accelerated towards his fleet. He glanced again at the timer, as it ticked away the seconds. "We wait," he said to Reese.

The Chxor force drew closer. In another ten minutes, they would be within missile range. "They're hitting us with targeting sensors." Reese said.

"Done!" Kandergain shouted. "Transmitting the jump calculations."

He looked at the clock, two minutes remained. "Message to all ships, jump to Shadow."

The transition hurt. Lucius felt his insides twist. He heard the ship groan. Then they entered shadow space and the gray nothingness surrounded them.

Reese spoke, his voice strained, "All ships reported jump successful, we're on course."

Lucius looked over at Kandergain, "Now where are we going?"

"I figured the gas giant Sanctuary would be far enough out the Balor wouldn't be looking there." She said. "I had to rush the calculations, that's why the transition was so rough. We may be off by a few hundred thousand kilometers, but I don't *think* we'll hit the planet."

Lucius hoped the last was a joke. "How long?"

"Fifty three minutes," She said.

"Message from Admiral Dreyfus, Baron," Reese said.

"Put him through."

The old Admiral actually looked angry, "What the hell did that just buy us?"

"Excuse me?" Lucius asked.

"I couldn't ask you why the hell we're running before, but I am now!" Admiral Dreyfus snapped. "Why the hell did we just abandon almost twenty million people!"

"Admiral, first off, you ceded command to me. I expect you to trust my decisions. I didn't want this job, but you damned well better believe that if I got it, I'd need your support." Lucius glared the older man into silence. "Second, we're not running. Kandergain did a system jump, that's why we tied up our communications and computers for so long. Third, I hope we just turned our enemies against each other."

Dreyfus frowned, "Explain."

"When I was at the academy—"

"Before you were expelled?"

"Before I was expelled," Lucius nodded and ignored the jibe, "I wrote a controversial paper on your battle against the Wrethe Incursion in what later became the Nova Roma system. In that battle, you took advantage of a military convoy that jumped in on the Wrethe's flank, and used that force to turn their flank and break them."

"Not that I don't enjoy the embellishment, but most of that was accidental, you realize. I had no idea Commodore Jacent's convoy would come in then."

"I know, Admiral. My paper was controversial because I derided the common notion that your genius won that battle. As a matter of fact, in my paper, I noted you would have lost the battle if not for that accident, primarily to underestimating the effectiveness of their bombers and poor deployment of your forces."

The Admiral winced, "Is that what I've come to? Being backstabbed by cadets?"

"Well, Admiral, they expelled me not long after. You're something of a folk hero for Nova Roma, and after my other issues there, the paper certainly didn't help me stay."

The Admiral chuckled. "Okay, so you're hoping, what, the

Chxor cooperate?"

"More, I'm hoping the Balor think that Chxor force are our ships, either captured or allied." Lucius said. "Think about it, they go behind that gas giant, seeing my strike force fleeing towards… something. They come out, and there's a force of thirty dreadnoughts, no sign of my ships, and no sign of a battle."

"It looks like you joined up with the larger force," Admiral Dreyfus said. "Either that, or you jumped out. Either way, if the Chxor and the Balor aren't working together, they're still two armed forces, neither particularly happy to see the other." The old Admiral nodded grudgingly, "I like it. I apologize."

Lucius nodded, accepting the apology. "Sorry I didn't keep you informed, Admiral, but time very nearly undid the entire plan." He realized, like the bruised navigation officer, he'd bruised the Admiral's pride in his hasty actions. "We'll emerge from Shadow in," he checked the timer, "forty two minutes."

"What's the plan, then?"

Lucius grinned slightly, "Plan, what plan?" They both chuckled slightly, "Well, assuming a couple things go our way, we'll see the Chxor try to implement our original plan, charging down the throat of the Balor." Lucius shrugged, "After that we'll see."

Admiral Dreyfus nodded, "Understood. I do think, however, it is best for you to transfer your flag, now, Baron."

"Excuse me?" Lucius blinked.

"The *Peregrine* is a fine ship, but it's not as tough as the *Patriot*. You're the commander of our forces, and the leader of a planet. How do you think things would go if a couple of Balor missiles get lucky hits on the *Peregrine?*"

Lucius looked away, "I think there's plenty of capable people to step up."

"I disagree. Leaving that consideration aside: my ship has better communications systems and computer systems. I understand your ships computer nearly crashed from the load. If you'd been aboard the *Patriot,* you would have been able to relay messages through the secondary computer system."

Lucius stroked the arm rest of the chair. He realized suddenly, the reason he didn't want to give up his position on the *Peregrine*. Doing so would be the abdication of his last ship command. On the *Patriot*, he'd be in the flag bridge. A ship only had one captain. Lucius spoke finally, his voice low, "I'll transfer over once we exit shadow space."

"Thank you, Baron." The other man smiled slightly, "Every good officer has to give it up sometime. My shuttle will be on its way the instant we exit."

***

The fleet dropped out of Shadow only a few thousand kilometers above the gas giant.

"Oh, *good!* We missed the planet," Kandergain said cheerfully.

"Commander Leone, do you feel Ensign Ferranti is up to taking over your position?" Lucius asked. At the other man's nod, Lucius turned to Daniel Beeson, "Well, Commander, looks like you're moving up in the world."

"Baron?" he asked

"You'll assume command of the *Peregrine*. I'm transferring over to command the fleet from the *Patriot*." Lucius felt his throat choke up with emotion. Departure from the *War Shrike* had been hard. To leave the bridge of his last ship command…

Lucius shook his head, then stood straight and saluted, "Commander Beeson, you have the conn."

"Baron, I have the conn." The young man returned the salute, looking stunned.

"Take good care of her." Lucius turned away and moved towards the airlock.

He found Colonel Proscia awaiting him there. "The Admiral and I had a bet, as to whether I'd have to come up there and drag you down here."

He heard Kandergain laugh behind him. "Ah." Lucius said, stepping aboard the shuttle. "How much money you make?"

"Two Republic scrip," Colonel Proscia said. "He gave me two to one odds."

***

He stepped onto the flag bridge and felt out of place as Admiral Dreyfus waved him to his own chair. "I hear I owe Colonel Proscia two drachma?"

Lucius shrugged, "If I'd known you only sent one man, I might have tried to fight him off." He felt a fluttery, uneasy feeling at the thought of commanding a battle from anywhere but the bridge of a warship. He nodded his head at Reese and Kandergain, "Do you have open spots at navigation and communications for those two?"

"I'm sure we can fit them in."

Lucius sat, but he felt his unease increase. He glanced over the controls and brought up the sensor relay. "We have a relay yet from the Emperor's ships?" His hands fumbled with the unfamiliar seat restraints.

"Yes, we got that up already. We'll watch the battle in near real time." Admiral Dreyfus said as he took another seat nearby.

Lucius stared at the screen and slowly, he smiled. The Chxor, at least, identified the Balor as a threat. They had altered course for a least-time intercept. The Balor had not altered their own course. The Balor would hit their maximum launch range soon.

"When's the last time anyone has seen a battle on this scale?" Kandergain asked.

"This many capital ships all in one place?" Admiral Dreyfus asked. "Never."

Lucius nodded, slowly, "There were a couple big battles at the fall of Amalgamated Worlds. When the Shadow Lords destroyed Earth's defense fleet... that might be as big."

"No," Kandergain said, "I was at that one. There were only a dozen dreadnoughts on either side." Lucius raised an eyebrow, but she didn't elaborate beyond, "I was there for an assassination."

"Whose?" Lucius asked

She shrugged, "Mine."

"How'd that go?" Admiral Dreyfus asked.

"It was complicated."

"So I'd guess," Lucius said wryly.

"Don't we have a battle to focus on?" Kandergain asked.

"Chxor are entering maximum missile range for the Balor's heavy ship killers." Reese said. "No fire yet."

They waited. A minute passed. The two fleets arced closer, "They might hold their fire to launch their heavies and lights at the same time," Lucius said.

"They're rate of closure is fast enough they might want to—" Admiral Dreyfus broke off as new icons blossomed.

"Multiple missile launches. It's—" Reese looked up, "Our sensor drones can't track all the launches. It's upwards of ten thousand."

"They launched their heavy and lighter missiles, everything, one launch." Lucius shook his head. He saw, now, that attempting to run that gauntlet would have smashed even the largest ships of his formation. He wondered if the Chxor would fare any better.

"I'm seeing counter-missile fire. Only a hundred." The Chxor ships didn't mount external racks, they had to use their main tubes.

"One minute to impact." Reese said, "The Balor just reversed course, they're maintaining the range."

The Balor weren't going to let the Chxor close nor to even fire a shot. Lucius shook his head. That was what his force faced, Lucius knew. He shook his head. How could they fight an enemy they couldn't catch, couldn't get range on?

The wave of missiles broke on the Chxor.

The sensors couldn't track the multitude of missiles. They couldn't differentiate the explosions of individual warheads in the hash of radiation as over ten thousand hundred-megaton and seven thousand five-hundred-megaton warheads detonated. For a few seconds, a new star blazed in the Faraday system. When that glare finally faded, a dozen wrecked warships emerged, leaking atmosphere and debris.

"I'm seeing only seven dreadnoughts and five cruisers left." Reese said.

"Those poor bastards," Lucius said. He almost felt guilty. The sensor data made the slaughter seem bloodless, but Lucius knew that aboard those ships, pain and blood existed in plenty. Bleeding and burned crew would be scattered amongst the dead. On ships like that, the injured would outnumber the hale.

"The Balor reversed course again."

Lucius watched as the armada turned and closed with the damaged ships. The Chxor either realized they had no escape or lacked any chain of command. They continued to close.

The Balor force closed and their heavy guns fired from twenty four thousand kilometers out. The two forces swept closer, but by the time the Chxor had range, three more of their dreadnoughts and all the remaining screening cruisers died.

The four remaining dreadnoughts fired. They targeted the larger Balor ships and Lucius saw two, possibly more hits. The shields of the larger ships absorbed the fire.

The two fleets interpenetrated. The fire continued from point blank. A Balor destroyer died. One of the Chxor dreadnoughts exploded. Shields around one of the battlecruisers flared and failed. A cruiser exploded.

Then the remaining Chxor dreadnought lost power. The Balor continued to fire. The hulk absorbed a dozen more hits before it came apart in a cloud of debris.

Lucius looked away, he'd just seen his own future. He caught Admiral Dreyfus's eyes and saw the other man knew it too. Any course they made would force them to run that same gauntlet of fire. That same destructive wrath would focus on his ships and the Balor would dance away until they decided to close and finish their game.

"The Balor have altered course, again." Reese said, his voice hollow. "They're making a least time intercept for Faraday. Looks like three hours till they reach maximum missile range."

"Their capital ships take, what, a half hour or so to reload their racks?" Lucius asked.

Admiral Dreyfus nodded. "They'll have their fighters reloaded in about the same."

At least when their turn came to run that gauntlet, they'd run into a smaller wave of fire. The destroyers didn't carry reloads for their external racks. Perhaps more of them would live to close with the enemy.

Lucius shook his head at the impossibility. The Balor's course, a predictable straight line, showed they'd finished with toying with Humanity. He didn't see a way to stop them, not without somehow jumping right in on top of them...

"Kandergain!" he jerked his head around, "Can you plot an intrasystem jump and overlay it on their current course?"

She frowned, "It will take me at least an hour."

"Reese, they're on a least time intercept course. Assuming they'll decelerate so they come in slow for a firing pass on the planet, plot their position in two hours." Lucius felt his thoughts crystallize. "Kandergain, can you do your magic and get us to come out on top of them?"

She frowned, "I can *try*."

"Do it." Lucius said. "Whatever you need, do it. Get us within ten thousand kilometers and we'll win this battle." The Balor's certain, predictable course gave him a slim chance of victory.

Admiral Dreyfus spoke, his voice thoughtful, "We'll drop out of shadow space with close to zero relative velocity. If we misjudge their position by even a little, we'll be sitting ducks for everything they have."

"And we could be way off on our estimate." Lucius said. "They might decide to make a fast attack run on the planet to avoid any planet-based defense. They might come to a halt at the edge of their range and volley missiles in at the planet till they destroy everything. They might alter course by a few degrees and we'll run calculations for a point several million miles off their actual course."

"But we can't do anything about that," Lucius shrugged. "If we can get in range, if we can put our superior weight of firepower into play, we can win this. That's the only way we can win this." He pointed at the drifting remains of the Chxor force, "Otherwise, we'll look like that. They outmaneuver us, they outrange us, and they can pull higher accelerations. We don't have any other option."

"Shut up, both of you," Kandergain snapped. "I think I can plot it so travel time will be only a few seconds. We'll know before we jump if this will work."

"Oh." Admiral Dreyfus said, then he frowned, "If the jump looks like it won't work, what's our back-up plan?"

"Really, as long as they move along that line, we'll be able to intercept them at that point." Lucius shrugged, "Otherwise... make a lot of noise out here and hope they turn away from the planet?"

"And then?"

Lucius sighed. He met the other man's gaze, and then quoted from memory, "Do you really want me to admit I'm making this up as I go along?"

Admiral Dreyfus frowned thoughtfully, "You would have to throw one of my worst quotes back at me." He growled, "I knew I should have pushed that reporter out an airlock."

"Probably." Lucius admitted, "He also immortalized your 'I'll keep fighting till I sober up and realize it's futile,' one from the Battle of West Eden."

"You're kidding!?" Admiral Dreyfus frowned. "I don't even remember saying that one."

***

"Jump calculations complete." Kandergain said, sounding tired. "It will take approximately thirty seconds, real time for us to cross the system and reach the coordinates. I've marked them 'Point Victory.'"

"They've maintained course, so far." Lucius said.

"Which probably means they'll alter it now." Admiral Dreyfus said.

"If they do, we're screwed." Lucius answered. "They've only got twenty minutes to do that. We briefed all the ships," He ticked off his list, a finger at a time, "All fighter squadrons are ready to launch, all missile racks are rearmed and we've done scratch repairs on what we could... am I missing anything?"

Admiral Dreyfus shook his head, "I think that's everything."

"Message from Emperor Romulus, Baron." Reese said.

"Good morning, your Highness." Lucius said.

"Admiral Mund just briefed me on your plans. I see a possible way to ensure they maintain their course." The Emperor said.

"What's that?" Lucius frowned.

"If my ships light off their drives and go out to meet them, they'll probably use a similar attack run as they did with the Chxor. I can time it so they reverse course in the same position."

"They'll only do that if they fire their heavy salvo at you first." Lucius said. "Out of the question, I'm not going to let you throw away your men—"

"Not your choice, Baron. I'm your ally, not your subordinate," the younger man said. "I can't save Nova Roma by myself. I need your ships. If you throw them away here, you won't be able to help me later."

"If you're *dead*, Highness, I won't be able to help you either!" Lucius snapped.

"I talked with Admiral Mund. If we light off our drives and plot an intercept course right about now, they'll alter their course and you'll be able to engage them at zero relative velocity when you emerge at Point Victory."

"Baron! The Nova Roma ships just went active, they're putting on full speed for an intercept course with the Balor. It looks like Captain Kral is taking most of the captured Chxor ships along,"

Reese called. "The Balor ships are altering course!"

Lucius felt a cold hand squeeze his heart. He looked at the sensors.

They'd altered their couse. "They're slowing." It took him a moment to plot the new course, he and Dreyfus spoke simultaneously, "They'll still pass through Point Victory."

Lucius watched. He knew that thousands would die to give them this chance. He looked over at Kandergain, "How close will we emerge to that point?"

She shrugged, "Hard to say. I've never tried to do this before. Plotting an intercept from shadow space to a moving force in real time... it's complex." She brought up some of her calculations, "We'll be within twenty thousand kilometers, at least. Maybe closer. We could emerge above them or below them or even in front of them, I don't know."

Lucius frowned, only those ships that used captured Ghornath tech had weapons that could range twenty thousand kilometers. His other ships would have to close the range as quickly as possible. "God I hate not being on a bridge." Lucius growled.

"Thinking you'd rather be at the helm?" Admiral Dreyfus asked.

"Absolutely." Lucius gnawed on his lip and stared at the two fleets approaching each other. The Balor fleet neared their maximum launch range. "If they launch like last time, we'll be among them before that flight hits." Lucius said. He felt a sense of déjà vu, only this time, it would be people on his side dying rather than an enemy force.

"Multiple launches." Reese said, his voice sad. "Total saturation, I can't track all the missiles. There's almost nine thousand, though." He cleared his throat, "We'll emerge at Point Victory a minute before impact."

Lucius watched in silence, they had two minutes before they jumped. He watched the formation alter, Kral pushed his heavier dreadnoughts and the thirty captured shield cruisers to the front of the formation. "He's setting up a screen for the Emperor," Lucius marveled. He never thought he'd see the day that a Chxor sacrificed himself for the Emperor of Nova Roma.

"At present velocity and deceleration, one minute to jump," Reese said.

"All ships, prepare to jump at my mark." Lucius said over an open link. "Fight for humanity, fight for your freedom, fight for your lives. Victory or death!" He took a deep breath, "All ships, commence jump to Shadow in three, two, one, mark!"

They jumped.

The transition went smoother. Lucius still felt the nausea, the unsettling body reaction to someplace not quite right. He felt the ship *turn* as Kandergain had done when they'd made their trip to seek allies. The gray on gray background altered. It pulsed... and slowly bars of green sprang into existence. He stared at the screen as the bars formed a grid of green lines, and the background of the alternate universe became a dull red.

He stared into the screen, for the second it took his mind to recognize the pattern.

Everyone on the bridge turned their heads as Lucius collapsed in laughter. He wiped at his eyes as laughed almost hysterically.

"What?" Kandergain asked.

"I—" Lucius sagged back into his seat, laughing harder. "We're—we've gone to ludicrous speed!" He couldn't help it, he lost it again. "Oh my God, we've gone to plaid!"

Dead silence met his exclamation.

He continued to laugh for several seconds, finally wiping tears away, "Good, God, doesn't anyone watch the classics?" He sighed, but couldn't repress a slight chuckle, "We should emerge in five, four, three, two, one..."

The timer read zero. The red and green of Shadow still remained. All the eyes on the flag bridge went to Kandergain. "I said thirty seconds would pass out there," she said. "I didn't say it would be the same for us."

Reese stared at her, "How can time be different? We're not traveling at high velocities in the real universe, there should be no relativity."

She sighed, "I didn't want to go into this again," she shot a glare at Lucius, "But essentially, time flows... differently in shadow space. Just like I plotted us a course through different dimensions of space in Shadow, I also plotted us a course taking time into account." She took a deep breath, "Pretty much, in order to make objective time as short as possible, I lengthened the distance we'll travel in shadow, and the subjective time we'll experience."

Lucius spoke, "Alright, how long, subjectively, do we spend in the plaid section of shadow?"

She shrugged uncomfortably, "Nine months."

"Nine *months*!?" Lucius demanded. He looked over at Admiral Dreyfus, "Do we have supplies for that long?"

The other man grimaced. "I don't know. I know some ships will be in trouble." Most ships stocked up rations for thirty days. Some of the ships in the fleet probably hadn't resupplied since the last operation, a week ago.

They both looked at Kandergain, "It would be very bad if the Fleet starved to death in thirty seconds."

She shrugged, "Hey, I'm sorry. If you want, we can drop out of shadow now and you could come up with another plan."

Lucius frowned, "Where would we end up?"

She shrugged, "Beats me. Normal Shadow, you'd emerge in the real universe somewhere. Out here... well, optimistically we'd end up in the real universe some*when*. Pessimistically... we could end up in another universe."

Admiral Dreyfus stared at her contemplatively, "You know, if we run out of food, I recommend we resort to cannibalism to survive."

"Bring it on, old man."

***

"There's something distinctly odd about this." Lucius said as he stared at a wall clock that showed the thirty second countdown. Six hours later, not even a third of a second had passed. He looked over the gathered officers, "What's the good news?"

Admiral Dreyfus slid a slim, gray, sealed plastic pillow down the table. "Hurrah, we're saved."

Lucius picked it up, he frowned at the small package, "What is it?"

"Marine Emergency Field Rations." Brigadier General Morris said. "We Marines keep a stockpile of them on hand. Each bag has enough calories for one person, for a day of strenuous effort. We've got enough to keep the Fleet fed for years."

"And the Marines save the day again." Lucius sighed. "What's the bad news?"

"We've only got fuel for the ships running fusion reactors for twenty seven days, with a transfer of fuel between those ships using hydrogen fuel." Captain Magnani said, her nasal voice sounding satisfied. "As I stated before, we'd have been better leaving such primitive—"

"Thank you, Captain." Admiral Dreyfus interrupted. "What have you done to find a stopgap measure?"

"I'd recommend we evacuate those ships." She shrugged. "Nothing else we can do."

Lucius sighed, opening a link to the *War Shrike*. "Captain Doko, please put me through to Engineer Harbach."

"What? Who is this? I was elbow deep on—"

"James, this is Baron Giovanni."

"Oh, what do *you* want?" The old professor whined.

Lucius rolled his eyes, "I have an engineering problem only you can address."

"Oh?" The old man's voice showed slight interest.

"In twenty seven days, all our ships with fusion reactors will be out of fuel." Lucius said. "We'll be in Shadow for nine months. How do I keep my ships flying?"

"Hmmm. That's a big problem. I'm not sure a mere commander could handle that."

"Excuse me?" Lucius asked.

"Well, you know," the old man's nasal voice whined, "I'm getting on in years. A nice little grant of land, maybe some money to keep me living well. Only fair, considering I've served so long and never gotten so much as a thanks."

Lucius clenched his fists beneath the table. He felt a vein throb at his temple, and he felt his left eyelid quiver. "Commander Harbach, if you think I'll let you blackmail this fleet…"

"Pretty spiteful not to give an old man a decent reward for saving a fleet, you know?" Harbach whined. "So… how about it?"

"You'll receive your plot of land and sufficient money for you to live comfortably," Lucius growled. "Now what's your solution?"

The old man chuckled, "Easy enough. We use some of those parasite frigates to provide just enough power to run the major systems. Two of them docked and running their plants over cables to the dock circuits will keep everything running fine. We just have to bypass the breakers so we don't cause a power failure. Otherwise—"

"Thank you, James. How long to do it?"

"Maybe two, three hours a ship."

Lucius turned to Captain Magnani, "Coordinate with Commander Harbach. Get all those ships hooked up as soon as possible."

She opened her mouth and shot a look over at Admiral Dreyfus. His glare shut her mouth. "Yes, sir," She said sullenly. She grabbed her notes and pushed away from the table violently.

Lucius waited for her to leave. "Any other crises?

***

Lucius looked around the palatial Admiral's Quarters aboard the *Patriot* and whistled. He heard the hatch open behind him, and turned. Kandergain leaned against the wall just inside the door, arms crossed. "Moving up in the world, aren't we?"

Lucius stared at her and smiled slightly.

"I was wondering if you rank any real food. I just had one of those MEF packages. I'm not sure starvation is so bad in the face of those."

Lucius's smile widened and he started towards her.

"Whatcha thinkin'?" Kandergain asked, also smiling.

"You know," Lucius said, "Ever since we got back from that trip, we haven't had more than a few minutes alone, together."

She cocked her head, "True."

"And now, we've got a nice, long voyage, with nothing in particular going on until the end of it."

She nodded, "Also, true."

Lucius walked forward. He reached an arm past her and flipped the lock on the cabin door behind her. "If I were a suspicious individual, I might almost think you might have seen that possibility when you calculated the jump."

"What, arrange things so they work out for the best *and* I get what I want too?" Kandergain smiled, "Why, Lucius, I'd *never* do something like that!"

"I didn't think so." Lucius said as he kissed her.

***

Lucius stared at the flat gray bar he held in his hand. "Just the opportunity for real food is going to be reason enough to win this fight." He'd never would have said he was overweight, but he'd lost some for certain over the past few months.

"Those things might have everything you need to survive," Admiral Dreyfus said, "But no wonder no one wants to be a Marine?"

Lucius chuckled at that. He tucked the bar away, "I'll go hungry a little longer, I think." Lucius said. He looked over at Kandergain, who sat in her chair awkwardly. "Are you going to be..."

"I'm fine." She snapped.

Lucius mentally cursed the situation again. Who could have expected this? Accidents happened, he knew, but the absurdity of this was too much for him. "I still think you should be in the infirmary."

"I still think you should shut up. I'll be fine." Kandergain didn't even look up from her console "Five minutes till we emerge."

Lucius looked across his boards, now become familiar. He felt glad he'd shifted over to the *Patriot*, now. He thought the similarity to the *War Shrike* and the familiar, unchanging surroundings for nine months would have driven him insane by now.

As it was, he knew most, if not all, of the twenty-nine thousand crew of the *Patriot* by name and face.

"One minute."

Lucius took a deep breath, and shot Kandergain one more worried look. Her condition caused him more concern than he knew he could afford to give on the eve of a battle. He wished the ship's sickbay had the right equipment, but well-stocked or not, they were not designed for these circumstances.

She wasn't the only person in the fleet so affected, he knew. Accidents happened.

"Emergence in five, four, three, two, one, mark!"

The ship shuddered and the plaid universe around them vanished. An instant later, they lay at rest, the stars of the real universe around them.

"Contacts, multiple contacts!" Reese said, excitedly, "We're right on! The Balor are five thousand kilometers ahead of us, just starting to turn!"

The *Patriot* hummed slightly as weapons systems came online, fighters and the parasite frigates launched and the engines kicked it forward. Lucius felt the tension ease in his chest, "Message to all ships, close with the enemy, envelope them and destroy them... attack pattern Alpha Two."

The *Patriot* mounted thirty two main turrets, with four colossal super-capital fusion lasers per turret. The secondary battery of slightly smaller lasers consisted of sixty four turrets. It carried two thousand Mark V missiles in vertical missile cells.

The Balor had begun to alter course to maintain the range between them and the force they'd just fired on. The appearance of the massive fleet at their rear came totally unexpected. The smooth choreography of their maneuvers faltered.

The ship thrummed as it opened fire. Around it, the other ships fired.

A wave of twelve thousand missiles surged out from the United Colonies Fleet. Three thousand of those missiles were the light Interceptor missiles. All five hundred of Lucius's fighters carried the lighter missiles, the better to sweep the enemy fighters out of the sky.

Shields flared and died. Ships shuddered. Debris and explosion haloed within the Balor formation. Then the missiles, unopposed by jamming and anything but sporadic fire, detonated in one long, ripple of explosions.

Lucius dimmed his screen, he wasn't sure if his gunnery officers still had targets or just fired blindly into that hash. Slowly the haze cleared somewhat.

Three of the dreadnoughts and seven of the battlecruisers remained, battered but still active. The ships began to return fire.

"Baron, their missile flight!" Reese shouted.

Almost half of the enemy missile flight had gone inactive. Those missiles drifted, drives silent. "But why..." He stared, thinking. "Their missiles are directed through command. We destroyed their ships, the missiles lost track."

A staggering number of missiles continued, still directed by the Balor ships. But as Balor ships died, more missiles went ballistic.

It might be enough, he decided.

The *Patriot* shuddered as Balor fire made it through the defense screens. Lucius picked out the battlecruiser that targeted them immediately. He opened his mouth to snap out firing directions, then realized he was on a flag bridge. He should be directing the *fleet*, not a ship.

He opened a link to a cluster of ships on the right flank, "Close the range further, their ships in your sector are trying to break away." When he looked back at the screen, the enemy battlecruiser broke up under the attention of the heavy guns.

Another of the enemy superdreadnoughts died. It exploded in a massive flash of energy.

A squadron of Kukri-destroyers began to close in on the flank of an enemy battlecruiser. They began to take direct fire. "Pull, back you've extended too far," Lucius said, too late.

First one, then a second died as they flared brightly under the battlecruiser's fire. The third exploded, as fire hit its antimatter plant. The last ship, heavily damaged, bulled forward, guns firing at maximum. It collided with the larger ship and a moment later, its antimatter plants let go. Lucius looked away, tears in his eyes for the bravery and loss of the crew.

The human fleet slowly enveloped the Balor force. The massed heavy fire eroded the alien shields. One of the remaining Balor superdreadnoughts fell silent; the colossal ship a gutted wreck.

The super-heavy ships of the Crusader-class continued to close, while the bulk of the *Patriot* followed sluggishly behind. Around them, squadrons of fighters crisscrossed. A dozen enemy Bane Sidhe fighters made a run on the *Patriot*. Their light guns strafed the surface. The multitude of close in weapons fired and half the squadron died. A group of Harassers pursued, and killed three more.

The fight became a melee, as the two fleets interpenetrated. Lucius bit back a curse as fire missed one of the Balor ships and struck the human destroyer on its flank. "Captain Crysnik, watch your fire. All ships, monitor your fire patterns!"

The last Balor superdreadnought shuddered under massed fire and began to break up. A series of secondary explosions rippled through the interior. The only remaining carrier exploded, violently, as something hit its magazines. When the glare cleared, two human destroyers had died with it.

The enemy fire dropped off. All the enemy capital ships lay powerless or as clouds of debris. Lucius stared, almost afraid to speak. "We've won."

"Oh, boy." Kandergain said, then gave a gasp.

Lucius looked over at her, then shouted, "Medic team to the flag bridge!"

***

CHAPTER XVI

May 3, 2403 Earth Standard Time
Faraday System
United Colonies

"Look at me, Kandergain, focus." Doctor Varene didn't even try to get him to leave.

She clenched his hand in hers, "I didn't think it would hurt so much."

The ship's surgeon spoke, "I can give you something—"

"No!" She shouted. "A psychic in pain is bad enough, a drugged psychic in pain is an accident waiting to happen."

The surgeon looked over at Lucius, "Sir, I'm really not qualified…"

"You're a doctor, right?" Lucius asked, no longer even trying to hide his own worry.

"Well, yes, but I'm a trauma surgeon, not—"

"Just do your job."

"Oh," Kandergain grunted.

Lucius clenched her hand, "Look at me, Kandergain. Focus on me." He winced as her grip on his hand tightened. He put his face over hers. Look at me, breathe. You'll get through this."

He heard the surgeon mutter. "What's that?" Lucius asked.

"Almost there."

"See, babe, we're almost there."

"I don't want to be almost there, I want to be done!" Kandergain grunted again. "Oh, this is so your fault!"

"My fault?" Lucius asked.

"Your fault." Kandergain grunted again. Lucius wiped some of the sweat off her forehead with the hand not held in a vice.

"Almost there." The surgeon grunted.

"Almost there, are you kidding, you said that an hour ago!" Kandergain shouted.

"It'll be fine, Kandergain." Lucius said, "Focus on me." He didn't want to think what would happen if she snapped and threw the surgeon across the room.

"Almost there."

"Stop saying that!" Kandergain and Lucius both shouted.

"She's away!" The surgeon shouted.

A second later, there came a shrill wail.

The sweating ship's surgeon stepped forward, "Congratulations, Baron, you're the father of a beautiful baby girl."

***

Lucius started awake at a soft noise. He opened his eyes, and realized he'd fallen asleep in his chair. The noise that awoke him was the soft sound of his daughter as she came awake in his lap. She stared up at him, piercing blue eyes stared sleepily into his heart.

Lucius felt tears in his eyes. "Hello Kaylee, welcome to the world."

He looked up, "Kandergain, look what…"

His voice died. The bed before him lay empty.

A plain paper envelope lay on the crisply made linens. He awkwardly opened it, while he held his daughter.

Dear Lucius,

It's a terrible thing to do, I know, but I have to leave.

I've never let myself love anyone before now. It hurts so much to go that I half wish I hadn't. But we made something beautiful, didn't we?

Anyway, I wish it wasn't so, but I do need to go. The main reason, as I'm sure you feared, is that I've got my own war to fight. It's been a long one. I hope, someday, that we'll have an opportunity to be a family. Until then... I love you, and I'll always cherish our thirty seconds together.

You know me, I cheated a bit. I don't know if you noticed, but all us powerful psychics don't seem to age much. We can control our metabolism. I altered yours. I could have made you a bouncy young man of eighteen, but I thought that might be hard for you to explain. You won't age, not a single day. When we finish our battles, Lucius, we'll have a long time together.

I would stay longer, but one of the things Lachesis *said was a warning to me. If I stay there, I'd be a direct threat to the Shadow Lords. The thing they fear above all else is a powerful psychic with access to a fleet like yours. If I'd lingered, they would have combined forces and come after us. The first thing I'm off to do is to personally warn them off you.*

Now, we come down to payment for my services. My first favor I ask is that you raise our daughter to be the woman she should be. She's inherited my abilities, though they won't manifest till she's older. Neither you or I had childhoods that we'd have wanted. Give her the one she deserves. Never let her doubt that her parents love her.

The second favor is this: on her eighteenth birthday, take her to Fey Darran, and find someone there to teach her. Don't go there until then. Trust me on this.

I'll keep my last favor in reserve.

*All my love,
Kandergain*

***

"Baron Giovanni, did you hear anything I just said?"

Lucius looked up with a start, "Sorry, what was that?"

Admiral Dreyfus sighed, "I know this is hard for you..."

Lucius shook his head, "I'm fine. My head's back in the game. Start from the beginning." He would not get melancholy and maudlin about Kandergain's departure.

"I said, we've finished damage estimates. The whole fleet's taken some heavy damage. The worst is with our Chxor converts—"

"How many Chxor volunteers did we lose?" Lucius asked.

"A lot. Their position and a majority of the missiles going ballistic sheltered the Nova Roma forces from catastrophic damage, but... a lot of Chxor died." Admiral Dreyfus shrugged, "They knew what they were getting into."

Lucius nodded, "I'll meet with Kral later, try to find out if there's anything we can do to honor them."

Admiral Dreyfus raised an eyebrow, "You think they'll want a memorial?"

"We'll have a memorial, regardless of whether they want one or not," Lucius responded. "If only to remind ourselves how close we came to defeat. But we owe those Chxor a debt, and I need to find out what we can do to repay that."

The other man stared at Lucius for a moment, "You realize you're talking about aliens from a race that's even now participating in genocide against a dozen worlds."

"Not these Chxor." Lucius said. "And even if it was... they just saved us."

Admiral Dreyfus shrugged, "Agreed." He cleared his throat, "Just the one dreadnought and the seven cruisers are salvageable. Recovery is still under way, but it's not likely they'll find many more survivors."

"The Marines are handling the Balor ships with caution. They're opening holes, venting compartments still under pressure, and then slowly moving through the wrecks. We'll have a lot of things, maybe even a few relatively intact ships for our scientists to look over." He paused, "The Nova Roma ships are back in orbit, receiving attention."

Lucius nodded. The Nova Roma forces, shielded by the Chxor, had survived with much less damage. None of their ships received crippling damage, anyway, though he knew hundreds of men had died in the Emperor's actions. "We owe them a debt too." He sighed, "We both know how we can pay that one."

Admiral Dreyfus nodded, "I've already got members of my staff considering how to run the campaign to liberate Nova Roma. I assume you'll want to move soon?"

Lucius nodded, "As soon as our own forces have repaired their damage. We also need to build the infrastructure to support that campaign, however." He frowned, "I don't know if we have the manpower for this."

Admiral Dreyfus chuckled, "Baron, with what I've seen so far, I think you'll manage."

Lucius snorted, "We've got a lot at stake here." He looked down at the infant asleep in his lap. "I've got a lot at stake here."

"We're building a future, of course there's a lot at stake." Dreyfus said. "But I think we'll manage now."

The com link buzzed.

Admiral Dreyfus flipped it over to speaker.

"Admiral, Baron, you need to see this, immediately."

"What is it," Admiral Dreyfus asked.

"A Balor battlecruiser just jumped into the system."

***

Lucius settled into the now-familiar command chair of the flag bridge, "What's the status?"

"It's... hailing us, sir," Reese said, plainly confused. "It's just outside of our missile envelope."

Lucius stared at the lone ship in confusion. "Connect them," he said.

A familiar human face appeared, "Baron Giovanni, this is General Shaden."

"General!" Lucius let out a relieved sigh, "You gave us a scare. We thought we had another Balor force inbound."

"Sorry about that. I would have called ahead, but I realized we never exchanged ansible codes. And... I came as fast as I could."

"I thought you had a battle elsewhere?" Lucius asked.

"The Balor never showed." The other man said, "As a matter of fact, they pulled back from attacks on a dozen systems in Republic space. They halted all their offenses, everywhere for the time being."

"Why?" Lucius asked.

"Because they threw a quarter of their fleet at you, here." Shaden Mirra said. "And you just destroyed it."

"A quarter?" Lucius asked, startled. "You mean they only have twenty four dreadnoughts total?"

"Had," Shaden nodded, smiling broadly. "You've set them back years, at least. Maybe decades. With this, the Republic warlords might be able to take the offensive. If I'd known they would send so much of their fleet here..."

"How long will it take them to replace their ships?"

"It took them two years to replace the one superdreadnought we've captured." Shaden shrugged. "Like I said, it could be decades. In the meantime, that's freed me up for a brief visit here."

"Going to lend us a hand with the Chxor?" Lucius asked, eyebrows raised.

"Ah... no. I don't have that long. Kandergain said you had a lot of Balor wreckage. I thought I'd loan you some of my engineers who've got some experience working with it." Shaden shrugged, "Best case scenario, a Shadow Lord won't be the only one with a Balor superdreadnought."

"I like the sound of that." Lucius grinned.

"I thought you would."

***

"The Emperor will see you now."

Lucius stepped into Romulus IV's office, and gave a deep bow. "Thank you for your time, your Highness."

The younger man spoke, "I hope we'll begin the offensive on Nova Roma now."

"Yes, your Highness," Lucius said, "The United Colonies Fleet will begin a campaign to free Nova Roma from the Chxor. Admiral Dreyfus and his staff are going over possible strategies as we speak." He sighed, "I want to personally thank you, and your men, for your actions against the Balor."

The Emperor shrugged, "Baron, I know you think me impatient and arrogant," the youth held up a hand to forestall Lucius. "Let me finish. Even with the ships I have, I must be a beggar, asking for help to save my people, my world. That's been hard for me. That the Empire my great-grandfather... *your* grandfather... founded has fallen so far…" The man shook his head. "On top of that, we both know how brutal life under the Chxor must be. They're killing our people, Lucius. They're killing them all."

"I know, your Highness," Lucius said solemnly.

"At first, I thought you were stalling, trying to use time as a bargaining chip." The young man shrugged, "Honestly, I thought you wanted the throne. It frustrated me because, when it came to it, if you'd asked, I would have given it to you."

"It's never been about that," Lucius said.

"I realize that now." The Emperor shrugged, "But even so, it's been hard to wait. Hard knowing that the people I'm responsible for are dying in the millions while I wait here."

"We're going to Nova Roma," Lucius said. "And when we do, we'll kick the Chxor Empire hard enough they'll never recover."

"We'd better," Emperor Romulus IV said, his sad eyes saw the mass graves that awaited his return. "We'd better."

***

EPILOGUE

"Daddy, tell me about Mommy."

"Again?" Lucius asked his daughter.

"Again."

Lucius looked down at her as she stared up at him with the solemnity that only a five year old can have. With her blonde hair, pulled back in a ponytail, she looked so much like her mother his heart ached. He picked her up, lifting her onto his shoulders.

"Your mother," Lucius said, looking up at the night sky, "is the smartest, bravest, most beautiful woman in the universe. And you're going to grow up to be just like her."

"Really?" Kaylee asked, in a small voice.

"Really," Lucius responded.

THE END

DIAGRAMS

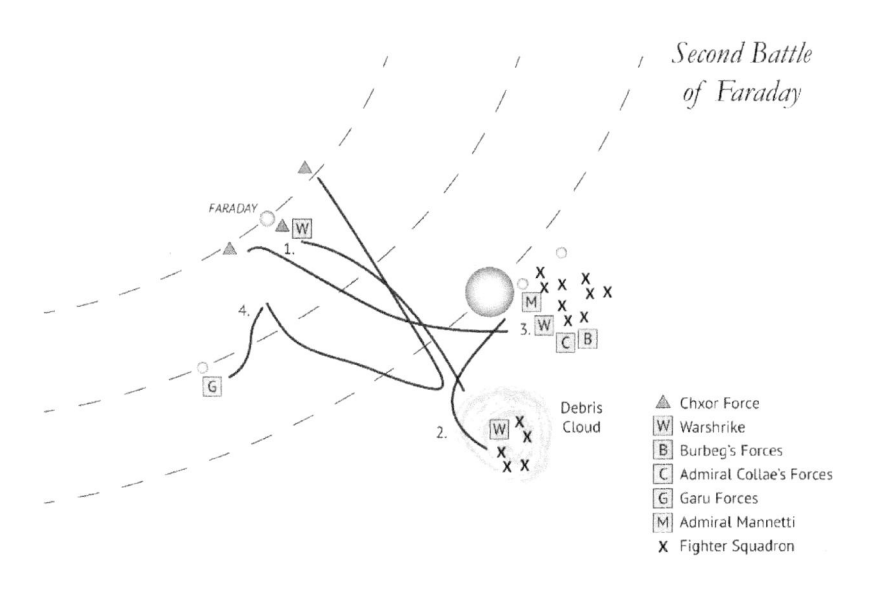

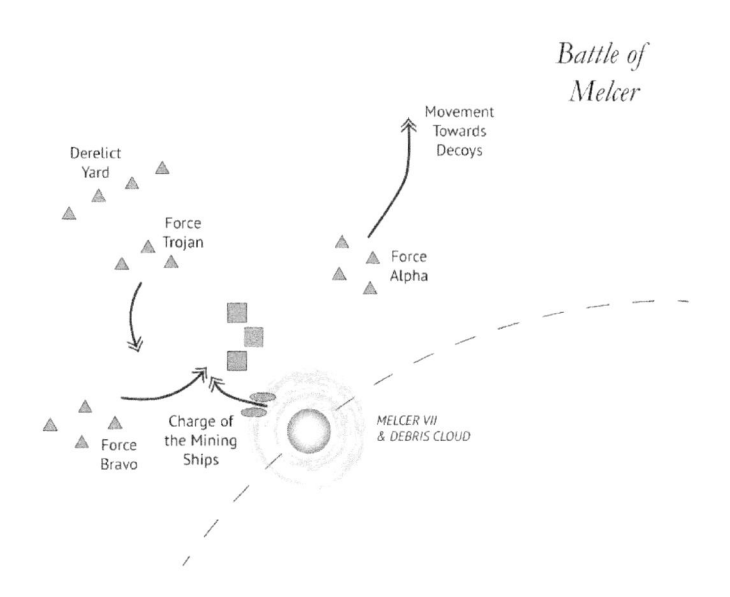

Second Battle of Faraday

- ▲ Chxor Force
- W Warshrike
- B Burbeg's Forces
- C Admiral Collae's Forces
- G Garu Forces
- M Admiral Mannetti
- X Fighter Squadron

Battle of Melcer

349

Third Battle of Faraday

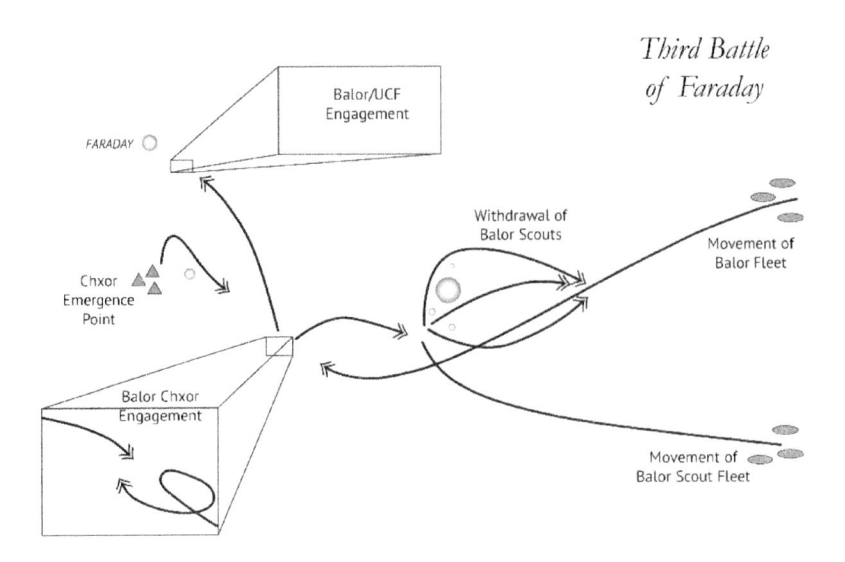

About the Author

Kal Spriggs started reading science fiction and fantasy in elementary school. Eventually he was the only eight year old with permission from the local public library to check out books from the adult section because he'd read everything else. He's written ever since he started running out of 'good' stuff to read when he was twelve, although he likes to think his writing has improved, if only slightly. His range of interests has since expanded to include computer and console games, tabletop RPGs, and strategy games.

An Army brat born overseas, Kal was born with a wanderlust to see what lies over the next horizon. Kal visited 22 countries on five continents before he turned 25, and hopes to add many more to the list, as well as revisit some of his favorite places. Spriggs loves to ski, hike, fish, and camp, especially in the Rocky Mountains where he spent much of his childhood.

Kal Spriggs is a graduate of the United States Merchant Marine Academy with an engineering degree. He followed in his parents' footsteps and joined the US Army after graduation and after spending almost a decade on active duty, he's now a reservist engineer officer. As well as earning a master's degree in environmental engineering, he's been deployed to both Afghanistan and Iraq.

Printed in Great Britain
by Amazon